The
Christmas
Company

alys murray

ISBN: 978-1-952210-71-6

www.hallmarkpublishing.com

To Mom, who taught me the magic of Christmas.

Chapter One
December 23

SOME MAY HAVE CALLED KATE Buckner biased, but she believed no one on planet Earth did Christmas better than the small town of Miller's Point, Texas. Okay, she was *totally* biased. After living there her whole life—almost twenty-seven years—she was allowed to love it, especially at this time of year. Miller's Point was a special place all year round, but it had a glow of its own once the weather turned chilly. Yes, even Texas got chilly, though Miller's Point accentuated the natural winter wind with more fake snow and crystal icicles than anywhere else in the world.

The town's glow was only *partly* due to the lights strung around the town square's famous Christmas tree. The rest came from the twinkling of thousands of others decorating every building in town.

Kate crouched precariously atop an eleven-foot ladder, her boots covering the "DANGER—DO NOT STAND ON TOP LEVEL" sticker. Her thighs burned as she reached out for her target… *Just a little further… A little more…*

"Hey!"

Kate froze atop the ladder. Even the subtlest of starts would send the ladder tipping, and she did *not* want to explain to Doctor Bennett how she cracked her skull open. Without moving anything but her eyes, she braved a glance down towards the cobblestones making up Main Street. In just a few hours, they would be covered in fake snow, but for now, they cleaned up nice, sparkling from last night's rainfall. The familiarly muddy boots of Carolyn Bishop, however, ruined the perfect cleanliness—and Kate's view. Kate would've smiled if she hadn't been deathly afraid the slight movement of muscles would send her toppling down to the cold, hard ground.

Her official job title was "Director of Festival Operations," but everyone called her Miss Carolyn, and for good reason. With her eternally good-natured smile and cracked skin testifying to how long she'd been living here, everyone generally considered her the town matriarch. The silver-haired woman with narrowed brown eyes stood lower than five-foot-nothing, but her presence towered over Miller's Point. Kate loved her almost as much as she feared her, which explained the slamming of her heart when she heard the worried accusation in Miss Carolyn's voice.

"What are you doing up there?"

"This light is out!"

Kate stretched her fingers. She was so close, and if she could only just reach… She grabbed hold of a tiny bulb and twisted it. Once, twice, three times. *There.* The light flickered on, joining the rest of its illuminated brethren on the thick green cord. It was only one piece of a very, very large puzzle, but Kate felt that the little details made all the difference. Miss Carolyn, for her part, didn't share Kate's enthusiasm for tiny lightbulbs or women who put themselves in dangerous situations to fix them.

"You've got to be the most hardheaded girl in town! Get down here before you fall and break your neck! No, you know what? A fall might actually do you some good. Maybe it'd knock some sense into you!"

As she made her way down the ladder, Kate couldn't help but survey the square surrounding her. She would never joke about something as important as Christmas, but she definitely wasn't kidding about the grandeur of Miller's Point. Every year, The Christmas Company—an event planning firm that was a subsidiary of Woodward Enterprises, the corporation that owned most of the ranching operations out here—transformed Miller's Point from one of the countless flyover Texas towns into a Dickensian Christmas wonderland. The square received a makeover, with Hollywood-style facades and enough fake snow to make their humble streets look so much like Victorian London that even a time traveler couldn't have told the difference.

From the day after Thanksgiving until New Year's Eve, the town banded together to host the Miller's Point Christmas Festival, where guests from all over the country flocked to join in the celebration. Everyone enjoyed the caroling and costumes, but the highlight of the festival—the real reason everyone went—was the immersive reenactment of *A Christmas Carol*. Every night, guests could follow Scrooge on his journey and watch him change from a bitter, hateful miser into a man with the spirit of the season coursing through his veins like an injection of sugarplum juice.

Their town square hosted such scenes as the Ghost of Christmas Present's journey through London and the final celebration after Scrooge's transformation. The Christmas Company spared no expense or labor in making it a dreamscape of holiday fantasy. Paintings on Christmas cards and backdrops in Bing Crosby movies couldn't compare. Lush green garlands wrapped in red ribbons adorned the storefronts covered in fake snow and frost. Countless fairy lights illuminated wreaths and holly, ornaments and decorations of every size and description. Outdoor lanterns and lampposts blazed. No matter where a visitor turned to look, the town simply glowed. It was the perfect backdrop for Tiny Tim to sit on Scrooge's shoulder and shout, "God bless us, everyone," and no matter how hard she tried to remain professional, Kate always cried when they got to that part.

When she finally set her feet on solid ground, Kate braced herself for an earful from Miss Carolyn. After volunteering with the festival since she was seven years old, Kate graduated to full-time employee status at nineteen, the youngest person ever hired by The Christmas Company, and as Assistant of Festival Operations, her list of duties was as extensive as it was satisfying. She ran into trouble, though, with her enthusiasm. As a volunteer, she scrambled to make herself useful, invaluable. Now, as an employee, she always found herself trying to do everything, a habit her boss hated. Miss Carolyn wanted her at her side, not off fixing the hem of Mrs. Cratchit's costume or refilling the mulled wine in Fred's apartment scene.

"What have I told you about getting up on that ladder?" Miss Carolyn asked, hands firmly on her hips, silver eyebrow firmly raised. Kate avoided her gaze. She focused instead on breaking down the ladder for storage, no easy task considering the ladder's height.

"Tomorrow's the big day and everything has to be perfect."

"There've got to be a thousand lights on that tree. How in Heaven's name did you spot the broken one?"

There were actually 12,460 lights on the Main Street Christmas tree, but Kate didn't want to correct her boss. Or look like the biggest festival nerd in town, though everyone probably already suspected as much. She shrugged.

"It's a gift."

To be fair, her eagle eye came more through experience than through some miracle of heavenly gift-giving. A lifetime of staring up at the tree with joy and awe had taught her the weak electrical spots. With the ladder broken down and folded, Kate scooped up the handle, groaning with the effort. She'd definitely feel the strain in her muscles tomorrow, but it was all worth it for that one tiny light. If the tree brought joy and the holiday spirit to even one person, Kate's mission would be accomplished. Christmas Eve was the night the crowds were the densest and most hopeful; Kate didn't want even one thing to go wrong for them.

She started off for Town Hall to return the ladder. With its balcony level and classic architecture, the main ballroom was used as Scrooge's house, but they used some of the anterooms and recreation rooms for storage and costume changes. Miss Carolyn followed behind.

"You're my best worker, kid, but you're stubborn as they come."

"We *make* Christmas for people, Miss Carolyn. What we do is important, right down to the tiniest little light bulb."

"You really love this, don't you?"

"More than anything."

Kate didn't need to think about that for more than a second. Her entire life revolved around the festival. As far as she was concerned, Christmas was the best time of year. Not because of the presents or the food, though those were certainly part of it. To her, Christmas was the one time of year when everyone put aside their differences and sat together at the table of humanity. Hope lit the lamps and compassion played the music. Christmas wasn't a holiday but a microcosm of the best of mankind, a reminder of what they could be if they only carried the spirit with them all year round.

It also made her excessively poetic.

"Well." Miss Carolyn cleared her throat and pulled Kate away from the side door. "I need you to come with me."

"Why?"

"We have a visitor from Woodward. And they're waiting on us."

The swinging of the heavy, oaken front doors of the town hall punctuated the ominous line. Heavy ladder still in tow, Kate stepped through the main marble atrium to see they were not entering some intimate meeting with their corporate overlords.

Judging from the sheer number of people present, the room looked more like an intervention than a meeting to discuss cost-cutting measures or whatever it was corporate decided to throw at them next.

Heads turned at the doors opening and a sea of worried, familiar faces turned to greet them. Mitch and Betsy Plinkett held hands and stared with distant eyes. Lindy Turnbull's perfect skin wrinkled with concerned lines. Even little Bradley Lewisham, their Tiny Tim, gripped his prop cane until his knuckles went white. Costumes mingled with plain clothes, but one thing was consistent: fear.

Something had happened. Or was happening. And no one had told Kate about it. Her stomach dropped too far for her to pick it back up. She glanced sidelong at Miss Carolyn. She was a rock of consistency and positivity.

If there was a North Star in this room, she would be it.

But when Kate looked, there was no guiding light to follow. Miss Carolyn's rosy cheeks sunk into a pale shade of gray. Her eyes hardened. Dread prickled the hairs on the back of Kate's neck. If whatever happened was enough to rankle their leader, it could only mean one of two things. Either someone had died, or they were getting shut down.

"Good evening."

Kate's head snapped to the front of the room, where a hastily constructed podium and a microphone stood. Too distracted by her friends and neighbors, she hadn't noticed the setup when she walked in, but now it was all she could do to even blink. Behind the podium stood a solitary man. Against the white walls of the atrium, his black suit and golden hair stood out with the entrancing shock of an abstract painting, as if he were nothing more than lonely brushstrokes on a canvas.

He was also, as far as Kate could see, the only person in the room without an identifiable expression in his face. For someone so young—he couldn't have been more than a few years older than her, if that—he had the practiced look of a lifelong poker player. She wouldn't have stood a chance against him in a game of Hold 'Em. His natural state seemed to be one of stone. Worse still, when he spoke, she realized it wasn't just a skin-deep distinction. His unavailable emotions went all the way to his core.

"My name is Clark Woodward, and it's my sad duty to inform you that my uncle, Christopher Woodward, passed away last month."

Gasps from every corner of the room, including Kate's. Mr. Woodward was a good, kind man. He lived in Dallas, but he made time every month to come and visit the ranches in Miller's Point, and of course he visited the festival every year. He even played Scrooge in the festival once, after the real Scrooge took ill and couldn't get out of bed. What he lacked in acting skills, he made up for with the biggest heart in all of Texas. Kate cracked at the news, but the young man behind the podium held his hand up for quiet, effectively silencing them with a single gesture. He wasn't done yet.

"As the new CEO of my uncle's company, it is also my duty to inform you that we will be shutting down The Christmas Company subsidiary, effective immediately."

CEO. Uncle. Shutting down. Immediately. The words all made sense individually, but when sliced into that order and delivered with such dignity, Kate wasn't sure she understood them. How could *this* man be Mr. Woodward's nephew? Who made him CEO?

Kate didn't even flinch when her shaking hands dropped the folded ladder with a room-shaking *thunk*, drawing the attention of a room full of her friends and neighbors. The other questions and confusions were nothing in the face of her biggest issue.

Destroying The Christmas Company would mean the end of Miller's Point as they knew it. Woodward's ranching operations made many of the families good livings, but the seasonal work meant working for The Christmas Company during the colder months was all that stood between many in Miller's Point and the stinging crush of poverty. Her chest tightened in pain at the reality of it.

Around her, the room erupted into conversation and denials, questions and protestations, each more vehement and heartbreaking than the last. But Kate remained squarely focused on their executioner as he dealt the final death blows, not caring if they could hear him over their distressed chatter.

"All salaried and hourly staff will receive a generous

severance package, and I will remain in town for the next few weeks as I oversee the dissolution of the company. Any questions can be directed to the phone number found on your severance letters, which will be in the mail in the next five to seven days. We thank you for your years of service."

With the crowd still reeling from the announcement, he stepped down from the microphone and moved to leave the room. Just like that. Without any warning and without any apologies, he marched down the hall's middle aisle towards the front door. People watched him as he passed, still talking among themselves, but no one said or did anything to stop him, not even Kate. She watched his mirror-shine shoes take command of the floor as if he owned the land he walked on. *Step, step, step, step.* It beat the tune of a song no one wanted to sing, the song of finality. A song that ended with the slam of the chamber doors behind him.

When there was nothing left of him but the faint whisper of cold air, the assembled crowd turned back towards Miss Carolyn. Some of them surely caught Kate in the periphery of their gazes, but she, too, stared at the weathered old woman for some sort of comfort. Miss Carolyn always had a plan. She had a plan and contingency for every scenario. The hall was silent. Kate couldn't even hear her own breathing. Everyone waited for Miss Carolyn's wisdom to save them.

But when she didn't speak and instead turned to Kate with wide, wet eyes, the younger woman understood their wished-for wisdom would never come. The dread fluttering in Kate's stomach turned to lead as the reality of their situation fully sank in. If Miss Carolyn didn't know how to save them, they'd already lost.

"I," she began, her voice wavering from tears. The room

seemed to lean in. Here it was. The big speech to rally the town and save Christmas. She opened her mouth once. Then twice. She scanned the room, meeting the expectant eyes gazing at her.

And then, just when everyone thought she'd give them all the answers, Miss Carolyn slumped. A wrinkled hand ran its way through her hair and she sighed deep enough and defeated enough for all of them combined. "I'm tired. I think I'm going home. Y'all should, too."

For a moment, no one obeyed. They waited for a punchline, for a "just kidding. Let's go punch the big city rat until he gives us what's ours." She met their hope with nothing but silence. Slowly people stood and collected their things, muttering well wishes for the season to their friends and neighbors.

Kate didn't move. Every time she blinked, more of her life crumbled before her. There would be no Christmas Eve festival tomorrow night. There would be no Christmas celebration. Scrooge would never again sing. The town would never celebrate its nightly tree lighting ceremony again. Friendships forged over the festival would dissolve. Some families would lose their main livelihood, others their supplemental income and others still would lose a reason to stay alive through the winter. The charities they supported would go unfunded. The town might not even survive without the tourist income. Kate's found family would disintegrate, just like that. Everything was lost.

As the thought occurred to her, a little sniffle made itself known. It was so clear and so loud she couldn't ignore it. Kate turned to find little Bradley hiding his tears behind his Tiny Tim cane. Kate wondered briefly how many other children had worn that cap before him. How many lives had been changed by those children?

What would those people have been without the festival?

Who would *she* be without the festival?

The questions were more convicting than the answers, and the brain-piercing goodbyes of her chosen family were one big key turning the ignition of her fury. This was her family. No one was going to tear it apart. Not as long as she had a say.

"Stay here, Miss Carolyn."

"Kate…what are you doing?"

Miss Carolyn's question wasn't going to stop her. Kate apparently no longer had a job to lose; she no longer had to listen. These people were her family, her community, and she wasn't going to stand by while some stick-in-the-mud Dallas boy tried to tear them apart and make this world a little bit worse.

With a spine as straight as a flagpole and chin held twice as high, she stormed out of the Miller's Point Town Hall. Her hammering heart joined the steady rap of her shoes as she jogged down the front steps towards the shadowed figure in the black sport coat.

"Hey!"

He was the only one on the street, hence the only one she possibly could have been talking to, but he didn't respond to her hail. The flames of frustration and anger licked at the back of her neck, threatening to consume her. She tried to keep them at bay and maintain some semblance of coolness—the last thing she wanted was to be accused of being an emotional or irrational woman by this stranger—but it was next to impossible. When she thought about all the lives this one tiny decision would touch, it burned up every sense of rational control she possessed.

"Hey, Woodward!"

Was it the use of his name, her razor-sharp tone or the

whipping wind that caused him to tense up like that? Kate didn't care, as long as he paid attention to her. She closed the small space between them, catching up to him just in front of the Scrooge and Marley office. During the off-season, it served as a general store, but she called it the Money-House all year round. Not even the sight of it, which usually sent a thrill of sentimentality through her, could calm her now. When he didn't turn to face her, she took the liberty of hopping down off of the curb so she stood directly in his eye line. This forced her to gaze up at him, but she didn't think there was anything doe-eyed about her. If anything, she felt like an avenging Valkyrie, riding for justice. No one, not even this arrogant stranger, would make the mistake of underestimating her.

"What do you think you're doing?"

His face remained as composed and disinterested as ever, but Kate spied the fingers of his right fist clenching and unclenching. She almost smiled. He had a tell; something was bothering him.

"I'm looking for my car," he announced.

"Your car?"

"Yeah, I parked my car here," he pointed to an empty space in front of Town Hall, "earlier today and now it's gone. It's a rental."

"It got towed, then."

"Towed?"

"We don't allow cars in town during the festival. It ruins the illusion."

Kate almost laughed as she said it, but quelled the urge to do so by crossing her shivering arms over her chest. Everyone with half a brain knew no cars could come into town during the festival. It was on every brochure and article ever written about their little Christmas town; plus, the Martins made a tidy penny renting out their field as a parking lot during the winter. Yet another source of income they'd lose if this guy managed to go through with his plan.

"You should be thanking me, then. I'm modernizing the place already." His tone managed to be smug even as she wondered if the slight shrink of his shoulders meant he might not entirely believe that. "Who do I call about getting it back?"

What arrogance! She'd come out here to give him a piece of her mind and he had the audacity to ask her about his *car*?

"I don't think you're going anywhere until you give us some answers."

"With all due respect, I don't owe you answers."

"Oh, really?"

"For my years of service focusing on profitable divisions of his business, my uncle left me the company and I'm doing my best to protect his legacy."

"His legacy? Look around you! This is his legacy!"

She said *is* when she supposed she should have said *was*. Though, in Kate's estimation, a man's legacy didn't die with him; it was a living, growing thing that outlasted him and stretched as long as other people cultivated it. Mr. Woodward would only really die if they let this festival die with him. It was yet another reason Kate continued to fight, even when this arrogant jerk couldn't stop staring down the bridge of his nose at her like she was no more than a receipt stuck to the bottom of his shoes.

"This festival isn't profitable."

"Maybe not in money, but—"

"What other kind of profit is there?"

Kate opened her mouth and closed it twice, not because she didn't know the answer to his question, but because she knew it wouldn't move him. He was a numbers and cents guy. Telling him what the festival lost in funds it more than made up for in revival of the human spirit probably wasn't going to do anything other than make her out to be some silly, sentimental woman.

Which she was. But she just didn't want him thinking it.

"No?" he asked. If she were the fighting type, she might have punched that smug, condescending smirk of victory off of his face, but she refrained. "Yeah, that's what I thought. Now, tell me who I call about the car."

"I could." Rather than violence, Kate decided to deal in bitingly sweet sarcasm. "But I have to do what's best for my town, just like you have to do what's best for your company. And I don't think it's good for us to have a lunatic like you out on the road."

"If I hear you out, will you give me the number?"

She'd meant her quip about him driving around town as a joke, but he responded as though they were finally speaking the same language: the language of transaction. In some ways, Kate had to admire him for that. He was as single-minded in his determination as she was; they shared a sincere faith in the rightness of their cause. Sure, he couldn't have been more wrong, but at least he believed in something, even if it was just the power and importance of money. He shoved his hands in his pockets.

"I'll consider it."

"Then I'm listening, Miss...?"

"Kate."

"Kate."

It must have been a strong, random winter wind sending chills through her body; it couldn't have been the almost tender way he said her name. She coughed and tightened her arms across her chest, hoping the pressure would stop the sensation.

"What should I call you? Scrooge McDuck, or…?"

To her surprise, he laughed. It wasn't an evil movie villain laugh or anything, just a nice chuckle with a warm ring to it. She dismissed how much she liked it as a fluke. Even cold, unfeeling statues sometimes looked almost human in the right lighting.

"You can call me Clark."

Kate didn't repeat his name as he did hers. It somehow felt wrong to call him by his first name; she felt more comfortable calling her former high school teachers by their first names than she did calling him Clark. It was such a wholesome, all-American kind of name. Clark Kent. Clark Gable. Clark Woodward wasn't the correct third for that trio.

"Listen." All of Kate's strength went into fueling her empathy for this man. Focusing on her friends and family would just leave her angry and bitter; focusing on him would give her a much better shot. Most men liked an appeal to vanity. Maybe it would work on him. "I don't know you. I don't know anything about you. But your Uncle Christopher was a good man. He believed in this town. I mean, your family basically built this place. The library is named after you. The school auditorium. The football field. The gazebo in the park, for goodness' sake. It's all yours. You can do whatever you want with it—"

"Great. You understand where I'm coming from."

"No. I mean, yes, but you don't understand where I'm coming from." He raised an eyebrow, which she took as a sign to continue. "You have a town full of people who stare at your name every day with hope. And gratitude. Are you going to betray all of these people? Take away their livelihoods?"

"I don't know any of these people. I don't care about any of these people."

Those two statements landed on Kate's jaw like a string of one-two punches. What kind of man just…didn't care?

"If they want jobs, they can herd cattle like the rest of my employees, but I can't waste money on this Christmas foolishness for another day."

"But your uncle—"

"I am not my uncle!"

It was a roar, a statement to the heavens; the force of it almost knocked Kate back a step. Somehow, she managed to hold her ground even as she couldn't quite understand the nerve she'd struck. Everyone wanted to be Mr. Woodward; he was as kind as he was insanely rich. The perfect combination. What kind of man hated a man like that?

"Clearly."

The sharp flash of emotion dissolved as quickly as it appeared. Clark straightened his jacket.

"I think I've heard enough. You can go ahead and give me that phone number now."

"One last thing," Kate said.

"Yes?"

"During your… During your little speech, you didn't even wish us a merry Christmas."

His refusal to do so left her with a nasty taste in her mouth. A small gesture it might have been, but its absence was so blatant she couldn't let it go.

"That's because I don't celebrate Christmas."

"Don't celebrate Christmas?" Kate choked.

"No. Now, give me the number."

Dumbstruck, Kate's brain didn't quite possess the processing power to say anything as she gave him the number. The cogs in her mind were too busy trying to puzzle out his declaration. But once he had the number, he was gone, leaving her with nothing but questions.

There was no goodbye. No, "for what it's worth, I'm sorry." Just a curt "thanks," as he walked away dialing. Kate stood alone on the sidewalk for only the briefest of seconds before a hand touched her shoulder. She didn't turn around or tear her gaze from the spot where Clark stood just a moment ago; she knew who would be there.

"How'd it go, dear?"

The pity in Miss Carolyn's question stung. Kate hadn't even realized tears were forming in her eyes until they left cold tracks down her flushed cheeks. She'd failed. She'd tried to save her town, and she'd failed. With a weak shrug, she decided a little gallows humor was probably for the best.

"Do you know if any places are hiring?"

Chapter Two
Christmas Eve

K ATE BUCKNER WAS ON A roll, as far as rants went.
Since arriving almost thirty minutes ago, she'd yam-
mered nonstop, flooding her companion and the empty
restaurant with her every stray thought. The faster she
spoke, the faster they came, leaving her to race to catch up.

"But you know what I really can't stand?"

It was 7:15 on the morning of Christmas Eve, and for
the first time since she was seven years old, Kate wasn't
ironing a petticoat or setting up trays of mince pies. For
once, she sat at the end of the bar at Mel's Diner, drinking
a steaming cup of coffee and relishing the hearty scents
of bacon and maple syrup. On a regular morning in, say,
March, the old diner was the greatest breakfast joint in
the known universe.

But this Christmastime? She hated it. Mel's was a staple
of the Miller's Point diet and she came in here at least once
a week, but that was part of the problem. Without the
festival, this felt like just another Tuesday. Bing Crosby's
holiday standards on the old jukebox just weren't enough
to convince her this was actually Christmas Eve.

"What can't you stand?"

Michael Newman, her breakfast companion and best friend since they were cast as Fred and Fred's wife in high school, couldn't have been more different than Clark Woodward. Where the out-of-towner played perpetual poker, Michael slapped himself open and let you read every page of him. He was the all-American type, dark-skinned with a smile that could light up a football stadium on its own, the exact image of a small-town golden boy. She'd always assumed he'd be mayor one day, but now she wasn't sure if the town would be around long enough for him to make the leap from ranch medic to political mastermind. For a long time, town gossip had it that the two of them, the town's two favorite children, would end up married, but she could never imagine it. They were like two trees planted too close together. Their branches intertwined and they shared the same soil, but they'd never become one. She only thought of him as a friend.

"What I *really* can't stand is that he has the audacity to stand there and mansplain to me about economics. Of course the festival doesn't make money for them, but it makes money for us, and that helps keep the town—the town where his business is, I'll remind you—afloat. What's he gonna do about workers when they all move to Fort Worth or something because there's not enough money circulating here? Huh?"

"I don't know, Kate."

The diner was completely empty, perhaps because it wasn't meant to be open. It closed on Christmas Eve and Christmas Day, usually because Mel, a rotund, redheaded man with a missing front tooth, always played The Ghost of Christmas Present, but this morning Kate had showed up at his front door with a determined knock and Michael in tow, ready to pay top dollar for black coffee and as many pancakes as it was humanly possible to consume in one sitting. She couldn't fathom sitting alone in her tiny apartment above the town's solitary bookstore for another minute, looking out onto the empty town square; the loneliness would have consumed her.

Now, all that consumed her was the frustration she'd been venting to herself all night. Saying these things out loud helped slightly, but as usual, Michael wasn't content to nod his head and agree with her. He just had to be difficult. The man never knew when to quit, an admirable quality he and Kate shared.

"And who doesn't celebrate Christmas? Christmas!" she exclaimed, waving her hands in her usual manner, the kind that almost always ended in her accidentally knocking over a salt shaker or a full glass of Diet Coke.

"Off the top of my head? Jewish people, Muslims, Jehovah's Witnesses, some other sects of Christianity, some atheists—"

The sass earned him a withering look.

"I don't know, Kate. Maybe he just doesn't like…" Michael picked at his biscuits and gravy, the first course of the six he'd ordered immediately upon sitting down at the bar. After half a lifetime of friendship, Kate had taught him these moods of hers meant he would need to be settled in for a long, long time. "I don't know. Trees. Maybe he's allergic to Christmas trees."

"He could get a fake one."

"Or he gets paper cuts from wrapping presents."

"He could use gift bags."

"What about eggnog? Maybe he's vegan."

"Then he needs to move out of Texas."

On some level, Kate knew she was being useless. Sitting in this diner complaining about the impossibility and injustice of it all seemed like a perfect way to get absolutely nothing done. On another level, the impossibility and injustice almost gave her permission to whine. Nothing could be done. Why shouldn't she just moan and groan and commiserate with her friend? She dropped her head into her hands.

"I don't want to be that guy," Michael said through a mouth full of biscuit, "but you don't look so good."

"I don't know why. I got a solid four hours of sleep last night. That's a full hour longer than usual."

Kate knew full well how she looked. Besides her daily uniform of jeans, a red flannel shirt, her reliable pair of sturdy-heeled boots and her dirty blonde hair tied away from her face in a sensible braid, heavy bags dragged her hazel eyes down and her splotchy skin spoke of a restless night. Michael was more of a solid eight hours of sleep kind of guy, so his surprise was understandable.

"What were you doing up that late?"

Kate brightened up. Her ideas may have been half-baked, but at least she had them. And even if it would never happen, she liked feeling useful.

"Brainstorming. I have tons of ideas to save the town." And only two of them involved hiring Bono and Beyoncé for a telethon. Most of the others involved social media campaigns and petitioning the federal government for a grant of some kind once she figured out how to write grants, but some of the ideas were sensible and others not cooked up. "We're gonna call the governor and petition to have the square designated a historical—"

Her ranting came to an abrupt halt as Michael's fork clattered to his plate and his jaw dropped halfway to the floor. He stared over her shoulder at something Kate couldn't see. She tried to make it out in the reflection of a window behind *his* head, to no avail.

"No way," he said.

"What?"

"Don't look now," he muttered, casually reaching for his coffee cup, "but your boyfriend from yesterday's meeting just walked in."

"My what?"

Kate spun in her seat, but Michael caught her shoulder and pulled her back to face front.

"I said don't look now!"

Thank goodness for the Bing Crosby Christmas hits. If it hadn't been for the loud crooning, Clark Woodward would've heard them. Mind racing, Kate tried to place the pieces of this puzzle together. This was their town and their diner. He must have thought himself as bulletproof as the real Clark Kent if he thought he could show his face in public after what he did yesterday.

"Why is he here?" Kate hissed, leaning into Michael to prevent herself from giving in to the temptation to glance over her shoulder at the intruder.

"I don't know. He's just sitting at a table, looking at a menu."

"What in the world does he think he's doing? Is he going to shut this place down, too?"

"Maybe he's just hungry."

"No." Kate shook her head. He wasn't a diner breakfast kind of guy. He was a protein bar and kale smoothie kind of guy. Dallas men always gave off a clean living vibe; it made them unable to function in a small town like Miller's Point. "He's got to have something up his sleeve."

"Shh. Mel's going to take his order."

They fell into silence as Mel's heavy steps took him towards the booth behind Kate. She tuned her ears for any whisper of underhanded moneygrubbing. The first time Clark tried to barter over the price of eggs, she was going to flip.

"Hi, stranger." Mel greeted him with the same warmth and openness with which he greeted everyone. His friendliness crawled under Kate's skin. Clark didn't deserve Mel's good nature. He deserved a one-way ticket straight out of town. She believed in universal good. Everyone had wonder and joy inside them. Everyone could be reached with kindness. But…this guy made her so mad she could spit. "What can I get you?"

"Yeah, can I have a double stack of buttermilk pancakes and a black coffee to go? With a side of bacon, too."

Even with her back turned, Kate could picture him in her mind's eye, sitting unmoved with the perfect winter backdrop behind him. His voice was as flat and lifeless as she'd heard it. Still, she applauded his order. Simple, direct, and he even got some of Mel's famous double-crispy bacon. Maybe he was human after all.

"To go? You off somewhere?"

"Work."

"Work? It's Christmas Eve, kid. Didn't anyone tell you?" Mel chuckled. He always made conversation with his customers. Maybe it was a small-town gossip thing or maybe it was a Mel thing, but he liked keeping up to speed with the movement of his community.

"It's a Tuesday. I work on Tuesdays."

Apparently, Clark didn't appreciate the perceived intrusion.

"Ah. I see." There was a pause, awkward in its length. Kate picked at her own pancakes to give off the appearance of not eavesdropping. "It's just…I don't know if anyone's gonna be in the Woodward office this morning. Most people would have the day off for the festival. Besides, even if anyone is in, they won't be there until nine, at least."

"All because of Christmas?"

"Yeah. Christmas is kind of a thing around here."

Understatement of the century. Christmas was a way of life, and Clark couldn't even begin to understand how terribly he'd disturbed it. A pang of sympathy tugged at her. His cronies in Dallas almost certainly worked on Christmas Eve, the poor big city stiffs.

"I'll just have my breakfast here, then. Thanks."

"Don't you have a family or anything to visit? I know it's not any of my business, but you seem pretty young to be wasting your holiday in a boring office."

"You're right." Newspaper pages rustled. "It isn't any of your business."

"Buttermilk pancakes, bacon and coffee." Another awkward pause spread between them like butter on a biscuit, ending only with Mel tapping his pen against his tiny ordering notepad. "Coming right up."

The interaction ended with Mel whistling as he returned to the kitchen and Michael turning back to Kate with untamed shock. He probably expected to see steam coming out of Kate's ears. If anyone had told her she wouldn't be hopping mad at Clark for speaking to someone in her town that way, she would have laughed in their face. But her mind caught on something and unraveled like a home-knit sweater.

Don't you have a family?

It isn't any of your business.

For the first time since meeting him, the anger and hurt serving as Kate's most recent and dear best friends were nowhere to be found. In their place stood a different creature altogether. She no longer hated the man threatening to take her life away.

She pitied him.

All of her assumptions about him had to be, on some level, incorrect. In her mind, she fancied him living the perfect, big-city rich boy life. A huge family who lavished him with gifts and privileges, love and understanding.

Yet, here he was. Alone. In a diner booth. On Christmas Eve. Waiting for his office to open so he could spend the day working.

How sad was that?

Kate's entire heart smashed open, and the blindness of her own rage smacked her in the face. Guilt bittered the coffee in her mouth, but it was soon replaced. Her eyes widened, she reached for Michael's hand, and let her hopes get as high as they pleased.

This was a solvable problem. Clark Woodward's loneliness was one hundred percent solvable.

"Can you distract him for a few hours?" she asked, knowing full well the monumental burden she'd shoved onto her friend's admittedly toned shoulders. Michael's eyes widened. As usual, he was an open book. Fear wrote itself on his every page.

"*What?*"

"I think I have a plan." Well, half a plan. Quarter of a plan. A fraction of a plan. She'd work out the rest on her bike. "Can you distract him until, like, noon? And then bring him to the old Woodward place? I think that's where he's staying."

"You wanna leave me with that?"

Kate stood and threw on her layers of sweaters and scarves, all while her mind wrote plans and made to-do lists. When she was done, she gave him a firm pat on the back for good luck. She wouldn't want his job, either, but he was the only person she trusted with the task. No one said no to Michael. Even in a world with Tom Hanks, Michael took the top prize for most effortlessly likable guy on earth.

"You're the best guy in town. If you can't do it, no one

can. I believe in you."

"But—! But—!"

His protests faded as she sprinted from the diner and hopped on her bike, which was waiting outside for her. As she pedaled towards the massive mansion on the far side of town, speeding past Dickensian facades and garlands, Kate's motives solidified. There was only one way to save Miller's Point. There was only one way to save the festival. There was only one way to save the solitary man in the diner from his own self-imposed darkness and isolation.

She had to make Clark Woodward believe in Christmas.

Chapter Three

I T WAS SO PROVINCIAL. CLARK Woodward couldn't think of any other word to describe Miller's Point. Provincial in every sense of the word. Nearly everything about them revealed how small they were, and what was worse, they reveled in their smallness. They clung to their superstitious belief in the holidays. They fought the inevitable march of progress he was going to bring to the company and their backwater enclave. The diner didn't even have avocado on the menu.

As he waited for his pancakes, Clark opened the newspaper. They didn't get the *Dallas Observer* out here, so the local gossip would have to do. He scanned the words, each one sinking in less deeply than the one before it. Out of the window framing his booth, he could see the entire town square, including the town hall, where only yesterday he and Kate—he never got her last name—had faced off.

Last night, he hadn't allowed himself the time or the thought to take in the beauty of the town's historic district. And it really was beautiful, even if it being beautiful just reminded him how wasteful the entire enterprise was. How much money did they spend on these facade recreations of London's Cheapside? How much of his family's fortune got washed away every night with those fake snow machines? And the lights! They might as well have built a fire out of all the greenbacks they wasted.

Wasteful and beautiful. The worst combination.

More dangerous, though, was thinking about the beauty who'd dared to challenge him. She'd burned herself into him yesterday with her persistence and the fiery passion behind her eyes.

He appreciated how strangely alike they were, even as they fought for completely different goals. If he hadn't been spooked by her insistence that his uncle would have saved the festival, he could have stayed on those steps and talked to her for hours. She was a sharp debater with a biting wit. In a town like this, he'd expected to be greeted as a king. His family, after all, was responsible for their survival. But she didn't bow and scrape; she challenged him.

She was wrong, of course, and he was right. But the challenge still thrilled him, even if he didn't dare let it show on his face. He didn't want anyone thinking they had any kind of power over him.

The most striking thing about her, perhaps, was her ability to embody everything he despised about Miller's Point. That dichotomy of wasteful and beautiful dwelled within her. She had much to offer; he saw that even in their brief interaction. Yet, she chose to stay in Miller's Point, where she could do nothing but waste her life putting up tinsel.

Clark knew he should push all thoughts of her directly from his head. A distraction like her would only get in the way of his plans. His mission was simple, but like a fine watch, even the slightest bit of sand carried the potential to destroy everything. In three steps, he could be done with this stupid festival. Step One: Dissolve The Christmas Company. Two: Sell off its assets. Three: Return to civilization and Dallas before New Year's. He could only do that if all distractions were kept to a minimum and all pieces of sand stayed far out of his way.

And he could only accomplish his three-step plan if people actually went to work instead of spending their Tuesdays watching Hallmark movies or whatever it is they did when they "celebrated" Christmas. Clark's mind boggled at the way this town shut down on this useless holiday. The McDonald's, where he first attempted breakfast, had locked its doors.

"But—! But—!"

Clark's head popped up from the blurred words of his newspapers at the loud shouting of a stranger. He whipped his head around just in time to see a flash of a red-scarfed woman dash out of the door and a desperate man sitting at the diner counter. Clark was aware of small-town manners. A good citizen would have invited the freshly liberated man to join him for breakfast, but Clark wasn't a good citizen, and even if he was, he didn't think anyone in Miller's Point would particularly want to share a meal with him.

"Can you believe her?"

It took at least fifteen seconds for Clark to realize the other man was talking to him. He focused on an article about a high school track meet. Apparently, this small town dominated at the recent district meet, held at Christopher Woodward Stadium. He wondered if they'd keep the name now that his uncle was dead, or if they'd turn it into the Christopher Woodward Memorial Stadium to acknowledge his legacy or whatever.

"I wasn't listening. Sorry."

Apparently, to the man at the counter, this was all the

invitation he needed to join Clark for breakfast.

"This seat taken?"

No, but it isn't open either. Please leave me and my pancakes in peace. Clark fought to keep the snark at bay. There was nothing he wanted less than company at the moment, especially when the entire town was afflicted with candy cane fever. He didn't want any of that foolishness rubbing off on him. But it didn't seem this guy was in the mood to take no for an answer.

"Go ahead."

"Thanks."

Balancing his array of half-finished plates across his forearms, he plopped into the seat, rattling the table. It took longer than a polite minute for the man to arrange his extensive breakfast, which only added to the heat flaring up the back of Clark's neck. His lips flattened into a thin line of displeasure when Mel appeared with a piping hot plate and mug. He placed them on the table, and Clark pulled them close, grateful for the distraction. He couldn't decide what the stranger across from him wanted, but if he thought he could convince him to change his mind about the festival, he'd be just as disappointed as Kate. Did these people have some sort of committee, dedicated to twisting the simplest of business decisions into a city-wide ordeal?

"One order of pancakes and bacon. And a black coffee. Syrup's over there. Can I get you anything else?"

Clark started to say no, but was cut off.

"Can I get some more coffee, Mel? Oh, and one of those blueberry muffins."

"They're about two days old."

"Can you pop it in the microwave for about thirty seconds, then?"

His easy intimacy with the diner owner put Clark's

transactional replies to shame. Without the protection of his newspaper, Clark had to actually interact with these people. His worst fears realized.

"You got it, kid."

Mel departed. As Clark dug into his pancakes, he hoped the only frustration he'd have to deal with was the treacle-sweet music pouring out of the juke box, but his new guest proved him wrong.

"You're that Woodward guy, aren't you?" he asked through a mouth of biscuits dripping with gravy.

"Clark."

"I'm Michael." Clark nodded once, an acknowledgment that he'd heard the introduction, but his new companion took his silence as an invitation for more conversation. "Some people call me Buddy, but I'll answer to anything, really."

The urge to roll his eyes was unbearably strong. He couldn't imagine anyone wanting to be called Buddy when Michael was perfectly suitable. Buddy wasn't a name for a man. It was a name for a puppy or a background character in a Flannery O'Connor novel.

"Small towns," he muttered.

"Buddy was my grandfather's callsign during the invasion of Normandy. He won a Medal of Valor."

Clark choked on his bacon, ready to splutter out some kind of tense take-back of the insult, but he was awarded with uproarious laughter from the man across the table.

"I'm just messing with you, Dallas. Buddy used to be my nickname, but getting a medical degree changes how people see you. I mostly just go by Michael now. How're the pancakes?"

"Good."

"Mel makes the best pancakes in the whole state, I think. On Christmas morning, he sets up an assembly line in the town hall and a bunch of volunteers chip in to help him make, like, two thousand pancakes so everyone in town can have breakfast before the festival starts. The 25th is our busiest day of the year." Michael's hurried excitement tapered off when he realized a tradition would be ending. He got a hollow look in his eyes, which Clark did his best to ignore. "I mean, he did. And it was. When the festival was still on."

The festival. He was tired of hearing about the festival. If these people loved the festival so much, why didn't they put it on themselves instead of using his family's money? Better yet, why didn't they raise the price from a measly ten dollars per person to twenty-five per person? A fifteen-dollar increase would've meant big things for their bottom line, yet when he'd proposed it to Carolyn, the Director of Operations, she'd assured him she'd rather quit the whole thing altogether than keep poor families out and only cater to rich folks. She then glared at him as if the mere suggestion of raising ticket prices cheapened the entire heart of her operation.

Clark said, "Listen, Michael. I'm not really looking for company. I'm fine on my own."

"Yeah. Of course. I was just thinking I could maybe show you around, you know, give you the lay of the land since you'll be here for a few days. I can show you everything. Library, bank, even the parking lots so your car doesn't get towed again."

News travels fast. He'd only told Kate and the tow truck guy about his car; twelve hours later, everyone knew. *If I walk around with you for twenty minutes, will you leave me alone?* Something in this town's water must have made them especially persistent. As with his first interaction with Kate, Clark saw no other way to get rid of this guy than giving him a little bit of his time.

"Sure," he agreed, trying to hide his displeasure behind a half-hearted smile, only to be practically blinded by Michael's blinding one.

"Mel! Make my muffin to go!"

What Clark hoped would be a brief twenty-minute introduction became an almost three-hour walking tour of the most important historical and contemporary sites Miller's Point had to offer. By the time Michael ran out of steam, Clark knew more about the remote ranching village than he'd ever known about Dallas. For example, he'd had no idea his family founded Miller's Point outright. He assumed they'd settled and prospered here, not set up the first encampments of ranchers.

At the first half-hour mark of the extensive tour, Clark considered bailing out and begging off to his office, but he couldn't actually find it in himself to do it. Save for the workers taking down the decorations in the town square (as he'd instructed the night before), the town was empty and Michael was every bit the enjoyable host. Not that he ever let on, but he actually had a good time walking around the town and taking in its sights, provincial though they were.

But he drew the line at a cemetery tour. Close inspections of ghosts and tombstones where Jesus wore cowboy boots did not fit his description of an acceptable way to spend a morning. He checked his watch.

"I have to go to my office. I have things to do," he said, curt and direct as possible. The tour may have been a fine diversion for a few hours, but it couldn't last all day. He needed to be in the office, taking care of work, even if no one in this town seemed to understand the concept.

"Great! I'll walk you there."

"I'm fine, thanks—"

"No buts! Besides, I know where they hide the spare key."

The Woodward Building was two blocks east off of the town square, and unlike the Dallas offices, it was not an imposing block of concrete and steel, made up in an intricate Art Deco style. It was a humble, two-story building with a flat roof and little else to speak of besides the embarrassment of Christmas lights decorating the front windows. A hand-painted sign with flippable numbers read: "0 DAYS 'TIL CHRISTMAS." Clark ripped it from its hook as Michael went for the spare key.

"You really aren't into this Christmas stuff, are you?"

Given he'd only known this guy for a few hours, Clark spared him the tragic backstory and instead took the key and let himself in. The building's exterior appeared humble, befitting a small-town center of business operations, but the inside ruined his every hope of a muted, respectable workplace environment. It was too fancy. Though years of red-clay-covered boots marked and stained the carpet, the wood finishes of the desks and the crown molding belonged in a palace rather than a satellite office building. Christmas decorations, no doubt charged to his family's accounts, cluttered every available space. Even the coffee machine was top-of-the-line, but something else bothered him more. He made a beeline for the wall beside the receptionist's desk.

"What are you doing?" Michael asked.

"Turning the heating off," Clark replied, searching for the temperature gauge instead of asking what in the world he was doing standing around here when Clark had made it clear their little tour had ended at the graveyard gates.

"It's, like, forty degrees outside."

"And we all carry coats, don't we? Heating is expensive."

The other man's shocked gaze bore into Clark's skin. He paid it no mind. He was a practical man in every sense of the word; he didn't indulge in luxury. He wore fashionable but reasonably priced clothes, even stitching buttons and cuffs himself when they showed signs of wear. He wore his father's timeless suit jackets, having them tailored to fit perfectly. He wasn't very well going to heat an entire building, especially when no one worked inside to enjoy it. Besides, chill increased productivity. Hundreds of workplace studies said so. He'd stopped heating the office in Dallas; everyone here would get used to it. His next order of business, while Michael underscored his movements with a warbling whistle version of "Baby, It's Cold Outside," was to find the receptionist's black book. When he finally procured it, he flipped through the pages, holding them close enough to his face to read them. He'd forgotten his glasses back at home.

"What're you doing now?"

"Calling my staff. *I* didn't give them the day off."

"You really think that's a good idea?" he asked. His boldness lasted up until Clark shot him a narrowed look over the secretary's desk. "It's just... They made plans. Want to see their families, you know."

"Why are you here? Why aren't you at work, I mean?"

"The foreman gave us the day off. We were all supposed to be out working on the festival to help with the Christmas Eve crowds. The 24th and 25th are packed. You wouldn't believe it."

"You work for Woodward?"

"Yep. On Ranch 13 on the Eastern lot."

Clark raised an eyebrow and flipped to another page in the contact book. No wonder the company suffered so much during the month of December. All of his employees were getting free passes from his foremen. If he had any say, everyone would be coming in to work this afternoon.

"I'll have to call him, too."

Passing pages upon pages of personal numbers and shoved-in food delivery menus, Clark finally reached the work associates section of the records and searched for his Head of Production's number. Whoever he was, he'd be getting an earful. Anyone who wanted to keep their job would be coming in, and that was final. Everyone in the Dallas office was working; there was no reason anyone else should have the day off. His fingers flew over the expensive black phone—only to receive the dial tone as Michael pressed down on the termination button. His eyes flashed with fear. Fear of what? Of hard work? This guy, with his big, calloused hands, didn't seem unaccustomed to hard work.

"Listen, I have to tell you something."

"…Yes?"

Returning the phone to its cradle, Clark waited for his companion to speak. Michael checked his watch, a gesture Clark couldn't help but note. Their tour had lasted an eternity without Michael checking his watch once; now he read the thing like the Gospel. The entire air hummed with nervous panic, though Clark couldn't for the life of him understand what Michael had to be nervous about. Surely the company's employees weren't this afraid of a hard day's work…right? Or did they really fear losing their precious day off so much?

"You know Kate Buckner?"

It wasn't the question he'd expected. Perhaps he should have. She'd been hovering in his thoughts like heavy-handed foreshadowing all day. He filtered her in his mind like sea water, never quite seeing her clearly.

"I've met *a* Kate," Clark offered. The taste in his mouth soured and he offered a silent prayer that Michael's sudden declaration did not concern the Kate who cornered him outside of Town Hall last night. *Dear God, let him be talking about a different Kate. Please.* If this strange small town had taught him anything so far, it was this: no one wanted to tangle with her.

"Pretty? Dirty blonde hair? Looks like she always wants to dance or fight?"

Clark wouldn't have put it that way. She never looked to him like a dancer or a fighter, though she carried herself with the natural grace of either. If he put any amount of real thought into her, he might have described her as a helper. She looked ready to help anyone and anything who needed her, even if helping meant she had to fight. It was an endearing quality; he would have admired it if he didn't think it was against her best interest.

"Yeah. I've met Kate Buckner."

"She's up to something." Michael spoke, gaining momentum with every word like a freight train. "She's at your family's house right now. I wasn't supposed to tell you, and I don't really know what's going on, but I think it's important you go home right now and check it out."

Truth be told, Clark hated that old place. He'd tried to avoid staying there the night before, but every hotel or bed and breakfast he approached informed him, polite as could be, they had no vacancy, so he'd bitten the bullet and returned to the mansion's creaking halls, choosing to sleep on a couch in the front living room to avoid diving too deep into the body of the house. He hadn't been there since he was a kid, and the memories wrapped around him heavier than the musty old blanket he'd slept under.

"The Woodward House?"

"Yeah."

He dreaded returning in the daylight, but he knew he had no choice. He didn't know her plan, but he couldn't let any harm come to the estate. The sham castle built on a hill still held the spirits of his family, and they required protection.

It was all he had left of his parents.

Collecting his coat, he tossed Michael the keys to his rental car, which he'd rescued from the tow yard this morning.

"Drive me there."

Chapter Four

"THIS ALL LOOKS AMAZING! CAN we move those candlesticks to the end of the hall? Oh, be careful with those ornaments! Just put the boxes down in the living room. We'll decorate the tree later."

Kate wasn't one to toot her own horn, but even she had to admit it: the Woodward House looked amazing. It wasn't all her doing, of course. She merely lugged a few boxes and used her copy of the house keys to let everyone inside. When she called Miss Carolyn to tell her of her plan, The Christmas Company phone tree went into full effect, and within an hour, most of the town's decorations were torn down from their places off of the square and almost one hundred people showed up at the Woodward House to ready it for Christmas. Thankfully, this place wasn't unfamiliar to the people of Miller's Point. Mr. Woodward had let them use it as a muster point for the festival for years, so once inside, everyone had a good idea of which archways and bannisters needed the most Christmas-ification.

It was a painfully simple plan, really, and everyone hopped on board quicker than she anticipated. All she had to do was teach Clark Woodward to love Christmas.

The process of that began with a Christmas makeover of his house. After seeing his pitiful slump at Mel's diner, she took to imagining quiet, lonely Decembers passing by him in a dark apartment in Dallas, complete with Hungry Man dinners and falling asleep on the couch. The sort of Christmas she only imagined in her nightmares. It was clear he'd fallen out of love with Christmas—Kate didn't believe anyone naturally disliked the holiday—because it'd been too long since he'd had a wonderful one. She was going to reintroduce magic into his life, and by tomorrow morning when she was done with him, he'd have to agree to putting the festival back on.

It would be difficult, but she had an ace up her sleeve. Some people claimed it was impossible to change someone's heart overnight, but Kate knew better. After all, she'd read Dickens.

"I think we're all done inside. They're finishing outside, but do you want to light 'er up in here?"

"Yes! Just one second…"

Kate sprinted for the top of the grand staircase, her muscles tingling. Everything had to be perfect, and this was the moment of truth. She nodded to Billy Golden, the load-in specialist for the festival, who'd been running point for her since his arrival that morning. He stood at the foot of the stairs with an electrical dial in hand, waiting for her signal. She held up her hands, as if preparing to conduct a symphony. "Okay. Now."

Kate blinked, fully expecting that in the split second of her eyes being closed, she would open them to find herself completely immersed in the winter wonderland of her own creation.

"What have you done?!"

Oh, no. The voice of her target echoed through the grand foyer of the Eastlake Victorian-style manor, shaking the paintings on the walls and knocking crystals of the chandelier. All movement—including Kate's heart—halted. Her eyes lowered, step-by-step down the carpeted, garland-strewn staircase, until she reached the tips of his mirror-shined shoes. She recognized his voice even without peeking at his face.

There was no noise but the driving, tinkling melody of "We Wish You a Merry Christmas." It wafted through the house like the smell of fresh-from-the-oven gingerbread cookies.

Apparently, Clark Woodward didn't appreciate music or delicious gingerbread because he let out another yawp of displeasure:

"And turn that music off!"

Without so much as peeking up from his shoes, Kate touched the pause button on the phone in her pocket, effectively silencing her Bluetooth playlist.

Once, when she was a kid, Kate had gotten caught trying on the Ebenezer Scrooge costume, fake beard and all. The man playing the miser that year had a lisp and a bit of a limp, so she was dragging her left foot around the dressing room saying, "Merry *Chrithhhmathh.*" To her everlasting shame and regret, he'd walked in on her mid-private performance.

She felt nearly as captured now.

Michael. She cursed his name. He was supposed to keep him busy until noon at least! Everyone was supposed to be safely back home so there would be no way of restoring the house to normal order. That was the entire point of the distraction. If Clark demanded his house be emptied of all Christmas cheer, the plan would be ruined.

You've got to do something, Kate's rational brain told her petrified tongue. *You can't just stand here like an idiot. It's starting to get awkward.* Hands shaking in her pockets, she wondered if she hadn't made a poor decision or two this morning. Not about the choice of an angel as a tree topper instead of a star—she stood by that. She wondered if she'd made a mistake in coming here at all. Was she beaten before she'd even started? Was she even strong enough to save her town? Why did she think she, the town's resident hem-stitcher and pie-placer, would be good or strong enough to defend them against disaster?

Kate straightened. It didn't matter if she wasn't strong enough. *He* didn't know she wasn't strong enough, and she could use that to her advantage. Besides, she had every right to be here. She picked her head up, adopting an impenetrable armor of optimism. This was Christmas Eve. These people were her family and friends. She *had* to save them all.

And she didn't know how to walk away from someone with eyes as cold as his. She'd just have to save him, too.

"Clark! How are you?"

Her smile sent him back a step. He must have expected her to whimper and scrape at his booming shouts. Good. She'd caught him off guard already. Once he'd recovered, he walked deeper into the foyer.

"What have you done to my house?"

"Your house? Does it have your name on it?"

Michael helpfully stepped forward.

"It does, actually. It's on the sign right out front."

"Don't you have a clock to check somewhere?" she snarked, sending him scurrying out of the front door, right behind Billy Golden.

With Kate at the top of the stairs and Clark at the bottom, she reveled in the literal high ground. All she had to do was hold onto it. She glanced out of the house's wide front windows. Though the decorations on the inside of the house were almost entirely complete, a near army of workers on ladders were still hard at work hanging lights outside.

"So." She placed a steadying hand on the top of the staircase banister, hoping it looked more like a power move than something necessary to keep her upright. "What do you think?"

"What have you done?"

"Is there an echo in here?" The quip, in her opinion, was brilliant, but he either didn't get the joke or purposefully withheld his laughter. Rude. She gripped the banister tighter and gave a sweep of the grand atrium with her free hand. The chandelier hanging in the high, vaulted ceiling had been dotted with poinsettia plants and evergreens, giving the room a sweet, rich smell. Kate was glad for their perfume; it meant she couldn't smell the smoke coming out of Clark's ears. She would've been lying, though, if she didn't secretly derive pleasure from his displeasure. He'd made everyone she knew uncomfortable when he ended their employment yesterday. Maybe he deserved to be uncomfortable, too, even if she was trying to heal what she suspected was his broken, used-up heart. "We decorated for Christmas. Do you like it?"

Don't shout. Don't raise your voice. Don't even let her know this is bothering you. Just be clear, direct, and get the job done. Clark's internal pep talk was strong, but not strong enough to hold his bewildered frustration at bay. He flexed his right hand, a nervous habit he'd spent almost his entire life unsuccessfully struggling to break, and tried to answer her question. Did he like it?

"I'd like it to be taken down."

"I'm sorry. No can do."

She stood at the top of the staircase like some silent film star, taking control of the garish scenery. He didn't need to look around him to see the marks of her handiwork everywhere. His family's house—that cold monument to excess and emptiness—had been transformed. In his memory, this place was always closer to Wayne Manor than Hogwarts—a shadowy prison for cobwebs and abandoned family photos.

When he'd driven up with Michael this morning, however, he'd almost turned around, convinced they'd made a wrong turn somewhere. Woodward today looked nothing like it did in his dark memories. With every turn of his car's wheels, they moved closer and closer to a postcard of a Victorian Christmas, not the palace of pity he'd always known the place to be. Though men and women still busied themselves on high ladders arranging wreaths upon third-story windows and hanging lights along the roof, the picture was clear.

Matters only worsened when he arrived inside to see a house overflowing with decorations and frippery. (Yeah, frippery. He was so enraged he'd had to dip into his grandfather's vocabulary for a word to describe it.) Fresh, fragrant greenery and cardinal-red ribbons brightened the sallow walls. Fake icicles hanging from the doorways danced in the heated breeze and caught the abundant light. A train—an honest-to-goodness train set—ran circles around the fir standing sentry in the open living room, sending out real puffs of steam from its working engine. And, if he wasn't going crazy—which, to be fair, wasn't entirely out of the realm of possibility—he could've sworn he smelled gingerbread baking somewhere.

The whole thing was enough to make him puke chestnuts.

"Take it down," he growled.

He could only hope the backdrop of tinsel and baubles didn't undercut the weight of his infuriated stare. This was his house. His family's house. And she had absolutely no business being in here, much less taking the whole place over for her personal art project.

"I can't." She shrugged and began a descent down the stairs, her high-heeled boots making authoritative thuds with her every step. "Not by myself, anyway."

Beyond the closed front door, a series of engines turned over and sputtered to life. Clark's stomach sunk.

"Let me guess…"

"Everyone's already leaving. They've got to go home for Christmas Eve. There's no way I could take all of this down by myself. It'll just have to stay up."

She landed on the step above him, and their body language echoed their last encounter. Back then, she was below him, asking for something she had to know he couldn't possibly give. Now, he was the one at a disadvantage.

Taking stock of himself, Clark tried to catalogue his feelings. In business, these sorts of exercises kept him from flying off the handle during negotiations. He treated his emotions like items on an inventory list. They first needed to be counted, weighed, measured, and then neatly put away to keep from overwhelming him. It would have been easy enough if her caramel-candy eyes weren't so distracting. The color was extraordinary, but it wasn't their beauty he kept tripping over. It was her unguarded warmth he couldn't quite wrap his head around. What gave her the right to treat him like an old friend, welcome to open the doors of her heart and make himself at home inside? Hadn't she ever been hurt before? Clark managed to put those thoughts away before he asked any of those questions out loud, opting to reach for the glass icicles over his head.

"Fine. I'll take it down," he said.

"And risk breaking everything before you can sell it?" Clark's expression and stiff arms must have given him away. She adopted an air of false modesty. "Am I wrong? I thought you wanted to make money off of this once you dissolve the company."

"It belongs to me." He returned his hands to his pockets. The icicles would have to wait. He didn't know the first thing about storing all of this holiday garbage, and no one would buy bits of shattered glass. "Why shouldn't I sell it?"

"Of course you should." A breeze of sarcasm blew behind her as she stepped down from the staircase and headed straight for the living room. He followed close behind, not wanting her to break or put her Jack Frost spell over anything else in this house. "But I'm afraid you'll have to wait until Christmas is over. The icicles are here to stay. Besides, you respect a contract, right?"

"A contract?"

"In your uncle's contract with the city, he stipulates that this home can be used as a muster point for all festival-related activities. I have every legal right to be here."

Uncle Christopher…why would you do this to me?

"Why are you doing this? What do you want?"

"Let me put it to you this way: the festival was my home. It's been my home every Christmas since I was seven years old. You took my home away, so I think it's only fair I get to take yours." The living room had received as much treatment as the rest of the house, plus it contained the *pièce de résistance*. The Christmas tree. Clark seemed to remember the ceilings in this house being fourteen feet high, which meant the undecorated fir was thirteen and a half feet tall. At least. The glistening angel almost brushed the ceiling. "Don't worry. I'll be out of your hair once the season's over."

Clark tightened his jaw to keep it from dropping to the floor. She couldn't possibly mean what he thought she meant, especially not with the nonchalant way she swanned around the room, adjusting the nutcrackers on the mantel as if she hadn't just invited herself over for Christmas.

"What do you mean?"

"I mean you're stuck with me."

The decorations, he could handle. He'd just sleep in his car the next two nights and wake up to the world returned to normal on Boxing Day. A strange woman with an affinity for decking the halls? He wouldn't and couldn't allow it.

"Oh, no. You're not staying, too."

"Of course I am. I bought us matching PJs and everything."

He didn't want to know if that was true. Picking up her jacket and duffle bag, he started to shove all evidence of her inside. The scented candles waiting to be lit, the pile of inventory papers tucked away on an end table… It all had to go.

"I don't want you here."

"I'm also non-negotiable. Contract says so. I'm the foreman."

"You *can't* stay here."

"Why not?" she scoffed, pulling the duffel out of his hands and returning it to its place in the corner of the room. "Don't you have a guest room or twelve?"

"Because you can't, all right? You just can't."

The last thing Clark was inclined to do was examine her question. *Why can't I stay here?* The question was more thorny than she probably gave it credit for, and he wouldn't prick himself on the brambles just to satisfy her curiosity.

"What? You're going to kick me out in the snow?"

"It's not snowing."

She clucked, leaning back on the couch, as comfortable and at ease as if she were in her own house.

"I wouldn't be too sure about that."

He didn't know what possessed him. His rational mind knew it wasn't snowing. Better still, he knew it couldn't be snowing. In Texas, even as far north as they were, the worst they usually got was the occasional cold wind, frosty pond, or hypothermic cow. Yet, his raging heart shoved him towards the window, where he threw open the curtains to reveal that, indeed, not only had the entire front yard of his home been covered in a thick layer of snow, but there was a gentle snowdrift passing by the window.

In a small, private humiliation, Clark's breath caught at the sight. Then, he remembered himself. Snow in Texas wasn't beautiful. It couldn't be beautiful because it wasn't real. He remembered the town square, which had been similarly covered in a layer of snow so thick and so realistic he'd almost reached out to touch it, and his awe dissolved.

"Fake snow?"

"It's not a Dickens Christmas without snow. Lots of it."

"I wouldn't know." He slammed the curtains shut, a gesture which resulted in little more than an impotent swaying of fabric. "I've never read it."

Back turned, he couldn't see the shock play on her face, but he did hear the genuine gasp of surprise she let out at this declaration. He shouldn't have expected any less from this Christmas freak.

"Never read *A Christmas Carol*? Well, thank goodness you're letting me stay." He turned in time to see her rustling about in her bag, determination written on her soft features, but even the softest, sweetest, most determined face in the world couldn't deter him. "I think I've got my copy in here somewhere."

"I'm not letting you stay. You're leaving." He scooped up her jacket and offered it to her. "And now."

"But think about it: do you really want to be alone in this big house on Christmas?"

"Yes!"

It came out as more of an emotionally charged, beastly roar than he anticipated, but if his own shaking voice shocked him, it was nothing compared to the surprise he felt as Kate's defensive charm softened into sweet sacrifice. Her smile morphed from practiced composition into something altogether more compassionate, tender.

She no longer armed herself or wielded her warmth as a weapon. She held it up as a peace offering. Peace with this woman scared Clark even more than the thought of battling with her.

"I'm not letting you. No one should be alone during the holidays."

He reached for his cell.

"I'm calling the police."

"Great idea. You can tell Chief Stan and Officer Harris I said Merry Christmas. I think they're on duty until midnight, then the Fitts siblings take over."

This woman was just crazy enough about Christmas to wish *anyone* a happy day, even the men he called to arrest her, but this wasn't a genuine request. She was reminding him where the loyalties of this town actually lay, and it certainly wasn't with the man who was going to end the town's most important festival. The police probably weren't going to be on his side, especially not if they saw Kate as their champion.

Besides, his uncle had signed that contract.

"You're not going to leave, are you?"

"I'm not a monster. I'm not trying to steal your house or anything. I'll leave after I have my perfect Christmas." Kate pointed to the kitchen, which was connected to the living room by a swinging servant's door. Clark was sure now he smelled fresh gingerbread cookies. "Can I get you some eggnog?"

"I don't want eggnog. I want you to put everything back to normal."

Clark examined his options—the few he had. The decorations and the woman were fixtures here, at least for another few days. So, he saw only two courses of action. He could leave. Or he could stay.

"You're in Miller's Point for Christmas, Clark," she said, not unkindly. "This is normal."

He'd have to stay. He didn't have to stay in *this room*, but he would have to stay. Cutting his losses, Clark walked for the door. He'd just go upstairs and find an office to work in. Normal in Miller's Point… What, all smiles and well-wishes and cartoon red-nosed reindeer?

"Yeah. That's what I'm afraid of."

Chapter Five

Y EAH, THAT'S WHAT I'M AFRAID of. He left her with that declaration, and all she could think was: *Well, at least I know you can feel something.*

No. The thought put him in an unfair light. He'd shown tiny flashes of emotions over the course of their two conversations. Rage. Annoyance. Frustration. Fear.

But the deep, aching loneliness she saw in him when she suggested he didn't have to spend Christmas alone resonated inside of her. Until now, this entire…spectacle was little more than a means to an end. She assumed he had to be, at least on some level, a lonely man. Does a content, happy, and fulfilled person *hate* Christmas? No. But she now realized her actions here could serve more than one purpose. She could help him and save the town. She could teach him the true meaning of Christmas while also restoring Christmas for the people she loved most in the entire world.

Despite what countless TV shows and movies had taught her, she really *could* have it all.

First, she needed to get him to come back into the living room with her. She knew that wouldn't happen just on its own. Shouting at him from the living room to come back and hang out with her so she could show him the beauty of the season probably wasn't her *best* bet.

"Think, Kate," she muttered to herself, pacing the living room. "Think."

Pacing the Persian rug, she surveyed the room. It was, in every sense of the word, rich. The house was built in a faux-Victorian style, an American collection of half-British angles and ornamentation, and the inside reflected Mr. Woodward's inclination to show off his wealth. He presented himself as a gaudy man, to say the least, and he never shied away from spending money or talking about spending money—a trait he clearly didn't share with his nephew. Kate's pacing only halted when she heard the movement of a loose tile in the kitchen.

"He's gone," she called. "You can come out now."

No sooner had she spoken than Michael burst from behind the swinging door, which smacked against the nearest wall. He huffed and puffed with the dramatics of an amateur opera singer, as if he'd been shoved into a tiny, airless closet instead of the well-stocked kitchen for the last ten minutes.

"What was *that*?" he spluttered, pointing at a random place in the room. Kate could only assume he meant to point at somewhere Clark stood, but she had no way of knowing for sure. It was obvious he'd been eavesdropping. She returned to her pacing, rolling over everything she'd learned about the man from their last encounter.

He was so cold. Not just in the way he spoke to her or saw the world, but in his eyes. He was frozen down to his heart. She just hoped a good Christmas fire could be lit and melt the ice and frost away, not just for their sake, but for his.

"*That*," she answered, a bit too smug for her own good, "was the first stage of my plan."

"And you just let him go?"

"Yeah." She ran a hand through her hair and checked her wrist for a ponytail holder she already knew wasn't there. Her dirty blonde hair was so long and thick it often broke the thin elastics, leaving her to fuss and fiddle with her locks whenever she got too nervous to think straight. Tugging on one strand of hair, as if to pull some wisdom from her own brain, she tried to lay down her plan. "He needs time to cool off. Nothing was going to get done by needling him."

"What's your genius plan now, huh?"

Genius. That was it. When she was seven years old, Miss Cartwright—owner of the music and dance studio near the center of town—told her she could be a genius piano player if she ever put her mind to it. When The Christmas Company said it would pay for her lessons if she used her skills for the festival every year, she'd readily accepted.

And as it happened, the Woodward House's living room housed the town's most beautiful and most expensive piano, which sat in the corner across from the Christmas tree, waiting to be played.

Kate wandered over to the ancient Steinway. Her fingers only just brushed the ebony cover. It shot a thrill through her, like touching a holy relic; she needed to approach with reverence.

"We're going to smoke him out of his room."

"How?" Michael asked, as she lifted the cover and took her place on the bench. Shaking his head, he immediately began a muttered stream of vain prayers. "Don't say with song. Please don't say with song."

Her fingers touched the keys. Out of tune. She winced, but pressed forward.

"With song," she confirmed.

It was perfect, really. So much had already been written and spoken about the power of music that Kate didn't think twice about this stage of her plan. Music spoke to the soul in a language unwhispered by any other tongue. Her screaming after him about the magic of the season wouldn't work, but her joyful voice raised in song might be enough to coax him out of his hiding place, wherever that might have been.

Michael didn't share her optimism.

"We're doomed. We're totally doomed. This isn't a song and dance kind of guy, Kate."

"I know." She cracked her knuckles. It was going to take a lot of singing to cover the flaws of this piano's lack of tuning, but she never backed away from a challenge. Besides, she listed "singing Christmas carols" as one of the Special Skills on her resumé. Without knowing it, she'd trained for this exact moment her entire life. "That's why this is going to work."

"And what's your plan after this, hmm? Make him fall in love with you and the town, like in one of those movies you love so much?"

"I'm *not* going to fall in love with Clark."

"Right. Because you're going to be an old maid and Miller's Point and the festival will be your family and your children. I've heard this speech before. Besides, I didn't say anything about *you* falling in love with *him*. I said *he* would fall in love with *you*."

"Love doesn't factor into this plan at all," she rushed out, eager to be done with this particular conversation. Whenever she and Michael broached the topic of her love life, they played out the same old song and dance. She reminded him that romantic, all-consuming, life-changing love never entered her mind as a possibility for herself. The pickings in town were slim and most of the people they went to high school with were paired off by the summer after senior year. And even if some handsome stranger did ride into town and she did want to fall in love with him, she wasn't even sure she knew how to go about doing it.

And then, he'd remind her that anyone could fall in love—no one *knew* how to fall in love; it just happened—and they'd go around and around in circles. She didn't have time for circles and talk of romance today, especially not in the context of Clark Woodward. "We're going to do Christmas our way. And…" Her fingers ran along the keys, testing them out one by one in no particular order. She struggled to articulate her thoughts. "He's got this thing about him. He's lonely. I can tell."

"He's inherited a corporation worth millions of dollars, at least. I think he cuddles a body pillow stuffed with hundred-dollar bills every night."

"The money doesn't matter."

"What do you mean, *the money doesn't matter?*"

Before this morning, Kate never would have made such a bold claim. She lived in a two-and-a-half-room apartment above the town's only bookshop. A broken lock barely kept her door closed and she existed on a steady diet of diner food and gas station salad bowls. If anyone knew the importance of money and the detriment of not having it, it was Kate. But when faced with Clark, she didn't see a rich man or a happy one. He was someone desperate to hide his own crippling solitary confinement. He believed himself above Christmas because he believed himself above people in general, a fact Kate was out to prove completely false.

"It doesn't. I mean, I thought it did, but there's something there. Or, something isn't there. And if we can give it to him…"

Michael nodded and helped himself to the opposite end of the piano bench as Kate continued to noodle some random melodies. She operated on muscle memory, barely pressing the keys for noise.

"He may just want to give us the festival," he said.

"And he'll be a better man for it."

Michael huffed a noise under his breath. Clearly, transforming Clark into a better man ranked low on his list of priorities. For a while, nothing passed between them but the music pouring from her fingers. Kate recalled Clark's enraged voice when he heard the music upon first entering the house. Once he heard the live thing, it would only be a matter of time before he sprinted down here to stop her. Then, she'd have him right where she wanted him. Michael gave her an unreadable look, creeping into the corners of her vision like rolling fog.

"If I didn't know better, I'd say you like him."

Kate choked on her own laughter. Clark Woodward was arrogant. Prideful. A complete miser with no regard for the happiness or safety of others. He was a tyrannical boss and a rude host. And he'd never read Dickens. Who graduated with an MBA without reading Charles Dickens at least once? She couldn't ever see herself liking someone who hadn't read the greatest in the English canon, even if he did light a fire of excitement in her every time they began one of their verbal sparring matches.

"I don't like him."

"Hmm."

"I don't dislike him either!" She covered for herself, resisting the urge to hold up her hands in a pose of joking surrender. "I feel—"

Michael cut her off.

"You feel for him."

"I feel *bad* for him," she corrected, even though it

wasn't remotely true. Or, rather, it was true, but it wasn't the entire truth. She did feel bad for him. It just wasn't the end of her feelings. Horror of horrors, she actually related to him. "Haven't you ever felt lonely?"

"Well, besides sharing a house with two brothers, I've had to deal with you basically my entire life. You never stop talking. No, I've never felt lonely."

"I have," Kate said, her head dipping down towards the piano keys.

"I know." Hard edges softened around Michael and he nodded in recognition. They would never speak of the thing that made her lonely, and he knew it. "I know. Just seems like a flimsy reason for you to want to help a guy."

"I can help him and the town at the same time. Those aren't mutually exclusive."

"I just want you to keep your eye on the ball," Michael said.

Kate didn't want to think about the sad things anymore. She wanted to sing. She wanted to play the piano until the lonely man upstairs was forced to confront them down here. She couldn't save the person she was when she was at her loneliest, but she could at least save him.

And her entire town and way of life, while she was at it.

With a blistering, face-cutting smile, Kate effectively ended their conversation.

"What do you think? 'Good King Wenceslas' or 'Here We Come A-Caroling.'"

After storming out of the room, Clark made a deal with himself: if he could survive the next two days without seeing Kate Buckner again, he would buy himself something nice. Something practical, of course. A watch, maybe. Or a new set of locks for his apartment in Dallas. A pair of shoes he didn't have to repair every other week because they insisted on falling apart at the seams when he walked too long or the temperature rose over seventy degrees. He rarely promised himself these sorts of rewards. His idea of a reward was sleeping in an extra fifteen minutes past his 6 a.m. alarm on Saturdays. But between the difficulty—maybe the impossibility—of avoiding Kate in his own house and the post-Christmas deals soon to flood the malls and shops back home, he decided it was worth it.

Here we come a-caroling along the fields so green!
Here we come wandering so fair to be seen!

He was sure he could do it until she started singing. There was music in his house. Not just any kind of music. Christmas music. When choosing a place to work from today, he'd made sure to pick the farthest room in the house from the living room. The second office used to host his uncle's secretary, if the discarded paperwork and bubble gum wrappers were any indication, and he assumed it would be a fine hideout for a few days. Its couch and proximity to a bathroom were convenient; he'd just have to make sure he snuck to the kitchen for snacks when he was sure Kate wasn't anywhere along his route.

A flawless plan…until she decided to go and fill the house with music. At first, Clark did his best to ignore it. He shut the heavy office door carefully, trying not to disturb the cheesy toy basketball hoop hung over the top—apparently, his uncle had hired an eight-year-old boy as a secretary—and returned to the whirring laptop. Maybe no one in this town was working, but he had a work ethic, and it didn't disappear because the weather got a little cold.

The closed door did basically nothing to prevent the music. If anything, it somehow managed to get louder. He shook his head and resolved to ignore it. He could manage distractions. He was disciplined enough to work over some annoying piano tunes.

Love and joy come to you! And to you glad Christmas too!

Clark tapped his foot. Maybe that sound would drown out their warbling.

And God bless you and se-end you a Happy New Year!

It didn't. He just managed to tap in time with them, giving them a beat. He covered his ears. Maybe *that* would drown them out.

And God se-end you a Happy Ne-ew Year!

It didn't. There was no drowning them out. Them, of course, because, as it turned out, he and Kate hadn't been as alone in the house as he assumed they were. Michael's slight drawl joined Kate's…competent singing. In a more generous mood, Clark might have described her singing as beautiful. Stirring, even. Not because it was technically perfect—it wasn't—but because there was a freedom to it. She didn't care about sounding good; she sang because it brought her joy.

Or something. Clark didn't want to read too deeply into it.

"That's enough."

Decorations and other passive, ignorable expressions of her Christmas obsession, he could handle. But indoor caroling? He couldn't allow it.

Leaving his work behind, he stormed downstairs. He flew past the miniature Dickens village set up on a long end table in the hallway, the popcorn garlands strung between overhead light fixtures, and down the garland-strewn grand staircase. Thank goodness his allergies didn't include pine or he'd be a dead man walking.

By the time he arrived in the living room, embarrassingly out of breath, they'd moved onto the slower, more somber "Silent Night," which Kate elected to sing in German.

Great. She knew German. The enemy living in his house was clever, talented, beautiful, *and* bilingual.

Not that Clark cared about any of that, of course. She was, above all, a nuisance. An obstacle to be conquered on his way to full control over his family's affairs. He had to think of her that way. He never thought about anyone else he did business with in warm or familiar terms. Why should he start now?

"What is this?"

"We're singing."

Apparently, the concept of a rhetorical question was lost on Michael, who answered with a big grin as Kate's song continued. Her head hung low over the keys and her golden-brown hair curtained her face, but the melody her lips offered wrapped around Clark with the insistence of prayer. He tried his best to ignore the clenching of his heart. The scene in the living room was something out of *The Saturday Evening Post*. Norman Rockwell couldn't have painted it better himself. A man and a woman sat, cozily enough, on a piano bench in the middle of a Christmas-covered living room. The fireplace crackled and the music hummed.

The picture-perfect image was enough to make Clark sick. It was enough to make Clark want to sing along. It was enough to make him wonder if Michael and Kate were together.

Again, not because he cared. Just because he needed more ammo against her. And he was curious.

"Singing's not allowed," he snapped, harsher than he intended.

Michael scoffed, undeterred.

"What is this, *The Sound of Music*?"

"I'm being pretty generous, letting you stay here. But this isn't an open invitation. You can't just have free rein in my house. And you know what?"

Clark's admittedly self-righteous lecture ended with the abrupt ringing of the doorbell. Truth be told, he was so oblivious to the workings of the house, he hadn't realized what their doorbell even sounded like, so the noise sent him jumping in shock.

"Oh, good!" Kate looked up from the piano keys for the first time since he arrived, her brown eyes alchemizing to a glistening gold. Michael popped up from the piano bench and ran towards the front door. For all of the excitement, a pit of understanding bottomed out in Clark's stomach. If he wasn't careful, his house would soon be overrun with townies. "Emily's here!"

"Emily who?"

"Emily Richards."

"I don't know who that is."

He didn't need an introduction. Emily Richards tottered through the living room door, juggling storage containers of brightly wrapped presents in her cocktail-straw-thin arms. The introduction wasn't necessary because Clark had actually met Emily the night before. She worked behind the check-in desk of the Miller's Point Bed and Breakfast. She was the one who had suggested sleeping in his car because "no one in this town is going to have room for you after what you did."

He hadn't taken her advice, choosing instead to return home for the first time in a long time, but that didn't stop her words and the hatred in her eyes from haunting him the entire way.

Emily Richards was a twig of a woman with high

blonde hair. She couldn't have been any more different from Kate if she tried. Where Kate was all curves and warmth, Emily was narrow and icy. Without knowing either of them particularly well, Clark could only assume their differences made their friendship work.

"Sorry I'm late. I walked all the way up the hill and it was *murder* on my calves. Where should I put these?"

"What are those?"

"Donation bins." Kate's deft hands continued their musical exploration of the keyboard, even as she afforded him the bare minimum of her attention in favor of Emily. "Go ahead and put them on the floor for now. We'll take them out with us later."

"Later? Where are you going?"

The suspense extended as Emily flounced into his kitchen without saying so much as a "hello" to him.

"Who wants eggnog?" she shouted.

"Three glasses in here please!"

Nope. Clark's foot needed to come down. He couldn't allow them to walk all over him and around him like this. He'd given her the run of the house, sure. But he did not agree to have his entire life overrun, not by Kate and certainly not by her friends. Every minute, she threw more and more illegal fireworks at him; soon, his annoyance would explode. His right hand twitched; he struggled to control his own breathing.

No one got under his skin like this. Not business partners, not rivals. And never a woman.

"No, no! No eggnog for me. Two glasses."

"But—"

"I didn't come down here for eggnog. I came down here to tell you to stop playing."

"It's not Christmas without music. C'mon," she said, her voice lighter than a chorus of bells. "Sing a song with us. It'll be fun."

"I don't sing," he growled.

"Everyone sings at Christmas," Kate said. Emily returned with the eggnog and requisitioned the overstuffed couch, plopping down on it and burying herself in the cushions. "Even Frank Sinatra sang Christmas songs and he could hardly carry a tune."

"Frank Sinatra was a *great* singer and this isn't a party!"

"Why not?" Her golden eyes twinkled with the edges of a private joke. "You look like you could use a little party." She'd wedged herself under his skin and she knew it.

You look like you could use a little party. The challenge repeated in his head, a maddening, singsong refrain he wished he could pluck out and erase from his memory. An unfamiliar feeling welled inside of him; every time he tried to place it, the name eluded him. It wasn't rage or dignified coldness; he could easily identify those, as they were his most common emotional responses to nearly any annoyance, even if he didn't let them register on his face. He felt altogether different than he could ever remember feeling before.

Fondness? Was it fondness?

Before he could answer, he turned tail. A hasty retreat would be best. Alone in his office, there was no way he could feel anything for Kate.

"I have to work. Keep the noise down and the disasters to a minimum, please," he commanded.

But he'd only made it three steps towards the exit when Michael sidled up beside him and dropped his voice to a conspiratorial whisper. Clark didn't often have occasion to feel like "one of the boys," but when Michael elbow nudged him, he could almost imagine it.

"Hey, Clark."

"Yes?"

"Can I give you some advice?"

Clark didn't want his advice. He knew the other man's advice would inevitably lead him to staying here, in this room, in close proximity to the undecorated Christmas tree and the beautiful, determined, open-hearted Kate Buckner.

"...Yes."

"Just go along for the ride. Your life will be much, *much* easier. I promise."

He huffed out a breath and scanned the room again. The living room of Woodward House always sunk under the weight of its own grandeur. Its stark beauty reflected its self-importance in its thick brocade furnishings and expensive finishes. The entire house suffered this design style; the office Clark holed himself up in, untouched by Kate's magical Christmas hands, was a sea of dark shadows and leather chairs. He glanced around this room. The new décor was—dare he say it?—tasteful. Small touches of holiday décor accented the mantelpieces and end tables, while a simple wreath hung above the fireplace. Even the Christmas tree was mercifully undecorated, strung with only simple garlands of white fairy lights. On the one hand, he resented the intrusion of brightness and levity to his dark world. On the other, could he really go back to his small room and listen to their laughter and song, knowing all the while he could be a part of it if he only said yes? Was he really content to sit in the darkness when light was just a step away? He knew he couldn't return to the shadows.

He just didn't want anyone else to know that.

Besides, the threat of memories in this place was too strong. Every corner of this house reminded him of the time *before*, of when he had a family here, when this season actually meant something to him. If he stayed here with Kate and her friends, then at least he'd have a distraction.

Steady as a tree, he returned to the fold of the living room party. He never once let his expression slip, but Kate seemed to see straight through him, as she had from the moment they met. She didn't look at him with judgment, though. There was something else in her soft tone. Understanding? Acceptance? Clark couldn't tell, and maybe he didn't want to. All he wanted was one uncomplicated day in the sun.

"Any requests?" she asked.

"I'm not singing. But I will stay." He tacked on another claim, just in case she thought she'd won something in this exchange. "Just to make sure you don't burn the house down."

A single nod and quiet smile were his only reward from Kate.

Emily picked up the slack. Popping up from the couch, she declared, "Great idea. I'll get you some eggnog after all."

Chapter Six

H ALFWAY THROUGH "GOOD KING WENCESLAS," the
clock above the fireplace struck noon, sending a
chorus of chiming bells announcing the time into the
room and disturbing the natural melody of their carol. If
all had actually gone to plan and Michael hadn't screwed
the entire thing up, they would have just been welcoming
Clark to the house right about now.

Kate structured her original plan, with its intricate,
timed details, to act in the same manner as a whirlwind.
They were meant to sweep Clark from one themed activity
to another, whipping him into a happy Yuletide frenzy.
She'd added Christmas caroling as a last-minute effort
to kill time before Emily arrived, and though it wasn't
a part of the original plan, Kate thought it fit right in.
Clark stood at the end of the piano, doing his best to
look every bit as stoic as a Mr. Darcy reenactor, but every
once in a while, Kate would look up at him from under
her eyelashes and catch him mouthing a phrase of a song
before catching himself and pretending it never happened.

He thought no one saw his slip-ups. He was wrong.
Kate caught them, and they fanned the flames of hope
in her heart, for her plan and for him. She tried her best

to hide her triumphant smile behind a curtain of hair. Spooking him could lead to disaster; she had to play her cards right if she wanted him to keep opening up.

In the middle of the song, Emily shot to her feet, checking her phone's clock against the one on the wall.

"That's the time? Kate, we've got to go if we want to make it."

"Make it where? Where are you going?"

If Kate didn't know better—and to be totally honest, she *didn't* know better—she would have sworn she heard a whimper of disappointment in Clark's voice, but she dismissed the thought as soon as it came through her head. Sure, maybe some of his edges had softened. Flickers of humanity peeked out from behind his stony exterior. That didn't mean he was suddenly an avid caroler, nor did he enjoy her company and want her to stay.

A stupid and exceptionally loud part of Kate's brain desperately wanted to hear what Clark's singing voice sounded like. Would it be thick and deep? Tenor and sweet? Would he be able to sing on key at all? She realized what a small thing it was, to want to know how someone sang, but she couldn't help wanting it all the same. In her experience, though, the smallest things were always the hardest to get in this life.

"Christmas isn't just a day for eating and eggnog," she said, leaving the piano and her dreams of hearing Clark sing behind.

"Though eggnog is a big part of it," Michael joked.

"It's also," Kate said through a laugh, "a day to do good."

"Well," Clark corrected.

"Not well. *Good.* Miller's Point is a great town, but there are still plenty of families that need our help. Every year on Christmas Eve, we do a big donation of Christmas presents and provisions for them, but no festival means no place to give out the donations, so a couple of us volunteered to pick up the slack."

One of the first thoughts Kate had after his announcement was for those families. Money was tight for her, but for some, it was even worse. Miller's Point wasn't a big town by any stretch of the imagination, and they didn't have a poverty epidemic like Clark might have seen in Dallas, but the few who needed help still mattered. If she couldn't at least help them, what good was she to anyone else? Kate reached for her coat as Michael and Emily started collecting the heavy boxes of presents waiting on the floor.

"We'll be gone for about an hour," she informed him as she wrapped herself in her favorite soft red scarf. Miss Carolyn knit it for her last year, and though it was full of holes and missed stitches, Kate couldn't bear to leave home without it. "Are you going to change the locks while we're out?"

"I could come with you."

Kate blinked. The offer… It *sounded* generous and kind. Which couldn't be true because she wasn't sure Clark Woodward had a generous or kind bone in his body. Kate's pulse quickened.

"What?"

"It's…" He cleared his throat. "Your things are heavy. I could drive you, I mean. That way you don't have to carry them back down the hill."

"Really?"

"It would be easier than taking this down by ourselves," Michael offered, though his skepticism was plainly written on every corner of his face.

"It will be good," Clark said. "You know, for the people in town to get to know me."

...*Before you take their jobs away.* Kate struggled with this Clark Woodward character. Every time she thought she got him, every time she saw some light poking out through the cracks in his walls, she remembered why she was here in the first place. He was close to destroying the town, trying to take away everything they held dear.

She wanted to see the best in him, and more than anything she wanted to find a way to make him happy in the same way his family had made this town happy for so many years. And yet...he seemed to go out of his way to make himself out to be the biggest jerk around. Until now. Until this moment.

"All right." Kate handed him one of the crates, groaning under its weight. What had they bought these kids, lead bricks? "Take this. And pull the car around. We'll be out in a minute."

They departed. Emily and Kate remained in the living room. When the door closed behind the two men, signaling that they were really alone, Emily's mouth popped into a perfect O and her eyes widened with fake horror.

"Wow. He's..."

Kate held up a silencing hand. She didn't need to like Clark to make her plan work, but she *wanted* to like Clark. No one deserved to be miserable at Christmas, not even the very cruel, but it would make things so much easier if she felt he had even a chance of being a good man.

"I've never heard you say a bad thing about another person. Don't start now."

"That's not true. You've heard me say many bad things about many people. Most people, actually."

"Still."

"I wasn't going to say anything *bad* about him. Just..."

"Just what?"

Emily's hesitation spoke louder than any condemnation

ever could. She was one of the most passive-aggressive, backhanded-compliment people Kate ever knew. You'd be on the receiving end of the world's most beautiful smile while being told you were a moron, but she'd say it so you thought she was lavishing praise on you. In the end, she picked up a storage tub, shook her head once, and said in the most piteous voice Kate ever heard:

"Bless his heart."

Even if Clark hadn't told her he'd rented this car, Kate could have guessed it. The sleek silver car hid a leather interior with a control panel so futuristic it might as well have been ripped out of a *Star Trek* ship. She could imagine him driving around Dallas in a usually broken-down clunker before she could imagine him forking over the thousands of dollars this car probably cost.

In the front seat, Michael guided Clark down the hill and the twisting, turning roads leading them to the back roads of Miller's Point. Out here, things were even quieter than in town, if such a thing were possible. Kate's request to turn the radio to 109.7, the local station that played *all the holiday hits from yesterday and today*, was firmly denied, and they rode into town in total silence, save for Michael's occasional navigation tips.

"Yeah, and just pull in here."

They turned up the familiar drive to the Lewisham house, where little Bradley and his family would be waiting for them. Sure enough, when they passed the tree line towards their humble house, Bradley sat on the front steps, tapping his feet and twiddling the famous Tiny Tim cane. Apparently, last night no one had the heart to tell him he couldn't bring the costumes home. Kate's gaze flickered to Clark. Was he heartless enough to take a fake cane worth less than three dollars from a little boy?

Probably not... Right?

Before the car even lurched to a stop, Bradley launched himself at it, shouting Kate's name as loud as he could. It was a good thing no one else lived out here, or he'd be disturbing the entire neighborhood.

"Miss Kate! Miss Kate!"

No matter how many times she heard it, she always got a thrill of the maternal every time one of the children in the festival called out to her. Leaving the donation tub behind her, she leapt out of the car and scooped him into her arms, hugging him tight.

"How's it going, Bradley?"

Bradley, as it turned out, wasn't interested in telling her about his day. Missing front tooth and all, he spluttered, "Are we going back? Is the festival back on again? Do I need to go get my hat?"

The belief in his eyes that everything was set right again stabbed a knife straight between her eyes. This boy with the saucer-big brown eyes believed she had the power to wave a magic wand and make everything well again.

She hoped she could prove him right.

"No, buddy. We're still working all of that out, but—"

"Will you tell me why?"

Still holding him in her arms—he was too big for it, but she indulged him anyway—Kate turned to watch the movement in the car.

"Sure. I'll tell you as soon as I can."

"Good. Because I have been working on my accent and," he dropped into a thick and terrible Cockney accent, "I fink it's going swell, I do!"

He continued speaking in his accent, but her mind

wandered. By the end of the afternoon, if they kept to their plans, they'd visit four houses with presents while a second group visited later in the evening with hot meals and frozen, reheatable food for the next day. If the festival had been going on, the food would have been served at the event and the presents doled out on Christmas morning, but given the unexpected changes, that morning they'd devised a new plan. In some ways, this might be better. More personal. On the other hand, Kate knew how deeply these families hated anything remotely resembling charity. In the friendly environment of the festival, where huge buffets of turkey and sweet potato pie ran through town hall like a deliciously fattening river, no one felt they were accepting charity because everyone shared equally. Bringing a bunch of food directly to a family with maybe six or seven days off a year so that they could spend their precious time together instead of cooking was targeted, singling out the people who needed the most help.

By the time she turned to the car, it was empty.

Well, empty except for one.

Clark, for his part, hadn't moved away from the car at all. He leaned against the hood, reading something on his phone and determinedly not looking anywhere but the dimmed screen. There was a strange duality to Clark. On the one hand, he clearly lived a frugal, tight-fisted existence. On the other hand, he had every luxury and advantage at his fingertips. He should have been a snob. Being a snob definitely would have explained his refusal to even interact with the Lewisham family or their aging but proudly kept home. There were only two motives she could see for keeping himself away from the people he'd driven here to help.

A) He was an unsalvageable, irreversible, cruel man

beyond salvation, who hated the poor, resented the working, and slept happily on stacks of money. He had to rest up, naturally, because he spent his days diving into money bins full of gold coins. Or:

B)…Something else. She wasn't entirely sure what that something else was, but there *had* to be a second option. She refused to see the worst of him and only the worst. Maybe he was allergic to the wildflowers in the front lawn? Maybe he didn't want to rub his wealth in their face?

She looked at his face. Tight. Strained. Maybe he was nervous?

"Hey, Bradley?"

"Yep!"

She released him; he plopped to the ground with the lightest thud she ever heard. Like a dedicated method actor, he leaned against his Tiny Tim cane, putting all his weight on it. Kate bent down to his eye level; she needed to impress upon him the importance of this mission. Just one little interaction could be the key to understanding the bank vault of a man who'd driven her here.

"If you do something for me, I promise I'll tell you everything. Deal?"

"Deal." Bradley brandished his cane like a sword. "Now, who do I have to fight?"

"You don't have to fight anyone. You see that guy over there?"

"Yeah."

"His name is Clark, and—"

"I know who he is!"

"Okay. Okay! What do you think about him?"

"He looks kind of lonely." Bradley shrugged. He matched his voice to the whisper of Kate's, keeping his tone low and confidential. "He's not your boyfriend, is he? Because everyone hates him."

Hate. What a bold, uncompromising word for a nine-year-old. A shiver gripped Kate's spine. The hairs on her neck raised.

"We don't hate him. We have to *help* him. Can you go over there and just…" She searched for the words to describe what she wanted. In the end, she landed on the one thing *she* wanted to do. "Just be nice to him?"

Bradley's face scrunched as he leaned on his cane, giving him the appearance of a curmudgeonly old man. A mini Scrooge. Of all the times not to have a camera handy.

"What, just like talk to him and stuff?"

"You said he looks lonely. Go be a friend."

"But everyone hates him! Everyone'll hate me next."

Hate, hate, hate. That wasn't Christmas talk at all. That wasn't Miller's Point talk. Kate couldn't let the poison of fear infect her town any more than it already had.

There was only one thing to do now: talk to the small child as though they were secret agents.

"No one's going to be mad…" She looked left, then right, as if checking for spies. "You're helping with the plan."

"What plan?"

"The *secret* plan to get the festival back. I can't tell you the specifics until you finish this mission. I have to know you can be trusted."

"Deal." Bradley started for the car, but stopped so hard he created a dust cloud. "And I want a candy bar."

"You can have a stick of gum."

He beamed.

"Deal."

Clark didn't often make bad decisions. At least, he told himself he never made bad decisions. Before coming to Miller's Point, the last bad thing he did was choose the cranberry orange protein bars instead of the blueberry protein bars during his last grocery shop.

But upon arriving at Miller's Point, he seemed incapable of making good decisions. Leaving his car on the street to get towed? Bad call. Letting Kate talk down to him on his first night? *Really* bad call. Giving Kate free rein over his family's house? Terrible call. Coming along on this charity mission? The worst call.

Like most things—including the cranberry orange bars, which had fifteen fewer calories than the blueberry—it started with good intentions. Good, stupid intentions. That was the reason Clark tried his best *never* to do anything with good intentions. He preferred neutral intentions. Good intentions always backfired. Neutral intentions weren't capable of backfiring, because no one had any skin in the game.

This decision was innocent and knee-jerk. He saw her struggling under the weight of packages, fighting to hold them upright, and eventually falling right down the steep hill from the Woodward House into town. He imagined being called to the hospital and having to identify her scraped-up face—a ridiculous thought, of course, since he would have been the last person she ever listed as an emergency contact. However absurd, the horrible images wouldn't leave his head, so he volunteered to drive her and her friends.

Now, he was here, in front of a tiny shack of a home. The second he pulled the key out of the ignition and got a good view of the place, not to mention the little boy with the Tiny Tim cane sprinting into Kate's arms, a swirling hurricane drew all of the energy from Clark's body and concentrated it in the pit of his stomach. His palms grew clammy, and as soon as he was finished carrying the heavy tub of general sundry and supplies up to the porch, he slipped on a reliably dark pair of sunglasses and focused his attention on his phone.

He knew how it looked. They would think him stand-offish and rude, superior and arrogant. He'd rather they think that than know the truth.

The truth was…he'd taken something important away from these people. The festival was stupid as far as he was concerned, but it clearly meant more to them than he realized…

He was used to being hated. Hatred was the cost of doing business. But hatred was always a distant thing brought on by business decisions. It wasn't up close. Personal.

When he came to town, he'd assumed he could hide from people. Dissolving the company would be easy enough; he was the boss. No one could openly hate the boss. But here at someone else's house, the house of a family who clearly loved the festival…

He couldn't face them. Hence the sunglasses. And the phone. And general *please don't come near me* vibe.

So, it surprised him when a small child ran up and stood beside him.

"Hey."

Clark did not respond.

"Hey, guy."

The child tugged on Clark's suit jacket. Still, he did not respond.

"Hey!"

When children shout, there's no choice but to respond. Raising one eyebrow over the top ridge of his pitch-black sunglasses, Clark glanced down.

"Yes?"

"My name's Bradley. And you're Clark Woodward, right?"

"Mm-hm."

He pocketed his cellphone. There was no reason to invest his time in this kid at all, but it would be worse to ignore him and have him run up to the house screaming about the mean man outside. Clark believed in his ability to be minimally polite.

"I knew that was your name. I'm really good at remembering stuff. That's why I got the part of Tiny Tim. I can remember all the lines. And I have a *ton* of lines. I'm good at remembering stuff and I'm really short. And poor. I guess it's at least a little bit because we're poor. I really get the Tiny Tim *thing*, you know?"

"Mm-hm." Clark bit his bottom lip to keep from laughing. Bradley was a character. It didn't surprise him he got cast as the lead in this town-wide play. His little face expressed a range of emotions in a second. The little boy huffed and leaned on some kind of roughly carved wooden walking stick. Not being familiar with the Dickens canon, Clark was vaguely aware the Tiny Tim character was disabled... Was this boy *also* injured, or did he just not want to let the role go?

"You're not making this very easy."

"Making what easy?"

With his free, non-walking-stick hand, Bradley smacked his face and sighed. Clark called him a character, but "ham" would have been more accurate.

"Miss Kate said I could have a candy bar if I came over and made you happy but you're not making it easy. Well, she actually said I could have a stick of gum. I don't think Miss Kate can afford candy bars either."

Ignoring Kate's desire to make him happy for the

moment, he caught instead on the insinuation of her poverty. She was clean and well-dressed. Her boots were scuffed and strained from wear, but that could just as easily be explained as she loved them too much to get rid of them, rather than them being the only shoes she owned or could afford to own.

"Why's that?"

"She lost her job when you cancelled the festival. It was kind of her life. She was the youngest person to work there, you know."

This is exactly why Clark avoided children. They didn't know anything about tact or keeping secrets or not punching their conversation partners in the stomach with their words. The only thing Clark knew concretely about Kate's relationship with the festival was that she loved it. Having deliberately kept his attention in the business to non-Christmas matters when his uncle was alive, he hadn't taken a look at the employee roster yet or familiarized himself with their staff, so he didn't know she worked there. Or that it was her life.

He didn't know, and he didn't want to know. *Change the subject, Clark. Change the subject.*

"Stay here for one second."

"Where're you going?"

Back in his car, Clark dove for the glove compartment. He usually took pride in its perfect organization—he liked his registration and safety manual where he could easily get them—but today he needed the one bit of clutter shoved in it. A white plastic bag with a blue outline of a tooth stamped on it. Out of that baggie came a silver-wrapped chocolate bar. Clark returned and handed it over to the wide-eyed boy.

"I got this at the dentist office the other day."

"You dentist gives you *candy?*"

"All dentist offices are rackets. They give you candy so you have to go right back and get more fillings. Make sure you brush your teeth."

Bradley ripped away the wrapping like a Roald Dahl character. He tore into the chocolate. Clark couldn't help but wonder when the child last had a dentist appointment. If they couldn't buy their own Christmas presents in a Christmas-obsessed town, who's to say they had enough money for dental work?

"Yes, sir. I will, sir." Bradley smacked his lips as he chewed, a pet peeve of Clark's he decided to ignore for the moment. After a contemplative silence, Bradley swallowed and spoke again. "You know…you're kinda like him."

"Like who?"

"Scrooge."

Clark didn't even have time to absorb the blow of those words. Kate interrupted their chat with Michael and Emily in tow.

"I think we're all done here."

Tucking his cane under his chocolate-holding arm, he held up his free hand.

"Gum, please."

"You think you earned it?" Kate chuckled. The sound was better than music. "He's not even smiling."

"C'mon, Mr. Clark. Give her a smile."

No. A line in the sand needed to be drawn. He'd been…polite to the boy and he was going to be stuck with Kate for the next thirty-six hours or so. None of them were going to walk away from this conversation thinking he could be manipulated. Not by gap-toothed children with chocolate-covered hands or beautiful women with laughter like wind chimes on a sunny beach.

"I'm not a trained animal. I don't smile on command."

The little boy dug his heels in to argue, but a call

from his father on the porch rescued Clark from any kind of debate.

"Bradley! Come in here and help your sisters set the table."

The boy groaned. Kate knelt down and handed him the stick of gum. In another scenario, Clark would have protested. He didn't earn the gum, and what kind of lesson was she teaching him if she gave him things he didn't earn? Maybe *that* was the problem with this town. Everyone here was too soft, too afraid of hurting feelings to say no.

"Here's your gum. Merry Christmas, B."

But…even he had to admit how sweet Kate looked as she ruffled Bradley's hair and sent him on his way. As he walked towards his tiny house, he gave one last goodbye.

"God bless us, everyone."

It didn't take a master of subtext to read into his declaration. *God bless everyone. Even you, Mr. Clark.* Once he disappeared behind the faded red door, Kate turned on him.

"You couldn't have even smiled for him?"

He didn't realize how long he'd been staring into the depths of her eyes, catching the flickers of mixing colors and light in her pointed gaze. When had she gotten so close? And why did he want to be closer? His gaze flickered down to her lips. Just a breath closer, just a heartbeat nearer to her and they'd be less than a kiss apart. And it shocked him how dearly he suddenly wanted that in this moment.

He coughed. Stepped away. And shook his head.

"No. No, I couldn't."

"What a shame." She smiled, a tease hiding in the corner of her mouth. "I bet you have a nice smile."

He coughed again and put as much distance between

them as he could, flexing and clenching his hand. The movement of muscles in his fingers did nothing to quell his desire to take her hand and hold it in his. As they got in the car, Clark recalled thinking coming to this house and meeting these people was the worst thing he'd done in recent memory. He knew now that wasn't true.

The worst thing he had done since arriving in Miller's Point was almost kissing Kate.

Or not kissing her.

He couldn't decide which was worse.

Chapter Seven

T HE AFTERNOON ROLLED PAST CLARK in a flurry of
cold, slushy rain and tittering laughter and conversation. He drove them to their next few stops, but
no longer got out of the car. He considered it a strategic
move. They would be safe from any near-miss kisses if
he did the noble thing of helping to bring the boxes to
the door and immediately returning to the safety of his
car. Insulated by the steel and leather interior, he couldn't
hear her laugh or smell the nutmeg in her hair. Every once
in a while, his attention snagged on bits of conversation
muttered outside of his window. Mostly insults about
him. *Why are you hanging out with that scumbag? Makes
sense he wouldn't want to come in and touch us poors. If I
didn't respect his uncle so much, I'd take him out back and
give him what for.*

Every year, *Texas Magazine* ranked the towns and
cities of the state by the kindness and friendliness of
their citizens. Miller's Point regularly came in at #1. The
nicest people in the entire state hated him. Normally,
he didn't mind hatred. He tried not to mind it now, but
he couldn't help but think, *I don't want Kate to hate me.*

When he didn't catch them saying cruel and utterly

justified things about his character, Clark captured little glimpses into the life of the woman who'd singlehandedly invaded his life. *Thank you so much for bringing my boy to the doctor last week. I couldn't have gotten the time off.* Or, *you'll never believe what happened last week! I took your advice and asked Laura out at her favorite place at the festival and she said yes! We're going out next week for New Year's.* Kate invested herself in these people, and not just for cheap displays of her own dedication to charity. Clark couldn't name a single neighbor in his apartment building, while Kate consistently remembered birthdays, anniversaries, breakups, and the name of every single person she came across. Small-town living came with perks and privileges not enjoyed by city folk like him, but he didn't suspect everyone in Miller's Point—or any small town for that matter—acted exactly like her. She was a creature entirely unto herself. He'd yet to meet anyone on earth, much less in Miller's Point, who rivaled Kate in any way.

Whether that was a point in her favor or a demerit, he couldn't be entirely sure.

The car's bells chimed as the doors opened and the ragtag team of daylight Santas, now relieved of their boxes and presents, slipped inside.

"That was the last one," Kate said.

Clark turned the key in the ignition and headed for town. Driving around today gave him a much better sense of the place, all of its hidden side streets and tangled roundabouts. Cell service cut out all over town, making his cell phone directions absolutely useless. Upon first arriving in Miller's Point, the maps would disappear and reappear at will, sending him on crazy routes until he finally gave up. Finding the town square last night was nothing short of a miracle.

Michael, on the other hand, knew every inch of Miller's Point and didn't require battery life or WiFi.

Conversation flowed easily between the three friends, leaving Clark to feel a bit like an out-of-the-loop Uber driver, an experience he only knew from the one time his bike got a flat tire in downtown Dallas and the public transportation workers spent the day on strike, forcing him to use the car-sharing service. In a city with plenty of bike racks and trams, Clark saw no reason to pay seven bucks for someone else to ferry him around.

"Wanna stop somewhere and get lunch?" Michael asked. "I'm starving."

"You're always starving."

"No one is starving. We all ate this morning."

"We could go to the diner."

"It's closed."

"You were literally there this morning."

"Mel opened it special for Kate and Clark sneaked in. Mel felt too bad to tell him to get lost."

The tips of Clark's ears reddened. He hadn't even noticed a *closed* sign. Was he really so entitled that he just waltzed in and assumed he'd be served?

"No." Kate inserted herself into her friends' conversation. Calm before the storm. "We can go back to Woodward."

Oh, no. That sounded like trouble. To Clark's knowledge, the kitchen hadn't been stocked since the last time his uncle visited the place. What was she planning to feed him? Canned chicken and bagged rice?

"What's at Woodward?" he asked, failing to hide his suspicion.

"You'll see," Kate replied.

"I'd really like to know…"

"You'll see."

He swallowed hard as the town passed by around him. Possibilities ricocheted against the walls of his skull. Was she going to make him go into the woods and kill a wild turkey or put him on a cabbage soup diet? Television ads around this time of year and NPR podcast sponsors assured him everyone ate instant stuffing and probably turkey for their holiday meal, but having eaten grilled cheese or zucchini lasagna on this day the last three or four years, he couldn't be entirely certain.

"I don't like surprises."

"Really?" Emily snarked. "You seem like such a zany, seat-of-your-pants kind of guy."

The burn effectively silenced Clark. No one was going to take his side in this. The urge to retort pried open his jaw, but when nothing came to mind, he closed it again. The board room at Woodward Headquarters had sharpened his wit, sure. Only no one there dared to take jabs at him. He mostly swung his verbal sword in their direction, not the other way around.

Knowing his own way back now, he turned into the town square. Without the festival, the streets opened themselves to cars again. In Dallas, the people would have thanked him for giving them the streets back, but not in Miller's Point. Driving through the square gave off an almost eerie, end-of-the-world vibe. Half of the decorations were gone—most likely taken down to be strung up in his house—and the sidewalks sat empty and unused. The tree, a monstrosity of fir and ornaments he couldn't even begin to calculate a cost for, lorded over the square, dark and unlit. Eerie, even for someone who hated this holiday and everything it stood for. The silence probably didn't help. Clark usually drove to NPR and various podcasts about business and finance, but after they'd asked for Christmas music he'd panicked and said he preferred to concentrate on the road.

When they started talking again, he'd have given anything for the sweet release of some kind of background noise. Every word they uttered dug into his skin, sharpened arrows built to pierce him.

"I can't believe everything's over." Michael clucked. "No more festival."

"Don't say that. Anything can happen."

Kate's reply embodied everything Clark knew about her so far. Foolishly optimistic. Beautifully wasteful. What did she think, he was going to cave and give in to their ridiculous whims? Waste money on something he saw no value in? Or did she think some other millionaire investor would sweep in and take the loss? Not likely. He'd already warned potential investors off the project when he decided to close the place down. Even keeping the place open for a few more nights, the rest of their season, would waste money in personnel and electric bills.

They finished the ride home without incident…until they pulled up to the house, and Clark's worst fears about Kate's "surprise" came to life through the clear wall of his windshield. During their brief time in the wilds of Miller's Point, the long driveway had turned into a parking lot. At least thirty trucks and SUVs made themselves very much at home on the pavement stretching almost a hundred yards from the street to the carriage-house-turned-garage tucked away behind the manor.

Clark pulled through the center clearing—thank God someone gave a thought to how they would all get in and out—and fought the quiver of anger in his voice. *Control yourself, man. You have always been able to control yourself before. Why can't you control yourself around Kate?*

"What's all this?"

"You'll see when we get inside."

He parked and they headed for the back door of the house, with Michael and Emily at the lead and him and Kate trailing behind. If Kate disturbed or confused them with this turn of events, they didn't let on. Clark didn't think anything about Kate would faze them by now. From what he'd seen of their friendship, Kate charged forward and everyone else hopped on board without a second thought. He secretly admired that about her.

"Why are there are people here?"

"You'll see. Just follow me. Everyone's inside."

Something strange happened then. Something Clark hadn't expected and didn't know he wanted. She reached for his hand, took it in her own, and led him forward. The contact didn't spark or crackle with electric shocks; the books and poems lied about that. She held his hand like she wanted to remember what it felt like. Like she wanted him to know every line in her palm and how her pulse danced against his. Holding hands with Kate Buckner was like falling into his own bed after a long day of work. A complete relief.

He ripped himself away, violently breaking up the sensation. It made Kate flinch, but her smile didn't falter or slip. She shook it off. She shook off everything he threw at her. He added another word to his description of her. *Endlessly* foolishly optimistic.

"I don't want people here. I told you this isn't a party."

Up the servant's steps and into the back hallway, Kate led him through the family house. How was it possible she knew this place better than he did? Up until his ninth birthday, he spent every Christmas here with his family. He should lead, not her.

"Okay," she began, popping with excited energy. "Every year, on Christmas Eve, we have a huge festival feast for lunch before we open the doors for the guests. I mean, it's huge. Everyone in town comes and we have everything you can imagine—"

"Last year, Buzz Schrute carved a Nativity scene out of butter. With a chainsaw," Michael called over his shoulder. They turned the corner to the main living wing, which housed the library, the study, the formal parlor, the living room, kitchens and formal dining room. The public wing of the house.

"Eating is as much a part of the Christmas experience as anything else. Everyone really opens up around the table. When you share a meal with someone, you're really sharing a part of your soul."

"Where are you going with this?"

They approached the formal dining room. *Oh, no.* The house no longer reeked of gingerbread or fir. Other smells swirled in dizzying circles around Clark's head. Garlic. Onions. Sage. Parsley. Paprika. Sweet potato. Brussels sprouts… Turkey.

"I wanted to show you what it's like. Give you a taste of the real Miller's Point Christmas experience. So, drumroll, please…" Kate shoved the French doors apart, revealing Clark's worst nightmare. He thought a redecorated house couldn't get any worse, but once again, Kate blew him and his expectations away.

"Surprise!"

The shout came not from Kate or her two compatriots, but from a room filled to the brim with Miller's Point Christmas nerds. In his rushed morning, Clark never inspected the formal dining room. He knew from his childhood that it accommodated almost forty-five people, though he'd never seen so many in there. Old, young, fat, thin, tall, short, black, white, in Christmas sweaters, in dresses. Everyone crammed around the table to surprise him and welcome him to his own personal brand of torture. Decorations covered the carved wood paneling of the walls and a miniature Christmas tree— apparently the towering monstrosity in the living room wasn't enough to sate Kate's lust for the noble fir—took post in the corner.

But ornate decorations were nothing compared to the table. Pages from Dr. Seuss stories were less cluttered and colorful. Anything ever featured on a Martha Stewart Thanksgiving special or on the cover of the November issue of *Southern Living* claimed space at this feast.

Stuffing. No fewer than six varieties of potato. Sweet potato casserole. Sweet potato biscuits. Green bean casserole. Cranberry sauce—homemade and canned. Cornbread. Corn pudding. Corn on the cob. Creamed corn. Mac 'n' cheese. Gravy. Brussels sprouts. Soup. Ham. Spinach dip. Broccoli salad. And on and on until the room nearly exploded with plate upon plate of delicious calories.

Three turkeys. Who needed one turkey, much less three?

It all looked so delicious. And so, so unnecessary. He clenched his jaw so tight he thought it might break his teeth.

"What is this?"

"It's a feast."

Kate joined the crowd, leaving him alone against a sea of strangers. He marveled. They all believed in this garbage. They all thought he would sit down at the table and suddenly be a changed man. Kate believed it. She was wrong. They were all wrong. He shoved his hands into his pockets so no one could spot their trembling.

"I can see that. Where did it all come from?"

"We ordered it. Well, some of it was already cooked and frozen for the feast, but we had to order some of it because—"

"Who paid for it?"

This time, Kate hesitated. The air in the room tightened, tense and uncomfortable. People shuffled, shifted their weight from one foot to the other, glanced uncertainly at Kate and coughed. With every tick of the grandfather clock placed against the far wall, as the inevitable explanation came closer and closer, Clark's pulse boomed in his ears. His right hand kept flexing and clenching against the lining of his suit pocket. One woman stepped back, apparently afraid he'd turn violent.

He wasn't a violent man, but he didn't rule out knocking over a gravy boat or two.

"It's part of the company expenses. We do this every year for the festival and—"

There it was. The explanation he knew was coming still managed to enrage him. His carefully constructed mask flew away, leaving nothing but the anger. He may have admired Kate, even liked her a bit, but she was still, at her core, stealing money from his company by disobeying his directive to cancel all festival-related orders. Stealing that which didn't belong to her all to prove some stupid point about a holiday he would *never* like.

"I'm dissolving the company because it's wasteful. This entire stupid holiday is a monument to *waste* and excess and it sickens me!"

A woman stepped forward, a coaxing but vain smile on her aging face.

"We worked really hard on this and—"

"Well that hard work was a waste of time because I'm not touching this. Go. Leave. Get out of here."

"Clark."

Kate threw him a lifeline. A chance to take it back and respond with a little bit of kindness. These people did nothing to him. They followed Kate and tried to help her. This was all her doing, really. He knew all of this intellectually, but his emotions either didn't get the memo or they got the memo and crumbled it into an unreadable ball before burning it.

"I didn't stutter. Get out of here."

When no one moved and all attention turned to the dumbstruck and now decidedly unsmiling Kate Buckner, Clark repeated himself.

"Get. Out!"

With that, the great exodus began. Everyone practically ran for their dishes, picking up what they could and filing out through the connected kitchen door, carefully avoiding Clark, who stood in silent rage. He'd deal with Kate once everyone else left. Only a few stragglers remained when Emily squared off with him.

She was ready for a fight.

"Hey, man. You're being a real jerk, you know that?"

She passed passive-aggressive and dove straight for aggressive-aggressive. Clark didn't care. He could be aggressive too.

"Am I? I feel like someone entered my family's house without permission and spent our money on things I didn't approve after she knew how I felt about it. How am I the bad guy here?"

"Because Kate's trying to do something nice for you after you ruined Christmas. I don't know why she's going to the trouble. You're the *worst*."

"It would have been nice if she'd left me alone, which is what I wanted. And what I still want."

Only the four of them remained, though Clark didn't give Kate a second thought. Nothing mattered now but his own self-righteous frustrations. He opened his mouth to release even more steam, only to be cut off by Michael.

"You know what…" He ran a hand across his short-cut hair, fake sincerity dripping from every syllable. "It's getting late, and I really need to go. You should come too, Emily."

"Great idea. Walk me home?"

They headed for the door. A little voice from the corner of the room tried to stop them. Kate's voice.

"No, guys… Wait—"

"You can come with us."

"You *should* come with us," Emily corrected. "This guy isn't worth your time. You can stay at my house and we'll have a real Christmas, just us."

The fire crackled. The clock ticked. Kate stared at her shoes as if they held the divine secrets of the universe. Maybe they did. Maybe that was the key to her eternal belief everything would work out in her favor: her boots told the future.

"No one should be alone on Christmas."

"He doesn't care about Christmas," Emily shouted, exasperation written in the creasing lines of her forehead.

"I don't," he agreed.

For the first time since their first fiery conversation on the steps of town hall, Kate's firm grasp on her wide-eyed optimism fractured. It was her turn to yell.

"But I do!" She flinched at her own voice, shock visibly rippling through her body at her own reaction. They stared at her, waiting with slack jaws as she ran a hand through her hair and collected herself.

When she returned to them, she was quiet, but no less emphatic, and to Clark's surprise, she didn't deliver the end of her declaration to the two lifelong friends currently begging her to spend her favorite holiday together. She spoke to him. "I believe in Christmas, and I don't think anyone should be alone like this. Even you."

She left chills up the back of his neck. She'd said the one thing he didn't want to hear. In the corner of his peripheral vision, Emily visibly deflated. Michael threw an arm over her slumped shoulders before walking her towards the door.

"Okay. We'll see you when we see you, I guess. Merry Christmas."

"Merry Christmas, guys."

They left, like the rest of the Miller's Point crowd, through the swinging kitchen door. Eventually, they'd find themselves either leaving from one of the servant's entrances or through the grand front entryway, but for now, their footsteps echoed in Clark's ears and their absence carved a chasm between him and the woman who stayed behind.

Stayed behind with *him*. Because she didn't want him to feel lonely.

Clark didn't know what to do with that information except hate her for it.

"What is your problem?"

"My problem?" he repeated, incredulous. He thought he'd made his *problem* exceptionally clear when he told her he wanted her out of his house, out of his life… and, yeah, out of his head. She'd only been around for less than a day, and still she consumed him. Clark often heard of people describing themselves as "walled off." They "built their walls" to keep themselves protected and others out. Clark's heart wasn't so much a walled castle as it was a vault in Fort Knox. With every word Kate said, he added another steel lock to the door. No one was going to catch him with his guard down, especially not the one woman who'd managed to get under his skin after twenty-seven years on earth.

"Yeah." She crossed her arms, an indication he'd be

seeing no more Miss Nice Elf. "I want to know why you're like this."

"I don't need to explain myself to you. This isn't tragic backstory time."

"I want to understand."

"There's nothing to understand."

"*Something* had to make you this way."

Clark paused. His blood rushed in his ears. He wasn't born this way. Statues like him were carved and sculpted and hardened over many years and many miseries. But he'd never told anyone why he hated this stupid holiday, and he wasn't about to start with Kate Buckner, who'd probably end up feeling sorry for him or kissing him or forcing him to let her into his Fort Knox vault of a heart.

"Some people are just the way they are."

"I don't believe that. No one is born lonely."

He'd given her too much room to breathe. The threat to expose his past, the intrusion into his life… It all added up to an attack he didn't know if he possessed the armaments to defeat. He could just push her away until she backed down.

"Christmas is a time where everyone spends money they don't have on people they don't really care about. Or, in this case, they spend other people's money on people they don't really care about."

"I care about you."

"What?"

"I mean…" She bit her bottom lip. "I care about everyone."

No matter what she said, all he heard was, "I care about you." The revelation plunged him into full-on defensive mode.

"I don't. I care about my company, my family, and my legacy. I don't care about Miller's Point. I don't care about your stupid festival. I don't care about Christmas. And I don't care about you. I said you could stay because I felt bad for you, but now I know…"

She stiffened. She froze. Something snapped behind her liquid-gold eyes. She seemed to consider her options. And then, without reaching for her coat or her scarf or anything belonging to her, really, Kate marched towards the nearest door.

"Where are you going?"

"Why are you even asking? You don't care."

The door slammed behind her. Clark knew he should have felt a rush of joy. He'd won. He'd claimed victory over the invading armies of Miller's Point and their fearless leader. But happiness eluded him. It sprinted in the other direction, leaving him empty. The sustaining belief in goodness she'd carried all through their time together dimmed.

He'd broken Kate Buckner.

He'd been trying to do it all day, but now that he'd succeeded, he felt nothing but disgust.

Chapter Eight

K ATE'S FIRST THOUGHT, AS IT always was when things went horribly, horribly wrong (or, to be completely fair, even slightly wrong) was, "How did I screw this up?" If a stranger's high heel broke or the set for the Fezziwig mansion got slightly burned by an errant candle fire or no one could agree on how to fairly split a bill at a restaurant, Kate's immediate reaction always passed go, did not collect two hundred dollars, and zipped straight to self-blame.

She abandoned Woodward House behind her, fully intending to return once she cleared her head. The problem with this entire plot of hers came down to one simple fact: being near him drove her crazy.

Crazy didn't accurately describe it. He just…robbed her of any ability she possessed to take decisive, bold action. Kate's performance reviews with The Christmas Company—both during her time as a volunteer and as an employee—always highlighted her excellent ability to think clearly, no matter the circumstances. During times of crisis or mild inconvenience, she took charge and steered the ship back on course. When she got near Clark, however…she might as well have tried to steer the Titanic through nighttime fog.

He made no sense. He surprised her with peeks of his heart and then tore it away when she stepped closer to get a better look. When he offered to drive them on their Christmas Box deliveries, when he gave Bradley that candy bar… Those actions pointed to something specific, to a truth he either wanted to hide or didn't know he had inside of him at all.

He was secretly a good man. He wanted to open himself up to others. But something—fear or pain or resentment—kept him from doing so.

This entire impossible-to-balance calculation led to Kate trudging through the back forty of Woodward House. Thin bands of frozen rain slapped her cheeks. After less than five minutes exposed to the elements, her bones themselves shivered from the cold. Texas never froze, of course, not properly. Snow happened rarely and people usually took it as a sign of the End of Days. But, on days like today, it did get cold enough for Kate to wonder if she would catch her death just trying to get some fresh air.

The forty acres of land stretched between the faux Victorian manor house and the edge of the hill overlooking Miller's Point upon which that house sat. It stirred Kate with its beauty. The old legend of the original Woodwards always included some storyline about Jedediah Woodward, the founder of the town and the company, who bought this land because his bride-to-be—whom he'd never met—apparently loved to paint. He thought buying her a landscape to explore and inspire her art might endear his unseen bride to him. Apparently, the gesture went over fairly well, seeing as she gave him thirteen children.

As she approached the end of the tree line, where a

log bridge crossed over an icy river, Kate gave Annabella Woodward some credit. If a man gifted this land to her, she'd probably give him fifteen children. At least.

Stopping at the river's edge, Kate leaned back against a granite boulder and surveyed the vast landscape around her. The rock was not exactly the most comfortable of recliners. She made do anyway. A view so beautiful deserved to be looked at. She could think of no better place to collect her thoughts. The tall evergreen trees followed the river down to a broad estuary in the distance. Unlike the half-frozen, half-cold spit rain, the river really had frozen over, halting the rushing water with a thin top layer of ice.

In the spring especially, she could understand the appeal of Jedediah Woodward's gift to his wife. In a time before flu medicine, one generally appreciated a warm, leafy landscape more than a cold, wet one. Today, with plenty of cold pills and doctors on hand in town, she enjoyed the view for its resilience. Everything froze. Everything died in winter. But that was all the more reason to flourish and blossom come April. Kate sat on the edge of it all, taking in deep breaths of fresh tree breezes as she reckoned with her failings.

She'd failed him, the man with eyes as cold as this landscape. Something in Clark wanted to come out. She saw the hesitant hope hiding in his distant eyes. So why was he being so cruel to her? What had she done to deserve his devil-may-care attitude? She ran circles around this question, poking and prodding and second-guessing every decision she'd made this morning. Every turn she took led her to another brick wall. Every time she thought she'd grabbed onto an answer, her hands clutched at empty air.

She'd been kind and open and honest with him. Maybe she'd been a bit pushy and he made her heart race when he even glanced at her with his hypnotic green eyes, sure, but overall, she'd done nothing but try to help him.

For the first time in a long time, Kate considered the possibility of someone else's failure. Maybe she hadn't failed him. Maybe nothing she could do would open him up. Emily could be right about him. Maybe he just…wasn't a nice guy. Maybe he'd been cruel to her to get her to leave.

With that horrifying yet liberating thought, the full weight of his insults bayoneted her in the chest. *You don't care about me. I don't care about Christmas. I don't care about you.* She heard them the first time, but blamed herself for their stings. Now, she accepted the full weight of his hatred. It burned her worse than the frostbite she was no doubt getting out here in this rain.

It occurred to her how every thought she had about him might have been the product of projection. She assumed everyone could be made to love Christmas because she loved it. She assumed he had a tragic back-story because she lived through a tragedy. She assumed he liked her because…well, against even her best judgment, she liked him. Sure, he could challenge the Grinch for grumpiness and Scrooge for Greatest Miser of All Time. But weirdly, she almost found it endearing, his little freak-outs any time she introduced something new and exciting into his world. He struggled with the basics of human interaction, but she swore he contained good inside of him.

Maybe she'd misjudged his character. Maybe he had nothing inside of him but hate and lumps of coal. She trudged through the woods to clear her head so she could eventually make her way back to the house with fresh eyes and a clear heart, ready to take on anything he threw at her. Now, she could only remember the words Michael always said when she ran to him for advice. *Sometimes,* he said, *you just gotta know when to quit.*

He said it knowing full well she'd never quit. But today…she considered it.

The crack and crunch of leaves behind her ended the internal debate. Kate spooked at the noise—she didn't think a murderer would ever come to a nice place like Miller's Point, but she'd watched enough Lifetime movies to know it was at least remotely possible—only to slump back down against her rock when she recognized the intruder. For some reason, the man who couldn't stand the sight of her and didn't care about her at all had tracked her down through the rain.

A cynical shade cast over his sudden appearance. Not literally, of course, as she stared out at the frogs sticking to the iced-over river instead of turning to give him her full attention. Was her being on his property a legal liability for him? Did he want her to sign some kind of injury waiver or something?

"H-hey. You're a fast walker," he said. Sudden arrivals didn't catch her attention, but labored, hard-fought gasping did. She turned her head just enough to survey him out of the corner of her eye. A small, eternally happy part of her almost giggled at the sight. Not only was he red-faced and anxious and bent over his knees to catch his breath, but the children of Miller's Point often pretended to be dragons when their breath puffed in front of their face. Imagining Clark on all fours, feigning a mighty dragon's roar, would've brought a less angry Kate to sidesplitting laughter, but as it was, she built a fence of hurt around her.

On the one hand, she needed him to save the town. And she couldn't leave him alone if she thought he had a chance of finding even a sliver of hope. On the other, she selfishly wanted an apology. Her love of Miller's Point and her belief in the goodness of the human heart would eventually dominate any selfish bone in her body, but for this one moment, she indulged in her own pain.

"Only when I'm running away from something. What are you doing here?"

"You're going to get sick."

"You don't care."

"You're still on my employee insurance until January 1."

"Good to know."

A pause. Kate didn't know what he expected by coming down here, and she didn't know what she expected him to say. She knew what she wanted him to say, but she couldn't imagine the words *I'm sorry* ever escaping his lips.

He circled her stone to stand before her, trying to force her to look at him. "Listen—"

"I listened to you all day. I listened to you trash and run over everything I tried to do to make you happy."

"You don't owe me anything. You don't need to make me happy."

"You don't get it, do you? It's not about you. It's about humanity."

"Great. Another soapbox speech about the magical healing powers of Christmas?"

"No. I won't waste it on someone who refuses to listen."

Kate kicked a pebble. It skidded along the dead grass down to the river, where it limply slid across the cracked-ice face of the still water. So, this was defeat. She'd worked so hard to avoid it, she hardly recognized the emotion. Defeat was wanting to scream the truth at the top of her lungs only to have him shove his fingers in his ears and refuse to listen. Defeat was standing in the rain and having someone else tell you it's perfectly dry.

He didn't get her, and she didn't get him. Defeat.

"I hear you." Despite the frost and the perfect cleanliness of his suit, Clark lowered himself to the grass. She couldn't escape his Ireland eyes and their self-serious absurdities. "I'm listening. It's just not for me."

"Christmas is for everyone," she said, for what felt like the millionth time since his arrival here.

"No, it's not."

"But it can be. Christmas is a spirit. Christmas is a way of treating people."

This was perhaps Kate's most deeply held idea about the holiday season. Christmas was there to celebrate the birth of Christ, of course. The name said as much, but because of that, not in spite of it, Christmas had to also embody all of the goodness of humanity. Christmas wasn't just about saying "God bless," but about going out into the world and living that message no matter the personal cost. The only way to truly celebrate Christmas, as far as Kate was concerned, was to stand up for people and love them completely…even if they hurt her.

"Kate…" Clark trailed off and suddenly forgot how to make eye contact. His big hands must have been very interesting, considering he wouldn't stop staring at them. "I think you're an…" He coughed. "I think you're an extraordinary woman."

"What?"

"You are kind and generous to a fault, even if you were generous with my money—"

"I only spent your money on you."

"You're funny and beautiful and witty and you clearly care about others and—"

He went on, but she stopped listening after beautiful. He thought she was beautiful? Even she didn't think she was beautiful. She tuned back in only after her ears stopped ringing.

"I can see what you're trying to do. I know you're just trying to help. It's a very kind gesture. I just don't want it. I have rules and standards for my life and they just don't include Christmas. Or wasting money. So, I think it would be better if you just go on ahead to your friends' place for Christmas. You'll have a better time."

Kate had only played dodgeball once in her life. This conversation reminded her of being the only person on one side while a barrage attack came from the other. He'd told her, in his stilted Mr. Darcy way, that he liked her, then immediately proceeded into why she needed to spend her holidays without him.

And he'd called her beautiful. His stream of consciousness declaration came out nervous and unfiltered. Had he even realized he called her that?

She changed the subject, if only to keep her heart from exploding with the possibilities. This time, she didn't attack him. A sigh, heavier than any winter wind, blew out of her, releasing the anger and hurt. Clark hadn't managed to say sorry, but he would. She believed in him. Besides, she didn't know how to hold onto anger. It wasn't in her character.

"You know, they're right. I've never left someone alone on Christmas."

"You probably bring them to the festival, don't you?"

"Not always." Kate took a chance. Clark hadn't responded to grand acts of magic or her charming personality. All she had left was her honesty. "Once, when I was eighteen, I'd finally gotten the part of Belle. She's Scrooge's love interest when he's younger. I'd always wanted to play her. She has this beautiful gown and she's just awesome, standing up for herself and breaking up with him when he's not good for her anymore—"

"You like her because she broke up with him?"

"It would have been easy to live with something bad. It took courage to break free and start over."

"I see."

He wasn't convinced, but she pressed forward. In her opinion, he could learn a thing or two from Belle.

"Anyway, this was the only time I was going to be able to play her. I was getting too tall for the costume. I only barely fit into it that year as it was..." She sighed again. "And then Michael broke his leg in the big State Championship football game our senior year of high school. He was going to just stay home that year by himself while everyone went to the festival on Christmas Eve because his parents were working there, but..."

"No one should be alone on Christmas," Clark finished for her.

"Yeah."

"You gave up your big dream just for him?"

Kate scoffed and rolled her eyes.

"My big dream is playing Scrooge. But unless I start growing a beard and some other chromosomes, I don't think that's going to happen."

"You know what I mean. You sacrificed for him."

"Yeah, I guess I did."

"Like you're sacrificing for me."

A clear delineation of thought erupted between them. Kate didn't see it as making a sacrifice. She understood she'd made a sacrifice, but she didn't see it that way or remember it that way. Like tonight, for example, she couldn't imagine ever looking back on it as, "that one Christmas I let a mean guy sneer and yell at me all day." She imagined she'd remember it as, "the year I helped save the town and the soul of a handsome but lonely man with a hidden heart of gold." In the same way, she remembered her eighteenth Christmas as the one where she and Michael played Go Fish until midnight and watched *The Muppet Christmas Carol* on repeat until four in the morning when they both fell asleep on the couch. She woke up with swollen feet because she'd slept in her shoes. She remembered laughing until her sides hurt and eating so much frozen pizza covered in turkey she almost threw up.

Instead of letting him in on this secret, she chose instead to tease him. She liked teasing him. The tops of his ears always turned bright red, a fact that tickled her and made her wonder how many people in his life ever had the guts to make jokes at his expense.

"It's not the same thing."

"Why not?" He furrowed his brow.

"Because I actually sort of like Michael." She shrugged. "Jury's still out on you."

"You don't like me?"

Kate didn't think of herself as a vengeful person, but she internally cheered at the hurt in his voice. It lasted only for a moment before she thoroughly hated herself for it. He'd hurt her when he said he didn't care about her. Part of her wanted him to hurt, however horrible that desire was.

"Have you done anything to make me like you?"

"Well…" He stumbled. "I mean…"

"Uh-huh," Kate retorted, triumphantly, happy to have a reason to smile again. She'd been frowning for too long. "So, why would I like you if you haven't done anything to earn it?"

"I can be nice."

"Yeah?"

"Yeah."

They sat in unmoving silence for one minute. Then two minutes. All the while, Kate stared. When he finally got uncomfortable with her gaze, he raised his eyebrows in confusion.

"What?"

"I'm waiting," Kate said, unable to help chuckling.

"Waiting on what?"

"For you to be nice!"

Clark joined her laughter. Not much. Not enough. But it was a start.

"Why don't we call a truce? A real one this time," he said, the ghost of a smile still pulling at his lips. "You can have your Christmas, and I'll have my peace and quiet in my study."

"My Christmas is the festival. Are you going to give me that?"

"No."

"But—"

The smile vanished. Clark's right hand flexed.

"We can't call a truce if you're going to be impossible."

"I am not being impossible!"

"You know I'm not going to give you the festival back. We can't afford it."

Here we go again, Kate thought. *Two steps forward, one step back.*

"That's not why we can't have it."

"It's a drain on our resources."

"Maybe, but that's not the real reason you're shutting it down," she retorted.

"Are we really going through this dance again?"

"I'll do it until you tell me what you've got against Christmas."

"You'll be dancing forever, then."

Kate explored two distinct possibilities laid out before her. Either he was a snob who would never attempt to open himself up to her or anyone else, for that matter—a possibility she found remote now that he admitted to liking her, something he never would have this morning—or he was going to flourish into the man she thought he could be. The man she saw hiding behind his thick curtains of cold detachment. Either way, she had to keep trying. The town hung in the balance and a man's soul was at stake. This was no time to hide at Emily's house and drink eggnog until she passed out, even if she wanted to.

"Why don't I make you a deal? Instead of hiding in your office like the saddest man in the world, you spend Christmas with me. Really with me. Not on your phone pretending I don't exist. And if you still hate it tomorrow morning, you don't have to tell me why. But if you like it, even a little bit, you have to fess up."

She wanted that secret. Knowing it could be the change in everything. It could make the difference.

"…Why do I have a feeling you won't take no for an answer?"

"Because I won't." She smiled and popped up from her rock. The cracked face of her childhood Mickey Mouse watch flashed in the dim light peeking from behind the towering fir trees. Already five o'clock? When had it gotten so late? There were so many Christmas Eve traditions to get through before the evening was out. Her mind raced with timetables and planning strategies as her boots crunched the frosty grass beneath her feet. The slight shower still trickled overhead, but she paid it no mind; they'd be warm enough once they made it inside and in front of a roaring fireplace. She rubbed her hands together to warm them, not considering the fact that she might look like a plotting, evil supervillain.

"Then I guess I accept your deal."

All at once, Kate bloomed into her normal self. It was Christmas. Anything could happen at Christmas. And what was more, she was *great* at Christmas. Renewed faith squeezed her chest.

"Then you'd better get ready for the best Christmas of your life," she commanded.

"That's an incredibly low bar to clear."

"Then you'd better get ready for the best Christmas of all time."

"You haven't convinced me so far." He smirked. "I accept your challenge."

Chapter Nine

H E ACCEPTED HER DEAL ONLY because he convinced himself it was impossible to falter. He would never like Christmas, and even if she did make him enjoy it a little bit, he could just lie and save himself the humiliation of telling his story.

And besides, he was a businessman. He didn't respect any deal not in writing.

When she fled the house, he had no choice but to go after her. Reason told him he couldn't let a woman wander around outside alone, especially not on his property. Reason told him she'd gone outside without a coat or an umbrella. She'd catch her death! She'd slip on the ice and fall and break her neck! She'd see a stray lightbulb and electrocute herself trying to fix it!

Reason instilled him with a sense of fear for her safety, but reason, if he ever decided to be honest with himself, only served as a justification for stepping out into the biting rain and following her footprints through the wet grass into the forest. As a kid, these woods had terrified him. He hadn't stepped foot past the treeline since his ninth birthday. Twenty years later, these woods still featured in some of his worst nightmares.

But he'd forged ahead anyway. Kate couldn't be out in the woods alone, not when he had been the one to push her out there.

Clark didn't have the time or patience for feelings like guilt. At least, he didn't until he met Kate. She was the human face behind his corporate destruction, and even if he still believed he was doing the right thing, she made him want to apologize. She made him wish there was another way.

So, that's why he said what he did about her, about her being kind and good-hearted. She needed to know this wasn't personal. She hadn't failed him. He just didn't buy into her gimmicks about the holiday season, that's all.

"We might as well get it over and done with," he said, picking himself up from the muddy forest floor. Usually, he preferred clean, Scandinavian office design to dirt and outdoors of any kind, but he made an exception for Kate.

"No need to sound so excited," she teased.

"I don't want this deal going to your head."

"Don't worry. I'm under no illusions you'll be an easy nut to crack."

"Good."

"But you shouldn't let this deal go to your head, either."

"Why?"

She spun on him, her long hair whipping waves of cinnamon and evergreen-scented air Clark's way. It stunned him as she leaned in close, too close for comfort. Not that he minded. With her this close and this mockingly intense, he could count the millions of near-gold flecks in her eyes and feel her puffing breath on his lips.

"Because you'll find I'm a very persistent gal."

"I already know that," he whispered, too low for her to hear, a fact he was grateful for. If she heard him, she might discover that *I already know that* was code for something else, an electric hum that stirred inside him every time she said his name.

Unfazed, she stretched her arms out. Arms open wide as if to hug the scenery around her, she tilted her head back and breathed. This place held nothing but anxiety and headaches for Clark, but Kate was perfectly at peace. Out here, away from the distractions of the Christmas lights and the electric bill no doubt climbing, he beheld her. Every soft curve of her beautiful face glowed against this frigid terrain. She smiled even as frozen raindrops slid down her skin. A cold would no doubt be in both of their futures if Clark didn't usher them back to the house soon.

A cold seemed a small price to pay to get to see Kate like this, surrounded by silver rain falling down in thin sheets against the emeralds and ambers of the woods towering around them. Set against this backdrop, she reminded him of a princess in a fairy story, one raised so deep in the forest she didn't even know she was royalty.

"This place is beautiful, isn't it?" she asked.

"Yeah," he breathed, never once glancing at the scenery. He was too wrapped up in her. "I guess it is."

"You guess? Don't you know?"

"I don't like these woods. Haven't since I was a kid. I got lost in them once."

The memories of that day still haunted him. He prayed she wouldn't pry.

"And…" She trailed off, her eyes narrowing in cautious suspicion, "you still came out to look for me?"

"It was the logical thing to do."

It wasn't *only* logical, but Kate didn't push. In the fashion of a distracted hummingbird, Kate broke the tenuous emotional connection between them. She changed the subject with surprising deftness, adopting a half-bent pose to examine his feet.

"What're your shoes like?"

"What?" An unapproved laugh escaped. How had he gotten from wanting to sweep her into his arms and kiss her in the middle of a drizzle to being asked about the quality of his shoes?

"Let me have a look at them," she demanded, bending down even further to pick up one of his legs. Clark gripped the nearest tree for support when his left leg was hoisted unceremoniously in the air. If Kate were any other woman, if this were any other day, and if he hadn't struck that deal, fury would have ruled him.

It was, however much he resented it, Christmas Eve. He did make a deal. And the woman holding his leg in the air was Kate, this strange, smiley, fireplace of a woman who weaseled her way behind his defenses.

"Why do you need to look at my shoes?"

She dropped his left leg and reached for his right. A sudden wave of embarrassment gripped Clark by the scruff of the neck, digging cold, sharp nails into the skin beneath his hairline. These shoes were—he mentally counted backwards—about twenty years old. He'd watched countless YouTube tutorials on cobbling so he could fix them up and keep them instead of spending a few hundred bucks on a new pair. Besides, they were his father's shoes. He didn't want to just throw them away. Could she tell they were holding together with shoe glue and a prayer?

"I need to make sure they've got enough grip on them."

"Okay. Wait, grip on them for what?"

Clunk. His right leg hit the ground, returning him to even footing. Kate rose, her cheeks flushed from the weather and whatever excitement bubbled behind that skull of hers. Having spent approximately zero time out in freezing rain before, the pink tint of her skin concerned him. His obliging attitude was going to land both of them in the hospital with a horrible flu or something.

Though he couldn't deny, at least to himself, how beautiful she was. With her hair now damp from the rain and her clothes sticking to her skin, a woman who should have looked like a drowned cat ended up glowing in the hazy sunlight like a beached siren. She kicked her own shoes against the nearest tree trunk, knocking out clumps of dirt and mud from between the treads. Her pink cheeks and nose belonged on a romantic Christmas card. Clark's confusion only grew.

"Are you up for an adventure?" she asked.

"Uh…" As much as he relished the golden thrill streaking through her gaze, he didn't like the sound of the word *adventure* on her red lips. "Not really. Why do you ask?"

Once again, Kate opened her arms to the scenery, only this time she didn't relish it or show it off. Clark followed her gaze out into the clearing before them. It was only now, with his attention fully focused on it, he realized this wasn't a clearing at all.

They'd reached the river.

"There's a family of cardinals across the water. Can you hear them?"

"Yes, but—"

"When I was a kid, one of my teachers used to hand-paint these Christmas cards with cardinals in snowy trees. We don't get snow here, but we've got to see if we can spot them."

Oh, no. Her voice recovered its bell-like ring, the same bell-like ring it got every time she wasn't going to take no for an answer. A snake of panic slithered down Clark's spine as she inched towards the long log bridge connecting the two banks of the still river; in less than a second, his anxious mind conjured up a list of at least twenty-eight things that could go wrong. He grasped at any reason not to follow through with this scheme.

"Don't you have a zoo around here? A bird sanctuary or something? You can see cardinals anytime."

"Oh, please," Kate scoffed and peeled off her now properly wet overcoat. It landed with a *splat* on her lounging rock. "Why would I go to a zoo when there's a perfectly good nest across the river?" When she sensed his hesitation, she sighed and extended her hand, her energy very much projecting a *just shut up and have fun for once in your life* vibe. "It'll be fun."

"That bridge isn't up to code."

"They're big old logs. It's probably been there for a hundred years. What more do you want?"

He pressed his back into the nearest tree. If wishes came true, the massive trunk would open up and swallow him whole. No such salvation came. He cursed this stupid forest; no wonder he hadn't come in here for almost twenty years. All the trees were jerks.

"Nope. No way." He shook his head, hoping his stern voice would be enough to indicate that he was putting his foot down about this one. He'd given her run of his house, his car, and his kitchen, but he really meant it this time when he said no. "It's not safe. Kate—"

Pleas fell on deaf ears as the woman in question took a challenging step forward, slapping her heeled boot onto the bark of the makeshift bridge. Clark's steady heartbeat picked up tempo and volume until it sounded like an overexcited drumline had taken a residency in his ears.

"You know you want to…"

Another step forward. Both of her feet were on the log now, only a foot or two above the iced-over water, but enough to worry him. Her smile curled upward.

She thought she had the upper hand; she believed he would follow her straight out over the river, bending to her will. Clark's fear kept him rooted to the spot even as his heart pounded against the cage of his chest, trying to escape and run straight for her. Across the river, the song of the cardinals—he assumed they were cardinals, at least—taunted him.

"I don't—"

Another step. She spread her arms out for balance.

"You're going to miss all the fun," she promised in a singsong cadence.

"You're going to be cold," he countered.

Another step. The heel of her boot narrowly missed a gap in the wood and his heart narrowly missed two beats. Her steps were small, cautious, and though she no longer looked at him, he would be willing to bet his fortune that she was smirking.

"You sure you don't want to join me?"

"Hey," Clark warned, this time moving forward in step with her. He kept his hands out in front of him in a show of surrender. Approaching her as if she were a wounded animal, he mentally begged her not to move another muscle.

"Just a little bit closer…" She crooned.

Clark halted in place. So *that* was her game. Trickery. He was *not* going to cross those logs. Games and sneaking around wouldn't work anymore than bribery or pleading would. Instead, he turned away from the river and headed for the path straight home.

He wasn't actually going to go home, of course. He just needed her to think he was so she would be inclined to follow him. Two could play at her game.

"I'm not doing this. You won't pressure me."

His reverse psychology failed. A huff from behind

him told him so.

"Fine! I'll just go by my—"

A crack. A piercing scream. A rush of water. Three sounds wrapped up in one cymbal crash of noise. Clark spun on his heel.

"Kate! KATE!"

But Kate was gone. She'd fallen. Broken the ice sheet. And the river—still only a second ago—now rushed away from him. Taking Kate with it.

He didn't think twice. He didn't have to. His body acted for him. Without a moment's hesitation, his powerful legs crossed the muddy ground and he dove head-first into the frigid water. It stung, a million frozen daggers cutting into his skin.

He crashed beneath the surface. His eyes opened, but the water was so black and cold he could neither see anything nor feel anything but pain. Slamming them closed again, he stretched his arm out before him. Once. Twice. His body shoved the water aside, searching for the one thing he needed to save. His lungs ached for air. His skin screamed from the cold. Currents pulled him, dragging him away, but he urged his muscles forward. He opened his eyes once, then twice, but besides the stinging this action caused him, he couldn't see a thing. He was swimming blindly, praying with every motion that he'd somehow find her. He *had* to find her.

Finally, his hand touched something warm and solid. Or, he tried to. Her body revolted against him, thrashing and shoving wildly as she fought to struggle towards the air above them. Gripping her by the waist, he swam upward, fighting with strained muscles to struggle against the punishing current. Everything was cold. Everything was painful. But he couldn't dwell. Thought vanished, leaving only the primal. It shoved him onward even when he wanted nothing more than to quit. *Survive. Save her and survive.* But with each passing second, her body grew more and more limp, and she fought less and less…until one cruel moment when she went still and slack in his arms.

"Ah!" He gasped when they finally hit the air. He drank it in, coughing and choking and spluttering. Kate returned to life, too, though not as violently as he. As he pushed their way crosscurrent to the river's dirty bank, Clark watched Kate's limp head barely suck in air. Her entire body shook with shivers, but at least she was breathing. Her eyes fluttered enough to tell him she was conscious. A small, desperate relief.

Clark moved quickly. They needed to get back inside. No time to waste, not when he'd been so supremely stupid. Every second they wasted not moving towards the house was a moment she wasn't getting the care she needed. Wordless and shivering himself, Clark scooped Kate into his arms, bridal style, and set his eyes on the peak of the house poking out from just over the trees in the distance. They left the clearing and the river behind, but not before he picked up Kate's coat, the one she'd discarded before her expedition across the log bridge.

Invisible needles stabbed him as his wet skin met cold air. He could only imagine what Kate was going through. Her now-pale body almost convulsed in his arms, though she kept the slightest of grips on his neck. The pressure provided him a small modicum of relief. As long as she touched him, he knew she wasn't under.

The forest that scared him so deeply as a child now served as mere window dressing. Nothing mattered but getting her home. As he walked, he tried to keep her awake. What little warmth he felt in her body slipped away with every step he took.

"All right, Kate. It's all right. We're gonna get you home and take care of you. I promise. I just need you to stay awake and stick with me, okay?" he muttered incoherently, not that it mattered. The words weren't important. He spoke to give her something to hold onto…and to keep his mind off of the fact that he let her get hurt. She could freeze to death or get hypothermia or lose her legs and it would be all his fault. All because he didn't want to sit around a warm fire and sing Christmas songs.

With one hand, Clark maneuvered the coat his hands until he was able to pull out the cell phone from her pocket.

"Kate, what's your password?"

"No password," she mumbled, her head curling into the space between Clark's shoulder and neck. Her breath tickled. At least it hadn't lost its heat yet. Her phone lit his face, clearly asking for a password. Did she not want to give it to him, or was she so out of it she thought she didn't have one? Clark racked his brain. He couldn't stop his walking and he needed help. He couldn't help her alone.

Then it came to him. And he pressed four numbers. They granted him access. 1-2-2-5. December 25. Christmas Day. She really *did* love Christmas as much as she claimed. During their tour yesterday, Michael informed him that the nearest hospital was in the next town over, meaning even the fastest ambulance would be miles behind someone who lived in town. They'd never make it in time to save Kate. He needed someone who could help. And he needed them fast. Making quick work of the damp phone screen, he clicked the first name he recognized. The voice on the other end of the line answered in one ring.

"I knew you'd come around! Want me and Michael

to pick you up—"

"Do you know a doctor?"

"What? Who is this?"

"Emily, there's been an accident. Kate needs—"

"Woodward? Is that you?"

"Kate fell into the river trying to cross this log bridge and she needs to see a doctor."

"Is it serious?"

"I don't know, but I need your help."

"Michael's a medic."

"Come to the house as quick as you can." She didn't respond. Desperation coursed through him. "*Please.*"

"We'll be there in ten."

Clark could only hope ten minutes would be fast enough. Michael's medical expertise was their only hope. He hung up and continued his journey.

When the tree line broke, Woodward House loomed into view. Clark, who had until now been walking as fast as his legs would allow, pulled into a dead sprint. Kate's hold on his shoulders had loosened. He was losing her to unconsciousness. Terror replaced his blood. The color evaporated from his world. He pressed onward into the house and upstairs to the first bathroom he could find. Shoving open the door with his shoulder, he entered and placed Kate on the counter, letting her body slacken against the wall. Her eyes slipped closed. They no longer fluttered. Clark fought the urge to vomit.

"Hey, hey, I need you to listen to me." He tapped her hand, perhaps a little harder than necessary. It twitched, a good response. As he continued to speak, Clark spun the bathtub faucet. A small chain—part of the ancient plumbing system in this house—needed to be pulled for the shower, but as the water heated up, Clark reached for the nearest towel and tried to figure out what to do next as he frantically rubbed the barely-conscious woman dry. He couldn't leave Kate in the shower alone. She'd drown. Waiting for Michael the medic would take too long. Kate needed warmth now.

With great care, Clark lifted Kate off of the counter, carried her to the steaming shower, and stepped inside with her, fully clothed.

The shower, like the rest of the house, showed its age. Glass and gold couldn't have been more out of fashion; the pipes groaned from the sudden use of the hot water. Clark only saw the woman in his arms. He placed her on her own two feet, but held her close, almost as if they were dancing. The hot water washed over them in a steaming, restorative rain storm. *Please be all right*, he silently begged her. *Please, please, please be all right*. He counted her heartbeats against his chest, marking each one as a victory, a sign she could make it through this.

Slowly, Kate's chattering teeth stilled. Her body ceased its convulsions. She looked up at Clark with an expression of half-awake awe, her heart hammering against his chest.

"You…" She trailed off. "You…"

Clark wanted to pull the rest of the words from her mind. What was she trying to say? Did she hate him for letting her fall down through the ice or love him for bringing her back or despise him for standing in the shower with her, even if they were fully clothed?

He would never find out. The bathroom door slammed open, revealing a red-faced Emily. Steam practically shot out of her ears, though Michael followed behind with level-headed stoicism.

"You!" Emily's voice ricocheted off the tiled bathroom walls. "What do you think you're doing?"

"I'm trying to help her."

"Help her? I think you've done enough. Now, go."

A protest shoved its way to the front of Clark's brain. He abandoned all thoughts of confrontation. As much as he hated to admit it, Emily was right. He put Kate in a terrible position and let her fall. If he stayed, the chances of him screwing it up even further only grew.

"Of course. Thank you for coming to help."

Awkwardly, he changed places with Emily. He walked his soaking wet body straight out of the bathroom and past Michael, without another word. The only thing he could do now was get himself cleaned up and wait.

About twenty minutes, a shower and a fresh set of clothes later, Clark found himself pacing outside of her bathroom door. He heard no sound, but it didn't deter him. He'd wait as long as he needed to see her, to make sure she was all right.

He didn't know how long he paced before a door down the hallway opened, revealing Emily. She hugged an oversized sweater to her chest.

"Is Kate all right?"

"She's fine. I borrowed some old pajamas from a drawer and put her to bed. Is that okay?" When Clark nodded, Emily glanced over her shoulder to make sure the bedroom door from which she emerged remained closed before leveling her uncertain expression at him. "Listen. I gotta talk to you."

"Yes?"

"I don't like you. I mean…" She rolled her eyes. A sigh blew rough between her lips. "I *didn't* like you. But Kate said you saved her from the river, is that true?"

Save. Clark knew how to destroy things. Subsidiaries and businesses. He knew how to dismantle them and sell off the parts. He wasn't sure he was comfortable being described as a man who saved anything, much less a woman's life. Much less *Kate's* life. He wasn't worthy of the distinction.

"She fell and I went in to get her," he said, diplomatically.

"And carried her all the way here and did everything you could to make sure she was all right?"

Clark merely nodded. Slumping back against the nearest wall, and disturbing an ancient painting of Clark's third great uncle Horace in the process, Emily released a long, low sigh of contradiction, not that Clark blamed her. He'd ridden into town, insulted everyone she knew, and gotten her friend almost killed. Him saving her life didn't change or negate the other facts of their interactions. But he did save her life.

"I can't believe I'm saying this, but thank you. Kate sees something in you I just don't. But I'm glad she was right."

"What does she see in me?"

"…She sees a good man somewhere inside of you. I thought she was crazy, but maybe she's onto something. She's got a good eye for that sort of thing."

It went entirely without saying that Emily thought Kate's idea of Clark as a good man didn't hold up to much scrutiny. He could accept that. He hadn't exactly been a good friend to anyone in this town; he deserved their ire, at least where Kate was concerned. Everyone here held her in such high regard. If he failed her, he failed the town. If he saved her, they didn't mind him quite so much. Before he could respond, Michael emerged from the door, backpack haphazardly slung over his shoulder.

"How is she? Can I see her?" Clark asked.

It was one thing to know someone was all right and quite another to see them with his own two eyes. Kate's cold, unresponsive body haunted him; her smile could cure the sickening fear humming beneath his skin.

"I think we should let her sleep. She isn't hypothermic,

thanks to your help, but she needs to stay warm and rest. She needs a little bit of peace and quiet after everything she's been through today."

"Okay. Thank you." An idea, a tentative, hesitant idea but an idea nonetheless. "Do you want to stay for Christmas?"

The pair shared a wary look.

"I'll drop by tomorrow," Emily said. "We have some things to take care of in town." They started to depart, but she stopped and turned before she went. "But thank you."

Since arriving in Miller's Point, Clark couldn't think of anyone thanking him. They hated him. Made snarky comments behind his back. Criticized Kate for spending time with him. No one ever thanked him until that moment.

As it turned out, he enjoyed being liked more than he enjoyed being hated.

Chapter Ten

K ATE DIDN'T KNOW WHAT MICHAEL put in that hot chocolate, but it must have been stronger than morphine and tasteless as water. One minute, she shivered under the covers and warmed her hands against the walls of the steaming mug; the next, she woke from a dream (where she starred as an animated Who in one of those Grinch movies) with a slight start. As she blinked against the darkness, it took her a moment to remember where she was and what had happened. The bedroom, with its crackling fireplace and slightly dusty fixtures—no one had been in here but the caretaker for almost a year now—engulfed her with its largeness. Kate cocooned herself in the warm covers, feeling more than a bit like Alice in Wonderland after downing the shrinking potion. Her entire apartment could fit in this one bedroom.

Against her better judgment, she had to wonder: how could a guy with a house like this be worried about money? Clark was, to put it mildly, a complete and total miser. A penny-pincher. The festival was just the visible tip of the iceberg. She'd even caught a glimpse into his car's trunk during their trip to bring food to the families on the outskirts of town. He claimed he intended to spend one week in town, but only packed one backpack's worth of clothes. Everything about him proclaimed his truth: money mattered, and he wasn't going to waste a penny of it, even if those pennies might make an entire community happy.

He had everything. But more than everything, he had nothing. Nothing of any value. Kate didn't have a lot—she worked for the festival because she loved it, not because the festival was paying her well—but even though she counted pennies and cut coupons so she could work in her dream job, richness filled her life. Emptiness filled Clark's.

Her heart bled for him.

"No," she muttered. "No more sitting around."

Admittedly, she struggled to make her heavy limbs rip the covers away and expose her body to the cold air of the old house, but she couldn't stay in bed any longer. Her eyes flickered to the clock above the mantel. Eight o'clock. Eight o'clock gave her... She counted on her fingers... Twenty-eight hours until the end of Christmas altogether. Twenty-eight hours to change a life, to fill it to the brim with magic.

Slipping out of bed, she marveled at the soft slouch of the pajama material against her skin. It served as a good distraction against the cold floor beneath her feet. It should figure Clark would have a massive, historical house with every modern luxury only to ignore the modern amenities like under-floor heating in favor of lighting a sooty fireplace.

As Kate crossed the room, she caught her own reflection in the mirror. Her makeup came off in the wash, her hair remained damp after her shower, and the pajamas Emily dug up from one of the wardrobes weren't the traditional Christmas pajamas she always wore because those were tucked in her overnight bag, which was subsequently shoved into a random closet on the first floor as Emily was in a rush to get her into bed.

Emily. Kate paused at the door. Before slipping into the oblivion of a Seuss-themed dream, Emily gave her explicit instructions not to get out of bed until Christmas morning, citing Kate-cicle's need to warm her bones and recover with some sleep. Kate cracked the oaken bedroom door slightly.

"Emily?" she called.

The house breathed in response, but no answer made its way through the halls. She cleared her throat, raising her voice lightly.

"Emily? Are you out there?"

Kate wanted to pretend her friend's protective, fiery nature didn't scare her, but that would have been a lie. This quiet, cautious check if the coast was clear was the only thing separating her from Emily's anger at being disobeyed. Kate counted to five. Then, to ten. When no voice or heavy footsteps answered, she took her first brave steps into the belly of the darkened house.

The darkness chilled Kate at first; it chilled her almost as deep as the frozen water. It pierced her skin. It amplified every creaking floorboard beneath her feet. Like a heroine in a gothic romance, she pressed on. Clark Woodward was somewhere in this house. She only needed to find him.

But finding him meant first finding a light. Any light. Kate groped around the pitch-black hallway, searching for a cord. Just this morning she did all of the wiring for the strung lights down this hallway. If she could only find the plug…

"There!"

Kate pressed the metal tongs into the outlet and the hallway burst back to carnival-like life. A sigh of relief escaped her. Clark had been miserly enough to turn off all the lights before 9 p.m. on Christmas Eve, but at least he hadn't taken them all down.

Guided by her new light, Kate pressed onward. Clark would be around here somewhere…she just had to find him.

The voices in Clark's head wouldn't stop yammering. For the past two hours, they argued and debated, sparred and grappled like two prize fighters trying to go the distance.

You should go check on her.

Emily said to leave her alone.

But it's Christmas and she's missing it.

You don't care about Christmas.

No, but she does… Maybe she'll be upset if you let her sleep through it.

If you wake her up, she'll probably be sick and then you'll have to put up with her making you do all of her tradition stuff all night.

…That might not be so bad.

Who are you and what have you done with Clark Woodward?

Christmas is pointless, sure. Wasteful and stupid, of course. But today's been the best Christmas I've had in a long time.

A woman almost died on your watch.

My comment still stands. Best Christmas since I was a kid.

That's an awfully low bar to clear.

I should go check on her.

She doesn't want to see you.

For two hours, it went on like that, all while he attempted to get some semblance of work done. With the office in Dallas closed after five o'clock and everyone home for the holiday here in Miller's Point, he had no one to do business *with*, but he still found paperwork to read and files to sort through. About an hour into his mental torture, he'd shifted from a secretarial office to his uncle's actual office, hoping to find more busywork there. It was eerie, being in a dead man's office, almost as strange as being in a dead family's house. Except for a few distant cousins, only Clark remained of the Woodward clan. He was the last of his kind, in a way. It made the wall of family photos lining his uncle's office all the more difficult to bear. Burying his head in the nearest drawer to avoid looking at them, Clark picked up stacks of paper at random and began sorting them. Busywork though it was, at least it was distracting busywork. His uncle had been many things, but a brilliant organizational mind, he most certainly was not.

Clark stacked papers into piles by subject matter, then date. When he'd accomplished that, he sorted by last name of the signatory partner, then date. He shuffled and re-shuffled and tried to get it into an appropriate filing system until finally realizing the filing system wasn't the problem.

He was worried about Kate. Not in the "she's a woman in my house and I need to make sure she's safe because that's what a good host does" way. Not in a detached gentlemanly way.

The longer she remained out of sight, the more he realized how wrong he was when he said "I don't care about you." He hardly knew her, but he cared about her. There was no getting around it or denying it.

Only one thing remained unclear: what to do about it. Caring meant investment. Caring meant friendship. For all he knew…if he spent more time here…caring could mean even more than friendship. Caring meant giving her things he didn't know he could give.

No. No. He couldn't do it. He'd just have to…lock himself in here until she gave up and abandoned him. It was the only way to move on. Maybe he was getting ill. Being sick always made him think crazy things. Maybe she bewitched him or something. Small towns usually had a witch, if made-for-TV movies had any truth to them. In any case, he couldn't be allowed to care for her. He'd just have to hide himself away until she shrunk and took up less and less room in his small, used-up heart.

After a day spent in this massive mansion, Kate assumed her hold on the geography of the place was pretty strong. Unfortunately, the house took on a life of its own after dark. Every gothic romance she read said as much, but she didn't believe it until she wandered the halls of Woodward House without a clue how to get around. This house needed a "You Are Here" map…or a logical layout. Whenever Kate thought she'd figured out where she was, she turned into what she *thought* was the living room, only to find she'd stumbled upon an indoor squash court or a stadium-sized library. Like a real-life episode of Scooby-Doo, she would enter a door and seem to come out halfway across the house. She didn't believe in curses or hauntings or anything so ridiculous, but if any house in the world was going to be under a spell, the old house on the hill of Miller's Point was probably the most likely of candidates.

It seemed to go on like that for hours, until she finally stumbled upon the staircase leading down to the first floor. Tripping down the stairs in her excitement, Kate rushed for the living room, practically slipping in her socks as she slid towards the living room and tossed open the doors.

"Hey, Clark!"

…she said, to an entirely empty, darkened room. A flick of the light switch revealed this was no prank. He just wasn't there.

Kate's stomach grumbled. Going to the kitchen would kill two birds with one stone; she'd have her fill of whatever she could find in the fridge, and the resonant noise from her singing against the tile floors and backsplash would carry easily to wherever Clark hid in this massive manor.

She waltzed through the swinging door. The kitchen was not as she left it this morning, hustling and bustling with overflowing platters and saucepans. Its tidiness smacked of Clark's presence. He'd been in here recently, and he'd cleaned the house of any trace of her guests and their feast. Kate's stomach grumbled, more insistently this time.

"Yeah, yeah. I hear you," she muttered, patting her own gut.

To her great relief, cobwebs and canned chickens were not the only thing lining the pantry. Leftover sundries and dishes from the luncheon—left behind by eager-to-leave guests—littered the cupboards and the refrigerator. Sating her hunger temporarily, Kate picked at a honey-roasted ham from the fridge as she explored the rest of her options. *Sweet potato biscuits… Apple pie… Garlic mashed potatoes… Roasted cauliflower… Turkey legs… Stuffed artichokes.*

When she opened the fridge, all debate ceased. Trays of frozen sugar cookie dough waited to be cut out and baked to golden, sugary perfection. A devious smile painted itself across Kate's hungry lips.

"Come to Mama…"

Clark's mental takedown of his errant flicker of emotion for Kate effectively ceased the worried voice in his head, finally giving him the clarity to properly order his files. First by department, then by date.

He continued on this way for too long before a distraction slithered under the door of the office, infiltrating his space and filling every corner. He couldn't escape it. He couldn't hide from it.

Cookies. Sugar cookies. His one weakness. The one redeeming quality of Christmas, as far as Clark was concerned, was the packets of frozen cookies with the Santa faces and trees pressed colorfully into the top. The smell of those cookies haunted him now, wafting through the walls of this old house like the ghost of a long-forgotten dream.

Leaping to his feet, Clark made it halfway to the door before realizing the dilemma he now found himself in: he could pursue his goal of falling out of like with Kate, or he could see her and have cookies. The voice speaking for his hidden emotions jumped at the first opportunity to speak again.

If you go downstairs, you can check to see if she's okay and you can have cookies. Kill two birds with one stone.

You'll regret it if you go down there. Wait until she leaves or falls asleep, then go down and get those sweet, sweet cookies.

If you wait, they'll be cold.

Put them in the microwave for ten seconds. Bam! Good as new.

It's not good as new, and you know it.

Is too.

Is-

"God rest ye Merry Gentlemen, let nothing you dismay…"

The voices silenced when one very particular voice reached Clark's ears. The confident tune joined the cookie-scented air in tying a knot around his stomach and pulling him exactly where they wanted him to go. Trapped in the hypnotic pull of her voice and his love of sweets, he left behind his doubts and followed them down into the kitchen.

After all, what was the worst that could happen? It's not like cookies would make him fall in love with her or anything.

Chapter Eleven

AFTER UNCOVERING THE FROZEN SHEETS of cookie dough resting atop some Tupperware containers of butternut squash soup and tubs of eggnog ice cream, Kate made quick work of baking, and within a few minutes, the marble counters turned snow-white and sticky. Without a cookie-cutter or can of baking spray in sight, she improvised, using a wire star ornament to cut out the dough. A brief dig through the pantry and the fridge rewarded her with flour and butter to grease the cookie sheets. The available dough was meant to feed at least forty people, so once the first batch entered the oven, Kate focused on the next twenty or so cookies.

Did she *need* to bake every single bit of dough left behind in the freezer? Of course not. Even at her most hungry, Kate's cookie-eating record never broke seventeen cookies in a single sitting. The end product of the baking wasn't the point, really. She baked because it gave her something to do, something to occupy her hands as she tried to plan her next steps. The night was still young, and she wasn't sure she'd made any progress with Clark earlier. Sure, he'd been slightly nicer to her than he was this morning, but he hadn't seemed any more sympathetic to Christmas or the cause of saving the festival. She certainly had her work cut out for her. If a redecorated house, a feast and a visit to the river didn't convince him, what would?

"Smells good in here."

The steaming tray of cookies in Kate's hands almost went flying across the room as a voice from the door behind her spooked her straight out of her skin.

"Sorry, sorry! Did I scare you?"

"I don't know." She dropped the steaming plate of cookies onto the counter as her free hand flew to her chest. She could feel her pounding heartbeat. Like being faked out by a horror movie jump-scare, Kate couldn't help but chuckle even as she shivered in fear. "Maybe you should ask my ghost. You can't just sneak up on people like that!"

Clark hovered in the doorway, halfway into the kitchen and halfway out, as if he couldn't decide whether or not to fully engage with her. Since waking to find him precisely nowhere in his own house, Kate assumed Clark had been hiding from her to avoid any more Christmas talk, despite his promise to at least try and enjoy her company. Thinking he hated her and her holiday so much had stung, and his arrival here and now soothed the wounds only slightly. To his credit, Clark gave off a sufficiently sheepish air. He filled the room with his uncertainty.

"I smelled cookies."

Oh. A stab of disappointment shot straight up Kate's arm, following the flow of her blood until it pierced and filled her heart. He hadn't come because he wanted to talk to her or come out of hiding. She'd angered him with more supposed "waste" of his family's resources. Kate turned her back on him. If he wanted to chew her out, fine. But she didn't have to pay attention. She transferred the steaming cookies from the baking sheet to the cooling rack she'd found in the back of a dusty cabinet.

"Don't worry. I didn't spend any of your money to make them."

"No, that's not why I'm here. I just wanted one."

"Really?"

"I like sugar cookies." He shrugged. "Is that a crime?"

"Not at all." If anything, the defensive admission only endeared him to her. Clark prowled around Miller's Point with all of the arrogant attitude of a demigod. Liking cookies made him more human in her eyes. She tried to imagine Clark sitting on a beat-up couch somewhere eating a plate full of cookies for Santa. The picture never came into focus. "It's just surprising, I guess."

"Why?"

"You don't like anything other people like. I just assumed you usually eat nothing but plain yogurt and protein bars. And water."

Given that he didn't know she'd been accidentally spying on him, she couldn't tell him she'd seen him order a plate of pancakes and bacon at Mel's, so she stuck with gentle teasing instead. As someone who ate almost every breakfast at a greasy diner in the town square, Kate couldn't think of anything more disgusting than plain yogurt and protein bars. She preferred her pancakes like Emily preferred her men: rich and sweet.

"There's nothing wrong with plain yogurt," was his weak defense.

"Yeah, if you enjoy things that don't taste good."

Clark reached for the cookies, stopping himself short in a "where are my manners" way.

"May I?"

"No, I'm sorry. They're all for me."

"You're gonna eat all…" Sweeping the cooling rack with his eyes, Clark gave a quick whispered count under his breath. "All twenty-four of these?"

"I'm hungry."

"Seriously?"

"No, not seriously," she huffed. "Eat as many as you want. Are you sure you want to though? I wouldn't want you to spoil your precious diet."

A diet program never came up in their conversations. It didn't have to. Despite those pancakes at the diner—which could have been explained away by a cheat day or the fact that Mel didn't serve healthy food—Clark was the kind of man whose tight belts screamed, "I had exactly 1.1 ounces of cashew nuts today as a snack. That's exactly 143 calories and lots of good fats to fuel my crossfit workout later this afternoon." The tips of his ears went red and he reached for the cookies anyway, taking one into each hand. Kate followed his lead.

"It's a holiday, right? I can afford the calories."

"Then you admit it. A holiday *is* happening."

"Just because I don't celebrate it doesn't mean it's not happening. Besides…" They shared a meaningful look. What kind of meaning, Kate wasn't sure. But it meant something. Her insides churned. "I promised someone I'd give it the old college try."

On the surface, she liked the sound of that. He'd come down here not to fight with her or start another argument, but because he wanted to honor his promise to her. His absence until now stuck in her craw.

"Then why were you hiding?"

"I wasn't hiding," he retorted, mouth full of cookies.

"You carried me through a storm and then I didn't see you again. You were hiding."

They both chewed, savoring the subtle flavors of the

fresh treats.

"I'm sorry about what happened."

"Why? I lived, didn't I?"

"Yeah, but—"

She flicked flour in his direction, failing to strike him with the white powder.

"I said I wanted an adventure, didn't I?" A big bite of cookie melted in her mouth. "Well, I got one."

"Listen." Clark clapped his hands together, ridding them of cookie dust and crumbs. "I promised someone I'd try this Christmas thing out, so what do I do?"

"Wanna help me make cookies?"

They didn't need anymore, but with three more trays of cookie dough and time to kill, Kate could think of no better option than this one.

"Is that a thing people do?" Clark raised an eyebrow; Kate almost choked.

"You're really out of the loop, there. Go into the other room and grab another one of these ornaments, will you?"

She raised the wire star she appropriated as a cookie-cutter. It glimmered in the low winter light. Clark left for the living room.

"You got it."

Kate dressed herself in a mothballed apron. In the next room, rustling and tinkling of ornamental bells danced in the air as Clark searched for a wire star. She continued their conversation through the door, raising her voice just enough to be heard.

"You're telling me you never made cookies around this time of year?"

A deep, masculine chuckle. "Are you fishing for my tragic backstory?"

"Only because I think you'll bite."

"You don't want to hear it."

He returned with the star in tow. Kate took her place at the long kitchen island, which looked like a tiny winter wonderland. Flour covered the surface like perfect snowcapped mountains.

"You're admitting there is a tragic backstory."

"I didn't say that."

"You don't have to tell me." Mr. Woodward, Clark's uncle, was one of the kindest men Kate ever knew. As much as she liked to tease Clark about what he called his tragic backstory, she had a hard time believing she was opening up old wounds by asking after it. How could a man as good as Mr. Woodward allow someone as close to him as a nephew endure a miserable life? Kate assumed Clark had some kind of stigma associated with Christmas—maybe a girlfriend dumped him around the season or he was allergic to pine or something—but those were all easily solvable problems. If she could replace the sad memories with beautiful ones, maybe she could take away the lonely emptiness in his eyes. "I was thinking if I knew, maybe I could help."

Clark didn't speak right away. He went into a cabinet and found an apron of his own. As he pulled it over his head and rolled up the sleeves of his blue collared shirt, Kate stopped herself from breathing too loud. She'd thought he was handsome since she met him, but this was something else. The clash of the domestic apron with his strong, exposed forearms, his willingness to open up and be sensitive around her… Her cheeks flushed, and it had nothing to do with the blazing oven. When Clark returned, he spoke again.

"I haven't had a real Christmas since I was nine years old. If I ever did make cookies, it was so long ago it's impossible to remember if I did."

"Really?"

"Yeah." He clearly thought that would be the end of it. Holding up the star ornament, he stared at Kate through its negative space like a rich man assessing a stranger through a monocle. "Now, what do I do with this?"

On the marble countertops before them, Kate set up their station. A frozen pad of cookie dough waited on the floured countertop and a greased cookie sheet waited for the cut-out cookies. She demonstrated the method, every so often glancing at Clark to gauge his reaction.

"You just sprinkle some flour on it and press it in. Like so."

"I don't know." He hesitated over the preparations, suddenly skittish. "I don't want to ruin it."

"You can't ruin it. Just press in…" She demonstrated again, "And pull it out."

Clark breathed in deep, as though he were diffusing a bomb instead of cutting out cookies. It was a cute image, in a way. He'd been out of practice in having fun for so long, he couldn't even take something as simple as cutting out cookies any less seriously than negotiating a huge business deal. He laid the makeshift cookie-cutter into the dough, pulled it out, and fumbled to pick the newly made star up. There weren't many ways to mess up using a cookie-cutter, so Clark's clumsy attempt came out fairly neat. Two of the star's points were lopsided and inconsistent with the rest. Clark deflated.

"I messed up the ends. What do I do now?"

"Just put it on the tray and try again with another one," Kate said, obviously.

"But—"

"Not everything's a disaster, Clark. You can always try again."

"I can't—"

He stopped himself short, hesitating to finish his

thought. Like a starving man given a bite of food only to have it taken away, Kate longed to hear it completed. What couldn't he do? And why couldn't he do it? She reminded herself to be grateful. For most of the day, he'd been as emotionally distant as he possibly could be. This was one of the first glimpses she got of his full emotional range. Even if his disappointment seemed silly to her, at least he was showing her some feeling. He could have kept himself closed off and private, deflecting her every attempt to get close to him. But he didn't. He was letting her see him for the first time. Kate stepped behind him, reaching her arms under his to better help him.

She didn't want to think about how good he smelled. Like an oaken whiskey barrel or a fresh forest. Nor did she want to think about how good his warmth felt mixing with hers. She didn't want to think about her desire to wrap her arms around his chest and hold him to her until he turned around and returned the gesture.

She didn't want to. But she did anyway.

"Let me help," she whispered, unable to catch her own stampeding breath.

Slowly, she guided his hands through the process, paying special attention to the tips of the stars.

"See?" She withdrew from him as he laid the star down on the cookie sheet, wanting to wipe the girlish swoon from her eyes before he could catch it. "Perfect."

"Thanks."

Was it her hope talking, or did he sound as breathless as she felt? Kate cleared her throat and returned to their task. Maybe talking about him would remove all of the magic tingles crossing her skin.

"Don't think you're getting out of it." She nudged him playfully with her shoulder. "Why haven't you had Christmas for twenty years?"

"I went to boarding school."

A diplomatic answer. Kate didn't accept it.

"And what? You never came back?"

"My parents died on New Year's. We'd just had our big family Christmas. I was only nine." Her lungs stopped working as he delivered his story with matter-of-fact sincerity. Her hands stilled over the cookies, but Clark went on cutting. "They were up in Eagle Point. I was here with my uncle. They went to a party and never came home. They told me a drunk driver lost control on a patch of black ice."

"Oh, Clark. I didn't mean... I'm so sorry. I didn't know."

Such a small way to apologize for something so massive, but Kate couldn't think of anything else to say. The gears of comprehension ground together in her head as information flew at her. She pieced it together. It all led to one heartbreaking picture.

"That's why I was so afraid of the forest. When they told me, I just ran out there. I didn't bring a flashlight or anything. I just ran through the rain until I couldn't see the house anymore. My uncle came out and found me eventually, but I was..." He rubbed a rough hand over his face. "He took custody of me, but I begged to go to boarding school. I didn't want to be here and remember. I didn't want The Christmas Company reminding me of what happened. That's part of the reason I hate it so much. I didn't want to think of Christmas ever again. So, I stayed at school almost all year round."

He shook his head. "On the one hand, it made me the man I am today. I pinch pennies because I'm afraid if I spend a cent out of line I'll lose the company. The only thing of them I still have. I wear my father's old suit jackets because I don't want to lose them. I stayed in school and worked all the time to make them proud, to become the great man they would have wanted me to be. On the other hand…staying at school made it easier to avoid thinking about it. No matter how much my uncle begged me to come home even for a weekend, I just couldn't face being here. I wanted to hold onto them, but I didn't want to remember them, either. It was too painful. Now, it's like I pushed it all away for so long, I can barely remember even when I want to."

"Why?"

"What do you mean, *why?*"

"I mean…why are you telling me all this? You could have just lied."

All at once, she became aware of tears blurring her vision as she gazed up at him. Tears for a man who'd lost everything. He'd been defeated by the world again and again, all while she'd been basking in the attention he'd been denied. The cookie-cutter remained useless in her limp hand. Clark sighed and put his own down to turn and meet her.

"Because this is the first Christmas no one let me be alone. The first time I pushed everyone away but…" They shared a meaningful look, one filled with the warmth of a freshly lit fireplace. "Someone stayed anyway."

She wanted to hold him. Or kiss him. Anything to show him he didn't deserve to be alone. Keeping her hands and lips to herself, she swiftly changed the subject, breaking the emotionally devastating mood with one joking question.

"How am I doing so far on that front? Have I made an elf of you?"

"You know, it's not so bad. I don't see what the fuss is all about yet, but I'm warming up to it. Keep feeding me these cookies and maybe I'll like it even more."

In a few swift movements, he placed the full baking sheet into the oven and plucked a few cookies off of the cooling rack.

"The good news is that we'll have enough cookies to last us three lifetimes."

"You don't know how many cookies I can eat."

He handed her a stack of five cookies, and Kate's stomach both curdled and leapt for joy. The idea of so many cookies was appealing, but the reality frightened her stomach. She almost refused the gift. Then, the smell hit her. She was powerless to the combination of sugar and butter cooked to warm perfection.

"If I eat more than twenty, drop a piano on my head," she encouraged, accepting the stack. "It's the only way to stop me once I get into a feeding frenzy."

"Deal." He laughed, a sound sweeter than any cookies.

They snacked in silence. Though this huge revelation hung between them, things seemed less fraught between them. Still, Kate couldn't help but sink in the sadness she'd heard in his voice. Cookies weren't enough to erase that memory.

"Hey, Clark?" she asked.

"Yeah?"

"What do you remember about Christmas? You said you don't remember much. Do you remember anything?"

Clark hesitated, then shook his head. "I haven't thought about it in so long."

"Do you want to remember? You don't have to. I know it's hard," she assured him.

Kate thought of her parents every day. She couldn't imagine the pain of wanting to forget them, of hiding away at boarding school so no one could make you think of them.

"I remember…" Clark bit his bottom lip. His hands flexed. He leaned against the counter for support. A tiny,

tiny smile glowed on his softened face. "My mother's perfume. Tuberose, I think. I remember them dragging me to go caroling. Every year, my mom would make a tub of hot cocoa and my dad would help her make cookies and we'd walk through the neighborhood caroling. None of us could sing, really. Dad was the worst of us, but it didn't matter. It was fun." He lost himself in the thoughts of his past. "When my mom would tuck me in on Christmas Eve, I remember she'd light a candle and put it on my windowsill. She told me it was so Santa knew where to find me."

"Those are beautiful memories."

"I miss them. I haven't let myself think about them like this in so long, but…I miss them." He trailed off, staring out into the distance. But no sooner had he withdrawn than he brought himself back, clearing his throat as if to clear the air of his very self. "Sorry. You don't want to hear this."

"I don't mind at all. In fact, it's pretty nice."

"Cookies and sad stories. What next? Champagne and a dentist appointment?" He chuckled, but the light didn't quite meet his eyes. Kate wanted nothing more than to sit here and talk to him about this forever. She wanted to know everything about him. What was his favorite shade of blue? What had his life been like after boarding school? What did he dream about?

For now, the questions would have to wait. As much as she wanted to keep talking, he needed something else. He needed a distraction. He still needed to fall in love with Christmas.

"Well." She smiled, her fingers brushing the top of his hand reassuringly. "The tree still isn't decorated."

New memories would never replace a lifetime of horrible ones, but Kate could at least give him one special night.

Chapter Twelve

I CAN'T BELIEVE I TOLD HER. *I can't believe I told her.*

For the entire thirteen-step journey from the kitchen into the Christmas tree-dominated living room, Clark could only repeat those words. Then the thought mutated. *I can't believe I'm happy I told her. I can't believe I'm relieved I told her. I can't believe I trusted her. And still trust her.*

Clark couldn't remember the last time he'd thought about his parents for any stretch of time, much less talked about them. He treated his memory of them like a precious, finite resource. The more he shared them, the less he had for himself. If he talked about them too much, he feared, he'd lose them forever. He wanted to protect the pieces of them he could.

But talking about them with Kate liberated him. Secrets he'd been jealously hiding all his life came to the surface, excavating the pieces of his heart he'd buried long ago.

Before his parents died, they spent most of their winter holidays here, visiting for a few days between Christmas and New Year's, reveling in the time they got to spend with their family. The living room hadn't changed. At least, it hadn't physically changed since Clark saw

145

it last. No one came in and threw extra tinsel on the mantel or hung more fake icicles from the ceiling. But as night cloaked the Woodward House, the quality of light changed inside the opulent family room. Instead of another room in a house on a cold winter's day, it grew into a safe harbor of golden light, a refuge from the black night settling in outside of the walls. Kate turned the key in the fireplace, igniting the flames within and adding to the invisible layer of coziness wrapping itself around Clark's shoulders. It reminded him of the time *before*, of the winter evenings spent here with his aunt and uncle, his mother and father.

"I'm guessing you haven't decorated a tree in a while, either?"

"I did a couple of times at school. That sort of celebration was mandatory."

As a kid, Clark did everything to get out of the festivities required of boarding school boys to make them feel more at home during the season. Thinking about Christmas brought up those memories he fought so hard to hide and hold onto; participating in the jolly holiday with his schoolmates only made things worse. He feigned illnesses. He tried to get in-school suspension. He claimed religious exemption, even going as far as to wear a yarmulke for three months. All to no avail. The administration allowed him to remain on campus for the holidays, but refused to excuse him from celebrating that same holiday during term time.

"I guess you made handprint wreaths and stuff," Kate ventured as she dragged a stack of boxes out into the middle of the room. Clark raced to help her, taking the top three boxes away to lighten her load. He followed her lead, opening the tops and exposing the blinding treasure trove of glitter, red paint, and homey paper stars tucked inside.

"We mostly made pinecone reindeer. Our teachers were not the most imaginative bunch."

"That's a shame. The teachers here in Miller's Point are amazing." Kate picked out a chain of paperclip stars. Their lopsided shapes assured him they were the handiwork of school children. He wondered if any of them hated Christmas as much as he had when he was a boy. Did anyone in Miller's Point hate the season, or was he the only Grinch in sight? "Help me untangle these?"

"Yeah, sure."

With delicate fingers, they picked apart the tangled knots of nickel. Clark paid special attention not to bend them out of shape. Frivolous as he thought the exercise was for a classroom—when he was a boy, he threatened to file suit because Christmas activities robbed him of the teaching time his family paid for—someone still spent their time and effort on this chain of stars. He didn't want to ruin them. As they worked, Kate talked, stupefying him more and more with every word out of her mouth.

"Miss Monzalno, the second-grade teacher, she teaches her kids how to make advent calendars. And Miss White takes her kids to Dallas every year to serve at a soup kitchen right before they get out for Christmas. I don't know if she still does it, but when I was there, Miss Elias took all of us to plant our own trees."

"You know so much about this town," he said, causing her to balk. A swift tug of her wrist sent the paperclip strand flying out of his hands.

She deflected. "It's mine. It's special to me."

"Not even Michael knew so much as you do."

"Miller's Point is my family."

"I don't know that much about *my* family."

He didn't mean it as an accusation. But she took it

as one.

"You're not the only one with a tragic backstory, Clark."

"You…?" She faced the world with the blinding optimism of someone who'd never been hurt before. He'd assumed she had a brimming family with many siblings. Every time he so much as imagined her home life, he pictured a Norman Rockwell painting, a white picket fenced house with a table of smiling cousins and grandparents.

She made herself busy with the ornaments, taking them out one at a time and arranging them on the tree's branches. They sparkled ironically as a shadow took hold of Kate.

"My mom wasn't ever really in the picture and my dad was…not a good father." Those words hung in the air for a moment before she amended herself. What came next was a confession, one he wondered if she'd ever shared with another person so explicitly. "He was an alcoholic. I started volunteering with The Christmas Company when my teacher—Miss Sanders—wanted to help get me out of the house. I liked it so much, I never wanted to go back home. The town became more of my family than my family ever was. Not exactly tragic. It's really a happy ending, if you think about it."

Each word was worse than a kick in the teeth. It took Clark a long, solemn moment before he recovered enough to speak again.

"Only you could see it that way."

"See it what way?"

"Horrible people treated you horribly and you think it's a blessing?" he asked, furrowing his brow. Kate only shrugged, picking up a small, golden star and hanging it up on a branch. The rustle of needles filled Clark's nose with the scent of pine, a scent he'd forever associate with this moment and this confounding, exceptional woman.

Her shoulders were so slender for someone who carried the weight of the world on them without so much as bowing beneath the pressure.

"If I was a normal person with a normal life, I never would have found anything spectacular. You know, bad things aren't the end of the story. Well, I guess they can be, but only if you let them."

A million incredulous, confused responses bubbled to Clark's lips. He didn't speak any of them. She offered him simplicity. What was the point in complicating something that clearly guided her and gave her happiness? Changing the subject before he could contemplate whether he could have lived his life like she lived hers, Clark reached for the nearest box of ornaments. He cleared his throat.

"How do you decorate this thing? And where did all of these come from?"

"It's all Christmas Company stock," she explained, "but we have this tradition where every year everyone who works for the festival brings one ornament and adds it to the collection. That's why they don't match."

"And what's the point of that?"

"I don't know. It's just fun."

"But why?"

"Because it's a tradition."

"But why is it a tradition? How did it start? What's the big deal?" Clark honestly wasn't trying to be an annoying jerk. He simply didn't get it, like his twelve-year-old self didn't get the point of the Christmas traditions at boarding school. Everyone bought into the rituals and empty gestures; he didn't understand why.

"It just is." Kate's hands hesitated over a small puppy ornament, searching for something to offer him. Clark held his breath. "Like your mom putting out the Santa candle. It didn't actually do anything. It's just meaningful for its own sake."

"Wait…you mean Santa isn't real?"

He chose to joke rather than acknowledge his own investment in his mother's tradition. That was different. It earned him a good-natured shove from his partner.

"Of course he's real. Shut up and decorate the tree."

Obediently, Clark collected a few ornaments out of the box, inspecting each one with keen interest. They didn't come out of a two-for-one sale from some big box store. Each one came from a person here in town. Each one carried meaning. They were, like the paperclip stars, special to someone. Maybe if he knew why, everything would become clear.

"Can you tell me about them?" he asked.

"The ornaments?"

"Yeah. Do you know anything about them?"

"I know them all. I keep the record books about who gives us what." She collected a few herself. "Why don't you start putting them up and I'll talk you through them?"

Clark nodded, then reached up on his toes to place a toy X-wing fighter up towards the top of the tree.

"What's the deal with this one?"

"It's heavy!" Kate held out a hand to stop him, her fingers barely brushing his. Panic gleamed in her eyes. Clark reminded himself how important these little trinkets were to her. Breaking even one would break a piece of her. "Put it on a low branch. The high branches aren't strong enough to hold it."

"Right."

Great move, Clark. Now she thinks you're a triple moron. You don't get Christmas and you made her confess her life story to you and you don't get basic physics. He placed the miniature space plane on the appropriate branch, ignoring the heat rising to the tops of his ears. If she noticed the red splotches undoubtedly forming there, she was decent enough not to mention anything.

"Teddy Cooper gave us that two years ago. He got it in a happy meal, said it was the "happiest meal of his life," and so he turned it into an ornament so he could always remember."

"Wow. Okay…" Clark scraped his memory for the last time he'd laughed as much as he laughed today, only to come up empty. Brushing that thought away, he picked up a tiny gold band turned into an ornament by an interlocked strand of clear fishing line. He dangled it so close to his eyes his lashes brushed the circlet of metal, trying to discern what it could possibly be. "What about this one?"

"Condola Walker. She broke off her engagement and that's the ring."

"What?" The urge to throw the ring across the room fought his urge to run into town and return the jewelry to this Condola person. Who would give up something so expensive when they could have just pawned it? Kate, unmoved by his indignation, rolled her eyes.

"It was, like, twelve dollars or something. Believe me, she was glad to be rid of it. Keep 'em coming. We'll never get this tree decorated at this rate."

Shaking off the abject strangeness of someone just giving away their engagement ring, Clark hung it up towards the top of the tree. It caught the light, spinning in the gentle breeze of the drafty old house. Even if he wasn't inclined to like her—which he was, he'd admitted defeat in his battle against his affection for Kate—he'd still be the first to admit how impressive Kate's instant recall of the facts of the town was. Like a close-hand magic trick, Clark all at once wanted to move in closer and step further back. Her confession about her childhood rattled him;

the distraction of decorating didn't prove as distancing as he hoped. She'd been so broken by her family that she'd devoted her life to everyone else in this town.

No wonder they all came at her call today. No wonder they decorated his house and cooked a banquet at her request.

"This one's a tiny fake tree," Clark said, twirling the small carving. Kate wedged herself between the wall and the tree, trying to decorate an unseen portion of branches, so this one demanded some description.

"Does it have little red baubles on it?" she asked, muffled by the tree between them.

"Yes."

"That one's from Mr. and Mrs. Simon. Their little grandbaby died, and Mrs. Simon built the coffin herself out of a tree in their backyard. She took a piece of the scrap wood and carved that."

Clark cradled the tiny ornament in the palm of his hands, staring down at it reverently as he searched for a word to properly describe the empty cavern opening in his chest. He hadn't felt this way in so long.

"That's sad."

"Don't worry. There are plenty of funny ones in there." Kate came to the rescue as Clark placed the tiny tree in a high place of honor upon the larger tree. "Do you see any paper flowers made out of thick paper? They should have music notes on them, if that helps."

Digging around, he finally found not one, but about twenty of those flowers tucked into a shoebox in the bottom of one of the ornament crates.

"Yeah."

"Those were given to us by Pastor Mark, but he didn't make them. He caught a bunch of boys making paper airplanes out of hymnal pages, so he decided if they liked folding paper so much, they would take all two hundred of the out-of-date hymnals and make paper flowers out of them. They spent six days of Christmas vacation making those things."

They carried on in this fashion for longer than Clark cared to admit; even worse, he hung on her every word. He actually invested himself in the intersecting and interweaving lives of these strangers. A born storyteller, Kate shared every story she remembered, dragging him deeper and deeper into the melting-pot mythologies of Miller's Point.

His attention slipped only once, when he pulled out what seemed like the millionth star-shaped trinket. Only, this one was different. It struck him. Multiple shades of ugly green and brown glass had been melted together to form a sort of patchwork glass star. Its edges created an outline out of twisted wire. The most similar thing he could think of was a stained-glass window, but those were beautiful. This wasn't quite beautiful. It was sublime, perhaps. Holding it up to the light, he let the color play on his face, losing himself in the warped surface of the star.

"What's this one?"

"That's one of mine," Kate said, her voice dipping low. The pride she'd taken only a few minutes ago in her stories and shared histories vanished.

"What is it? Did you make it?" Clark squinted, coming up closer to a raised etching along one of the corners. He could hardly make it out. "Is this a whiskey label? I didn't know you drank."

"I don't."

"Was this like an art project or something?"

After hours of learning about her town and these ornaments, he should have known none of these were *just* anything. They all carried their own weighted tales.

To think Kate's wouldn't was the height of foolishness.

"When my dad died, right after my eighteenth birthday, I went to his apartment and cleaned it all out. I hadn't been living there for, like, two years. Emily's family took me in. So, I went through the whole house, throwing almost everything away. And then I got to my old bedroom. It was covered in broken bottles, like he'd just thrown them all at the wall and let them shatter. There had to be a hundred of them. He used my room as a garbage can, basically." She laughed a wry laugh.

It occurred to Clark then how unfamiliar they were, and yet how close at the same time. They'd only met yesterday, but they'd both exchanged their most painful memories without a second thought. Maybe it was the magic of the season or her persistence or a little bit of both, but they trusted one another even when they had every reason to protect their own secrets.

He'd broken her once. He told her he didn't care. He lied. But this moment was different. She wasn't broken; she wasn't hiding. But he still wanted to wrap her in his arms and hold her together.

"Kate—"

"Anyway," she brushed him off. "I cleaned the whole house, but I couldn't get rid of all that glass. I mean, I could have. But when the whole house was clean and I was left with a handful of broken glass shards, I didn't want to. I wanted something of his, even if he hated me. I asked Michael to help me make this. My dad wasn't a good dad. Or really a dad at all. But he was mine. And I didn't want him to be erased. I wanted to always look at the tree and remember."

"Remember what?"

Her arms froze over the tree. The whiskey bottle star halted over the greenery. Her face knitted tightly in an expression he'd never seen come across her face before.

"I don't know," she confessed. "Remember him. Remember that I survived. Remember that I forgave him and loved him even if he wasn't good to me."

"You forgave him?"

Kate blinked. Her long eyelashes were wet with tears, but none fell down her cheeks. Her stare melted into confusion, as if he was a student who'd just asked what the capital of their own state was, as if the answer was so obvious as to render the question absurd.

"I had to."

"Why?" He asked.

Somehow, Clark and Kate had gotten so close he could feel her breath on his skin. He wanted to kiss the wrinkle between her eyebrow away. He wanted to hold her and tell her nothing could ever hurt her again.

"Because we can't survive if we're always carrying dead bodies around, you know? That's no way to make a happy life." The sting of conviction stole the breath from Clark's lungs. He was guilty. He'd been dragging around dead bodies his entire life, robbing himself of any chance of happiness just so he could forget his own pain. Kate rolled her eyes, an attempt to clear the air of tension. "Besides, he was kind of a jerk. He probably would have resented my forgiveness. No better way to get revenge, right?"

She moved to step away, but Clark caught her. He couldn't help but touch her. Their intimacy demanded it. His cold hand reached up for her left cheek; he cradled it, commanding her eyes. Her breath hitched. His heart stumbled. *Kiss her, you moron* argued with *don't ruin what you have by kissing her, you moron*. He'd gone most of his life without friends, and tonight he'd found one. Learning from her and basking in their friendship had to be more important than kissing her.

"How do you do it?"

"Do what?"

"Stay as hopeful as you do. I don't understand how it's possible for one person to be this optimistic all the time. I was awful to you and you didn't flinch. Your life hasn't been great but you count it as a blessing… How do you do it?"

"You really want to know?"

"Yeah."

She bit her lip, an adorable gesture Clark never got in movies but now understood completely. She grew increasingly sheepish as she interrogated his motives.

"You promise you won't make fun of me? It's pretty cheesy."

"Promise."

"Cross your heart?"

"Yeah."

She shot him a look. Apparently, she wanted him to *actually* cross his heart. He did so, all while struggling to maintain a dignified, solemn expression. When she was satisfied, she shoved her hands into her back pockets, staring up at the tree. In the glow of the lights, she looked more than beautiful as she whispered the simple truth that had sustained her through her entire life.

"I keep Christmas with me all year long. It's the one time of year when I find it impossible to think the worst in people. If I pretend every day is Christmas, it makes life so much easier to live. And people so much easier to love."

"I wish I could do that," Clark breathed. He tried to move his hand away from her cheek, but Kate got there first. She held him there, this time forcing him to give her his eyes. A sweet smile encouraged him. Challenged him. Filled him with hope.

"You can."

Chapter Thirteen

TREE DECORATING GAVE WAY TO black-and-white
movies and popcorn, which gave way to leftover
turkey sandwiches with cranberry sauce which inevitably
gave way to heavy eyelids and almost naps. Conversation
and laughter flowed easily between them, though Kate
got the distinct feeling Clark was out of practice when it
came to having a friend. The defenses he threw up against
her only this morning diffused, leaving them only with
his rusty attempts at humor and near-constant questions
about Christmas and its traditions. Kate didn't mind at
all. In fact, she suspected this Christmas would go down
as one of her favorites. Not because it was perfect—it
definitely wasn't—but because she'd never experienced
anything quite like this, something this pure.

The Festival was her life. Everyone who worked on
it was her family. She was immeasurably glad for the
security they gave her. The problem came on Christmas
night, when her entire year had been leading up to a
grand spectacle of the season. She loved the spectacle,
but there was something beautiful and singular about
sharing a private Christmas with someone who'd never
had one before. For the first time, Kate saw the holiday

not through her eyes, but his. The beauty of this holiday she loved so much now engulfed her. The lights shone brighter. The classic lines of *It's a Wonderful Life* cut deeper. Her faith renewed.

When *It's a Wonderful Life* went into its encore showing, Kate stretched her tight muscles along the overstuffed couch. Clark, for his part, sprawled out in a distinctly Victorian armchair. Wide, decorative walls of the chair obscured his face behind their panels while the roaring fireplace illuminated his long limbs.

"Clark? Clark, are you awake?" she whispered. Half of her didn't want to disturb him, while the other half of her demanded she wake him up. It wasn't even midnight, after all. There was so much Christmas left and so little time to prove its worth to him. Fortunately, he saved her the trouble of waking him.

"Yeah, I'm awake," he whispered back, as though they were in a crowded movie theater instead of his own living room.

The next phase of Kate's plan wasn't really for him. It wasn't even part of the plan. She'd been doing Christmas without parents for most of her life, which meant she was fairly stuck in her ways. There was one tradition she refused to compromise on.

"I was wondering… Do you have a copy of *A Christmas Carol*?"

"No idea. Why?"

"I read it every Christmas Eve."

She thought she'd brought her own copy for such a scenario, but a quick scan of her backpack earlier in the evening revealed only pajamas, a change of clothes for Christmas Day, a toothbrush, and a box of white chocolate pretzels. Perhaps during her packing she assumed the multimillion-dollar mansion would contain at least one copy of the greatest novella in the English canon; if she had a manor and an estate, she'd have a million copies. It was, after all, her favorite book.

"Really? But don't you…" Clark leaned forward, popping out from behind the panels of his chair to scoff in disbelief, "You basically watch *A Christmas Carol* every day for like, a month and a half, don't you?"

"Yeah, but…" Kate played with her hands. One of the reasons she'd gotten the job at the festival was her reputation in town as the "Dickens-obsessed girl." She could practically recite the original book by heart. What they didn't know was that after the festival ended on Christmas night, she tucked herself into her bed at her dad's house and read the book over and over again, just so she could pretend she was still in a magical world of hope and joy, rather than a booze-soaked nightmare. Kate didn't feel inclined to tell Clark the entire truth, so she danced around it instead. "Usually, once the festival is over, I go home and I'm too keyed up to sleep. It's my favorite book, so it puts me in a good mood."

"Follow me," Clark said, rising to his feet.

"Where are we going?"

"If it's anywhere, it'll be in the library. C'mon."

Kate caught a passing glimpse of the library earlier, but walking in and fully immersing herself in it almost knocked her back a step. She'd never been in this room before. It was off-limits during all Christmas Company events. Belle's library in *Beauty and The Beast* had nothing on this beautiful collection of leather-bound tomes. The Woodward Library in the center of town, until now Kate's favorite place in the world, paled in comparison. She thought back to the stack of three rotating library books on her bedside table and her falling-apart copy of *A Christmas Carol*. Rich people may not have had it easy, as Clark's stories about his childhood suggested, but they *did* have an endless supply of books, which Kate could absolutely get on board with.

"There must be a million books in here," Kate said, awed.

"I think it's closer to two thousand. Let's check the card catalogue."

"There's a card catalogue?"

"How else would you find anything?" Clark arrived at a carved wooden chest pockmarked with orderly drawers. Each was labeled with a series of letters. He rifled through the *Da-Dl* drawer, moving the cards with practiced efficiency. Kate could only assume he was too cheap to digitize his office. Everything in Woodward Enterprises probably operated on card catalogue. "Dickens… Dickens… *Oliver Twist. Tale of Two Cities, A… Pickwick Papers…* I'm sorry. No *A Christmas Carol.*"

To his credit, Clark really did sound sorry. This morning, he probably would have jumped for joy and rubbed the absence of the classic story in her face. The taste in Kate's mouth bittered with disappointment.

"Maybe it's somewhere else?"

"No, I don't think so," Clark said, even as he dug through the catalogue for a missing or misplaced card. "But why don't you read it off your phone?"

"That's not the same."

She realized how petulant and selfish the refusal made her sound; she didn't care.

"It's a shame. I've never read it."

They'd discussed this character flaw of his before, but now Kate felt she could really shine. All her life prepared her for this moment. Adopting a practiced British accent, she dipped into the same performative storytelling style she often did when reading the abridged children's version to the little ones in the festival cast.

"*Marley was dead: to begin with. There is no doubt whatever about that. The register of his burial was signed by the clerk...*" Kate stopped. That wasn't right. "No. *Was signed by the clergyman, the undertaker...*" Again, she messed up. "No..."

When she looked back up, Clark graciously hid his laughter behind a hand clenched over his mouth.

"Are you trying to recite it right now?" He managed between tightly gritted teeth.

"I used to have it basically memorized."

"Is that a brag?"

"It's a tradition," she defended as they made their way through the illuminated house back to the pine-scented living room.

"Then read it on your phone."

"You don't get it. The book itself is important. It takes me to Victorian England. Reading it on my phone reminds me I'm here in this time and this place. The paper is a medium across time."

"Listen. I like you, but you are a huge nerd. You know that, right?"

Despite her disappointment, Kate laughed. It wasn't the first time she'd heard that and it wouldn't be the last, but coming from Clark who cobbled his own shoes and whispered when the TV was on, it was a hilarious accusation to hear. "No one knows better than me."

But if loving Christmas and trying to get others to love it too made her a nerd, then she gladly accepted the title, and nothing could ever make her give it up. Especially now, when Clark looked at her the way he did, like she had all the answers to his questions about finding joy in this world.

Her mission for a copy of *A Christmas Carol* thoroughly

defeated, they returned to the living room, though for what, Kate couldn't quite decide. Going to bed now would be akin to admitting defeat. She still wasn't convinced he cared enough about this day or this town or the festival. And, if she was being honest with herself, she didn't want to leave him. He was, against all her better judgment, fun to be around. She was enjoying herself, even without the trappings of her usual traditions.

Emily, no doubt, would have accused her of seeing him with rose-tinted glasses. Emily *always* said Kate's willingness to like people without any proof of their goodness was a sign of her naivete. Maybe she was right. Kate saw it a different way. She didn't need proof of someone's goodness. Their being a person made them good; she just had to find where that good was buried. Today, Clark's humanity peeked out through her excavation of his heart.

On second thought, maybe it was better to think about him like a butterfly stabbed on a cork board. If she thought about him that way, she'd stop thinking about wanting to kiss him or hold his broken pieces back together.

As they navigated the maze of hallways and doors between the library and the living room—Kate finally understood how the game *Clue* came about; if the house in that game and movie was anything like this house, in that game and movie was anything like this house, it's a wonder they ever found the body at all—Kate whistled absently to herself, a habit she'd had since she was a kid. It got her in trouble with teachers, her father, and coworkers, so when she realized she was doing it now, she braced herself for the worst. Clark didn't like music, especially Christmas music. The worst never came; the whistling only stopped when they walked into the living room to the sound of the mantel-place clock tolling the hour. It matched her heartbeat, vibrating at the same frequency. *Bom… Bom… Midnight. Bom… Bom… Midnight. Bom… Bom… Midnight.* Unlike Cinderella, Kate's magic remained when the clock stilled, and the prince didn't disappear.

Not that she saw Clark as a prince. Definitely not. Of course not.

"What now? What do we do now?" Clark asked, a jagged edge serrating his enthusiastic voice. Did he… Did he think they were going to kiss? Like on New Year's Eve? Quick thinking would be needed to avoid any confusion. A list of random activities ran out of her, activities she could use to wedge herself even closer to him without actually getting *close* to him. In this scenario she'd gotten herself into, Kate existed in the middle of a seesaw. Tipping too far to one side would keep her from her task, from saving her town. Tipping too far to the other would leave her vulnerable to Clark's half-smiles and thawing eyes.

"There's plenty we can do." She paced. "Sometimes people toast marshmallows. Or get out a telescope and look out for Santa. We could call NORAD."

"What do *you* usually do at this time on Christmas Eve? You're the expert. Let's do what you do."

Rats. She was hoping he wouldn't ask that. The midnight tolls on the big clock in the center of Miller's Point always meant one thing, and one thing only on December 24: the midnight ball. On a night when the festival *wasn't* cancelled by a profit-hungry but secretly beautiful-souled out-of-towner, every volunteer and staff member would get dressed in their 1843 best and go straight to the town square, where the guests would be invited to join them for a traditional Victorian ball, complete with warm mulled wine, a live string band, and a fake snowdrift. As the last official event of the night, the twirling and dipping and bowing and swirling lasted well into the early hours of the morning. It wasn't unusual for the younger members, Kate included, to dance until their shoes broke and the sun rose over the tops of the buildings. Then, they'd welcome Christmas morning with hot chocolate and leftovers from the previous day's feast before preparing themselves for the Christmas Day crowds.

But dancing would mean getting close to Clark phys-ically…and that would mean the possibility of getting too close to him emotionally. She'd read and believed in enough Jane Austen books to know it only took one dance to fall in love with someone. One minute you're dancing, the next everything else in the world disappears but the one person you're meant to be with.

If she danced with him, she could lose her heart to him.

…It also occurred to her she might have been overre-acting about the entire thing.

It just wasn't a chance she was willing to take.

"I don't think it's really your kind of thing," she brushed him off, searching the room for something else to do. Popcorn garlands? Gingerbread houses?

"None of this is my thing. I hate all of this. But I'm trying it for you."

"Why?"

"Because I promised I would."

"You still don't like it?"

"I still don't like it." His hands flexed. "But I don't hate it either."

Worse people hurled worse things at Kate on a regular basis. Out-of-towners coming in for the festival called her crazy, a zealot for Christmas. They tacked horrible names to her when she pulled them out of the crowd after overindulging on mulled wine or when she confiscated their flasks from their bags. Yet, Clark's tacit admission sliced her in half. She was failing. He still didn't believe.

Fine. If he wanted it that way, if he wanted to throw her through the motions without ever really opening himself up to genuine change, fine. She could play his game. Her hands gripped the material of her jeans at the hips.

"We dance. There's this big dance in the center of town. Everyone goes."

"I don't dance," Clark said, just as she knew he would. Almost every activity she proposed received some sort of push back from him; she expected nothing less from this challenge. If he didn't cut loose enough to know how to decorate a Christmas tree, of course he wouldn't dance. Dance required an openness of the heart she wasn't convinced he actually possessed.

"No?" she pressed, biting in her own confidence even as he sunk into the nearest chair and seemed content to stay there forever, if possible.

"No."

As Clark sank into the armchair, he wondered vaguely if he could literally melt into the fabric and disappear. When that line of thought proved frivolous, he made himself a promise: *You will not get up and dance with her. No matter how much she might want you to. Don't you dare do it. You've made a fool of yourself a hundred times over today, but draw the line here. Dancing is a stupid, pointless activity and you're not—I repeat, not—going to do it. Especially not with Kate.*

His place in the corner of the room afforded Clark

the perfect view of Kate's preparations. Bickering words popped between them like whacked baseballs as she dragged furniture towards the walls. A few hours ago, a move like that would have earned her Clark's annoyance, annoyance he now knew to be fruitless. She'd gotten her way all day. Objecting earned him no points with her.

This time, though, she wouldn't get her way. Let her turn the room into a pseudo-ballroom if she wanted. He wouldn't join her.

"Why don't you dance?" she asked. The smug smile tugging her pink lips told Clark everything he needed to know. She thought she was going to get her way with enough prodding. Well, the joke was on her. He was in his chair and in his chair he would stay.

"I just don't."

"You don't do Christmas either," Kate reminded him.

"I'm putting my foot down at prancing around the room like a drunken reindeer."

"Someone's grumpy."

"There's no way you're getting me to dance."

The coda of that sentence, *with you*, never made it out of his mouth. In his mind, there was a distinct difference between not wanting to dance at all and not wanting to dance with her specifically.

Floor clear, Kate pulled off the little slip-on red and green shoes she'd been wearing with her pajamas, leaving her feet covered by an equally busy pair of socks covered in a pattern of Santa sleighs.

"I didn't want to dance with you anyway. I can dance on my own."

"Good. Enjoy yourself."

He reached for a nearby newspaper. The headline read something about the end of The Christmas Company. That page ended up discarded on the floor; the comics section always interested him more than any part of a newspaper, anyway. Determined to ignore Kate and whatever stunt she pulled, Clark only glanced up in time to see Kate walk over to the couch and coquettishly solicit an imaginary suitor for a dance.

"Me? You want to dance with me?"

"Really?" Clark deadpanned.

"I'd be delighted," she told the imaginary man as she took his invisible hand and led him to the newly made dance floor. Without a triumphant smirk in his direction, her lips wrapped around the whistling notes of a Christmas tune Clark heard a million times before but couldn't quite place off the top of his head.

"You're making a fool of yourself."

"I think you're making a fool out of yourself. You're letting a beautiful woman dance alone."

Beautiful woman. She was that and so much more. Clever. Decisive. Loving. Damaged and beyond hopeful. Over the top of his newspaper, he watched her, this woman who invaded his house, his life and perhaps his heart. Watching her directly would make her think she'd won. Discretion was key here.

Clark lived firmly in the real world. Two feet on the ground. Head firmly out of the clouds. Business. Practicality. Frugality. These ideals guided his simple, prosperous and quiet life. He didn't like superhero franchises or any books about unrealistically clever detectives. Movies rarely made an appearance on his weekly leisure schedule. Television, even less frequently. He saw the world and everyone in it as they were, not as how they wanted to be seen or as he wanted to see them.

…Then Kate curtseyed to an imaginary partner, and Clark's firm grip on reality dissolved in a haze of magic, magic he didn't believe in or trust, but that took hold of him all the same.

Before his eyes, the world changed, as easily as turning a page in a book. Kate no longer stood in socked feet on an ancient rug. Her partner wasn't invisible. Her pajamas were replaced with a ball gown. Her hair swept up into an elaborate updo. The living room was a ballroom, decorated even more grandly for Christmas than before. An orchestra replaced her whistling. A handsome man lifted her and swanned her around the room, making her fall more and more in love with him every step they took together.

And Clark was jealous. Jealous of an apparition. His throat dried. His chest tightened. Leaving her to dance with this imagined rival was no longer possible.

He stepped into this new reality, this historical fairy tale he conjured around them. He crossed the ballroom. His heart pounded louder than the orchestra. And he tapped the stranger on his black suit-clad shoulder.

"May I cut in?"

When Kate's face sparked into an all-consuming smile, his heart rate quieted and the music once again dominated the room.

"I'd be delighted."

The language was as dated as the fantasy, but she was very much real, a fact only confirmed when her warm hand found its way into his while the other placed itself on his shoulder. His found her waist. They drew close. Close enough to fall in love.

"I don't know how to dance like this," he confessed.

"Just follow my lead."

Kate stepped simply, nudging him along. Never judging his lack of confidence or shouting out when his foot accidentally grazed her toes. Soon, he got the hang of it, and they flew across the floor like dolls in a music box. His heart grew. And grew. And grew. Until he thought it would explode right out of his chest and hand itself over to her forever.

In this dance, he saw everything he'd been denying himself his entire life: the chance to be free. Not only of his past, but of his own fears and hatred of the world. By trying to protect himself, he'd robbed himself of simple, easy joys like dancing.

And falling in love.

Not that he would have fallen in love before this moment. There was no one on earth like Kate Buckner, and even if he'd been looking for love before now, he wouldn't have found it. It existed in her and her alone. And now, he'd found it.

As they twirled and tripped and floated across the floor, Kate whistled the tune, her eyes never leaving his face and his never leaving hers. Could she feel his heartbeat? Could she hear it? Could she make out the Morse code of its beating? *Bum... Bum... I think I... Bum... Bum... Love you.*

They spun out and stopped their movements when Kate's song wound to a close. Unmoving, they held one another as if they hadn't stopped the waltz. Her eyes seemed to be made for him to admire. The perfect color. The perfect shape. The perfect windows into a perfect soul.

Was he crazy enough to think she felt this way too?

"I have some bad news," Kate whispered, too close to him to speak at a normal volume. Clark's hands shook.

"What's that?"

A glance upward. A guilty smile.

"We're under the mistletoe."

Sure enough. Green leaves and white berries dangled overhead.

"You know the tradition, don't you?" she asked.

Nodding, not trusting himself to speak, he waited for her to answer the unspoken questions hovering in the air between them. There was no way she didn't hear his heart now.

"Would you…" The whisper trailed off. Clark moved a tiny bit closer. "Would you like…" Another trail off. Another bit closer. "Would you like to…" She trailed off a third time. He was so close he could count the tiny wrinkles in her lips. Another breath closer, and their souls would collide as they fell into a tender, sweet kiss.

"Yes." He saved her from asking as he tightened his grip on her waist. "Yes, I would."

RIIIIINNNG! RIIIIINNNNNGG!!!

The moment shattered. The possibility of a kiss died. Kate fled Clark's arms, diving across the room to collect her cell phone from the nearest table.

He never knew two hands could feel as empty as his did when Kate left him like that.

Chapter Fourteen

S HAKING SO VIOLENTLY SHE ALMOST dropped the phone twice, Kate scrambled to answer the call while trying to brush the stardust from her eyes. She almost kissed Clark Woodward. She wanted to kiss Clark Woodward.

"Hello?"

"Kate!"

Her lifelong friend Michael's voice couldn't possibly be mistaken for anyone else's, even when it was dominated by loud background noise. In the split second of his greeting, Kate picked out bits of sound with surgical precision. Laughter. A Santa going ho-ho-ho. Music. So much music and conversation everything mixed into a chaotic, cacophonous mud of sound.

"Michael? Where are you?" Kate pressed her free ear with a finger, hoping the closeness would help her hear his shouting voice.

"Are you still with Public Enemy Number One?"

"Yeah, he's in here with me. And don't call him that."

Kate didn't dare look at him. He'd wanted to kiss her, too. The very thought weakened her knees and blew on the embers inside her heart.

"Great. Get into the car and have him drive out to the

location I'm texting you, okay? You should be able to get there if the roads in his backwoods are clear."

A ding from her phone alerted Kate to a text message. She glanced at the GPS signal Michael sent and furrowed her brow. A random spot in a random field.

"Why are we going there?" she asked.

"Just do it, okay? You'll see. Trust me."

"Okay… If you say so."

"Don't sound so glum! If this doesn't make him fall in love with Christmas, nothing will!"

"I'll ask him if he wants to go."

Fingers still shaking, Kate ended the call. They'd planned something, a secret kept even from her…what could they be up to?

"What's up?"

"Do you want to go on a little drive?"

Everything about him—his stance, his mouth half-opened and ready to ask a million questions she didn't have the answers to—told her he wanted to talk about what just happened between them. The kiss. Well. The almost-kiss. The kiss she desperately wanted. The kiss whose absence tingled on her lips. She could only hope everything about her told him not to push his luck.

"Yeah. Yeah." His head dipped in disappointment as he dipped out of the room. "Sounds good. Let me get my coat."

Ten minutes later, they sat next to each other in the front seat of the car. The GPS gave muted directions to Clark, who had to navigate by headlights because the back forty didn't have any lights to speak of.

"Do you know where we're going?" he asked, scrunching his face as he tried to see further ahead of them than the light would allow.

She shrugged and leaned into the impossibly comfortable seats of Clark's car. They needed to get there soon. Any longer in this quiet, dark, comfortable seat and she'd definitely be asleep.

"I don't know. Maybe they're having a bonfire or something."

"On my property? Without my permission?"

"I can't think of anything else they could be doing. It's a big, empty field."

Kate kept her arms firmly tightened across her chest and her eyes anywhere but Clark's direction. Pretending to be endlessly fascinated by the dark blurs passing them outside wasn't easy. It was, however, necessary. She didn't have the time to parse out her feelings about her impulsive desire to kiss him. She'd only come here to make him fall in love with Christmas and her town, not to make her fall in love with him.

"Maybe Santa's real and he's coming to personally give us our presents," Clark joked.

"Or maybe there's a freak snowstorm and we'll get to have a snowball fight."

"Snow in Texas? Better chance of Santa coming to town."

Another stretch of silence met those words as Kate didn't know what else to say. The only words she could come up with were: *I really like you and I want to kiss you, but I don't think it's a good idea because you're trying to destroy my town and maybe liking you means I won't mind if you do. I have to love my town more than I love you or I'll lose everything.*

An impulse moved her hand to the dark radio. Some music would distract them both. She almost pressed the power button before remembering his stern words against Christmas music this morning. They'd ridden in silence all the way through Miller's Point because he hated it;

she didn't need to invite more conversation or conflict with a stupid choice.

"What's up?" he asked, when her hand retracted.

"Oh, sorry. I know you don't like the music."

A pause. Then:

"Go ahead. I don't mind so much anymore."

"Really?"

"It's growing on me."

And you're growing on me. As she turned on the radio and switched the dial to her favorite Christmas station, she kept that particular opinion to herself. It wouldn't make a difference anyway. She was going to show him the meaning of Christmas (somehow, and apparently with Michael's help), he was going to give them the company back, and then he'd be gone. Back to Dallas where he belonged. This would be nothing more than a memory. A cocktail party joke he could tell about that time he almost kissed a poor, provincial, Christmas-obsessed girl in Miller's Point.

But at least she'd have the festival, right? That had to matter more than anything, including this crush she'd fallen headlong into.

The problem with breaking the crush completely was that as they drove deeper and deeper into the darkness, Clark started tapping the steering wheel and humming off-key with her favorite song. *I'll Be Home for Christmas.* It was so sweet, so unexpected, she almost cried. And if she hadn't been careful, she definitely would have fallen in love with him right then and there.

"Well."

Upon their arrival, they found no bonfire, no Santa, and certainly no snow. They didn't even find a single other human being. Only a large, dark, grassy field.

"Are you sure we went to the right place?"

"Yeah. This is where the GPS took us."

Her illuminated phone was meant to take them straight to the coordinates sent her way by Michael, but he must have gotten them wrong. Or perhaps the dense forest kept the location services from working properly. Kate squinted at the screen and checked her roaming settings. No, this seemed to be the right place. Only, it couldn't be. There wasn't anything here. She shot off a quick text to Michael.

Why'd you send us out to a random field?

The three little dots appeared. A text followed shortly thereafter. *Walk to the edge of the hill. Overlooking town.*

"He wants us to look down into town, I think."

Miller's Point was something of a geographical oddity. More accurately, it was a linguistic oddity due to its actual lack of a point or nearness to a point. Essentially landlocked and settled into the valley between two high, forested hills, Miller's Point was a fraud. Miller's Valley was actually correct, though it didn't have quite the same ring to it. Kate led the way to the edge of the hill, less than fifty yards ahead of them. When the light from the car's front bumper finished guiding them, the ambient light from the town below led them the final distance, until they could see Miller's Point down below.

And that's when Kate realized Michael's plan.

"Wow." To her surprise, Kate realized she wasn't the one who said that. Clark did. Whipping her head back to see him a few paces behind her, she spotted him, illuminated by the light of the town, the image below reflected in his emerald eyes. "What is happening down there?"

In his official letter of dissolution of The Christmas Company, Clark demanded the immediate removal of all decorations from the town square. They were to be put in storage immediately. And to their credit, the grounds crew team of the festival, both paid and volunteer workers, all stayed through the night to get the job done. The only thing not packed away for storage was the Christmas tree itself, which stood unlit in the center of town. Not a single decoration accented the square. The only lights that should have been coming from town were the actual lights of the houses down below. People should have been tucked away in their living rooms or in their beds, ready to celebrate tomorrow's holiday.

Only, they weren't all tucked in their beds. They weren't silently waiting for the morning to come and the now private festivities to commence. The town square of Miller's Point was alive, as active and full as any evening of the actual festival. Without the decorations or trappings of the season, they made their own color and illumination. Tacky Christmas sweaters and red and green tights were lit by hundreds of white candles, held by singing people. Even here, high upon a hill just on the edge of their village, their voices rose up to Clark and Kate's ears.

Kate realized her misplaced cynicism in Michael. He hadn't organized this for their benefit. He'd been invited and wanted them to share in it. It wasn't a trick to get Clark on their side; it was a sincere expression of a town's faith.

O Holy Night
The stars are brightly shining.
It is the night of our dear savior's birth...

Their voices didn't ring out in perfect harmony. The song was at times too fast and at times too pitchy to be easily recognized as *O Holy Night*, but Kate's soul still moved with the music.

The lesson Clark was, no doubt, brought here to learn hit her just as hard. She'd been so certain Miller's Point needed the festival to stay together, never once considering that it wasn't the festival keeping them together at all. It was their love for one another. Nothing could break that, not even a businessman with a heart of steel.

"Do you…" His voice shook. A grumbling sound came from his throat as he attempted to no avail to clear it. "Do they do this every year?"

"No. This is the first time they've done this. At least, I've never seen it before, and I've worked with them since I was seven."

"So, they just came together on their own? To celebrate?"

"Yeah. I think so." When he didn't reply, she gave him a slight nudge. There was emotion in his eyes she'd never seen before, a fullness she didn't recognize. "Are you okay? Do you want to leave? Do you want *me* to leave?"

Clark ran a hand through his golden locks and stammered, two things Kate wasn't sure she'd seen him do.

"No, please. Will you…" He trailed off, voice thick with emotion. "Will you sit here with me for a while? I need to think. I want to watch."

At the edge of a hill that might have been the edge of the world, they sat in the damp grass, not caring how the wet seeped into their clothes. They shared in the awe of the sight before them. Clark promised to take everything from the people of Miller's Point. Kate promised to do everything to get it back. Yet, there they were. Spending the most sacred night of the year being in fellowship together, lifting their voices up and coming together as a community. There was nothing there but their love for one another and their belief in the goodness of this holiday.

Kate's humility consumed her. She thought she needed to save the world, but really…what was she doing? Trying to make herself the town hero? Trying to force herself into the center of a conflict that wasn't really there? Was she really so self-obsessed to think anyone in this town needed her? That it would die if she didn't save the day? She swallowed hard to hide the tears. She didn't want Clark to see them.

"What's wrong?"

Rats. Too late. Clark saw everything; Kate considered it his worst quality. Too perceptive. She sniffled.

"It's just beautiful, that's all."

Until now, they'd been sitting an honest distance apart. Close enough to feel his heat, but far enough that she thought he couldn't easily reach out and touch her. Another miscalculation. His warmth wrapped its way around her as his arm crossed her shoulders and pulled her into his side. At first, she resisted. But it felt so nice. Beyond nice to be held when she wanted to fall apart in her own shame. She'd lived in Miller's Point her entire life and still didn't understand anything about it. Collapsing into his side, she welcomed his chaste embrace. There wasn't a bit of harm or prowl in it. It comforted her.

"I've never seen anything like this."

"Me either."

"I thought it was just for the money, you know? A way to drum up tourism for a few months a year, but you all really love Christmas, don't you?"

"We love each other." All the ways she could think of to describe the sensation either fell short or sounded profoundly cheesy. Better to be accurate. "I think Christmas is just the excuse to love each other publicly."

The empty field whistled behind them, and their voices stayed in whispers. Being overheard was an impossibility here. Still, they couldn't help but confide in one another as though they stood in the middle of a crowded room. Time danced on the edge of a cliff while Clark's chest tightened and his heart hitched in his chest, a movement of muscles Kate heard loud and clear. Her head on his shoulder felt better than any pillow.

"I can't imagine loving anyone that much. Or being loved by anyone that much. It's almost freezing, and they're out there singing."

"Really? You've never loved anyone that much?"

What a sad, empty life. Kate could barely imagine the darkness of a life lived unloved. No wonder he resented them so much at the start. Kate's nightmares could only conjure up who she'd be without the love of her town.

"My parents, but…" She marveled at the careful way he considered his words. Upon meeting him, she pegged him as the decisive, cold type who spoke and assumed his words would have the desired impact because he said them with such authority. "I think sometimes I forget what loving them felt like. Like, I buried it so deep for so long that it doesn't feel right anymore. I'm remembering a memory of a memory so I don't know if it's real or imagined."

From her place on his chest, Kate couldn't get a good view of him. Maybe it was for the best she didn't. He needed her compassion, but he didn't need her romance. Torn between his bewitchingly handsome face and her convicted town, she settled for playing with a loose thread on his hastily acquired overcoat.

"I think anyone's capable of that kind of love," she said.

"Even me?"

She'd never heard two words so filled with the promise

of hope if confirmed and the threat of despair if denied.

"Especially you."

Neither of them were wearing watches. They didn't dare look at their phones. There was no way of marking time except for the passing of songs from the assembled crowd below. Kate and Clark remained frozen in their poses, two breathing statues carved from flesh and awe, entranced by the groundswell of spirit coming from Miller's Point.

"Do you want to go down there?" Kate asked as the music paused long enough for someone—Kate swore she recognized Miss Carolyn, with her fake antlers stuck on her head of silver hair—to walk up to the podium for a reading. Michael sent them up here to see the festivities, but Kate didn't want Clark to miss out if he wanted to join in. She hesitated to encourage it, just in case his presence sent a ripple of rage through the crowd, but wanted to offer all the same. "It could be fun to be right in the thick of it."

"I'm happy where I am, thanks."

He saved her from the freezing water. He tolerated Christmas, maybe even learned to like it… The dance. The almost-kiss. He wanted love. Her love.

For the first time in her life, Kate didn't know if she wanted to share her love with another person. A friendship was one thing, romance was quite another. Especially on Christmas. Christmas gave everything a Heaven-touched glow; it sang of forever.

Her thoughts tore at one another in a bench-clearing brawl as Miss Carolyn stepped down from the podium and the crowd returned to their singing.

I heard the bells on Christmas Day
Their old familiar carols play
And mild and sweet their songs repeat

Of peace on earth, good will to men.

"I don't know if I like that song," Kate said, scrunching up her nose. She never met a Christmas song she didn't like, but this one always rubbed her the wrong way. Clark chuckled, sending white puffs of warm air out into the dark night air. The temperature was dropping rapidly. Kate didn't know how much longer she could hold out before shivering took hold of her, especially after her dip in the river this afternoon. Billy McGee at the general store had sworn up and down this coat would protect her against any weather Miller's Point could produce. She'd have to call him up about his 30-Day Satisfaction Guarantee.

"Why? What's wrong with it?"

"Peace on earth, good will to men," Kate shrugged and finally sat up. After goodness-knew how long resting on his chest, she finally stitched herself together enough to support her own weight again. Instant regret flooded her. A chill a minute ago turned into full-on shivering with the sudden loss of their shared body heat. "They don't seem to care about women."

"I care about one of them."

A bolt of light broke the darkness around them, invisible to anyone but Kate. Her foolish, wanting heart wanted to throw herself in his arms and kiss him. It clung to that light, never wanting to let it go. Her frightened, skittish self retreated into the shadows.

Dangerous. Risky. Impossible. Loving Clark Woodward was all of these things. She couldn't let herself want it.

"Clark," she admonished, pushing herself to standing. The more distance between them, the safer she'd feel. "You really shouldn't…"

"*Shouldn't*? I don't understand. All day you've been

showing me what it means to love someone and now that I want to, you're saying I shouldn't?"

He followed as Kate strode closer to the cliff. Surely, he wouldn't follow her off a cliff? A hundred possible tactics flew at her and she grabbed hold of the first one she caught. Play dumb. Be obtuse. Deliberately obfuscate.

"You should care about everyone. All of those people—"

"I do care about them, but I don't… I'm not falling in love with them. I'm falling in love with you."

She froze at the edge. He stood behind her, not near enough to touch but somehow near enough to reach into her chest, grab her heart and hold it so tenderly the heat of oncoming tears burned her eyes.

"You barely know me."

"You don't feel the same way?"

"That's not the point."

It was as good as an admission, but she couldn't even think the words. She marveled at the ease with which she said, "I love you," and "love ya," to her friends and neighbors, only to balk now when something real and magical waited just three steps away from her.

"Then what is the point? You love so many people. Why not me?"

"…It's scary."

"I know." He breathed a laugh. "Why do you think I've been avoiding it for so long?"

His soft words coaxed some truth out of her, a stammering, hard-to-admit truth, but a truth nonetheless.

"When I love someone, I can focus on them. I can make sure they're safe and comfortable and happy. I'm very good at loving—"

"But not so good at being loved." The breath left her body. He soldiered on. "Because that means being vulnerable. Being taken care of. When was the last time someone took care of you, Kate? Or listened to you the way you listened to me today?"

He stood in front of her now, his back to the cliff's edge and framed by the light of the town below. Still, she stared at her shoes.

"What?" She could almost hear his hand flex with nervous energy. "Do I need to go find some mistletoe for you to look at me now?"

You can just run now. Run into the forest and call someone to come and find you. You could just jump off the cliff. A fall from this height probably wouldn't kill you. A body of broken bones only marginally less appealing than facing her feelings, Kate looked up.

"I see you," he whispered.

And I see everything about you, Clark Woodward. You have so much love and compassion bottled up, so much you've hidden and want to give now you know how. What if I disappoint you? What if I fail and don't live up to the me who exists on December 24? What if the magic dissolves on the 26th and you go back to Dallas and I'm alone in a crowd again? She didn't ask any of those questions. And he didn't answer. What he gave her, as he closed the gap between them, was so much better.

"I never knew I could feel this way. I thought I was trapped, but you opened my entire world up. And filled my house with so many pine needles I don't think I'll ever get them out."

"It's easy, you just take a high-powered vacuum and—"

"You've made this stupid holiday into one of the best days of my life. You made me feel something, Kate. Do you know how long it's been since I've let myself feel anything?"

"I'm happy I could help," she said, ever the diplomat even as his nose almost brushed her with its closeness.

Her heart—oh, her poor reckless heart—threw itself against her ribcage, banging to get out. A strong hand landed on her right cheek. His pulse was as fast as hers.

"Why did you come to my house in the first place? And why did you stay?"

"I just didn't want you to be alone anymore."

"And I don't want to be alone anymore. But I don't want you to be alone anymore either," he said.

A pause. A lifetime of happiness hung in the balance of that pause. Kate said nothing. She didn't know how.

"May I kiss you?"

"Only if you want me to fall in love with you."

Chapter Fifteen

DESPITE WHAT HIS BOARDING SCHOOL roommates or overly friendly colleagues in the office thought, Clark had kissed women before. They never set his soul on fire as they seemed to do in the movies, nor did they live up to the locker room banter thrown around by the men in his acquaintance, nor was it a gentlemanly thing to do, so he never bragged about his romantic encounters.

Now, he thanked his past self for never inflating the memories or exaggerating the stories. They only would have cheapened the most perfect kiss in all the world.

His lips brushed hers, featherlight at first, not wanting to push his luck. Everything about her was soft, the perfect contrast to his rough edges and tough exterior. His hands moved to gently cup her face and he drew her lips into his for real this time. The slightest pressure, and the kiss exploded into a final firework of connection. His heart caught fire and his eyes were blinded to everything but her as she responded in kind. The kiss spoke louder than any words they could have said or wishes they could have made.

Given how much he despised it, he never expected the most important moment of his life to happen with

Christmas songs being sung in the background. This morning, the moment would have been ruined by the inclusion of "O Come, All Ye Faithful." But then again, this morning, he wouldn't have fallen in love with Kate Buckner.

He was so glad not to be the same man he was this morning.

When the kiss broke—too soon, as far as he was concerned—the dark world brightened and he tipped his forehead against hers. Thoughts like stars hung around his head, too many to count or hold onto. He wanted to kiss her again and again and again and ask her everything about her life. Did she like gray or blue better? When did she last laugh so hard she snorted? What movie always made her cry? How did he start to make her as happy as she'd made him?

"Wow."

Clark couldn't count on one hand how many times before today he'd ever said wow. He added it to the list of things Kate inspired in him. He now understood how to let go of his need to seem above everything. He embraced wonder.

"Yeah." A disbelieving sigh came from her smiling lips. How many times had she been kissed? However many it was, he hoped she liked his kiss the best. He was a competitive type. "Wow."

Turning her so they looked out over the town again, Clark pulled Kate in close, throwing an arm over her shoulder again. He loved this pose. So protective. So close. In this position, she could listen to his heartbeat and know it was real, know she made it race every time she spoke. He swept his free arm across the glittering landscape of houses and businesses, all lit from the inside. Identifying with a building didn't seem a particularly smart thing to do, but Clark did all the same. Each of those houses looked so dark on the outside. Night painted their exterior walls. But their windows revealed the truth. The light within spilled into the streets, promising warmth and comfort inside. He felt like that now, trapped in night but carrying a raging fire in his chest. A fire Kate started.

"I think I see what you're talking about with this Christmas stuff now."

"It's amazing, isn't it?"

"It's magic."

"No." She gave him a little shoulder shove. The smile she no doubt wore echoed in her voice. "It's love. Better than magic."

"I don't like telling people they were right and I was wrong," he admitted. Kate changed his life, sure. She opened up new worlds of possibilities in just a day... Still, old habits die hard. In business, he never said sorry or admitted fault. He barreled forward without regard for those beside or behind him. With Kate, he wanted to accept her love of him and this holiday, but he wasn't sure if his lips knew how to form the words necessary to admit his fault.

"You don't have to tell me. I already know." By now, he knew any time she sounded smug, she was really teasing. He groaned anyway.

"That's even worse."

"Then go ahead. Tell me I'm right and you love Christmas now and you're a big fat softie," she punctuated those last three words with pokes right into his gut. "Who believes in miracles and that you deserve good things."

You deserve good things. The pokes to his gut didn't knock the wind out of him, but that sentence certainly did. A lifetime of neglect told him the exact opposite.

"I wouldn't go that far. I'm just not used to being

given anything. Even though my uncle did try, I didn't *want* to be given anything. When I was young, I was always battling a ghost, you know? I worked myself to the bone at school and college and then at work because I needed to make my parents proud. I needed to carry on their legacy, and I had to fight every step of the way to do it. You're just giving me all of this, and it's… I don't know how to handle that." He stumbled over the words. Rolled his eyes. Old habits die hard, and one of his oldest habits happened to be not letting anyone into the inner workings of his mind. He'd lost countless girlfriends, friends, mentors and roommates that way. His last relationship ended with her saying she didn't want to be with him anymore because of his lack of emotional availability, to which he responded *yes, that's probably for the best.* Kate's presence threatened the fabric of his entire personality. "Look what you've done to me. I'm a sentimental mess now."

"You can be a sentimental mess. I won't judge."

"It's just that I care. My whole life, I just wanted to care about me and my own baggage and duty and responsibility. I didn't know how to care about other people," he declared, a little too loud but not afraid to let the entire world know his secret. "And now I understand what it means to. I care about you. And this stupid holiday. And your town."

"So," Kate breathed on his skin. "Do you think you could give us back the festival?"

"Come again?"

He hadn't quite heard her. Or, at least, he couldn't have heard her right. Why on earth was she still talking about the festival? They were together. The town clearly didn't mind functioning without the festival. They should have been walking on cloud nine, apart from every worry and care of the mortal, un-in-love world. She must have said something else.

"If you get it now, don't you think you could consider giving us the festival back?"

"I don't understand."

"You took it away because you didn't understand what it means. Now that you get it, I thought maybe you could, y'know. Help us out."

"Help you out."

He separated the words. Help. You. Out. Each of the words, he understood individually. In that order, they no longer made sense.

"Yeah." She nodded.

"I didn't cancel the festival because I don't *get* Christmas," he explained. In one motion, he extricated himself from their sideways embrace so he could get a good look at her. He turned his back on the singing town. The skin just under his collar started burning. "I cancelled the festival because it's a financial liability."

"Right, but it pays back in what it gives to the town. And the people who visit. Like you."

His stomach dropped.

"Oh."

"What?"

He saw her clearly for the first time, and he saw himself. The world—spinning with joy only a minute ago—screeched to a slamming halt. Vertigo overtook him. He blinked to steady his vision.

Once, he'd gone on a field trip to a 3-D planetarium on a school field trip. The shock of taking off the glasses during the middle of an illusion had rocked him.

He felt that same way now. All of his illusions and understandings about Kate Buckner turned out to be nothing more than blurry projections, useless colors splashed on a paper-thin screen. Fake. Incorrect. Pathetic of him to buy into it. God, it hurt.

"I'm an idiot," he declared, meaning it in every sense of the word even as it stabbed him to say so.

"No, you're not."

"Yeah. I am." Swallow. Breathe. Don't raise your voice. Just state the facts. Letting go of your tight control over yourself is what got you in this mess in the first place. "You're a liar."

"Me?"

She had the good sense to balk at the accusation, but Clark didn't buy it, just like he shouldn't have bought anything she sold him all day. The first thing he would do when he got back to Dallas was head straight for the optician's office. Only a blind man couldn't see the con played out so deliberately in the lithe body of this beautiful woman.

"You're good, don't get me wrong. But how did I not see straight through you? You were using me."

"Using you?"

"Don't play dumb," he snapped. His entire body ached with the pain and the weight of it; it consumed him too much to keep from barking at her. "I see it now. You wanted to wrap me around your finger, giving me all of this garbage about not wanting me to be alone because you thought you could manipulate me. You made me start to…*feel for you* so you could use me to get your festival back."

"I didn't—"

"Not even a little?"

She stammered. Staggered backward. That told him plenty, but not nearly enough to bring him the pain necessary to break away from her. He'd need to hear it from her lips, to hear the confession of the betrayal before he could trust himself not to fall into her arms again. The irrational, stupid part of him that got him into this mess in the first place wanted nothing more than for her to tell him it was all a misunderstanding and explain how none of his suspicions were correct. The smart, detached part of him knew he needed to cut this cancer out before it infected all of him. He'd been right all along. Love—if it existed at all, and that wasn't even something he was sure of—was a tumor, not a cure.

"I wanted to be close to you."

One of his assets as a businessman was his ability to see a situation clearly and choose a plan of action. Kate's motives, cutting as they were, made perfect sense. They were logical. He saw the path through them clearly.

"So you could use me to get what you wanted. You are a liar." He repeated it and watched it slice straight through her. Now he questioned everything he knew. Were those tragic stories about her family even real, or did she make them up for sympathy? The ornaments, did she make up those stories about them on the spot? Did he know anything real about her, or had he been falling for a fiction this entire time?

"I'm not a liar. I just needed to do what was best for my town!" She raised her voice. Clark didn't give her the satisfaction of doing the same, no matter how much he wanted to, no matter how red his skin grew under his collar. Doing the best thing for her town was as good as a confession. Another one. She didn't give a lick about him. He was a useful, lonely idiot willing to believe any affection tossed his way after a lifetime of being starved for it.

"You admit it."

"But when I saw you at the diner, I realized you had never had what we had. I wanted to share it with you."

"Yeah. Because you wanted to use that to your advantage." The next revelation hurt the most. No one in his life ever liked him. But he was stupid enough to believe she might be the first. He'd fallen, all right, but not for her. He'd fallen for her trap. Hook, line and sinker.

"You convinced me you liked me."

"I do!"

Any better and she'd win an Oscar. The woman even managed tears. They puddled in her eyes, refusing to overflow. Clark paid them no attention. They were just another tool in her deception.

"You only stuck around because you had an endgame. Was all of this," He pointed an accusing finger down to the town. They still sung, the lemmings. "part of it, too?"

"No!"

"Convincing." Clark laughed derisively.

"Honestly, Clark." Her small hand flew to his chest, the pleading gesture of a woman broken by her own game. "This wasn't me."

One look down the ridge of his crooked nose and he removed the desperate hand. He never wanted to be touched by her again. If Miller's Point knew about her plan to con him out of his own company, they probably organized this entire thing to trick him. To give him a childish love of a stupid farce of a holiday so he would fall over himself to give them this expensive, two-month long game of Charles Dickens dress-up. Even if she didn't call this sing-along, she was complicit in it. As the mastermind of this scheme and the pied piper of Miller's Point and all her people, he felt no guilt in holding her responsible, not when his heart was the prize she'd incidentally managed to seize.

"Maybe not, but it was them. They were in on your plan, weren't they?"

"It isn't like that," she ground out between gritted teeth.

"What is it like then? Explain."

Her mouth opened and closed, invisible, soundless words came out, but nothing else. For the first time, Clark raised his voice.

"Explain yourself!"

Her shiver of fear would have made him feel like the biggest heel on earth if she hadn't started it.

"I wanted to get the festival back, yes. But I wanted to help you, too."

"Two birds with one stone, huh?" He snorted, crossing his arms to keep himself from shaking with cold. A cold winter night to reflect the cold heart of this woman.

"I'm not going to deny that Miller's Point is always my first priority, but I never lied to you. I want to be with you." Again, she reached for him. He backed away before she got the chance to touch him. "I'm falling for you. Please don't let this get between us."

"You're just saying that because I haven't given you what you wanted," he said, no uncertainty wavering his stern voice.

"No. I'm saying it because it's true."

True. She made countless spoken and unspoken promises today, and she'd broken every single one by lying to him. If she would go to these lengths to win back a stupid festival, what kind of person was she really, deep down in her heart? He thought of his parents. The stories he'd told her about them. He kept them so close to his heart no one ever saw or heard about them, yet he'd opened his mouth and blabbed his tightest held secrets. As much as he despised her in this moment, he hated himself the most. His lifestyle of cold calculation wasn't a bug; it was a feature that protected him from heartbreaking blunders like this one.

Why did this hurt so much? How had he given her so much power? He wanted to crawl under a rock and never re-emerge almost as much as he wanted to sell her beloved festival off piece by piece in front of her just to show her how spiteful and cruel he could be, in spite of her assertions to the contrary.

"I don't think you know what that word means. I opened up to you. I told you things I've never told anyone. For what? So you could use them against me?"

This fight began with his decision to remain rational and unattached, to tell her how badly she hurt him without ever allowing him to show her how badly this betrayal pained him. But the more he spoke, the faster his avalanche of anger grew. She'd quivered in fear when he raised his voice earlier; he wanted her to do it again.

"I did it so you could finally understand what it's like to have a friend."

No. He wouldn't listen to that line again. He wouldn't be a victim twice. She said this stuff because she needed him. He was nothing more than a pawn in her game, a piece she could move around to get what she wanted. The glory of having saved Miller's Point.

Did she even like Christmas? Or was her slavish devotion to the rituals and false promises of the season nothing more than a ruse, too?

"I don't need friends. And I don't need you."

"Clark. Please don't…"

"You know what, Kate Buckner." He spit her name. It would be the last time it ever crossed his lips and he wanted her to know how much he hated it in the deepest pits of his being. Once it was spoken, he straightened, pulling on the hems of his coat to give him a more dignified, regal appearance. He was once again the Clark Woodward of this morning, the Clark Woodward he would be forever. "You did make me believe in something today. Love or whatever you want to call it is just as fake as Christmas. And I don't want anything to do with it. I was right when I said I didn't care about you. I wish I'd listened to my gut."

"You're just saying that to hurt me," she said, though the defense, like the flicker of compassion in her eyes, was weak. He turned his back on her. His car lay less than fifty yards away; he'd use it to head straight for Woodward House. Tonight, he could remain in the terribly decorated manor, a reminder of his failures, but tomorrow he would depart for Dallas and send an assistant in his stead. His direct involvement in the Miller's Point branch of Woodward Enterprises could easily be handled by anyone on earth besides him. He'd never come back to this place. They didn't deserve each other.

"And you just said everything you said to use me. If I hurt you, well. I guess we're even now."

He imagined she would follow him. Stay persistent. Turn him around and kiss him full on the mouth because she really did love him and he was being too stubborn or too blind to see it. He imagined a last-minute reprieve from the pain of losing her this way. It didn't come. A little voice almost got lost in the wind, and the crack of her boots against stray twigs and leaves signaled her departure from the scene and from his life. A fact he should have been glad for.

"Fine."

This time, when she went into the deep, dark forest of the back forty, Clark did not follow her. She and her stupid holiday could jump into a hundred icy rivers for all he cared. He was going home. He was going to take down the decorations. And he was going to go back to his lonely life. He would be alone, but at least he would be safe.

Being alone meant never having to open up to anyone. Being alone meant never having to take care of anyone. Being alone meant security. Tranquility. Ease.

Being alone meant no one could see tears trickling down his face.

Chapter Sixteen

KATE DIDN'T GET VERY FAR into the forest. The flimsy light on her cell phone couldn't contend with the creeping darkness and generally left her feeling like the first victim in a direct-to-video horror movie. Of all the ways she conceived of dying, she never dreamed it would happen in the middle of the Woodward family's back forty while crying over a stupid man.

A stupid, beautiful man whose heart she'd broken.

She paused in the middle of a circle of trees long enough to consider her options. All of her things sat back in Woodward House. Her wet clothes and toothbrush and the now ill-advised present she'd left for Clark under the tree.

Oh, the present. She'd give anything to be able to slip in through a crack in a window and steal that back before he got a chance to open it. Would he even open it at all? Or would he toss it in the nearest fireplace and watch it burn to ash? Her gift joining the embers broke her heart, but her gift would no doubt insult him. She couldn't decide which outcome she dreaded more.

No, she couldn't go back for her stuff. If he was any kind of man, he'd send it into town or send her an

Amazon shipment of new clothes and toothbrushes. Any further encounter between them would be pointless. But she couldn't keep randomly walking through the woods in the dark. The mental Rolodex in her mind spun, searching for the least embarrassing person she could call to help her out of these woods—physical and emotional. Michael would be glib and make too many jokes about it. Emily would probably drive straight for Clark's house and beat the daylights out of him. In a town of less than ten thousand people, Kate knew there was only one woman she could call on for help.

"Hello?"

Miss Carolyn answered on the first ring.

"Miss Carolyn?" Try as she might, Kate couldn't keep the miserable sob from cracking the words. In the background of the other woman's side of the call, Kate could make out the general merriment of the town square. Like an ironic fairground soundtrack playing in the background of a melodrama, the carol singing and laughter creeping through the phone mocked her, underscoring her pain. "I think I need you to come pick me up."

Michael would've asked what was wrong. Emily would've asked who hurt her and what they were going to do about it. Miss Carolyn?

"Send me your location. I'll be there in ten minutes."

True to her word, no less than ten minutes later, Miss Carolyn's red pickup truck screeched into the muddy field where only a few minutes ago Kate and Clark watched the sing-along down in the valley. As she walked out from the forest towards the glow of the headlights, Kate reeled. To get this far from town that fast, she probably didn't even pause for stop signs.

Miss Carolyn ran to meet her, scooping her into one of her world-famous hugs. For the first time in her life, the woman's warm embrace did nothing to soothe Kate's cracked heart.

"You're gonna freeze to death out here," Miss Carolyn said. "Let's get you in the car."

"Yes ma'am."

Kate followed the older woman's lead. Her swishing silver hair glowed in the moonlight, leaving a distinctly witchy vibe in her wake. As grateful as Kate was for Miss Carolyn's rescue from the forest, the worry lines creasing her face dropped a pile of lead into the pit of her stomach. A pair of reindeer antlers sat crown-like upon her silver hair and a tacky Christmas sweater replaced her usual red flannel, a uniform Kate probably would have replicated if she hadn't spent the entire day falling head over heels for the perfectly wrong man. The initial appeal of calling Miss Carolyn was her sage advice, the wisdom she'd always offered Kate through her life. Now, Kate didn't want advice. She wanted to shut herself off from the world and forget everyone else existed.

They settled into the cab and took off into the night. The Woodward House was private, fenced-in land, but if anyone knew the way to sneak in and out through a broken or missing stretch of fence line, it was Miss Carolyn. That woman knew everything.

"You warm enough?"

"Yes ma'am."

Snuggling into the familiar tobacco and air freshener scented seats, her shivering finally subsided. Though she'd stopped crying a while ago, her face was caked with the salt from her teardrops, as if she'd been swimming in the ocean all day and forgotten to shower. Kate no longer wanted to sob and weep over Clark Woodward, but the salt cracking on her skin almost reminded her of armor.

She marveled, in the beginning, at Clark's ability to

feel nothing. It frightened her more than anything; she swore she'd never let herself get to that point, where she so spurned the idea of feeling that she simply chose to avoid it all together. Tucked in the cab of Miss Carolyn's car, Kate realized the choice wasn't a conscious one. She hadn't decided to die inside. It just happened. Somewhere between hanging up the phone and finding her way into this truck, she just stopped caring. About everything.

What had caring gotten her? What had caring gotten Clark? A big, fat nothing.

"Want to tell me what happened?" Miss Carolyn asked.

"No ma'am."

"You sure?"

Kate squirmed. The day's events weighed squarely on her shoulders, pressing down until she feared they might flatten her altogether. Her heart—like the flat line of her voice—remained placid and unbothered, but the pressure on her back increased.

"No. I'm not sure," she confessed.

"Tell you what. Why don't we go to the square and get some hot chocolate and some songs into you—"

"No." Kate barked. Off of Miss Carolyn's shocked look, she attempted to recover. Just because she no longer cared didn't mean she had to forget her manners. She corrected herself. "No, thank you. Just take me to my apartment, please."

"Your apartment?" Miss Carolyn spluttered.

"Yes ma'am."

"By yourself? On Christmas?"

"Yes ma'am."

Eyes trained forward, hands folded in her lap, Kate didn't dignify Miss Carolyn with a response to her clear shock. She would not be deterred, even if the older woman gripped the steering wheel as if she drove the escape car from a botched bank robbery instead of through the empty streets of Miller's Point. Going to the town square to feign happiness as she sang lying songs about all of creation singing *gloria* appealed to her about as much as diving into a pit of live, starving snakes.

Her initial assessment proved incorrect. She wasn't actually empty or dead to the little voices interpreting her body's reactions into categories like sadness or rage. All of those things existed within her, they just couldn't be heard over the one dominating force controlling her entire view of the world at present.

Bitterness.

She was, plain and simply put, bitter.

"Are you feeling all right?"

"I failed," she said, twisting her hands together. Her voice was black coffee. Her eyes were probably darker.

"Oh, honey. You didn't fail."

Miss Carolyn's pity burned her, hot acid on her skin.

"I let everyone down. I tried to get the festival back and I failed."

"Michael and Emily told me about your plan."

"But that wasn't all. He was so broken." She placed a hand over her own icy heart. "Frozen. I thought maybe if he understood what I saw in this holiday—"

"He'd understand why we love our festival so much."

"No!" What had she done in her life to make everyone think she couldn't possibly really care about this man? Or did everyone, including Clark himself, think him so beyond redemption the idea of her trying to rescue him from a life of loss and misery was completely outside of the realm of possibility? "I thought maybe I could save him. I thought maybe he was just a Scrooge, you know? He needed to see the value in people. And himself. And he'd just open himself up."

To love. To me.

"What happened?"

Kate snorted. The more she encountered the memories she made today, the more childish she saw herself. She really thought she could protect a man's soul by putting up some Christmas lights and serving some turkey? What a dumb, naive girl she was.

"I was almost right. It almost worked. But I messed it up. He thought I was just using him. And it undid everything."

"Did you explain yourself?"

"Yes ma'am."

Miss Carolyn, in her capacity as Director of Festival Operations, always asked three questions in any dispute. What happened? Did you explain yourself? Did you apologize? For reasons unknown to her, the third question went unasked as they crept closer and closer to Kate's apartment. She readjusted her hands on the steering wheel. From the corner of her eye, Kate peeked long enough to see her press her lips into a thin line.

"I really think you should come to town and be with all of us. You shouldn't be alone tonight."

"Why? Because I'm a pathetic mess?" Kate bit questions with the irrational force of a rabid dog. Miss Carolyn scooped her out of the freezing forest and brought her home. She wasn't her enemy. But Kate wanted to push her away; she wanted to forget her own foolish attempts to change her small slice of the world.

"No, because no one should be alone on Christmas Eve," Miss Carolyn echoed Kate's own words back to her just in time for Kate to say something she'd never before said. Not in her entire life.

"I want to be alone."

"A little company and a little cheer will do you good."

"It didn't do Clark any good."

"Then he's not worth your time."

Not worth her time? What happened to the *find the good in everyone* lessons their A Christmas Carol festival taught throngs of people every year? If Scrooge was meant to be redeemable, so too was Clark.

And if Clark couldn't be saved… If Kate failed… It meant everything she believed was a lie. Christmas. Love. Salvation. The fragments of her deeply held convictions crunched into dust beneath the weight of her newfound cynicism.

"We tell people things that aren't true, Miss Carolyn. We tell them this holiday has magical powers that can save anyone, but that's a lie. I don't want to go into town, okay? I don't want any cheer or any uplifting stories. I don't want to hear any more garbage about how people can change through the power of love. I want to go home and I want to sleep until January second."

"This isn't like you," Miss Carolyn said, her eyes as sad as Kate ever saw them. She ignored their sting and repaid their compassion with a stab of her own.

"We all have to grow up. Thanks for the ride."

The car hauled to a stop in front of Kate's building, and she practically threw herself out of the cab without saying goodbye. She lived in a tiny, closet-sized attic above the local bookstore, a fact she never minded and certainly didn't now. The room barely fit her and all her furniture; it certainly had no room to fit all of her fears and worries and memories and disillusions. In a place as small as hers, she could dive under her bed covers and forget the rest of the world.

Kate entered through a side door and climbed the rickety set of stairs up to her apartment. The attic had been divided into three sections by thin walls, separating out a kitchen, bathroom and bedroom. Even with the limited space—her bedroom, after all, had enough space for a mattress, a side table made out of a milk crate and a lamp—she'd gone all-out decorating for Christmas. Lights. Tinsel. Wreaths. The room reeked of pine and cinnamon. Kate's stomach turned, and she knew what she had to do.

With her foot, she opened the empty kitchen garbage can. Time to work. She started with the tinsel. Then the lights. Wreaths. Paper flowers. Finally, the miniature tree. They all met their fate in the bottom of the bin. After a minute of struggle with the lid, she succeeded in closing it.

Her apartment was clear. Clean of all Christmas foolishness and frippery. Now, instead of a sad apartment made merry by decorations, it was simply a sad apartment.

Too lazy to get undressed and into pajamas, she dragged herself into bed, peeling off only her coat before tucking herself between the covers. The place had no heat, which meant she never went to sleep with less than two layers on anyway.

Laying on her side, she found herself face-to-face with The Book atop her makeshift bedside table. *A Christmas Carol* by Charles Dickens waited there, begging her to open it and read it as she had done every year since she turned ten and saved up her pennies for this very copy. Its frayed edges and taped-over spine whispered to her, begging her to breathe in its tale.

Kate got out of bed. Picked up the book. And put it where it belonged. In the can with the rest of the trash. She was done with Christmas. She no longer had any use for its lies. Its betrayals.

Only then, with the last evidence of her belief in humanity safely discarded and the town outside her window still singing those blasted carols, did she return to her bed for a long, dreamless sleep.

Clark Woodward would curse the name Kate Buckner until the day he died for making him feel this way. No, scratch that. For making him feel *anything*. As he drove back to his family's cold and empty home, he could think of nothing else than the new parameters of his existence. She'd opened up his heart and demanded he let everything flow freely both in and out of it, leaving him completely vulnerable to the pains of existence. Now that he'd broken through the dam, nothing could stop the flow.

It all rushed past him and around him and through him until all he could see was the road before him painted with projected colors of rage and pain and longing and sadness. Trying to push it away worked, but only for a few seconds at a time before it pinned him to the mat once again.

It only got worse when he arrived at the house and found the facade still covered in the remnants of Kate Buckner's invasion. He could no longer think of her as Kate, the girl he thought he fancied himself in love with. He could only think of her in formal terms, with a full, unbreakable name like a super villain. Lex Luthor. Inspector Javert. The Wicked Witch. To hold her personally and remember her humanity only broke him further because it was all fake, and he was a fool.

She and her team of scheming townsfolk rigged the Victorian-style manor with hundreds of flood lights and millions of tiny stringed lights, which brought out each painstaking holiday detail they'd hung outside. Giant wreaths, wrapped and bowed with red ribbons, hung between each of the fifty north-facing windows. Two proud Christmas trees—decorated with identical gold baubles and red toppers—flanked the front doorway.

It was as beautiful as it was welcoming. As welcoming as it was sickening.

Clark yanked the car into park and jumped out. He wouldn't stay in a house like this. With the temperature rapidly dropping, he couldn't stay in the car either, but he could not stay in a house covered in the fingerprints of the woman who ripped out his heart, lit it on fire and roasted chestnuts over it.

Great, now he was describing things like she would have.

Storming across the frost-strewn lawn, Clark made a beeline for the first wreath on the first floor. Earlier today, she'd told him taking these things down would be an impossible job for one person. She lied about everything else. Why would she lie about this? He reached for the four-foot monstrosity and tugged. And tugged. And tugged. Until finally it let loose. The momentum shot him back a few steps until he tumbled to a halt, gripping onto the wreath for dear life.

With a minor success under his belt, he went for the rest. In a snowstorm of rough pulls and tugs, he yanked and pulled and ripped at each one in turn. By the fourth, his arms ached and when he fell backwards, he landed flat on his back with a face full of wreath pressing him down into the damp grass.

Fine. He could stay in this house for one night. One night in a house where every ware reminded him of Kate Buckner wouldn't kill him.

It might break his heart even worse. It would no doubt keep him up all night. He wouldn't be able to escape the pain. But it wouldn't kill him.

He abandoned his pursuit of a fresh, un-Jack Frosted house. The wreaths stayed on the front lawn or at their window-side post and Clark took himself inside, where the fires Kate tended still burned hot and her decorations twinkled even more brightly as the night darkened and grew denser around the house. Room by room, Clark made the journey of extinguishing Christmas from the place. He took nothing down—he didn't want to touch anything, while the memories and pain burned fresh— but he unplugged the lamps inside tiny porcelain villages and flicked off breakers controlling scores of hung fairy lights. The formal dining room. The kitchen. The downstairs study. The hallways. One by one they fell to his power until Clark reached the closed French doors of the living room, the one room he'd been dreading all along. Where Kate told her story about her family and how much the festival meant to her. Where they watched *It's a Wonderful Life* and laughed at the plot holes while debating if George Bailey was a real romantic at heart. Where they decorated the tree.

Where Clark realized he was falling for her.

He considered leaving it, but knew it would only hurt worse in the morning. Might as well rip it off, Band-Aid style. The doors spread for him, spilling golden light into the hallway.

All at once, his body deadened. He couldn't lift his arms. His feet refused to obey commands. His own skeleton revolted against him, forcing him to stand in the frame of the doorway and revel in all the ways he failed himself today. Ghosts of them together flitted around the room, teasing him with the promises of what might have been.

If he hadn't believed her. If she hadn't been lying. If he'd just listened to her explanation. If she'd said sorry. If. If. If.

Maybe he wouldn't have tried to tear down all remnants of her and maybe they wouldn't have spent Christmas apart from one another. Maybe he still would have believed everything she told him, about love and Christmas and all the rest of it.

But Clark learned long ago his life wasn't a movie and it didn't follow his whims or wishes. He was a sailboat at the mercy of its whims. All he could do was try not to capsize.

The fire. It needed dampening first. Then, he moved onto turning off the television, blowing out the candles, ripping down the mistletoe from the doorway. Piece by piece, he deconstructed her fairy tale until he stood alone in a dark room with nothing to guide his way but the bulbs on the Christmas tree. He ducked to unplug those too, but stopped when something strange tucked behind the tree caught his eye. A flash of red, sparkly paper caught the light, and he reached back to investigate. After a moment of grappling, he finally caught the hidden object and pulled it up to his face for inspection.

A small package, wrapped in red wrapping paper, tied with white and green curlicue ribbons. A practiced hand made the lines of the wrapping absolutely flawless. It could've been done by someone behind the wrapping department at Macy's, though Clark knew immediately only one person could've done this.

Kate Buckner. Kate Buckner had given him a present.

Clark couldn't remember the last time someone—not a business colleague, not a client or prospective partner—got him a present. Even his secretaries knew not to bother because he wouldn't open them anyway. Anything he got went straight to one of the lower-level directors who would no doubt enjoy tickets to the Cowboys game or a wine tasting trip for two more than he ever would.

Throw it away, reason said.

Open it, sentimentality replied.

For some stupid reason, he listened to sentimentality. For some stupid reason, Clark glanced up at the clock on the wall, checking to make sure it was *really* Christmas. Snake though she may have been, he didn't want to insult her by opening a Christmas present before Christmas morning. But at almost 1:30 a.m., it was most decidedly Christmas morning. Early, early in the morning, but morning all the same.

Rusty from years of not opening presents, Clark struggled with the paper. At first, he attempted to lift the wrapping off at the tape lines so as not to completely destroy the stuff, but when the tape proved tougher than anticipated, he ripped straight through it, revealing the gift inside. It wasn't a box at all. It was a book. The red leather-bound cover gave no hints about the contents inside, so Clark picked himself off the floor and found a seat in his favorite chair by the now-darkened fireplace.

He opened to the first page, though the words were not type-written and official as he expected. Instead, a dark blue pen swooped cursive handwriting onto the first blank page.

Dear Clark,

The same compulsion telling him to light the fire and throw the book straight into it also told him to stop reading there, but his curiosity tamped down all of that. He read on.

Dear Clark,

I don't know you very well. Yesterday, we didn't exactly get off on the right foot. You want to destroy my town. I was rude and abrasive. We both made mistakes. But this morning, I saw you eating breakfast alone at the diner in town and my heart broke for you. Everyone in this town thinks you're a villain. And maybe they're right. But I don't think they are. And I'm hoping I can prove it.

Or, maybe better, I hope we can prove to you that you're not a villain. If, in the end, I fail to do this, I hope you'll read this book. It's made me see the best in people all my life. Maybe it can do the same for you.

Yours Most Sincerely,

Kate Buckner.

He parsed her words, picking them apart alongside everything he now knew about her. Everything in him wanted to stay angry with her, to cling to that pain that shot straight through him when she'd asked about the festival. It was no small thing for him to open up, so it was no small thing to be betrayed.

But…what if she *hadn't* betrayed him? The gift had been sitting there since her arrival that morning. She'd written all of this before they'd known each other, wrapped it with care when the last time they'd spoke he'd carelessly insulted her home and everything she cared about… Even then, she didn't think he was a monster. Even then, she saw good in him. And gave him something without any expectation of a return.

Clark sunk to the lowest pits of despair. She'd been honest all along. Sure, the festival was important to her, but this morning before she even knew him, she wanted to help him. He'd misjudged her character. He'd failed her, not the other way around. He would not cry. He would not cry. He would not cry. He just needed to see what was so special about this book. He sniffled, holding back his torrent of angst as much as possible. Delicate as he could, Clark turned to the title page and read the bold print declaring the name of Kate Buckner's favorite piece of literature.

A Christmas Carol.
In Prose.
Being a Ghost Story of Christmas.
By Charles Dickens.

Oh, no… He'd have to read this thing, wouldn't he?

Chapter Seventeen

Christmas Day

"**K**ATE! KATE!"

To her profound disappointment, Kate Bucker did *not* sleep until January second as she'd been hoping. Groaning from her place under the blankets, she reached a single hand out and shooed whoever thought it smart to intrude this morning. No doubt word of her story and failure with Clark made its way around town by now—Miss Carolyn was many things, but discreet could not be counted among them—and she did not want to spend her new least favorite day of the year listening to her friends try to comfort and console her. For the first time in her life, Christmas Day would be hers to do with exactly as she liked. With no festival to plan and run, she could stay in bed until well past noon and listen to heavy metal or whatever it was anti-Christmas people listened to on December 25.

"Go away."

The security in her apartment didn't exactly rival Fort Knox. On most nights, since she didn't have a working lock on her front door, she usually kept a can with a bunch of coins in it directly in front of the door as a kind of makeshift alarm system. Apparently, she'd forgotten to put the can out.

Some mumbling voices, dampened by the comforter pulled over her head, didn't make enough sense for her to understand their words, but she did recognize the voices. Emily and Michael. Those two. The best friends a girl could have…except for when she didn't want any friendship. Petty though she knew it was, she wanted to wallow in her own self-pity, not accept it from anyone else. She'd always been the reliably cheerful, good ship lollipop kind of gal, but for once she had a real reason to disappear into her mattress. The mumbling stopped, only to be followed by the clicking of heels against hardwood and the sound of a closing door.

Wish granted. She was alone once more. Moments passed with no noise.

"Emily?" she called. No response. "Michael?" Again, no response.

The covers flew away from her body as she sat up and faced the day, but when Kate opened her eyes, something strange happened. Her little apartment didn't look as she'd left it. Decorations that had been shoved into the bowels of her trashcan—now crumpled—were placed back on her walls. Light shone through her windows though she could have *sworn* she closed the curtains before she fell asleep. Everything was almost exactly as it was when she woke up on Christmas Eve.

Why was her apartment back to normal? She shot up to sit in bed, giving herself a head rush. Spots appeared in her vision. She never slept well, so the sensation could almost certainly be caused by oversleep. The clock on the wall read 9:30. When had she *ever* slept that late?

It was then, as she checked the clock, that Kate noticed

that something *was* out of place. There, on the windowsill, sat a book with a sticky note upon it. Sunbeams played on gold lettering.

"READ ME," it said.

A stubborn denial locked Kate's limbs. She recognized that book. Of all the books in all the world, it was the one she'd recognize anywhere. And she wasn't interested in reading it ever again. With a single bound, she was on her feet, ready to throw the book back into the garbage where it belonged—her best guess was that Emily or someone heard about her night and snuck in to make her feel better, a losing proposition—but then something hanging over her front door halted her stomping.

Her heart clenched. She gasped.

The Belle dress. The one she'd never gotten to wear after staying with Michael after he'd broken his leg, with its green velvet and perfect bustle, hung from a satin hanger over the lip of her door, complete with a corset, stockings and those shoes she'd always wanted to steal. Makeup and a curling iron, along with a plastic box of bobby pins and hair ties sat on her kitchen counter. Tacked to the dress waited another note, this time reading, "WEAR ME."

She had to be dreaming. She had to be.

Her fingers reached out to brush the lush material of the gown. It ran like water beneath her skin. Quickly, as if afraid someone would come in and take it from her, she held it up to her body and rushed to examine herself in the bathroom mirror. Yep. Definitely a dream. The Belle dress for the festival stopped fitting after her growth spurt in junior year of high school.

No. It wasn't a dream. If it was, she would have woken up by now. She didn't know who had gifted her this dress, but if the festival was closing and all its assets sold, she was going to get one good Christmas Day use out of this gown. Even if she hated the book from which it came—which she did—it was too beautiful to pass up. Her practiced hands flew through the motions of dressing and preparing herself. Years and years of helping Belles fit themselves in the fabric guided her until she looked the part. Victorian curls framed her face, crowned by a halo of holly, a customary feature of Belle's costume. Bright red lipstick brought some color to her otherwise pale skin. A red and gold brooch glowed at the base of her throat, pinned to the lace collar of her gown.

Oh, the gown. It fit as if it had been made for her. She spun, letting the skirts swirl up and reveal the petticoats and shoes hidden beneath. Even if everything was falling apart, even if her heart still felt half-stitched together, even if she didn't want to believe in Christmas anymore, her girlhood dreams were coming true.

She looked better than beautiful. And she felt it.

"Extra! Extra! Read all about it!"

Her vain inspection smashed to a halt with the intrusion of a squawking voice; it filtered through her thin window panes, a little, booming cry from the streets down below. Doing her best not to trip over her own feet—she couldn't remember the last time she'd worn heels that weren't her sturdy work boots—she scrambled for the window, stopping only for the briefest of moments to grab the READ ME copy of *A Christmas Carol* waiting on the sill. Costume firmly in place and book tucked under her arm, Kate opened the panes and looked down below, searching for the source of the newsboy cries.

Only, she didn't see the source. Not at first. Instead, an uncontrollable, unstoppable gasp flew from the depths of her chest as she stared out at the town square. It was there. Everything was there. As if Clark Woodward never demanded they take down the sets and facades and decorations, the square looked picture-perfect and ready for Christmas. As she leaned out of her window, she realized she was leaning into Dickensian England, with all of its beauty and wonder.

They'd put it back. They'd put it all back. She just didn't understand why. But there, on the corner between the facade of Marley and Scrooge's office and the butcher's shop, Kate spotted Susan Cho, a nine-year-old who played one of the Cratchit daughters in last year's festival. Dressed in one of the countless street urchin outfits Kate put together over the years, she held a newspaper high over her head. From this angle, Kate couldn't make out the headline or even if it came from Dallas or their stock of Dickens-specific recreations of London newspapers.

"Merry Christmas, London! Extra! Extra!"

"Susan! Come over here!"

As if she'd been walked through this a dozen times, Susan hustled down the block to stand beneath Kate's window, tucking the newsprint under her arm. If this were the festival come back to life, Kate would have scolded her for getting newsprint on the costume, but her confusion and awe at the entire situation overtook any practical thought. It didn't matter if the costumes got dirty or the fake newsprint smudged, not when there was so much outside at which she could marvel.

"Morning, miss!" Susan lisped through her two missing front teeth and tipped her newsboy cap. "What can I do for you?"

"What in the world is going on here?"

"Sorry, Miss Kate. Can't talk now. I have to stay in character," she stage-whispered before returning to her strolling and hawking. "Extra! Extra!"

For her part, Kate remained rooted to the spot.

"But if I *was* able to talk to you, I'd say you should

come downstairs."

"What?" Kate whispered back, starting a complete conversation in hushed tones.

"You're supposed to follow me."

"Oh." Whatever was happening here, whatever character Susan was meant to keep and whatever was happening to this town, it was clear there was a plan and an order in place. Kate just didn't know them. But if she knew anything from a lifetime of working with and around children, it was to play along with their games. "Okay. I'll be right down."

She gathered up her skirts and did as she was told, skidding down her steps towards the town square. Once out on the street, following close behind the little girl as she hawked her papers, Kate couldn't contain her curiosity.

"Hey, Susan?"

"Yes, ma'am?"

The little girl must have felt Kate's distress radiating off of her because she dropped her character in order to answer. God bless children and their inability to pay attention to anything for more than ten minutes.

"Is this a dream? Am I dreaming?"

She didn't exactly believe she was dreaming, but it seemed as likely as Clark suddenly having a change of heart and giving her the festival back.

"Hmmm." The little girl tugged on her cap, considering the question. "I don't think so. If you were I hope I'd be wearing something much cuter."

Unconvincing as the argument should have been, it swayed Kate. After the events of last night, would this bizarre journey through Miller's Point be something she would dream about? Unlikely.

By Sherlock Holmes logic, it meant she was definitely, for real, walking through the festival facsimile of *A Christ-*

mas Carol in a sweeping ball gown on Christmas morning.

Susan led her around the empty square, all while Kate puzzled out what little she understood about her surroundings. Dickens. Susan. None of it made sense, but she decided she saw no harm in playing along. Her heart broke yesterday. It couldn't re-break. Besides, the pieces were too small to be crushed into anything else. What did she have to lose?

When they reached the corner beneath Scrooge's house, Kate turned to Susan for instructions. Susan, for her part, tapped her toe on the sidewalk and stared up at the closed windows.

"What are we waiting for?" Kate asked.

"I'm *really* not supposed to break character, but—"

"You there, boy!"

System overload. Kate's processing power extinguished itself within one second of hearing that familiar, booming voice fill the square. Like staring at a box of puzzle pieces, she understood the picture in front of her in fragmented snippets. She knew that line. It was Dickens. No one knew A Christmas Carol better than she; it only took three words for her to identify his speech. And when Kate followed the conversation up and up and up the wall of the building she stood in front of, she was greeted by the unfathomable puzzle piece.

Clark Woodward. Leaning out of Scrooge's window. Wearing the Ebenezer Scrooge costume. Screaming Scrooge's Christmas morning lines.

Rats. Somehow the cut of the Victorian era costumes made him even more attractive. Great. Just great.

"What's the day today?"

Nope. Susan couldn't be right. This had to be a dream. Nothing else could explain it. Forget Sherlock Holmes logic. Not only was Clark wearing the Scrooge costume, but he somehow got at least one person in town to trust him enough to play along with…whatever this charade was?

No. Wrong again. If this was her dream, Clark would get the lines absolutely right instead of paraphrasing them. This was *definitely* happening, but why?

"Uh… Christmas Day, sir? What're you, crazy?"

Ah, Susan caught the paraphrasing bug, too. As the Assistant of Operations, Kate always stayed on book and gave the performers line notes at the end of each night, ensuring vigilance and protection for the Dickens text. This morning, protecting a long-dead author seemed everyone's last priority.

Kate knew everything there was to know about this scene. Pick any random scene in *A Christmas Carol*, she could have recited the dialogue, at least, entirely by heart while visualizing its exact place in their version of Victorian London. Here, after waking up very much alive, Scrooge renews his lease on life and decides to live every day as if it's Christmas, beginning by employing an errand boy to fetch him the biggest turkey in London.

What a crock.

Caught between her desire to continually roll her eyes every time they spoke and her rapture at watching the most wooden, stoic man in the world wildly shout about turkeys with a face-splitting grin on his face, Kate leaned against the nearest lamp post for support.

His smile, rare and pure, weakened her knees. Her last thoughts before falling asleep last night were, I'm so glad I got Clark Woodward out of my system, but the longer he smiled and the longer she stared at it like a snake charmer's victim, the more untrue that statement became. He hurt her. He hated her. But he was not out of her system.

Dickens's dialogue—or this interpretation of it—flew past her like a familiar song, allowing her to just drink him in. A dangerous prospect. If this was a dream, she'd dream something stupid like falling into his arms, and if this was real, she'd endanger her heart. And then probably stupidly fall into his arms.

Unable to speak during the performance, a hurricane swirled inside her. Remnants of her feelings for him yesterday swirled with her anger at not being able to fight them off well enough.

At the end of their scene, Susan took the oversized bag of gold coins and rushed off, leaving Scrooge and Belle—Clark, who had somehow made his way down to street level, and Kate—very much alone, but that didn't break his concentration.

"I must go see the charitable gentleman. And Fred and his wife. Oh, thank you, Spirits!"

Apparently, these were cues of their own as out of nowhere, Doctor Joe Bennett appeared, dressed as the charitable gentleman Scrooge denies a donation earlier in the book. In real life, Joe played this role every year as a bit of a charitable scheme in and of itself. As the Chief Physician of the county's charity hospital, the festival always donated a little something to the cause. But when Clark approached him and shook his hand, he did not pull out one of the phony-baloney bank notes used during the regular festival. Clark instead handed the man a very real-looking check, and the man's shock wasn't the well-rehearsed expression he used every year during this big moment in the narrative.

"Hey, man…"

The line was most definitely, *Lord bless me!* Yet another clue the check in Clark's hand was real.

"And not a penny less. I owe you many, many back-payments, and this is just the beginning."

Doctor Bennett rooted himself to the spot, jaw nearly scraping the floor, while Clark-as-Scrooge hummed to himself and scooped up several brightly wrapped presents on his way down the slowly filling street towards Fred's house. Familiar faces of the town started to mill about in their costumes, just as they would any other Christmas morning. As if this all were very normal indeed. Without the slightest clue what else to do (she thought she might need to stay and give the doctor a dose of oxygen to combat the symptoms of his shock, or at least stick around long enough to see if the check really was real and how much it was made out for, but ultimately decided against it because she didn't want to get stuck taking care of a fussy doctor type), Kate followed them.

The scene in Fred's house always pleased crowds, and this morning was no exception. Kate giggled as Fred's wife fainted at the sight of Scrooge and Scrooge scrambled to help her—a comedic diversion not written into the original text, but added at a much later date by Miss Carolyn in order to beef up the character when Kate played it at sixteen—and followed along as Scrooge proceeded to collect people, imploring them to bring along foodstuffs and presents, treating them all with the charm and guile of a newly risen king. Such generosity, such goodness was an unnatural fit for Clark, but perhaps that was why the cautious parts of her hated how much she wanted to believe it.

In spite of her newfound hatred for this bogus holiday, the naive glass shards of her heart longed for him to be the real-life Ebenezer Scrooge. She wanted his smiles and his warmth to be real.

But it wasn't. And when she examined things more closely as Clark picked up small children and spun them around or joined in carols, Kate realized she didn't care for this at all. The spectacle was just that: a spectacle. Fake. Phony.

He had an angle. All of this was part of some plot. To humiliate her or to make fun of her or to stomp on her one more time… She didn't know. But he was working a fix and she wouldn't fall into its trap. With that, she folded her arms across her chest and resolved to give off the most unsympathetic, hateful, grumpy vibes she could manage.

Basically, she channeled him from one day ago.

"Can you show me the way to Bob Cratchit's house?"

All at once, he was there, directly in front of her, asking for directions to Bob Cratchit's house. Oh, yes. He was real. And so, so unfairly handsome. She'd never seen his eyes catch the light like this or his smile relax into an effortless assurance of his goodwill.

Kate urged herself not to give in. And she didn't. Something was going on here, and she could indulge it for the sake of her festival family, but she didn't have to invest herself in it. Blindly, Kate nodded and took the arm he offered her. Soon, she found herself leading a parade of Victorian-dressed characters carrying presents and goose, pies and wreaths like some kind of out-of-place drum major. Behind her, they sang in unison, a feature of their penultimate scene. They did it every year. This was the ending of *A Christmas Carol*. Clark, somehow and for reasons passing understanding, brought the end of the festival into his home and let it take life there.

The doors to the Cratchit House stood closed, and, against her will, a familiar rush of joy fluttered in Kate's stomach. Whether or not Clark knew it, this was her favorite part of the entire story. The beauty of the tale and the reversal of fortunes for the Cratchits made the entire journey worth it. In the novella, the confrontation between Bob and Scrooge happened at the office, but for the sake of bringing Tiny Tim back for one final "God Bless Us, Every One," they transposed the encounter to Bob Cratchit's house instead.

As Scrooge always did—Kate would know, she'd trained six different Scrooges—he waved away the crowd, they feigned hiding, and he settled an angry scowl upon his brow before knocking upon Cratchit's door. *Boom! Boom! Boom!* Goosebumps raised the hairs on her arms.

She just hoped she wouldn't break and cry. She always cried at this scene.

The Cratchit family generally consisted of a real-life husband and wife and whatever children could sit still the longest and memorize the most dialogue, but when the Cratchits appeared today, Mr. and Mrs. Isaacs were not standing there in their costumes, ready for their close-up. Kate's breath hitched.

There, framed by the holly-lined doorway, stood Michael and Emily, dressed up in the poor clothes of the clerk and his wife, while the usual suspects of children cowered behind them at the mean ol' Uncle Scrooge. The last time Emily got in front of a crowd, she picked up the lid of a piano and vomited into it, so her appearance here caught Kate off guard.

If she had a heart any longer, it would have warmed and stretched with love for her friend's courageous appearance, made all the more amazing by her genuine acting chops.

"Bob Cratchit!" Clark-as-Scrooge boomed. "You did not come in to work today."

Michael cowered, his knees shaking in a mockery of knocking together.

"But it's Christmas."

"I never gave you the day off."

"You did, sir." To his credit, Michael appropriately stammered and stuttered over the words forcing them out between his teeth with all the joy of poisoning himself. He even wrung his hands. Kate couldn't have directed this scene any better. The children in the back did their part, too, huddling together as their mother grew in anger. "You just said to be in earlier tomorrow."

"Oh, I'm going to throw the book at you, you lazy layabout!" Scrooge shouted, shaking his walking stick for emphasis. Kate would have directed against that particular choice, but hamming it up seemed to be Clark's style of the day, a noted change from the man who wouldn't even smile at a little boy yesterday after he begged him to do so.

"Lazy layabout!" Emily charged forward, her thick curls shaking under her bonnet. She shoved up her sleeves as if to instigate a fight. Kate almost laughed. Almost. "I'll have you know—"

"I'm going to give you everything I've got!"

"Please don't! I'll come in now! I can—"

Scrooge cut him off.

"I'm going to raise your salary."

"Pardon?" Emily and Michael said at once, a unified explosion of shock.

"I'm going to raise your salary and take care of you and your family for the rest of my days. And," Clark waved his hands, calling the crowd from the shadows, filling the room with rich aromas and colors the likes of which contrasted deeply with the Cratchits' costume design, as was Kate's plan when she helped pick those outfits. The sight of the swarm of well-wishers sent Kate's temperature skyrocketing. Her stomach turned. "We will discuss the entire thing over the most beautiful Christmas dinner ever brought forth in the whole of Christendom!"

A cheer. Little Tiny Tim leapt into Scrooge's arms and he lifted him high upon his shoulders.

"Mr. Scrooge!"

The room filled, leaving Kate distinctly apart. A viewer of this spectacle. The object of their collective stare as much as they were an object of hers.

She wanted to vomit.

What on earth could have possessed them to all come here and be a part of this? Maybe it was Miss Carolyn. Surely Clark didn't do this all by himself. Miss Carolyn must have threatened to throat punch him if he didn't comply. They were trying to fix her Christmas cheer, surely. Or bring her back into the fold after a tough night of disillusionment and Clark was a part of that. They all bought into the dream, a dream she no longer knew how to be an active participant in.

Next in the story came the "Scrooge was better than his word" speech. Another surefire "Kate always cries at this part so make sure someone has Kleenex handy" moment.

It felt like Christmas. It looked like Christmas.

And she couldn't stomach it. She didn't know what Clark was doing in the middle of all of this. She didn't know what his game was. She didn't know what he wanted from her or why he seemed intent on hurting her through the one thing she used to love most in this world.

All Kate knew was that she needed to get out.

Chapter Eighteen

CLARK SPENT HALF OF HIS morning memorizing this Dickensian text, only for the woman he memorized it for to storm out of the house before he could even get halfway through his final speech.

The door of the Cratchit house slammed behind her, silencing the small living room as fifty heads turned to him in hushed anticipation. Paralysis set in, even as he clung to little Bradley, who waited patiently on his shoulder for his final cue. For a moment, the room could have passed for a ride at one of those high-priced theme parks, where the guests floated through fantastical scenes with broken animatronic characters who could only blink and jerk their heads. The heat of the room's bated breath left beads of sweat on Clark's forehead, trickling down his forehead as his only indication of the passing of time. He couldn't wrench himself away from the closed door; the place where Kate once stood now tortured him endlessly. The absence of her ripped at him; a punch in the gut would have been less painful and robbed him of less breath.

After too long a silence for the little boy's taste, Bradley clonked the top of Clark's head with his cane, a new brand of pain almost bold enough to shake him from his stupor.

"Hey." Clark blinked. Another clonk. Bradley addressed him in a stage whisper through clenched teeth, a manner of confidentiality he probably mimicked from a million Saturday morning cartoons. "Hey, Mr. Clark. I think they're waiting for you to say something."

Michael caught Clark's eye first, a small miracle. After staying up to read his present from Kate, he tracked the young man down. A frantic phonebook search later and he had both Emily and Michael in the living room of Michael's cabin, where he told them the entire story. Being the sort of guy who never spilled his guts, Clark struggled, but eventually explained everything.

They didn't get on board with his plan, however, until he told them the entire truth. *I think I'm falling in love with her and I don't want to lose my one chance because I was too blind to see that some people are good people.* Halfway through the Dickens book, Clark started to understand why he'd been so happy to assume the worst of Kate, even when everything she said and did instructed him to believe the best.

He couldn't believe what a jerk he'd been.

Once Emily and Michael got on board, they went to work buttering up Miss Carolyn who did *not* care for him, expressing frequent and blatant desires to punch him in the throat. In the end, she only agreed to the entire scheme because Emily convinced her it was the only way to save Kate from her disillusionment...

Well, that and Clark allowed her one free punch to his stomach. The old woman had surprising strength for her age; no doubt a bruise started forming almost immediately. The rest fell together at Miss Carolyn's instructions. She yanked children out of bed and hustled parents into costumes. They organized a feast and reset everything in the town square.

And by the time the clock struck nine that morning, everything seemed poised to work. Clark would win the girl, save the town, and give them all the Christmas they deserved.

Only…it didn't work. Kate stormed out before he could even tell her the good news. Before she even had time to hear his apology. Or fall in love with him again.

"All right, everyone." Clark cleared his throat, a strangled sound as his trachea contracted and tightened. "I'm going to go—uh, to go investigate."

Depositing Bradley—who gave him an unsubtle wink and thumbs up once he landed safely on the ground—Clark bolted. He didn't know how to lose her like he'd lost her yesterday.

The streets and buildings around him blurred as he picked up speed (no easy feat in the Ebenezer Scrooge costume, which rarely saw this much physical activity), and he blew past every door and obstacle on his way. Even if she was halfway to Argentina by now, he was determined to find her.

Determination went unrealized when he skidded to a halt in front of the gazebo in the dead center of the town square, where he found Kate, facing away from him, sitting in a puddle of skirts on a set of wooden steps. She flinched as his footfall hit the wood a few paces behind her.

"I don't have a car and these heels are killing me. That's the only reason I'm still here."

It was then he realized she hadn't been shaking with noiseless sobs, but fooling with the difficult laces of the Victorian heeled boots on her feet. From directly behind her, he couldn't tell the difference, but once he stepped to the side, he saw the fight firsthand and the determined way her teeth dug into her bottom lip. In the cold, her skin both paled and reddened at the same time, the high contrast giving her an otherworldly glow amid the thousands of lights strung up across the square from the buildings on either side of them. Clark didn't want to think about the electricity bill they'd rung up over the last few days.

"Can I sit down with you?" he asked, pointing to the sliver of space between the end of her billowing skirt and the side railing of the gazebo's steps.

"Why?"

Good question. A smarter man might have gotten down on his knees and begged forgiveness. Right? Clark didn't watch many movies, so his vocabulary of romantically tinged apologies was severely limited.

"I was hoping to talk to you," he said. A cringe bunched his shoulders together just beneath his neck. He'd never done anything like this; this limb upon which he was reaching out bowed under the weight of his own insecurity.

"You can't talk standing up?"

His chest tightened. After his cold dismissal of her last night, he didn't blame her. She had every right to despise him. Knowing the right was hers didn't make it hurt any less. He'd orchestrated this entire Christmas miracle for her, to make her feel better, not worse.

"I can, but you seem pretty upset."

"Well, I'm not."

"I've never seen you like this."

"I'm fine."

He could hit himself. Everything out of his mouth turned out to be the exact wrong thing to say.

"Okay. Okay." He breathed in a deep lungful of country air. Dallas never smelled this good, nor did it ever crackle inside him like the first spark of a fire. It cleaned him from the inside, clearing his head. A path presented itself, so he took it. A risky move, but one he had to take. "I'll just stand up here until you're ready to talk."

One of the few memories of his mother he held close to him was a story she used to tell about a woman who was separated from her love, and she sat by the banks of the river every day waiting for him to return. His mother held it up as an example of true devotion, sacrifice and love. Though he hoped she wouldn't, he would wait a lifetime if Kate asked. Out of his own selfishness, he'd caused her pain; the least he could give her was devotion and a little bit of patience. He counted the minutes by the twinkling of the timed, dancing lights overhead. One cycle. Two cycles. Three cycles. And finally:

"Fine. You can sit down."

The space between the hoops of her skirt and the side railing barely fit, but Clark sat on an angle to speak to her, only to open his mouth and find he had nothing to say.

"Kate. I think—"

Good thing he hesitated. An explosion of hot air and frustration flew from Kate's lips, pouring out steaming accusations as she gesticulated wildly. Though it was hardly the time or place to do so, Clark couldn't help but store away Kate's habit of talking with her hands as one of his favorite quirks of hers.

"What is it with you, huh? Why are you doing this? What is all of this about? I don't understand."

A reasonable question, one he wished she'd asked before storming out of the house and out here into the cold where she would almost certainly catch her death only one day after he saved her from it.

"I got your present."

"Present? What present?"

Slipping out of his coat, he pulled a red-bound book from the breast pocket, which he handed to her. Distracted by the slender volume, she barely reacted to him as he laid his coat over her shoulders and wrapped his red scarf around her throat. He took pains to brush her skin as little as possible, a task that proved almost impossible and left him with tiny electric shocks every time they *did* touch.

"The one you left under my tree yesterday."

"Oh."

As reverent as opening a prayer book, Kate turned over the pages until she stared at the title page engraving, a picture of an old man with a small boy on his shoulder. Clark didn't concede to wearing old age makeup as Emily suggested, but if he had, he and Bradley would have looked almost identical to the picture she traced with her red-painted nails now.

"*A Christmas Carol*," she muttered.

"Good title."

His quip went ignored as she thumbed the pages. Clark tried to rescue the moment.

"No one's ever seen me before. Or wanted the best for me. And you were right yesterday when you said I took your Christmas away, so…I thought it was only fair I try to give a little bit back to you."

"Why? Because you want to rub it in my face or what? You hated me yesterday."

"I was wrong."

"Yeah? Maybe I was wrong, too. I liked you and you treated me like dirt. You thought I was trying to manipulate you when all I wanted was the best thing for everyone." She'd long since given up trying to take off the uncomfortable shoes. Curling up under herself, she drew her knees into her chest, making herself as small as possible. Clark couldn't begin to see a way out of this. He'd taken a willful, loving woman and broken her like he'd been broken. The whispers in town were right. He was a monster. Kate sniffed and turned her head away from him, resting her head on her knees. "All I wanted was for everyone to be happy."

"I know. And that's what I didn't understand. I've never known someone who genuinely wants good things for other people. I wanted to be right. I think I wanted to believe you were only out for yourself and your town, that you didn't really care about me at all."

"Why?"

Another breath. Deep. Calming. Since putting down the book last night, he framed most of his decisions by following Scrooge's example. It took courage to admit his own fault and apologize to the Cratchits. Clark needed to find some courage of his own. With gentle fingers, he tugged on the end of his red scarf. Kate took the hint and turned her head back towards him. It still waited on her knees, as if her misery weighed too much to keep her head upright, but it was a step in the right direction.

And if this was the last time she'd ever let herself get caught dead in his presence, at least he'd have one last chance to look at her beautiful, bewitching eyes.

"So I could stop feeling things for you. So I could put you in a little box and forget you. Because I've never been in love before and falling in love is terrifying for someone like me. I like being in control. I like knowing exactly where I'm going and when I'm with you... You've turned everything upside down for me. It scared me. It still scares me, but—"

Once he started talking about her, he found it impossible to filter himself, but one purposeful look from those striking eyes silenced his rambling.

"I've never been in love before either."

"Really?"

He found it hard to believe on two levels. One: no one in the world carried as much love inside of her as Kate Buckner. How in the world had no one ever unlocked it and treasured it before? Two: she'd never fallen in love before and yet she chose him? Impossible.

"No better time than Christmas, huh?"

A dreamlike haze settled across her face, only to be torn away with a shake of her head.

"No. No." She held up her hands, brushing away invisible cobwebs. "You're not smooth talking your way out of this. I have to protect myself."

Yesterday, Clark would have shouted. Been indignant. Rejected her and all she stood for. Today, he slid down to the step below where she was sitting so he could look up at her, all while softening his sympathies.

"I'm sorry. Is that what you want to hear? I'm sorry I pushed you away. I'm sorry I shut you out and threatened to take away everything you love out of spite. And if you never want to see me again, I will walk out of this town forever but I can't do that until I know I've made it right. Until you've had your Christmas and until you know you've changed my life."

"That sounds a little dramatic," she said, even as she hugged his heavy wool coat closer. He didn't blame her for thinking it a bit farfetched. When had a man ever changed in one night?

Oh yeah. In *A Christmas Carol.*

"It's not dramatic. I mean it. I wouldn't say it if it wasn't true."

You saw me yesterday, he implored silently. *You saw me when I couldn't even see myself. Please see me now.* Unlike

Clark, she only hardened, a caustic undertone taking over her entire being as she tightened her arms across her chest. Did she feel the need to hold herself together? Did she feel as close to shattering into a million tiny pieces as he did?

"You're telling me you did all of this so you could get me back? Like...to win me?"

"No, I did all of this so you'd know you changed me. After what I did..." Clark loved the way she talked with her hands. When it came to his own twitches and ticks, he despised the way his hands flexed, an instant tell at how nervous he was. "I know I don't stand a chance. I have too much to learn about being a good man to deserve someone like you. I just needed you to know and leaving a sad voicemail at 2:30 in the morning wasn't splashy enough." Kate fiddled with her velvet skirts, but Clark spied her blinking furiously. Did she have a tell of her own? "Now can I ask you a question?"

"One," she conceded.

"Why are you so upset? I know I hurt you, but you stormed out of *A Christmas Carol*, and I honestly thought that was the one thing you'd never do."

With a furrow of her brows and a sigh telling him she only answered because she promised she would, Kate laid herself bare. At this point, he couldn't tell if he made any progress with her or if she only hated him all the more now for all of his confessions.

"Last night, I swore off of you. And Christmas. So, to wake up this morning and be here with all of this," she motioned to the green dress gracing her body. When Clark saw it on the rack, he couldn't help but think, *is that really the dress she obsessed over?* He understood the appeal as soon as she waltzed into his view. She made a plain green frock glow brighter than any emerald. "It sort of makes me feel like Charlie Brown. The second I start believing in you, you'll pull away the football and I'll be on my behind wishing I had never tried at all."

"I'm not going to pull away the football." In a moment of stupid bravery, he placed one of his hands atop hers. "I swear."

"Can I tell you a secret?"

"Do you trust me with one?" he asked, afraid of the uncontrollable undertones of bitterness in the question.

Her hand moved beneath his, sending up red flags and storm warnings in every corner of his body. *She's taking her hand away. She hates me. She's going to tell me to get lost and I'll be stuck with this big, dumb, broken heart.* Then, she turned her hand over and properly held his. The tender gesture grew his heart three times bigger than it had ever been before. Though she stared down at their intertwined fingers, Kate's growing smile couldn't be hidden behind her curtains of curls.

And with four words, she changed him forever.

"I really like you."

A brass band took over his heart. Fireworks replaced his pulse. Christmas really was magic. Scrambling back to sit on an equal step with her, Clark prayed this wasn't a dream. Or if it was, he wanted to live in this dream forever.

"I really like *you*," he replied. She tried to hide her smile, something he couldn't possibly attempt.

"And that was…" She paused so long Clark thought he would die from waiting. This time, she gave him the privilege of viewing her entire face; the shy smile reddened her already flushed cheeks. "That was a really good apology."

His jaw dropped. He'd been convinced she'd run him out of town on a rail.

"Was it?"

"Yeah, but I have one question."

"Shoot."

Anything. Anything. I'm all yours.

"Why am I in this ridiculous costume?" she asked, ruffling the skirts with a laughter-tinted huff.

A moment of panic. Clark remembered her telling a story about outgrowing the Belle costume—her favorite—so he arranged for it to be let out and altered by Miss Carolyn. Had he gotten it wrong?

"What? Don't you like it? I thought you said Belle was your dream role in the festival."

"It is, but…" Kate sighed, her fists wrapping into the velvet. "But…"

"But what?"

"But Belle and Scrooge don't end up together."

No sooner had she spoken than she scrunched her face in humiliation, slapping a hand over her face to cover the spreading blush. Adorable. Kissable. His heart opened wide to her.

"I've got news for you." He tugged her hand away from her face and tipped her chin up. "We aren't Scrooge and Belle." He pressed a kiss to her forehead. "But we can be. During next year's festival, if you want."

"Next year's festival?" The halting words left tracks of white air in their wake as her warm breath spiked the freezing wind around them. Unspoken hope brought out the muted green flecks in her golden eyes as she looked up at him. Clark knew how she felt. Desperate to believe, terrified to be disappointed.

"Next year's festival," Clark confirmed, jumping to his feet and taking her with him by their interlocked hands. "And you can make that call because you, Miss Kate Buckner, are the new Director of Festival Operations for The Christmas Company."

"Me?" She choked on the word, yanking her hand back so she could place it firmly over the place where her heart beat, presumably to keep it from running out on her.

"Miss Carolyn's looking to retire. She wants to enjoy the festival as a guest next year, and she recommended you for the job." The idea came to him this morning when Miss Carolyn complained about hurting her back moving one of the props around the town square. She muttered something about getting too old for this, and Clark offered her a generous retirement package. Apparently, she'd been wanting to quit for some time but didn't have the money. Now she did, leaving an opening for an upstart Christmas fanatic to take over. "I don't think there's a person in the entire world who would lead this company better than you."

Even when presented with her dream job, Kate stayed hung up on one thing in particular. She held his hands so tight he wondered if she was trying to keep herself from flying into the clouds with joy. He certainly was.

"You aren't ending the festival?"

"You were right all along. The festival is good for the soul. Even if it loses Woodward Enterprises a few dollars every year."

In the grand scheme of a billion-dollar company, that's all it was. A few dollars to make people happy and sustain an entire town? Yeah, now Clark saw the appeal of such a setup. Kate swallowed hard.

"I don't know what to say."

He pulled her close.

"Say you'll make next year the best Christmas ever."

"Nothing could ever beat this one."

Her head rested on his chest, where he hoped it would always remain.

"Miss Kate Buckner, would you do me the honor of giving me a second chance?" All of a sudden, music struck up from the bandstand at the far end of the square, grand and sweeping, as Clark ordered. The finale was meant to happen at 10 o'clock sharp, and a check of his watch affirmed Miss Carolyn's devotion to timeliness. "And dancing with me?"

"I'd be delighted."

They swayed in the cold air, accompanied by the roaring band down the street. Completely content. Completely at peace. Clark never knew such happiness. Not in his entire life.

As the song barreled towards it climax, Kate's eyes widened in awe and she pulled away from his chest so she could open herself up to the heavens.

"Snow!" she exclaimed, another delicious smile overtaking her bright features.

"Yeah," Clark confessed. "I told them to turn on the fake stuff. I thought it would add to the atmosphere."

"No, Clark." Kate took his hand and opened it to the sky. "It's not fake. It's really snowing."

Sure enough, one by one, tiny flurries landed on his palm before melting into his skin. This wasn't the sticky soap bubble snow or the false stuff covering every surface of Miller's Point to give it the illusion of snow. This was the real thing.

"Snow in Texas on Christmas Day," he marveled.

"See?" Kate returned her head to his chest. "Miracles do happen."

And for the first time in his life, as he danced with Kate Buckner in a gentle snowdrift, Clark Woodward believed.

The End.

Sweet Potato Biscuits with Country Ham

A Hallmark Original Recipe

In *The Christmas Company*, Kate and many other people in town surprise Clark with a lavish Christmas feast. It includes every holiday treat imaginable—including sweet potato biscuits and ham. Our recipe would be a brilliant use of leftovers from your own holiday meal, and a perfect main dish for a Christmas brunch or lunch.

Yield: 10 servings
Prep Time: 15 minutes
Cook Time: 20 minutes

INGREDIENTS

Sweet Potato Biscuits:
- 2¼ cups flour
- 2 tablespoons brown sugar
- 2½ teaspoons baking powder
- 1 teaspoon kosher salt
- ½ teaspoon baking soda
- ½ cup (1 stick) unsalted butter, cold, diced into pieces
- 1 cup cooked mashed sweet potatoes, chilled*
- ¼ cup cold buttermilk

- 14 to 16 ounces sliced country ham (about 2 slices)
- 1 tablespoon butter
- as needed, honey
- as needed, country Dijon mustard
- as needed, blackberry preserves (or apricot preserves)
- as needed, butter

DIRECTIONS

1. Preheat oven to 450°F.
2. To prepare sweet potato biscuits: combine flour, brown sugar, baking powder, salt and baking soda in a food processor bowl fitted with a steel blade and pulse to blend. Add cold butter pieces and pulse until mixture resembles coarse cornmeal.
3. Add mashed sweet potatoes and buttermilk to flour mixture and pulse just until mixture comes together and forms a dough.
4. Turn the dough out onto a floured work surface. Gently knead just until smooth; pat into a circle to a thickness of ¾ to 1-inch. Using a 3-inch biscuit cutter, cut out biscuits. Arrange on a baking sheet lined with baking paper. Gather

left-over dough into a ball, pat into a circle and cut out remaining biscuits (recipe makes ten 3-inch biscuits).

5. Bake for 15 minutes, or until golden brown, rotating the baking sheet halfway through baking.

6. While biscuits are baking, cut ham slices into 2 to 3-inch pieces. Melt butter in a heavy skillet over medium heat; add ham pieces and cook on each side for 2 to 3 minutes, or until sizzling and golden around outer edges.

7. Split sweet potato biscuits horizontally, layer ham on bottom halves of biscuits and close with top halves. Arrange on a serving tray with choice of condiments.

* Recipe uses left-over plain unseasoned mashed sweet potatoes. Or roast a whole medium to large-size sweet potato (enough to make 1 cup of mashed sweet potato, without the skin) at 400°F for about 1 hour or until tender; cool, peel off skin and roughly mash sweet potato.

Thanks so much for reading *The Christmas Company*.
We hope you enjoyed it!

You might like these other books from Hallmark
Publishing:

Journey Back to Christmas
Love You Like Christmas
A Heavenly Christmas
A Christmas to Remember
Christmas in Evergreen

For information about our new releases and exclusive
offers, sign up for our free newsletter at
hallmarkchannel.com/hallmark-publishing-newsletter

You can also connect with us here:

Facebook.com/HallmarkPublishing
Twitter.com/HallmarkPublish

About The Author

Alys Murray was born and raised in New Orleans, Louisiana, and will always be a southern girl at heart. A graduate of New York University's Tisch School of the Arts, she travels with her fiancé as much as she can and writes as many love stories as she can.

you might also enjoy

ON CHRISTMAS AVENUE

A feel-good small-town romance

NEW YORK TIMES BESTSELLING AUTHOR
GINNY BAIRD

Chapter One

MARY WARD STARED AT HER boss and blinked. "Where did you say I'm going again?"

Judy cocked her chin and her asymmetrical bob swung sideways. She had a slender section of her black hair pinned back on top, offsetting her dark brown eyes. "To Clark Creek," she repeated matter-of-factly, like she'd just said Atlanta or some other highly recognizable place. In addition to being Mary's boss, Judy Ramos was also her bestie, and had been for a decade—ever since they'd been roommates in college.

They stood in Judy's tenth-story office in a corporate building on the outskirts of Richmond, Virginia. Snow fell beyond the floor-to-ceiling windows, coating the pines abutting the parking area. Davenport Development Associates specialized in fundraising initiatives for nonprofit entities, but generally not towns, so this wasn't a typical assignment.

"Well, I've never heard of it."

"Neither had I," Judy said, "before I got their mayor's cry for help." She stepped toward Mary, extending her cell phone, and Mary had to crouch down to see. She towered over her shorter and more athletically built friend.

Judy pulled up a map of Virginia and tapped at a spot

in the state's western portion.

Mary's brown curls spilled forward and she held them back with one hand, attempting to get a better view of the screen. Nothing obvious jumped out at her, besides mounds of mountainous terrain. "I'm not sure I—"

"Hang on." Judy enlarged the map on her navigational app and a tiny dot appeared. The name *Clark Creek* sat adjacent to a curvy blue line, indicating a narrow body of water connected to a larger tributary.

"That looks like it's in the middle of nowhere."

"Not completely nowhere," July replied. "The Blue Ridge Parkway's nearby."

Judy was big into hiking, kayaking, and skiing...all sorts of things that meant spending time outdoors. She'd been president of the sporty Outdoors Club at their university. Conversely, fair-skinned, easily-sunburned Mary was more of an *indoor* yoga person. The only club she'd belonged to in college was the Christmas Club she'd started.

While other charities donated seasonal gifts and meals to those less fortunate, few delivered uplifting decorations, like live Christmas trees and festive garlands, to folks who wouldn't otherwise have them. Mary had been pleased to learn her club had continued operating even after she'd graduated from college.

For her part, she'd never really gotten out of the habit of buying Christmas decorations whenever she found them on sale. She loved saving them up to drop off at nursing homes or other places where they were appreciated. Her apartment closets were so jam-packed they couldn't absorb any more holiday cheer, and the cargo area of her SUV was loaded.

Judy motioned for Mary to have a seat in the chair facing her desk, and Judy sat behind it. A small plastic

Christmas tree stood on its corner wrapped in colorful lights, and the wreath above Judy's bookshelf behind her showcased a red-and-green-checkered holiday bow.

"What's going on in Clark Creek?" Mary asked her.

"Not nearly enough." Judy sighed. "The email from the mayor was honestly a little sad, and a lot frantic. Clark Creek barely has enough reserves to fund its daily operations."

"Oh no. You're talking local government?"

"I'm talking all of it. Government operations, the sheriff's office...and the shops and restaurants are hurting, too. The town council learned about our company's reputation for raising capital quickly and reached out to us for help. If they don't get relief soon, the whole town will go under."

"Bankrupt?"

Judy nodded. "Everything will take a hit in that case, including funding for parks and schools."

That sounded perfectly awful for the poor people of Clark Creek.

Mary shifted in her chair, growing uncomfortable. She normally helped smaller organizations like charities run their fundraisers, functioning as part of a team. Lately, she'd been spearheading those teams. But none of them had tackled anything this big.

"How many of us will be on this?"

"I tried to suggest sending you, Natalie, and Paul—at a minimum." Judy grimaced. "But the mayor said they can only afford one consultant."

"One?" Mary swallowed hard. "I don't know, Judy. This sounds like a challenge."

Judy scanned something on the laptop in front of her, then shut it. "Since when have you backed down from a challenge?"

Mary chuckled, feeling called out. "Never."

"See? You're perfect for the job. Smart. Determined. Innovative! Plus, you can think on your feet."

"Let's hope I land on them, too."

"You will." Judy took on a serious tone. "I'm not supposed to tell you this," she said in a whisper. "But if you pull this off in Clark Creek?"

"Yeah?"

"It could mean Seattle."

Mary's heart thumped. "What?"

"Headquarters," Judy confirmed. "And a promotion to program manager, like me. You won't even have to apply. Upper management already has their eye on you. All you need is this major victory to seal the deal, and my recommendation, of course. Which you know you have."

Anticipation coursed through Mary. This was just what she wanted—what she *had* wanted for the past year, ever since Judy had been promoted ahead of her. They'd started at the firm at roughly the same time as implementation specialists, after both having earned their MBAs and working for different universities' development offices.

Mary had been glad to move to Virginia, and extra happy about working with Judy, who'd already accepted a position at Davenport. Things became privately awkward for Mary when Judy got named her boss. Even though Judy was always kind and fair about it, being her subordinate felt weird after being equals and friends.

Then again, Judy was more assertive than Mary, and not afraid to advocate for herself. Like she had when she'd applied for the supervisory position she currently held.

Mary frowned. "But that would mean leaving Virginia. And you."

"Don't be silly, Mary! We'll keep up like we did before. Besides…" Judy playfully rolled her eyes. "You've got to know, if the shoe was on the other foot—"

"You'd jump at the chance in a heartbeat."

"Yeah."

Mary knew this was an opportunity she couldn't refuse. She really did love rising to a challenge, and moving to the West Coast sounded exciting. Virginia was great, but she'd already lived here for nearly two years, and grass was growing under her feet. While Mary wasn't stellar at maintaining long-distance connections, she'd always managed to stay friends with Judy—in part, due to Judy's bullheaded persistence. Mary loved her to death for her loyalty. Judy was the closest thing to a sister she had.

"So all I've got to do," she said, "is present this little town with some new strategies?"

"For fiscal viability, yes. That's what they're counting on. An economic reboot."

Mary inhaled deeply, thinking things through. She could do this; of course she could. Given enough time to strategize. "Okay. Why don't you send me the particulars: demographics, chamber of commerce information, that kind of thing. Oh! And forward that email from the mayor. I'll do some research on Clark Creek and come up with a proposal to run by you before presenting it to the mayor and the town council."

"Super. As soon as it gets their approval, you can go on site to implement your plan."

"How long have I got?"

"They're wanting results by Christmas."

"Christmas?" Mary's stomach clenched. That sounded impossible, even to her. She was accomplished at her job, but she wasn't a miracle worker. "That's only two weeks away."

Judy shot her an encouraging grin. "Sounds like you'd better get busy."

Evan Clark's mom greeted him as he approached the courthouse. Snow drifted through the air. A fine white powder dusted the town square with its stylish gazebo and seasonal outdoor skating rink. The impressive façade of the library stood across the way, marked by its tall ivory columns and ornate windows. Beyond the smattering of town buildings behind the library, clouds cloaked a snowy mountain ridge.

"Oh, Evan! I was looking for you earlier. Itzel said you'd stepped out," his mom said, mentioning his administrative assistant. Connie Clark wore her winter coat and held up a small umbrella while grasping a paper cup of coffee in a gloved hand. Her dark blond hair skimmed the edges of her fake fur coat collar and her blue eyes sparkled when she smiled. Despite the crows' feet at their corners, she looked a lot younger than her age. She'd been mayor in Clark Creek these past ten years.

"Yeah, I had to stop by the bank." As Evan walked with his mom up the courthouse steps, he angled his sheriff's hat forward to keep the snow from hitting his face. It was driving down harder now and growing icy, which would mean slick streets. Folks would need to take care. "What's up?"

"This is about, you know…" She dropped her voice a notch. "That little issue we have going on."

Read the rest! *On Christmas Avenue*
is available now.

Beijing

Beijing

3 9082 08880 3732

Text by JD Brown
Edited by Richard Wallis
Updated by Matthew Ippolito
Photography: Nicholas Sumner, pages 4, 9, 10, 12, 18, 23, 27, 30, 31, 41, 45, 53, 64, 80, 83, 85; JD Brown, pages 3, 5, 6, 17, 20, 24, 28, 32, 36, 37, 39, 49, 50, 51, 55, 58, 62, 67, 71, 75, 76, 79, 90, 96; China National Tourist Office, pages 68, 93
Cover photograph by Marcus Wilson-Smith
Photo Editor: Naomi Zinn
Layout: Media Content Marketing, Inc.
Cartography by XNR Productions
Managing Editor: Tony Halliday

First Edition 2003

CONTACTING THE EDITORS

Every effort has been made to provide accurate information in this publication, but changes are inevitable. The publisher cannot be responsible for any resulting loss, inconvenience or injury. We would appreciate it if readers would call our attention to any errors or outdated information by contacting Berlitz Publishing, PO Box 7910, London SE1 1WE, England. Fax: (44) 20 7403 0290;
e-mail: berlitz@apaguide.demon.co.uk

090/201 REV

CONTENTS

• A  in the text denotes a highly recommended sight

Beijing

BEIJING AND ITS PEOPLE

As the nation's capital for the past 600 years, Beijing has been the center of gravity for all things Chinese. Its imperial treasures are unequaled, and today Beijing is the most visited of all Chinese cities. The Forbidden City, where the emperors resided from 1420 to 1924, remains intact, and the best-preserved portions of the Great Wall still guard the northern approach to Beijing. Inheriting the best of Chinese history and art, Beijing protected them during the deaths of dynasties and through the throes of revolutions. Today, as the capital of a new China, Beijing can set these accumulated treasures before the eyes of the world as the last relics of Old Cathay.

As you cross the vast courtyards of Beijing's palaces and pavilions, you can almost hear the heart of the Middle Kingdom beating. As you peer into the fragrant recesses of tile-roofed halls, you can imagine the shadows of the emperors rising from the Dragon Throne. For five centuries this was the home of China's most powerful dynasties, including the Ming and the Manchu. China's last emperor — together with his eunuchs and concubines — abandoned the Forbidden City early in the 20th century, his dynasty destroyed. But the imperial walls have survived, as have the palaces of the "Great Within." The imperial architecture of Beijing offers a rare opportunity to see and feel this China of our dreams.

The ancient parks of China's capital have also survived. The Temple of Heaven, where emperors performed the annual rites to ensure the prosperity of the Earth, still stands at the southern end of the Imperial Way in Beijing. The royal processions from the Forbidden City no longer travel this route along the main axis of the old capital, but thousands of tourists make the pilgrimage.

The Summer Palace, formerly a lakeside resort reserved for the imperial court and the private playground of the notorious Empress Dowager Cixi during the twilight of the last dynasty, has endured, to the delight of modern visitors. The once-exclusive shores of the Back Lakes and of Beihai Park, just north of the Forbidden City, are also open for our pleasure today. Dotted with temples, pagodas, imperial altars, classic gardens, and aging mansions, the lakes and parks of old Beijing provide pathways into China's romantic past. They contain rare but sumptuous scenes from a civilization that is a world apart — a world apart not only from anything left in modern China, but from anything that ever existed in the West.

While Beijing's chief attractions are these exotic monuments to the past, such dazzling surfaces are but one aspect of the Beijing experience. Modern Beijing exerts its own appeals: its streets hold a fascination that is distinctly Chinese. Beijing is famous for its courtyard houses located in tiny alleys (called *hutongs*) outwardly changed very little since the Qing Dynasty. In Beijing's *hutong* neighborhoods — and indeed on its busiest shopping avenues — East and West engage in a tug of war on every corner. Fortune-tellers haunt the doorsteps of the latest European boutiques and itinerant vendors hawk baked yams at the entrance to Beijing's newest McDonald's outlet.

The capital is still the best place in China to take in a performance of the centuries-old Peking Opera or to feast on a banquet of authentic Peking duck, but Beijing is also the best place in China to shop at a mega-mall, ride the subway, dine on nouvelle French cuisine, or watch professional basketball live from the US in the familiar surroundings of a sports bar.

What most surprises Beijing travelers is the capital's modern appearance. China's greatest city is flat, sprawling, and not terribly attractive. Much of the cityscape is dominated by monotonous rows of highrise hulks fashioned from unpainted concrete, a legacy of China's first phase of modernization. At that time, the architecture of "socialist realism" practiced in the Soviet Union served as the model.

The most recent phase of construction follows the steel-and-glass skyscraper school that dominates the modern skylines of the world's big cities. At first glance, Beijing looks like any other world capital in any other developing nation, an ugly duckling of ul-

City sights: a man stops for a quick street-side haircut.

tramodern hotel towers, aging tenements, and massive construction zones encircled by elevated expressways clogged with vehicles mostly manufactured in China. Add to this universal urban stew a pronounced, often all-too-visible air pollution problem, and Beijing quickly sheds much of its imagined charms.

Part of this urban blight is the result of Beijing's sudden economic boom. In scarcely a generation, it has leapt from the depths of a poor, pre-industrial metropolis to the heights of a major world capital, becoming the administrative center of the largest consumer market in the world. Finally securing the wealth and political will to modernize itself in the 1990s, Beijing has pulled out all the stops, rather as Tokyo, Taipei, Hong Kong, and other Asian cities did after World War II. What sets

A shop in Liulichang, a restored shopping street.

Beijing apart, however, is that it retains significant sections of its pre-industrial neighborhoods, its ancient parks, and its imperial monuments. Old Beijing has not been bulldozed or reconstructed out of existence — at least not yet.

The Beijingers themselves are extremely proud of the old capital but not nearly as sentimental about their past glories as outsiders are. They support unfettered progress, rapid modernization, and willy-nilly Westernization because these volatile processes are eliminating centuries of severe poverty. The old courtyard houses in twisting alleyways might be picturesque, representatives of a profound Beijing tradition, but new apartment towers promise decent living space, modern plumbing, clean heating, and other comforts previously enjoyed only by emperors. Beijingers are practical. They are also warm, outgoing, and frank — frank enough to tell visitors that material progress for their families takes precedence over an Emperor's silk robe, a Buddhist's decaying shrine, and perhaps even the quality of the air.

More than 11 million people now live in the greater Beijing metropolitan area, with 7 million packed within the city limits. This makes Beijing the world's 12th largest city. It is quite crowded in the streets, living space has not increased in years, there's a severe housing shortage, and the per capita income is about US$1200 a year. The minimum wage is barely above a dollar a day. Beggars huddle around temples and tourist sites. Beijing's large "floating population" — consisting of those who arrive from the countryside illegally in hopes of finding work — circulate in the streets, looking to become maids or construction hands.

> Among world capitals, Beijing might have the most bicycles. But it also has more taxis (over 70,000), which charge 20 percent more at night.

Yet despite these conditions, Beijingers are regarded as extremely prosperous within China, far better off than those on the farms or in other cities lying inland. In fact, there is a rising middle class in Beijing, made up of the well-educated and those who succeed in free enterprises. The capital has its poor by the millions, but it also has its overnight millionaires. The traveler will find most Beijingers exceptionally optimistic about their prospects, pleased that they are better off than ever before, and full of hope for the future. Beijing has become a spirited city, a city certain of its future.

Beijing is also one of the few cities in China with a sustained exposure to the outside world. It has long been the primary host of foreign delegations. In recent decades, Beijing has welcomed from abroad more diplomats, scholars, experts, artists, business travelers, and tourists than any other Chinese city. Today, over 100,000 Beijing residents are foreign-born, most of them employed by overseas businesses and agencies. Beijing contains China's leading universities, governmental agencies, and foreign business offices. In short, Beijing is more and more an international city.

The curious thing is Beijing's essential otherness. Despite its Western appearance, despite its international politics, despite its dedication to Western business practices and free enterprise, and despite its admiration for imported movies, fast food, new cars, and personal computers, Beijing is at heart a fully Chinese city, with its own ways of doing things.

Beijing has its own language and cuisine, both of which give it an exotic feel. Travelers who restrict themselves to hotels, tour buses, hired guides, and major shops and restaurants will encounter few language problems in Beijing. But everywhere else throughout the city, the sounds and signs are all Chinese. Beijingers speak a local dialect, which happily for them is very close to the official dialect, known as *putonghua* (Mandarin). The rulers in Beijing, of course, were the ones who determined just which of the many varying regional dialects of spoken Chinese became the official version.

Chinese food is more familiar to outsiders than is the Chinese language, but the cuisine of Beijing is also quite distinctive. The flavors are those of North China, seldom resembling

Serious fun: time out for a game of Chinese chess in Tiantan Park, Beijing.

the Westernized "Mandarin" fare of Chinese restaurants in North America and Europe. Chopsticks are the common way to consume a meal, although Western tableware is becoming widely available. The food and the language are both alien elements but must be counted as attractions rather than as obstacles. In Beijing, these and other cultural differences remain solidly in place, along with customs that Western contact and modernization have not erased.

A multitude of historic sights, scenic parks, old neighborhoods, and ancient temples are scattered throughout modern Beijing. For sightseeing today, buses, taxis, the subway, or perhaps a rented bicycle have become necessities. Getting around town can be a tedious affair. There are more new vehicles than new roadways, making traffic jams common. The heart of the city is still where it's always been: at the Forbidden City, directly across Chang'an Avenue from Tiananmen Square, the largest public square in the world. The Temple of Heaven is to the south, the Summer Palace to the west, and the Great Wall looms to the north. The city retains the checkerboard layout with which it was endowed by its Ming emperors.

> Cars, trucks, and bicycles have an absolute right-of-way in the streets of Beijing, even when the light favors pedestrians. Follow the lead of native walkers.

While Beijing is China's leading imperial treasurehouse, no other city in China is modernizing so rapidly, sometimes with little regard to preserving its splendid past. Beijing is a city undergoing a massive reconstruction designed to put forth a powerful new face for the 21st century, an up-to-date international face with no trace of emperors or teahouses. If you want to see China from two intense perspectives — that of its graceful past and that of its frenetic future — Beijing lies at the most striking point of intersection imaginable, and it is still a city of dreams.

A BRIEF HISTORY

Beijing has frequently been at the center of Chinese history, from the rise and fall of dynasties to the recent triumphs and tragedies at Tiananmen Square. Each great phase left visible marks on Beijing, and the capital is a virtual museum devoted to the world's oldest continuous civilization.

Peking Man

The skull and bones of China's oldest prehistoric resident, Peking Man, were discovered 50 km (30 miles) southwest of Beijing in 1929. This excavation at Zhoukoudian, estimated to be 500,000–690,000 years old, constituted one of the major chapters in modern paleontology, since it was the first evidence that early man *(Homo erectus)* might have evolved in Asia as well as Africa. The Peking Man Caves and Museum at Zhoukoudian are still a major Beijing tourist site, although many of the important fossils are in collections outside China.

Within Beijing itself, there was no evidence of prehistoric settlement until the accidental discovery in 1996 of a Stone Age village barely 1 km (half a mile) from the Forbidden City and Tiananmen Square. The stone implements and human fossils at this site, beneath the new Oriental Plaza office and shopping complex, are now on public view in a basement gallery. They push the known human settlement of central Beijing back to 20,000 B.C.

Capital of the Khans

There are records of a town existing at Beijing as early as the Western Zhou Dynasty (1100–771 B.C.), but the growth of the city did not begin until the end of the Tang Dynasty (A.D. 618–907). Invaders from the north, the Khitan, swept down

Historical Landmarks

500,000 B.C. Cave dwellers reside southwest of Beijing.

20,000 B.C. Village established near Tiananmen Square site.

A.D. 916–1125 Liao Dynasty locates northern capital at Beijing.

1275 Marco Polo visits Kublai Khan's capital, Khanbaliq (Beijing).

1402–1420 Ming Dynasty builds the great palaces of the Forbidden City.

1644 Manchus claim Beijing as capital and begin the Qing Dynasty.

1860 European forces invade Beijing and open Foreign Legation.

1903 Summer Palace rebuilt by Empress Dowager Cixi.

1911 Qing Dynasty falls; Republic of China is declared.

1919 Protests in Tiananmen Square against foreign treaties.

1924 Puyi, China's last emperor, expelled from the Forbidden City.

1928 Chiang Kai-shek makes Beijing China's capital.

1937–1945 Beijing occupied by Japan.

1949 Beijing becomes capital of People's Republic of China under Mao Zedong.

1966 Cultural Revolution begins: many of Beijing's historic sites are closed, damaged, or destroyed.

1972 US President Nixon visits Beijing, establishes diplomatic relations.

1976 Chairman Mao dies.

1989 Pro-democracy demonstrators evicted from Tiananmen Square.

1996 Funeral for Mao's successor, Deng Xiaoping.

1999 Beijing celebrates 50th anniversary of People's Republic at Tiananmen Square.

2001 Beijing is chosen to host the 2008 Olympic Games, the first Games to be held in China.

and made Beijing their secondary capital, from which they controlled much of northern China. This period was known as the Liao Dynasty (A.D. 916–1125), but there are almost no traces of it in Beijing today. The Liao capital at Beijing, then known as Yanjing, occupied the southeast region of what is the modern capital today, with the Fayuan Temple the only surviving monument.

Another swarm of nomadic invaders eventually routed the Khitan, establishing the capital of the Jin Dynasty (1115–1234) on the outskirts of Beijing (which they renamed Zhongdu, or Central Capital). The Jin capital was in turn completely razed by a fresh batch of northern nomadic usurpers. They were the Mongols — led by Genghis Khan — who would leave a more lasting and extensive mark on Beijing and all of China.

Genghis Khan laid the groundwork, gradually uniting all China under his rule and leaving it to his famous grandson, Kublai Khan, to secure the Yuan Dynasty (1279–1368). Kublai Khan erected his own capital in 1279 on the shores of Beijing's Beihai Lake, where some of his imperial treasures remain on display today. It was to these same shores that Marco Polo claimed to have journeyed at the end of the 13th century, where he won the support of Kublai Khan. He made Beijing, then known as Khanbaliq (Khan's Town) or Dadu (Great Capital), the base for his extensive travels in China as emissary of the Khan. Of the 13th-century capital, Marco Polo wrote that "the whole interior of the city is laid out in squares like a chessboard with such masterly precision that no description can do justice to it" — a pattern Beijing retains to this day.

The Ming Period

The Mongol rulers of the Yuan Dynasty were eventually undone by indigenous Chinese rebels who established one

of the most renowned of all imperial lines, the Ming Dynasty (1368–1644). The capital was again razed and rebuilt, and Ming Emperor Yongle gave it a new name that would stick: Beijing (Northern Capital). By 1420 he had finished constructing the city's most famous surviving monument, the Forbidden City. This was accompanied by other monumental projects. The Bell Tower, the Drum Tower, and above all, the graceful Temple of Heaven were built in the early 15th century. Many of Beijing's major temples also date from the Ming Dynasty.

Monumental Mings: the Drum Tower recalls the impressive Ming Dynasty.

The Ming rulers cautiously welcomed a few Catholic missionaries from Europe to Beijing. In the 17th century the Jesuits, headed by Matteo Ricci, had a profound influence not so much on Chinese religion (they made few converts among Beijingers) as on science, mathematics, astronomy, art, medicine, and other forms of knowledge that had never before been infused with Western ideas in China. Perhaps the greatest project of the Ming, however, was the restoration and extension of the Great Wall north of Beijing. For the first time, brick was used to finish these magnificent fortifications. It is the Ming Dynasty Great Wall that millions visit today at Beijing.

The Golden Stream wends its way through the glorious grounds of the Forbidden City.

The Qing Period

The Ming rulers were understandably nervous about yet another invasion from the north and took defensive measures by extending the Great Wall. They were nonetheless undone by precisely what they feared most: northern invaders. This time the conquerors were the Manchus, who established a dynasty that proved as long-lived and as glorious as the Ming.

The Manchu rulers of the Qing Dynasty (1644–1911) were wise enough to adopt Chinese ways. They kept the capital at Beijing but, unlike preceding dynasties, did not raze it. Instead the Manchus preserved and restored China's past. The Forbidden City, the Temple of Heaven, and Beihai Lake were maintained as imperial strongholds. Old temples were renovated, and the *hutong* neighborhoods of courtyard mansions were developed.

Two of the greatest Qing emperors, Kangxi and his grandson Qianlong, maintained the Ming Tombs and saw to the building of the Summer Palace, while the last great imperial ruler of China, the Empress Dowager Cixi, kept the Summer Palace and the Forbidden City in splendid condition into the early 20th century. These and most other historic sites at Beijing were either preserved or created by the Qing rulers, including their own imperial tombs, which rival those of the Ming.

The Qing Dynasty is also celebrated for its elaboration of the artistic traditions it inherited from the Ming Dynasty. What we know as Peking-style opera and still see performed today in the capital became formalized under the Qing, although its roots (and costumes) go back to Ming and earlier eras. The Ming were also noted for their superb ink paintings, cloisonné enamel work, furniture design, and lacquerware — but above all for their porcelains of the "five-colors" and "blue-and-white" schools. At the end of the Ming, these porcelains with landscape and garden designs became all the rage in Europe, where imitation "Chinese" pottery began to be produced. The Qing continued these artistic traditions, adding increasingly rich and dense ornamentation and applying new colors, many of them clashing or gaudy.

This absorption in overly elaborate artwork, combined with heavy demands for imperial luxuries, finally coincided with a decline in the dynasty itself. In the 19th century the Qing rulers faced a new legion of invaders, not from the north (as in the past) but from the West, and they were unable to resist the tide.

Since the time of the First Opium War (1839–1842), Western nations had been pushing China to open its doors to foreign trade. In 1860, during the Second Opium War, British and French troops forcibly occupied Beijing and exacted

For almost 500 years it was closed to the public, but now you can see for yourself all the treasures of the Forbidden City.

treaty rights. Foreign delegations, businesses, and missionaries poured into the capital, taking up residence in the Legation Quarter, located just southeast of the Forbidden City.

In 1900 the Legation Quarter was attacked by the Boxers, a radical nationalist group that had the tacit support of the Qing court. In retaliation for this unsuccessful attempt to expel Westerners from Beijing, military forces representing the eight foreign nations resident in the capital went on a rampage, destroying the national library and even setting fire to the Summer Palace. Thereafter, the Legation Quarter exercised complete control over its own affairs, becoming its own foreign city within the city of Beijing. Many of the European-style embassy buildings, offices, banks, hotels, and mansions of the period have survived, although all have been converted to other uses since the revolution of 1949.

Republicans and Warlords

China's history of imperial rule is far older than Beijing's reign as capital, but it was at Beijing that the last of

China's dynasties was destined to fall. The Qing rulers were overthrown in 1911, and the Republic of China, led by Sun Yat-sen, was declared. A period of regional civil wars and power struggles among rival warlords ensued.

Great Names of Beijing

Marco Polo *(1254–1324)*. Italian author and merchant, Marco Polo traveled the Silk Road to China and back (1271–1298), claimed to be an emissary of Kublai Khan, and wrote the first popular account of China in the West. Many scholars, however, doubt his account.

Matteo Ricci *(1552–1610)*. Most famous of the Jesuit missionaries to China, Ricci lived in Beijing from 1601 until his death. He served as mathematician and astronomer to the imperial court.

Kangxi *(1654–1722)*. As second emperor of the Qing Dynasty, Kangxi refurbished many of Beijing's major temples and imperial sites, built the Old Summer Palace, and created the imperial retreat at Chengde. His great works continued under the reign of his grandson, Emperor Qianlong. Both emperors ruled for about 60 years.

Empress Dowager Cixi *(1835–1908)*. Former concubine and the power behind the throne during the twilight of the Qing Dynasty, the Empress Dowager is renowned for her extravagance and the rebuilding of the Summer Palace.

Mao Zedong *(1893–1976)*. A founder of the Chinese Communist Party (1921) and supreme ruler of the People's Republic from its birth, the "Great Helmsman" is both revered and reviled for his accomplishments. His body lies in state at Tiananmen Square.

Deng Xiaoping *(1904–1997)*. Mao's successor, Deng spearheaded the economic reforms that transformed China. He also ordered the crackdown on the 1989 pro-democracy movement in Tiananmen Square. Deng's reforms have been continued under the leadership of Zhang Zemin.

Students used Tiananmen Square in 1919 as the stage for their protests against post-World War I "unequal treaties" that favored Japan, a patriotic demonstration known as the May the Fourth Movement. In 1928 Beijing was re-established as the national capital under the Guomindang (Nationalist Party), led by Chiang Kai-Shek. For the first time in Beijing history, the imperial strongholds, from the Forbidden City to the Temple of Heaven, were no longer forbidden to China's masses.

Progress and freedom were short-lived in Beijing. Japan invaded northern China on the eve of World War II, seizing the capital in 1937 after a valiant battle at the Marco Polo Bridge (one of many new monuments added to Beijing in the 20th century). The Japanese occupied Beijing until the war's end in 1945. Nanjing became China's new capital under the ruling Nationalist Party, but revolutionary change was in the air.

Communists and Capitalists

On 1 October 1949, a new nation — the People's Republic of China — was declared from the podium facing Tiananmen Square, and Beijing was again to serve as China's capital. This new China was indeed radically new. Led by Chairman Mao Zedong, it was the largest communist state in the world, and it would soon begin its own program to reverse and destroy the "feudal" legacy of thousands of years of imperial rule.

The Chinese Communist party first initiated a popular program of reconstruction to transform and modernize the nation. In Beijing, the ancient city walls were pulled down and the city moat was filled in. Only a few of the venerable city gates and towers remain standing today. China's first subway system now makes a loop that retraces the foundations of the city walls, with the subway stops named for the ancient city gates. Tiananmen Square was substantially en-larged, Chang'an Avenue widened, the Great Hall of the People built, the Museum of History and the Museum of the Revolution opened — all in the 1950s. Old neighbor-hoods began to be replaced by modern brick-and-concrete highrises. Beijing became its own powerful municipality (not part of any province), the seat of the new revolutionary government for the nation.

The Cultural Revolution (1966–1976) closed Beijing's doors to the outside world. Mao and his most radical follow-ers shut down the nation's institutions and went on a witch hunt for those alleged to harbor politically incorrect thoughts, behaviors, or backgrounds (which at times seemed to include anyone not waving Mao's *Little Red Book*). Many of Beijing's temples and historic sites were not only closed but severely damaged, all in the name of making a complete break with the feudal, superstitious past. Renovations as a result of this era of cultural destruction are not yet com-plete, and some ancient sites have never reopened.

Nevertheless, after the death of Chairman Mao (whose mausoleum on Tiananmen Square has be-come a much-visited mod-ern monument to China's modern "emperor"), Beijing

*Workers of the world unite!
This statue sets the tone
outside Mao's mausoleum
in Tiananmen Square.*

Enshrining the past: Confucius Temple honors China's great philosopher.

entered a period of liberal economic reform that has again transformed the capital. Under "supreme leader" Deng Xiaoping, China opened its doors to Western investment and culture in the 1980s.

By the time of Deng's death in 1997, Beijing was firmly reshaping itself as an international capital in the Western mode, complete with expressways, skyscrapers, shopping plazas, luxury hotel chains, rock concerts, and state-of-the-art computer technologies — not to mention rising crime rates, soaring pollution levels, increasing unemployment, and income disparities sharp enough to make Mao turn over in his crypt.

The skyline of the capital rises higher and higher each year, glass and steel replace brick and mud in the old courtyards, cars replace carts in the streets, and computers replace abacuses in the schools. Today's Beijing would seem to have little in common with the Beihai lakeshore of Kublai Khan and Marco Polo, the Forbidden City of the Ming, the Summer Palace of the Qing, the Temple of Confucius, or even the patriotic tomb of Chairman Mao. But China's capital has not escaped the history that shaped it, be it ancient or modern. Visitors can still see both today.

WHERE TO GO

Beijing has fascinating districts and neighborhoods to stroll. However, the main attractions are scattered throughout this sprawling city, so you'll be taking frequent taxi, bus, or subway rides no matter where your hotel is located. Following the ancient city plan, we have divided the capital like a compass, with the downtown sights in the center surrounded by quadrants to the north, south, east, and west.

The main urban area of Beijing covers 750 sq km (290 sq miles), with the Forbidden City and Tiananmen Square at the center. Chang'an Avenue bisects these two sites and forms the capital's long, wide east–west axis. A north–south axis runs 8 km (5 miles) from the Temple of Heaven through the Forbidden City to the Drum and Bell towers. Old Beijing, once surrounded by massive city walls and nine towering gates, is now encircled by a modern subway and a major expressway, the Second Ring Road (23½ km/14½ miles).

In turn, a Third Ring Road, 48 km (30 miles), encompasses most of urban Beijing, although the city is bulging outward toward the Fourth and Fifth Ring roads.

The Forbidden City and Tiananmen Square, separated by the main east–west thoroughfare, Chang'an Avenue, stand at the center of downtown Beijing. They are convenient references for locating the attractions in the north, south, east, and west districts of the city.

CITY CENTER

The center of the city contains Beijing's outstanding historical site, the Forbidden City. Across Chang'an Avenue to the south is the capital's premier modern site, Tiananmen Square. Just east of the Forbidden City is Beijing's most im-

Beijing Highlights

Beihai Park. *Downtown, northwest of Forbidden City.* The capital's oldest imperial park, with large lake, white pagoda, pavilions, and gardens.

Forbidden City. *Chang'an Avenue, center of Beijing.* This vast complex of imperial palaces and courtyards was the home of Ming and Qing rulers for six centuries.

Great Wall. *Two-hour drive north of Beijing.* You can visit celebrated Ming Dynasty portions of China's greatest tourist attraction at Badaling, Mutianyu, and Simatai.

Hutongs. *Back Lakes area north of Forbidden City.* These are the narrow, twisting alleys in Beijing's old neighborhoods, where traditional courtyard houses make for a fascinating tour on foot or via pedicabs.

Lama Temple. *Northeast of Forbidden City.* The city's most popular temple complex: resident monks, local worshippers, and splendid halls with Tibetan Buddhist statuary.

Liulichang Culture Street. *Southwest of Tiananmen Square.* The historic Dazhalan neighborhood is a restored avenue of tiled-roof antique shops, arts and crafts vendors, teahouses, and silk fabric stores.

Summer Palace. *Seven miles northwest of city center.* China's premier imperial garden — seasonal residence of Qing emperors and empresses — is Beijing's most beautiful park, filled with historic pavilions, bridges, and covered walkways.

Tiananmen Square. *City center, south of Forbidden City.* World's largest public meeting place, with Mao's tomb, Great Hall of the People, and Museum of Chinese History nearby.

Temple of Heaven. *South of Tiananmen Square.* Large park, popular with locals, contains remarkable round Hall of Prayer for Good Harvests, the emperor's shrine for imperial rituals since 1420.

White Cloud Temple. *West Beijing.* Beijing's top Daoist temple, thick with incense and ancient superstition, the best place to mingle with fervent local worshippers.

The Forbidden City was home to Ming and Qing rulers.

portant shopping street, Wangfujing Dajie. These three places happen to be within walking distance of each other, a rarity for sightseeing in the capital.

Forbidden City

Completed by the Emperor Yongle in 1420, the **Forbidden City** (Zijin Cheng) in the center of Beijing was home to 24 consecutive rulers of China during the Ming (1368–1644) and Qing (1644–1911) dynasties. The 9-m (30-ft) walls enclose 74 hectares (183 acres) of magnificent halls, palaces, courtyards, and imperial gardens, and the rooms and chambers number nearly 10,000. The Chinese call the Forbidden City the Palace Museum (Gu Gong Bownguan), and it is indeed a museum of imperial architecture, artifacts, and private collections of the emperors.

Mao's portrait graces the The Gate of Heaven, a large archway which marks the main entrance into the Forbidden City.

The main entrance is from the south, through the **Gate of Heaven** (Tiananmen), the large archway decorated with Chairman Mao's portrait facing Chang'an Avenue and Tiananmen Square. The ticket booth is due north along a central corridor at the Meridian Gate (Wumen), where audio tapes can be rented in a variety of languages. Beyond the Meridian Gate is the Outer Court, which contains three magnificent ceremonial halls and their vast courtyards. The Meridian Gate is connected to the first great hall by the Gate of Great Harmony, which has five white marble bridges.

The first hall of the Outer Court, the Hall of Great Harmony (Tai He Dian), contains the emperor's Dragon Throne. The second hall, the Hall of Middle Harmony (Zhong He Dian), contains a smaller throne, from which emperors addressed their ministers. The final hall of the Outer Court, the Hall of Preserving Harmony (Bao He Dian), is where emperors received China's best students from the annual imperial examinations that determined who would enter the bureau-

The Palace Eunuchs

For nearly 2,000 years the emperors of China required that all male servants be eunuchs, thus protecting the honor of their wives and numerous palace concubines. Working closely with rulers and members of the royal family, some of these castrated servants rose to positions of high power, amassing large fortunes and sometimes directing affairs of state. Ming Dynasty rulers were said to have employed as many as 20,000 eunuchs in Beijing's Forbidden City. The numbers gradually dwindled to just 1,500 when the last dynasty fell in 1911.

Eunuchs came from the poorest ranks of the population, often snatched as children by buyers. The Lin and Bi families of Beijing performed the official castrations, supplying certificates of authentication to the court. Educated eunuchs might become secretaries or teachers in the Forbidden City, but most ended up doing palace dirty work in the kitchen or gardens. They could be beaten for the slightest mistake by their masters — or even put to death.

Those few eunuchs who rose to position and acquired wealth in exchange for their influence were able to buy houses, land, and businesses outside the Forbidden City. Upon retirement, the wealthiest often moved to Buddhist monasteries where they had made large contributions.

While the success of the castration procedures was quite uneven (and rumors of romances between eunuchs and palace maids were constant), the eunuchs were universally pitied, often reviled and despised. In a nation where the family is the central unit and producing sons is the highest goal, the eunuchs were condemned to be outcasts — although the richest not only maintained mansions outside the Forbidden City but set up elaborate "paper" families consisting of legally registered wives and adopted children, a retinue of servants, and even their own harem of concubines.

cracy. All three halls date from 1420 but were renovated or rebuilt under the Qing emperors.

Between the Inner and Outer courts are the Eastern Exhibition Halls. The Hall of Clocks, located in the Hall of Worshipping Ancestors (Feng Xian Dian), contains the imperial collection of timepieces, many of them 18th-century gifts from England, America, and Europe. Nearby is the Hall of Jewelry, housed in the Palace of Tranquillity and Longevity (Ning Shou Gong), with another display of royal treasures, including robes worn by the Empress Dowager Cixi. The Empress Dowager's private theater, Emperor Qianlong's rock garden, and the Nine Dragon Screen (Jiu Long Bi), a 30-m (96-ft) ceramic mosaic created in 1773, are also located in this section of the Forbidden City.

Three private pavilions make up the Inner Court, located on the central axis in the northern portion of the Forbidden City. These halls were used as residences by the emperors and their families. The imperial concubines and eunuchs also lived here, with household staff often numbering over

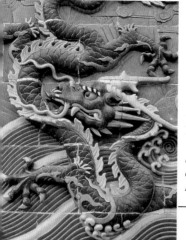

1,000. The first pavilion is the Palace of Heavenly Purity (Qian Qing Gong), the private residence of the Ming emperors. The second is the Hall of Union (Jiao Tai Dian), which contains the throne of a Qing empress. The final hall is the Palace of Earthly Tranquil-

Spot this fellow and eight other friends on the Nine Dragon Screen.

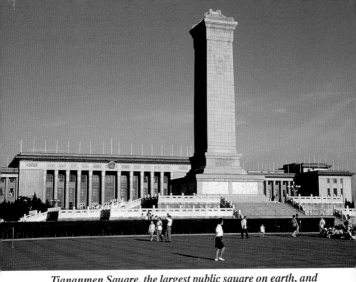

Tiananmen Square, the largest public square on earth, and site of the tragically famous 1989 student uprising.

lity (Kun Ning Gong), where the last Chinese emperor, Puyi, was married as a child in 1922.

Near the northern gate to the Forbidden City is the **Imperial Garden** (Yu Hua Yuan), filled with small pavilions, ancient cypress trees, and complex rookeries, all built during the Ming Dynasty. The final major pavilion is the Hall of Imperial Peace (Jin An Dian), a Daoist temple to Xuanwu, the God of Fire.

Tiananmen Square

Occupying 40 hectares (99 acres) directly south of the Forbidden City, **Tiananmen Square** (Tiananmen Guangchang) is the largest public square on earth. This vast expanse did not exist during the time of the emperors, but in the 20th century it became China's primary public meeting place for national ceremonies and political demonstrations. It was enlarged to its present size under Mao Zedong. To celebrate the golden anniversary of the founding of the People's Republic on 1 October 1949, Tiananmen Square was renovated, with granite replacing the old paving blocks.

The 500-year-old **Qianmen** (Front Gate), one of the original nine gates of the city wall, still stands at the south end of Tiananmen Square (next to the Arrow Tower). Most of the other gates fell when the wall was demolished during the modernization of Beijing in 1958–1959. This towering edifice, which houses a photographic exhibition of old Beijing, can be climbed for a view of the capital. The imperial court once passed through here on its annual procession to the Temple of Heaven.

Also located on the south side of Tiananmen Square is the **Mao Zedong Mausoleum** (Mao Zhuxi Jinian Bei), opened in 1977, a year after the Chairman's death. Especially popular with Chinese tourists, it consists of a reception hall — with a statue of the Great Helmsman seated on his "throne"

An imposing presence, the Great Hall of the People stretches nearly 1 km across the west side of Tiananmen Square.

— and an inner chamber, where Mao lies in state in a crystal sarcophagus. Visitors maintain a respectful silence and are quickly ushered through to a gift shop at the back.

The **Monument to the People's Heroes** (Renmin Yinxiong Jinian Bei), on the west side of the square, became internationally renowned when it served as the command post for pro-democracy demonstrators during the 1989 occupation of Tiananmen. The granite obelisk, 38 m (124 ft) high, was erected in 1958. It contains calligraphy carved in the hand of Chairman Mao and is engraved with stirring scenes of a century of Chinese revolutionary history.

The massive **Great Hall of the People** (Renmin Dahui Tang) borders the west side of Tiananmen Square for nearly 1 km (over half a mile). It opened in 1958 and has served as China's legislative headquarters ever since. Whenever the National People's Congress is not in session, the Great Hall is open to visitors, who can enter its banquet halls, 32 reception rooms (one for each province and region), and glittering main auditorium, which holds up to 10,000 delegates.

The east side of the square is home to the large courtyard halls of two museums. To the north is the **Museum of the Chinese Revolution** (Zhongguo Gemin Lishi Bowuguan), with over 10,000 items that document revolutionary politics, most focusing on events in the early history of the Chinese Communist Party (1919–1949).

The **Museum of Chinese History** (Zhongguo Lishi Bowuguan), to the south, is of more general interest. It ranks among China's top museums and has the nation's largest holdings. Its 300,000 priceless artifacts, displayed on two levels, are arranged chronologically from the Stone Age through the final dynasty, the Qing. Although bereft of up-to-date display cases and featuring explanations written in Chinese only, this museum provides the most exhaustive overview of Chinese civilization — illustrated with national treasures — of any gallery in China.

Wangfujing Street

Beijing's top shopping street is also the site of many cultural and historic attractions. **Wangfujing Street** (Wangfujing Dajie) begins a few blocks east of the Forbidden City and runs north from Chang'an Avenue.

The **Beijing Hotel** (Beijing Fandian) began as the "Grand Hotel de Pekin" under foreign management in 1917, has had several wings added over the decades, and is worth strolling through today as an architectural museum of Beijing's evolution in the 20th century. Wangfujing itself has a long history, serving as the exclusive neighborhood of the well-connected and the rich during the Ming and Qing dynasties. Westerners moved to the district in the late-19th century, and the street was known as Morrison Street for a time, after a *London Times* correspondent. Tradesmen had long done business in the neighborhood's tiny attached lanes, which are today filled with an assortment of tea shops, silk stores, art galleries, street markets, and modern shopping plazas.

The south end of Wangfujing Street is dominated by the new malls at **Oriental Plaza,** a sprawling two-floor complex featuring designer outlets and a food court on the lower ground floor with a fantastic selection of Chinese dishes from all over the world. Located on the bottom level is the "Old Beijing Street", a recreation of a former Qing-era marketplace where you can find bargain chops, fans, and other gift items. Ironically, the brand new Oriental Plaza is situated on the capital's oldest site, the recently unearthed remains of a 20,000-year-old Stone Age settlement, complete with human fossils, buffalo bones, and hunting tools. Sun Dong

An Plaza (at No. 38 Wangfujing) has seven levels of boutiques, supermarkets, and fast-food oulets. Farther up the street is Beijing's best stop for book browsers, the Foreign Language Bookstore (at No. 235), boasting the capital's largest collection of non-Chinese books and magazines. Cross the street again to find **St. Joseph's Catholic Church** (Dong Tang), the "East Church" that was leveled during the Boxer Rebellion (1900) and immediately rebuilt; it is now open for Sunday masses (in Chinese and Latin only).

At the north end of Wangfujing Street is the **China Art Gallery** (Zhongguo Meishuguan), the national art gallery of China. Within this monumental museum, built in 1959 in the Chinese style, are 14 galleries with contemporary as well as traditional artworks. There are artists at work in its studios, and recent works can be purchased in the gift shop.

> Lobby cafés in the international luxury hotels on Wangfujing Street make fine places to take a break during downtown sightseeing.

One block west, on Dongdan Street), north of Oriental Plaza on Wangfujing Street is the **Capital Hospital** (Xiehe Yiyuan), which has an emergency clinic for foreigners. It was founded in 1915, located in the mansion of a Qing Dynasty prince, and underwritten by American millionaire John D. Rockefeller. It was previously known as the Peking Union Medical Hospital.

NORTH BEIJING

The neighborhoods north of the Forbidden City are the most scenic in Beijing, encompassing imperial parks and lakes, temples and towers, princely mansions, and some of the city's most interesting older neighborhoods. An atmosphere of imperial leisure is cast by **Jingshan Park** (Jingshan Gongyuan), also called Coal Hill (Meishan), rising immedi-

*Worth the walk: Jingshan (Coal Hill) Park summit affords
a spectacular view of the Forbidden City.*

ately north of the Forbidden City. Jingshan was built by hand
from soil dredged out of the palace moat in the early-15th
century. A ten-minute hike to the summit at the Pavilion of
Everlasting Spring (Wanchun Ting) is rewarded by the finest
view possible of the Forbidden City and its golden-tiled
palaces. To the right (west) of the old Forbidden City is a new
version, Zhongnanhai, where China's communist leaders are
ensconced today (strictly off-limits to all visitors).

Beihai Park

Beijing's oldest imperial garden, **Beihai Park** (Beihai
Gongyuan), was built on the capital's largest lake over 800
years ago. Near the south entrance, in the Round City (Tuan
Cheng), is a large ceremonial vessel of green jade presented
in 1265 to Kublai Khan, who built a palace here and entertained Marco Polo on these lake shores in the 13th century.

Scenic Hortensia Island (Qionghua Dao), built from the soil
excavated to create Beihai's lake, is crowned by the **White
Pagoda** (Bai Ta), one of Beijing's landmarks. Tibetan in style,

this *dagoba* commemorates a visit by the Dalai Lama in 1651 and measures 36 m (118 ft) in height. At its foot on Jade Hill, to the south, is Yongan Temple (Yongan Si), a well-preserved Lamaist Buddhist complex. The north shore of the island is bordered by a covered walkway, known as the Painted Gallery, and a cluster of Qing Dynasty imperial halls. Located here is a traditional restaurant, Fangshan, founded by chefs who once cooked for the last emperor in the Forbidden City.

On the western shore of Beihai's lake are several pavilions and gardens built during the Qing Dynasty, including a fine rock and water garden, Hao Pu Jian, where the Empress Dowager Cixi listened to music. The Studio of the Painted Boat (Hua Fang Zhai) is another shore garden, built by Emperor Qianlong in the 18th century, famous for its large square stone pool. On the northern shore of the lake is the Studio of the Serene Mind (Jing Xin Zhai), a favorite retreat of China's last emperor, Puyi.

On the eastern shore is a double-sided Nine Dragon Screen, created in the 18th century from glazed tiles, similar to the more famous version in the Forbidden City.

The pavilions, pagodas, and rookeries on the northeast shore are known collectively as the Gardens Within Gardens, where the imperial court once enjoyed the lake. Its most arresting site is

Beihai Park's White Pagoda honors a 1651 visit from the Dalai Lama.

Little Western Heaven (Xiao Xi Tian), which consists of a square pagoda and four towers, erected as a shrine to the Goddess of Mercy (Guanyin) in 1770. Tour boats depart the eastern shore from Five Dragons Pavilion to Hortensia Island. Today, Beihai lake is no longer restricted to the imperial court, and it is the most popular spot in Beijing to rent a rowboat in the summer or to ice-skate in the winter.

Back Lakes and Hutongs

Central Beijing's three front lakes, Nanhai, Zhonghai, and Beihai, run along the west side of the Forbidden City from Chang'an Avenue north to where they connect with the three **Back Lakes** (Shi Sha Hai), known as Qianhai, Houhai, and Xihai. These lakes once comprised the route used to ship grain and luxuries via the Grand Canal to the Forbidden City. Later, this was the waterway employed by imperial barges when the emperor desired an outing. These interconnected lakes are marvelous places to stroll. The Back Lakes District contains many landmarks of old Beijing — from mansions to old temples and gardens — but it is best known for its colorful alleyways and traditional courtyard houses.

> Don't drink the water unless it's from a sealed bottle. Beijing's tap water, even in the top hotels, is not sanitary enough to sip.

At the northern tip of the Back Lakes is **Huifeng Temple** (Huifeng Si). Perched on a tiny rocky isle in Xihai Lake, it is a wonderful spot for a lake view and a picnic. East of this temple, on the north side of the Second Ring Road, is Deshengmen Arrow Tower, a gate and archers' tower from the Ming Dynasty that survived the demolition of the great city wall. Inside is a small museum devoted to the history of the local *hutong* neighborhoods. In the gate's courtyard are a coin museum and antiques market.

On the eastern shore of Houhai Lake, the middle of the three Back Lakes, is the **Soong Ching-ling Residence** (Song Ching Ling Guzhu), where the famous Soong sister who married Sun Yat-sen lived from 1963 until her death in 1981. Her estate and its 200-year-old classical garden are now a museum, filled with photographs and heirlooms of her remarkable life. On the same lake shore is **Guanghua Temple** (Guanghua Si), a small Buddhist complex that has returned to life after being severely damaged by rampaging Red Guards during the Cultural Revolution (1966–1976). Nearly two dozen monks reside here.

Sacred and scenic: Huifeng Temple is perched on a tiny rocky isle in Xihai Lake.

A few blocks east of the Guanghua Temple are Beijing's historic **Drum Tower** (Gu Lou) and **Bell Tower** (Zhong Lou). Both can be climbed for splendid views of the Back Lakes District. The Drum Tower (open 9am–4:30pm daily; free) is the more interesting of the two. The capital's first Drum Tower, from which the hours of the day were signaled with drums, was built here by Kublai Khan in 1272, rebuilt by Ming Emperor Yongle in 1420, and renovated under the Qing emperors. A side stairway leads to the balcony, where one of the 24 original watch drums remains, along with what's claimed to be the world's largest drum (made in 1990).

Qianhai, the most southern of the Back Lakes, connects to the lake in Beihai Park. It is famous for its views of the Western Hills. Under the willow trees on its western shore, vendors set up an enormous outdoor market (known as the Lotus Flower Market, or Lianghua Shichang), which sells food and hosts amateur Chinese opera singers in the evenings.

On the west side of the Back Lakes is **Prince Gong's Mansion** (Gong Wang Fu), Beijing's best-preserved example of an imperial mansion. Prince Gong, brother to an emperor and father of China's last emperor, Puyi, occupied this estate in the mid-19th century, making use of its 31 halls and pavilions as his private residence. The estate contains numerous courtyards, arched bridges, ponds, rock gardens, and its own pagoda.

The neighborhoods of the Back Lakes District are filled with the *hutongs* (alleys) and *siheyuans* (courtyard houses) that were characteristic of urban Beijing during the Ming and Qing dynasties. They are common even today, with nearly half of the capital's population living in some form of rectangular courtyard compound.

> Beijing's narrowest residential lane is Qianshi Hutong — 38 cm (15 inches) wide at one point. Its shortest is Yichi Dajie — just 9 m (30 ft) long.

Nevertheless, *hutongs* and *siheyuans* are endangered symbols of Beijing's past, constantly under threat of urban renewal. Fewer than 2,000 courtyard dwellings are preserved in cultural protection zones. Although it would have once been occupied by a single rich family (plus servants), a courtyard house today is shared by many families.

The *hutongs* can be toured on your own — on foot, by rented bicycle, or by hiring one of the canopied pedicabs in the area. But most visitors prefer a guided tour. The Beijing Hutong Tourist Agency (Tel. 6615-9097), which books tours through hotel desks, has a fleet of red-canopied pedicabs led by an English-speaking guide. Its *hutong* tour combines many of the sights in the Back Lakes District with the opportunity to step inside a courtyard house and talk with its modern-day residents.

Lama Temple and Confucian Temple

Beijing's most popular Buddhist complex is the **Lama Temple** (Yong He Gong). Built in 1694 for a prince who became the Qing Emperor Yongzheng, it was converted to a temple in 1744. Under the reign of Qianlong the temple served as the chief center of Tibetan Buddhism (Yellow Hat sect) outside of Lhasa. The Lama Temple is large and ornate, with about 200 monks in residence today.

Its five central worship halls are spacious. Between the first and second halls is the capital's oldest incense burner (1747). The throne of the Dalai Lama is in the fourth worship hall (Falun Dian). The final hall contains the Lama Temple's most revered statue, a 23-m (75-ft) image of the Buddha carved from a Tibetan sandalwood tree, its head peeking out of the pavilion's third story. The side halls have large collections of cast and carved Buddhist figures, includ-

The ornamental gateway at Lama Temple. This is Beijing's most popular Buddhist complex and home to 200 monks.

ing many Tantric statues whose more explicit features are discreetly draped in colorful silk scarves.

Across the street from the usually packed Lama Temple is  the serene **Confucian Temple** (Kong Miao), the largest shrine to the great philosopher outside of Confucius' hometown in Qu Fu. Built in 1302, the complex was long part of the Imperial College (Guozi Jian), and its courtyards teem with scores of carved stone tablets honoring students who passed the nationwide civil service examinations from the time of Kublai Khan.

The most interesting display is located in the long side building on the eastern wall. It is a museum of Beijing history that furnishes a comprehensive overview, with signs in English and Chinese. In another hall of the Confucius Temple is a complete edition of the Confucian classics carved in stone. Near the entrance of the temple (just inside the main gate) is the Donald Sussman Center for Chinese Antiquities, opened in 1995. At the north end of the complex there is a statue of Confucius and a collection of 18th-century stone drums used in Confucian ceremonies.

SOUTH BEIJING

Few tourists venture into the Xuanwu and Chongwen districts south of Chang'an Avenue and Tiananmen Square except to visit the Temple of Heaven and perhaps to walk along the charming Liulichang Culture Street. But there are other sights of interest.

The **Foreign Legation**, where foreign governments maintained their own autonomous quarter in Beijing from 1860 to 1937, lies east of Tiananmen Square. No longer the location of the diplomatic compounds in the capital, this district still contains many former embassies, clubs, barracks, churches, and commercial buildings, most now converted to Chinese institutes, banks, and offices. The architecture is fascinating.

Located along Taijichang Dajie (the former Customs Street), directly south of Dongchang'an Jie (Chang'an Avenue East), are the old Austrian Legation (now the Institute of International Studies), the Italian Legation (now the Chinese People's Association for Friendship with Foreign Countries), the private Peking Club (now the Beijing People's Congress), and the French Legation and French Barracks (now the offices of the Chinese Workers Union).

Westward along Jiaominxiang toward Tiananmen Square are the neo-Gothic St. Michael's Church, built in 1902 by the French and still active. You'll also find the German Hospital (now the Beijing Hospital) here, and the former embassies of Germany, France, Spain, Holland, and Russia. North up Zhengyi Lu (the former Canal Street) back toward Chang'an Avenue are the former Japanese Legation (now the Beijing Mayor's office) and the British Legation, once the largest Western stronghold in Beijing (occupied from 1860 to 1959), now the stronghold of the Chinese security services.

Southwest of Tiananmen Square, in the city's Xuanwu District, is the **Ox Street Mosque** (Niu Jie Qingzhen Si), the center of Beijing's most vibrant Muslim quarter. Here the capital's 200,000 people of the Hui minority — largely indistinguishable from Beijing's Han Chinese majority — practice many of the ways of Islam, which arrived in China from the far western regions of the Silk Road during the Tang Dynasty (618–907). This mosque, originally constructed in the year 996, is Chinese in style but contains a six-sided astronomical tower, a bathhouse, an Islamic prayer hall facing Mecca, a minaret for calling the faithful to prayer, and tombs of Moslem leaders dating to the time of Kublai Khan.

Southwest Beijing is also the location of the city's main Catholic church, **South Cathedral** (Nan Tang), also known as Mary's Church. It was constructed on the site of missionary Matteo Ricci's residence in 1650 and rebuilt for the last time in 1904 after being destroyed during the Boxer Rebellion. Offering masses in Chinese, Latin, and English, South Cathedral has a rock garden dedicated to the Virgin near its southern entrance on Qianmen Street West.

The **Temple of the Source of Law** (Fayuan Si), near the Ox Street Mosque, dates from the Tang Dynasty (696) and houses a national Buddhist college and religious publishing house. In addition to dozens of novice monks in training, this large temple is famous for its Ming- and Qing-era statues and bronzes, carved stone tablets, bells, paintings, and incense burners. The last of its six halls contains a large reclining Buddha 6 m (19½ ft) long.

Grand View Park (Daguan Yuan), located at the southwest corner of the lower Second Ring Road, was opened in 1986 on the former site of the imperial vegetable gardens. Built to re-create the classic garden portrayed in the popular Chinese novel *The Dream of the Red Chamber,* it is filled with traditional features of 18th-century Mandarin estates: lakes, pavilions, arched bridges, and pagodas.

The Chongwen District of southeast Beijing contains three popular attractions. Panjiayuan (known variously as the Dirt Market or Ghost Market) is the capital's top open-air market for antiques and curios, best visited as early as possible on Sunday mornings. The **Natural History Museum** (Ziran Bowuguan) has China's best display of dinosaur skeletons. It is located outside the west gate of the Temple of Heaven (Tiantan).

☛ Temple of Heaven

The Temple of Heaven (Tiantan), built under Ming Emperor Yongle in 1420 as a site for sacred rites, is located directly south of the Forbidden City. Today the site is called the **Temple of Heaven Park (Tiantan Gongyuan). The emperor would lead a procession from the palace to the altar here to perform the annual rites and sacrifices to heaven. One of China's most remarkable architectural works survives from that era of imperial ritual, the **Hall of Prayer for Good Harvests** (Qinian Dian), a circular hall with blue-tiled roofs capped by a golden sphere. The entire shrine was constructed without nails or cross beams, its magnificent arched ceiling supported by 28 carved pillars. This hall survived until 1889, when lightning burned it to the ground, but the reconstruction is superb, and the round hall has become an emblem of imperial Beijing. Unfortunately, its ornate interior can only be glimpsed from outside, since visitors are no longer allowed within.

Two other important monuments survive in Tiantan Park, both located on the axis running south from the Hall of Prayer for Good Harvests. The **Imperial Vault of Heaven** (Huang Qiong Yu), built in 1530, resembles the Hall of Prayer; stone tablets used in the winter solstice rituals were once stored here. It is surrounded by Echo Wall, into which visitors attempt to whisper messages that can be heard by friends at distant points along the wall. The

The crown jewel: the Hall of Prayer for Good Harvests is a Ming masterpiece.

southernmost monument is the **Circular Altar** (Yuan Qiu), an open platform dating from 1530 where silk was once burned as a sacrifice to the heavenly powers. Its acoustics are said to allow orations to be broadcast for miles in all directions.

Temple of Heaven Park is an excellent place to take a morning stroll. It's popular with locals, including students seeking a quiet bench for reading and citizens performing their morning *tai chi* exercises.

Liulichang Culture Street and Dazhalan Mall

The flavor of the old capital's commercial districts is best preserved along Liulichang Culture Street (Liulichang Xijie and Liulichang Dongjie) and the Dazhalan Mall (Dazhalan Jie), two conjoined avenues south of Tiananmen Square that run east-to-west for over 1½ km (1 mile).

☞ **Liulichang Culture Street**, the shopping haunt of scholars and antiques fanciers since the Ming Dynasty, was restored in the 1980s. Its tile-roofed shops sell curios, antiques, traditional art supplies, scrolls, paintings, prints, and old books. Among its renowned shops are Rongbaozhai (art and art supplies), the China Bookstore (old books), Jiguge (a teahouse featuring clay figures from tombs), and Wenshenzhai (former purveyor of fans and paper lanterns to the Qing Dynasty).

> Tipping is officially forbidden in China. However, exposure to Western ways has made it quite common to tip bellhops, hairdressers, and tour guides.

Liulichang merges with **Dazhalan Mall**, a cobblestone street closed to motor traffic that offers still more window-shopping: historic outlets for traditional herbal medicines, shoes, pickles, and silk fabric and clothing. Among the outlets is a charming Tibetan store with friendly Tibetan staff. The east end of the Dazhalan pedestrian mall is intersected by Zhubaoshi Jie (Jewelry Street), once the major theater and brothel district of Beijing and now the site of a lively sidewalk bazaar. Zhubaoshi Street connects Dazhalan directly to Qianmen and Tiananmen Square.

EAST BEIJING

The areas east of Tiananmen Square along Chang'an Avenue and northeast up the Third Ring Road (both sections of the vast Chaoyang District) have received the brunt of Beijing's modernization. Here Chang'an Avenue changes its name to Jianguomenwai Dajie, the location of some of China's finest

Bicycling Beijing

Beijing is a city devoted to bicycling. The capital's 1,000,000 motor vehicles, including its 70,000 taxis (the most of any world capital) are dwarfed by a bike population that exceeds 8,000,000. Foreigners can rent bicycles — including new multispeed mountain bikes — by the hour or day from many hotels, shops, or rental lots. Nearly every block has its sidewalk bike repairman on hand who can quickly fix flats and other ailments on the spot at unbelievably low prices.

While the crowded streets of Beijing look chaotic and dangerous, it is surprisingly easy to join the flow of other bicycles. You should give cars and pedestrians the right of way when possible. Beijingers do not ride fast, so just follow along. If your bike has a bell, clang it at intersections to warn pedestrians. Helmets are not required. Beijing's major streets have spacious separate bicycle lanes which cars, trucks, and buses are not supposed to use (but sometimes do).

Despite the superior number of bicycles, there are signs of their demise. China's output of new bikes has recently taken a spill (down to just 20 million annually), and late in 1998 Beijing actually banned daylight bicycle use on one of its busiest streets (Xisi Dong Lu, near the Xidan shopping district). It was claimed that the 100 bikes per minute there obstructed the timely flow of motorized vehicles.

international hotels and Beijing's best shopping opportunities. The same can be said for the northeast section of the Third Ring Road, where major hotels and shopping plazas are also concentrated, along with China's first Hard Rock Cafe. Located between these two stretches is the Sanlitun Diplomatic Compound, which has the capital's liveliest nightlife. The shops, cafés, parks, and historic sites of east Beijing attract thousands of international visitors by day and after dark.

Jianguomen

The eastern section of Chang'an Avenue, between the Second and Third ring roads, is known as **Jianguomen** (after one of old Beijing's nine city gates, now the site of a subway station). A number of international hotels have located here, and there also numerous shopping opportunities

At the intersection of Jianguomenwai Dajie and the Third Ring Road East there is a major shopping mall in the massive **China World Trade Center**, where outlets range from China's first Starbucks coffee shop to an ice-skating rink. Additional shopping options along Jianguomenwai Dajie include the Friendship Store, the best place to browse for Chinese gifts and souvenirs, and the **Silk Alley Market** (Xiushui Shichang), the city's most popular open-air clothing market. Once celebrated for its silks and bargain prices, the crowded Silk Alley stalls are now filled with name-brand, logo, and knockoff designer sportswear. Running north for several blocks from Jianguomenwai Dajie, Silk Alley is a lively bazaar requiring abundant bargaining and haggling skills; there are no set prices. The market leads into a quiet, modern foreign diplomatic quarter, home to embassies including those of Ireland and the US.

Just north of Silk Alley and the Friendship Store is **Ritan Park** (Ritan Gongyuan), location in imperial days of the

Silk Alley Market, once home to purveyors of the fine fabric, is now the place for designer knockoffs.

Altar of the Sun. The altar — where the emperor performed annual rites — was erected on a hill in 1530 and is today crowned by a pavilion. Ritan Park contains a serene rock garden and fishing pond in its southwest corner. On its northwest side is the large Russian Market (Yabaolu), where Chinese vendors cater to Russian traders with carpets, crafts, and clothing, including leather goods, furs, and boots.

Ancient Observatory

Beijing's **Ancient Observatory** (Guguan Xiang Tai) was built in 1442 under the Ming Dynasty. It is at the intersection of Chang'an Avenue and the Second Ring Road East; almost immediately below it is a Beijing subway station. The observatory supplanted one created by Kublai Khan. Inside the brick tower, which looks like a remnant of the old city wall, are astronomical displays, including a gold foil map of the heavens as they were plotted in China 500 years ago. On the open roof is a fine collection of Qing Dynasty bronze instruments (copies) devised by the Jesuit missionaries who resided in Beijing in the 17th century. The view from the terrace of downtown Beijing, the Forbidden City, and Tiananmen Square is superb.

Sanlitun

Located in the heart of a large foreign diplomatic district between Dongzhimenwai Dajie and the Liangma River, **Sanlitun** has become the nightlife district of Beijing. Many of its 60 or more small cafés — offering international cuisine by day and drinking and music by night — are located on Sanlitun Lu, which has been officially named Sanlitun Bar Street (Sanlitun Jiuba Jie). Many of Beijing's expatriates and foreign tourists, as well as the city's younger Chinese, gather here each summer for the sidewalk drinking, dining, and people-watching. Sanlitun cafés and bars now stretch southeast of Sanlitun Lu down a small lane called Dongdaqiao Xie Jie.

This leads to the Workers' Stadium area and Beijing's oldest expatriate American-style bar and grill, Frank's Place. While Sanlitun is devoid of historic sites, it stands out as modern Beijing's most international neighborhood.

WEST BEIJING

Two of Beijing's top attractions, the Summer Palace

Seeing stars: the Ancient Observatory, another remnant of the Ming Dynasty.

and the Western Hills, are located northwest of the capital's relentless urban sprawl. This is the beautiful, hilly countryside of the Haidian District (home to China's top universities and computer technology developers). And closer to city center, the western precincts of Beijing are the site of four major temples, the Beijing Art Museum, and the Beijing Zoo.

 ## Summer Palace

The site of imperial palaces since the reign of Kublai Khan, the **Summer Palace** (Yi He Yuan) achieved its present form during recon-

Must do: stroll through the extraordinary Long Corridor of the Summer Palace.

structions from 1749 to 1764. Emperor Qianlong saw to the expansion of the park, its hills, and its lake, and he added pavilions and halls that stand today. The imperial court used the Summer Palace as its summer home, escaping the heat of central Beijing and the Forbidden City. Today, it is the playground of locals and tourists alike. Many say it is the most beautiful imperial garden in China — a large-scale garden equivalent to a park or estate.

The Summer Palace was twice destroyed after its expansion under the early Qing emperors. In 1860, during the Second Opium War, British and French troops invaded Beijing and ransacked and ruined many of the buildings. Empress Dowager Cixi saw to a complete restoration in 1886, but the

Western armies returned in 1900 in retaliation for the siege of the Foreign Legation during the Boxer Rebellion. Undaunted, the Empress Dowager completed a second restoration in 1903. The Summer Palace became her countryside version of the Forbidden City, her residence of choice even when the heat of summer diminished. Like the Forbidden City, the Summer Palace was opened to the public in 1925.

The 280-hectare (700-acre) Summer Palace is dominated by **Kunming Lake**, which itself is subdivided into West Lake and South Lake by several causeways. **Longevity Hill** rises above the north shore. Behind its peaks is a version of Beijing's Back Lakes, created during the Qing Dynasty. The main strolling area is along the north shore of Kunming Lake, where the pavilions and courtyards are linked by the **Long Corridor** (Chang Lang). This covered promenade stretches 777 m (2,550 ft) from the Eastern Halls west to the Marble Boat. First built in 1750, it consists of 273 crossbeam sections and 4 pavilions. Nearly every exposed portion of its beams, panels, and pillars is decorated with a painted scene from Chinese myth, history, literature, or geography — 10,000 brightly painted panels in all.

Among the important imperial buildings on the east side of the Long Corridor, four are worth viewing. The Hall of Benevolent Longevity (Renshou Dian) is where Empress Dowager Cixi received court members from her Dragon Throne (which is still in place). The Hall of Jade Ripples (Yulan Dian) is where Cixi confined her nephew, Emperor Guangxu, while she ruled in his place. The Hall for Cultivating Happiness (Yile Dian) served as the Empress Dowager's private viewing box for performances in the adjacent three-story theater, which was built to honor her 60th birthday. Cixi celebrated many of her birthdays at the Summer Palace, and she was especially fond of theatrical performances, in which she sometimes played a role. This theater now contains some of her imperial garments, jewelry, and cosmetics, as well as a Mercedes-Benz said to be the first passenger car in China. The Long Corridor begins at a fourth Qing building, the Hall of Happiness and Longevity (Leshou Tang), where the Empress Dowager slept. The curtained bed, the lamps, and most of the furniture are original.

Midway along the Long Corridor at the foot of Longevity Hill is the Hall of Dispelling Clouds (Pai Yun Dian), where Cixi held her birthday parties. This hall now houses a collection of birthday gifts, including the portrait of the Empress Dowager painted by Holland's Hubert Vos upon the occasion of her 70th birthday in 1905. The Long Corridor ends at the Pavilion for Listening to the Orioles (Tingli Guan), where there is now a restaurant serving Qing dynasty imperial dishes.

Just beyond this point is the most famous (or perhaps notorious) monument in the Summer Palace, the **Marble Boat**, known officially as the Boat of Purity and Ease. To Beijingers, it is China's "ship of fools." Rebuilt with lavish materials (stone and stained glass) by the Empress Dowager in

The Marble Boat, testament to what some consider the Qing's excessive penchant for luxury at all costs.

1893, this 36-m (118-ft) statue of a boat was restored (it is said) with funds meant to shore up China's woeful navy, but it was not long before Japan completely humiliated China in battles at sea. Cixi has been blamed ever since for her profligate and selfish ways, combined with her Machiavellian rise from concubine to Empress, popularly held to be the cause of China's weakness and the fall of the last dynasty. The Summer Palace remains as visible testimony to the extravagance of the late Qing Dynasty at the expense of China's freedom and prosperity at the beginning of the 20th century.

While many scholars doubt that Empress Dowager Cixi played such a villainous role, her Summer Palace is undoubtedly lavish enough to have launched countless tales of luxury and decadence. Even today the view of Longevity Hill and its scores of tile-roofed pavilions and towers, enjoyed from a pleasure barge drifting across Lake Kunming, is a scene from a dream of old China in which emperors and empresses led lives in gardens of unimaginable splendor. Here even the bridges — connecting lake isles to the palace shores — wouldn't be out of place in a Ming or Qing scroll painting, particularly the celebrated **Seventeen-Arch Bridge** (Shiqi Kong Qiao), 150 m (492 ft) long and built of white marble.

Not far from the Summer Palace is the site of the **Old Summer Palace** (Yuan Ming Yuan). When Emperor Kangxi built this imperial park in the 18th century, it had no equal. However, after its destruction in 1860 by French and British troops, it was left to decay, and the court's attention turned to restoring the new Summer Palace. All that's left now in the Old Summer Palace are some of the most haunting ruins in China, particularly in a section known as the Garden of Eternal Spring (Changchun Yuan), where European-style halls, marble fountains, mazes, and a concert stand are now a broken jumble of ornately carved columns and arches. Every few years there are fresh announcements that the Old Summer Palace will be restored to its former glories. For now, it provides a quiet picnic grounds amidst the ruins of an empire.

Western Hills

When China's rulers really wanted to escape the heat of the city, they went farther west than the Summer Palace to the **Western Hills** (Xi Shan), romantically known today as **Fragrant Hills Park** (Xiangshan Gong yuan). Imperial villas first dotted these hillsides — 27 km (17 miles) from Beijing

Autumn at Fragrant Hills Park: history and nature achieve aesthetic balance.

— more than 800 years ago. But it was the Qing Emperor Qianlong who converted the Western Hills into a formal mountain retreat for the enjoyment of the court, complete with its own temples, lakes, gardens, and even a zoo. Late autumn is the favorite season for park visitors these days, when leaves turn a fiery red. However, locals as well as tourists come to the Western Hills year round for the natural beauty and historic sites.

Two renowned temples still survive in the Western Hills. Near the park's north gate are the four great halls of the **Temple of the Sleeping Buddha** (Wo Fo Si). In the final hall (Wo Fo Dian) there is a 5-m (16-ft) lacquered statue of the reclining Buddha (dated 1321) about to attain nirvana.

Inside the park's north gate is an even larger complex, the **Temple of the Azure Clouds** (Biyun Si), which ascends the hillside. The body of Sun Yat-sen, founder of the modern Chinese Republic, once lay in state here before removal to Nanjing; his hat, coat, and coffin are still at this temple. So, too, is the fascinating **Luohan Hall**. *Luohans* are followers of Buddha who achieve enlightenment but choose to stay on Earth to show others the way. The 500 *luohans* portrayed in this temple's carved figures range from the ecstatic to the gruesome, from the common to the surreal. Topping the temple is the Diamond Throne Pagoda (Jinggang Baozuo Ta), built in 1748 in the Indian style, with four pagodas and two stupas surrounding a 35-m (115-ft) white pagoda.

The most popular site in the Western Hills is natural: a summit known as **Incense Burner Peak** (Xiang Lu Feng), named for the image created when fog comes sweeping over it. There is a winding path to the top known as Gui Jian Chou ("Even the Devil is Terrified") as well as a chair lift (20 minutes each way). At the 557-m (1,827-ft) summit there are pavilions, vendors, and small paths into surrounding forests. There are also fine views of the lakes, temples, pavilions, and pagodas below, which can be explored upon return. On a clear day, one is tempted to linger. Here, there's an emperor's view to the southeast, commanding both the pavilions of the Summer Palace and the skyscrapers of downtown Beijing.

☛ White Cloud Temple

Beijing's most active Daoist complex, Bai Yun Guan, is better known as **White Cloud Temple**. This is also the capital's most fascinating religious site, a place of superstition and incense, mystery and spirited worship. As China's leading indigenous religion, Daoism differs from Buddhism (transplanted from India) not so much in the architecture of its temples and the art of its statuary (these are often quite similar in style) as in its practices and beliefs. Daoism emphasized nature, the individual, and the Way, but in its orga-

The Harvard of China

China's top institution of higher learning, located not far from the Summer Palace, is Peking University. For over a century it has been the prime school for Chinese intellectuals and political theorists, as well as the source of student protest movements that have changed the course of the nation.

Founded in 1898 as the Imperial University, it was renamed Peking University in 1911 with the fall of the Qing Dynasty. Mao Zedong worked here as a library assistant in 1918. In 1953, when Mao had moved up the ladder a bit (from library assistant to supreme leader), the university was moved to its present campus, where lakes and tile-roofed pavilions could still serve as models for ink-brush paintings of classical gardens.

But Peking University's students have seldom been regarded as passive mandarins or privileged Confucian idlers in love with the China of the past. They first took their progressive agenda to Tiananmen Square in 1919, denouncing World War I treaties imposed by the West and decrying China's weakness and corruption. Students appeared at Tiananmen again in 1976 to implicitly denounce the policies of Chairman Mao and his followers. Finally, in 1989, Peking University students spearheaded the occupation of Tiananmen Square, calling for greater economic and political freedoms.

Peking University today is no hotbed of political dissent. The university's new US$1.2 million library is the first of several dozen building projects that are giving the venerable campus a modern makeover. Students of "China's Harvard" seem more inclined to pursue business careers than to organize political protests.

nized form it relies on a huge pantheon of gods, goddesses, and supernatural icons promising miracles.

At Baiyunguan the first courtyard features the Wind Containing Bridge, where visitors attempt to ensure their good fortune by striking a 17th-century copper bell with coins. In the Spring Hall for the Jade Emperor, worshippers touch the golden feet of statues representing the gods of wealth. In the side halls there are shrines where the devout can appeal to the proper god to cure eye problems, ensure the birth of a son, pass an examination, get a good job, and increase longevity. Every one of these "wishing halls" is usually jammed with locals, who are often dressed in their most expensive clothes for the tour. Festivals on the first and fifteenth of the lunar month are especially lively times to visit. At the rear of the complex there is a large rock garden, a courtyard, and classrooms where many novice monks are trained in Daoism.

Baiyunguan was founded in 739 and received its present name in 1394. Most of the halls date from the Qing Dynasty, although Yuanchen Hall, where visitors try to locate the deity on the zodiac of their birthday, dates from the time of Kublai Khan. Just south of this temple complex is Tianning Si Ta, the Temple of Heavenly Tranquillity Pagoda, built during the Liao Dynasty (907–1125), making it Beijing's oldest surviving building. The 13-story tower is 58 m (190 ft) high and is decorated with fine Buddhist carvings.

Baiyunguan Temple, Beijing's principal shrine for Daoist worship.

White Pagoda Temple

Extensively renovated and enlarged in 1998, the **White Pagoda Temple** (Bai Ta Si) is renowned for its Tibetan-style pagoda (usually called a *dagoba* or stupa). The white pagoda at this temple is larger than the more famous one in Beihai Park. In fact, it is the largest of its type in China, built in 1279 during the reign of Kublai Khan.

The main gate of the White Pagoda Temple (located on the north side of Fuchingmennei Dajie), the first courtyard, and the museum are new. The museum houses many Buddhist artifacts and statues discovered on the temple grounds, as well as a *sutra* copied out by Emperor Qianlong. This rare manuscript, unearthed in 1978, was composed in the emperor's own hand in 1753. Beyond the museum to the north are three finely restored prayer halls. The Hall of the Great Enlightened Ones is stuffed with thousands of little Buddhas. The white pagoda itself, rising 51 m (167 ft), is last and, like most *dagobas,* remains sealed, its holy treasures and relics somewhere beneath or inside the imposing structure.

Five Pagoda Temple

North of the Beijing Zoo, across the Nanchang River, is one of Beijing's most beautiful sights, the **Five Pagoda Temple** (Wu Ta Si). Its singular main hall consists of a square stone building 7½ m (25 ft) high, its outside walls decorated with one thousand niches, each containing an engraved Buddha. The hall is crowned with a cluster of five elaborate towering pagodas, with stairs inside leading up to a view from the roof. The five-pagoda building is more Indian than Chinese in style. It was built in 1473, during the early Ming Dynasty.

The temple was originally part of the larger Zhengjue Temple complex (built during the reign of Ming Emperor Yongle in the 1420s and sacked by Western troops in 1860

Beijing's Temples, Churches, and Mosques

Big Bell Temple (Da Zhong Si). *31A Beisanhuan Xi Lu, Haidian District*. Open 8:30am–4:30pm daily. Admission 10 yuan.

Confucian Temple (Kong Miao). *13 Guozijian Jie, Dongcheng District*. Open 8:30am–5pm daily except Monday. Admission 10 yuan.

Five Pagoda Temple (Wu Ta Si). *24 Wutasicun, Haidian District*. Open 8:30am–4pm daily. Admission 3 yuan.

Huifeng Temple (Huifeng Si). *Second Ring Road North, Xihai Lake, Xicheng District*. Open 8am–8pm daily. Admission 5 jiao.

Lama Temple (Yong He Gong). *12 Yonghegong Dajie, Dongcheng District*. Open 9am–4pm daily except Monday. Admission 15 yuan.

Ox Street Mosque (Niu Jie Qingzhen Shi). *88 Niu Jie, Xuanwu District*. Open 9am–sunset daily. Admission 10 yuan.

South Cathedral ("Mary's Church": Nan Tang). *141 Qianmenxi Dajie, Xuanwu District*. Weekday services at 6am (Latin), 7am (Chinese); Saturday at 6:30am (Latin); Sunday at 6am (Latin), 7am (Latin), 8am (Chinese), and 10am (English).

Temple of the Azure Clouds (Biyun Si). *Fragrant Hills Park, Haidian District*. Open 7:30am–5pm daily. Admission 10 yuan.

Temple of the Great Transformation (Guanghua Si). *Ya'er Hutong, Dongcheng District*. Open 8am–5pm daily. Admission 2 yuan.

Temple of the Sleeping Buddha (Wo Fo Si). *Northeast of Fragrant Hills Park, Haidian District*. Open 8am–4:30pm daily. Admission 5 yuan.

Temple of the Source of Law (Fayuan Si). *7 Fayuan Si Qianjie, Xuanwu District*. Open 8:30am–11am and 1:30pm–4pm daily except Wednesday. Admission 10 yuan.

White Cloud Temple (Bai Yun Guan). *6 Baiyunguan, Xuanwu District*. Open 8:30am–4:30pm daily. Admission 8 yuan.

White Pagoda Temple (Bai Ta Si). *Fuchingmennei Dajie, Xicheng District*. Open 9am–5pm daily. Admission 10 yuan.

and 1900). On the same grounds today is the **Beijing Stone Engraving Art Museum**, an open-air display of over 500 ancient stone carvings and inscribed stone pillars.

Big Bell Temple

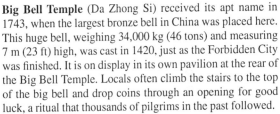

Big Bell Temple (Da Zhong Si) received its apt name in 1743, when the largest bronze bell in China was placed here. This huge bell, weighing 34,000 kg (46 tons) and measuring 7 m (23 ft) high, was cast in 1420, just as the Forbidden City was finished. It is on display in its own pavilion at the rear of the Big Bell Temple. Locals often climb the stairs to the top of the big bell and drop coins through an opening for good luck, a ritual that thousands of pilgrims in the past followed.

Since the early 1980s the Big Bell Temple has served as China's bell museum, with over 700 bells in its collection. A few of the bells are modern (cast to commemorate recent events), and some are from foreign countries, but most are Chinese antiquities. Among the bells displayed in the various halls and pavilions are some that are 4,000 years old. For a small fee, visitors can sound a set of stone chimes that date from the Warring States Period (475–221 B.C.).

Beijing Art Museum

Doubling as museum and temple, the **Beijing Art Museum** (Beijing Yishu Bowuguan) is housed in the halls of the **Wanshou Temple**, the Temple of Longevity. Although the temple, renovated in 1761 by Emperor Qianlong, is no longer active, it contains many old structures, including the bell and drum towers in the first courtyard, which date from 1577. The Empress Dowager Cixi used to lodge overnight in this temple on her voyage by royal barge from the Forbidden City to the Summer Palace. The museum was closed for renovation at the time of writing, but the temple and museum will re-open late in 2003.

No longer used for worship, Wanshou Temple is still a sacred space — it's the Beijing Art Museum.

At the rear of Wanshou Temple is a large rock garden with shrines to the gods of three of Buddhism's sacred mountains in China, two pavilions built in 1761 (one housing a stone tablet with the engraved signature of Emperor Qianlong), and two arched gates constructed in the style of 18th-century Europe.

Beijing Zoo

The **Beijing Zoo** (Beijing Dongwu Yuan) is the creation of Empress Dowager Cixi, who in 1908 converted this private Ming Dynasty garden estate into a preserve for some 700 exotic animals imported from Germany. The entrance gate dates from the late Qing Dynasty, and many of the exhibition halls seem nearly as old. Even the outdoor pens seem quite dated. With some 6,000 animals the zoo is the largest in China, but despite its notable collection of giant pandas, Siberian tigers, golden monkeys, and red-crowned cranes, the facility is in need of modernization. Few foreign visitors are happy with the size and condition of the cages, although the new Panda Garden, featuring a half-dozen adult pandas and twin babies, is a bit more spacious and a step in the right direction. The adjacent Beijing Aquarium, a state-of-the-art marine park, has over 50,000 aquatic species in residence.

EXCURSIONS

The Great Wall is China's most popular attraction. From Beijing, splendid sections of the wall can be enjoyed at several locations. Less visited (and less crowded) are two of China's greatest imperial cemeteries: the Ming Tombs and the Eastern Qing Tombs. Two other major excursions from Beijing are the Peking Man Museum at Zhoudian and the vast imperial retreat and temples of Chengde.

Great Wall

Construction on the Great Wall began as long ago as the fifth century B.C.; it winds across northern China for over 10,000 km (6,200 miles). However, the **Great Wall** (Wanli Chang Cheng) that most visitors see consists of a few beautifully restored segments near Beijing that were built, extended, or refortified during the Ming Dynasty (A.D. 1368–1644). The Ming builders were the first to finish these massive earthen fortifications with brick. They built a new section of the wall running for 630 km (390 miles) just north of Beijing as a massive buffer and early warning system against invaders from the north. This stratagem was to fail, as the Manchus eventually broke through, overthrew the Ming, seized Beijing, and established the Qing Dynasty in 1644 — China's last imperial line.

Hundreds of thousands of laborers were conscripted over the centuries to extend and repair the Great Wall, and many of them lie buried in its ruins. In the seventh century A.D. over a million workers were said to be involved in this project, but in the centuries since — until the Ming Dynasty — much of the wall fell into ruin. Even today, most of its length has not been kept up, the earthen remnants barely visible. While it is often reported that the Great Wall is the only manmade object visible from the moon, the claim is dubious at best. Still, it is China's grandest achievement, on par with Egypt's pyramids and a handful of other ancient wonders of the world.

The Great Wall is best appreciated at four main sites north of Beijing: Badaling, Mutianyu, Juyongguan, and Simatai. Three of these four segments have been carefully refurbished, with the exception of Simatai, which is largely untouched since the days of the early Ming Dynasty. The earthen foundations of the wall and watchtowers, as well as much of the brick-work, are

Parks and Attractions

Beihai Park. *1 Wenjin Jie, Xicheng District*. Open 6am–9pm daily. Admission 10 yuan.

Beijing Zoo. *Xizhimenwai Dajie, Xicheng District*. Open 7:30am–6pm daily. Admission 15 yuan (adults), 8 yuan (children).

Great Hall of the People. *West side of Tiananmen Square, Chongwen District*. Open 8:30am–2pm daily, except during legislative sessions. Admission 35 yuan.

Qianmen Gate. *South end of Tiananmen Square, Chongwen District*. Open 8am–sunset daily. Free admission.

Temple of Heaven Park. *Qianmen Dajie, Chongwen District*. Open 6am–6pm daily (until 9:30pm in the summer). Admission 35 yuan.

Western Hills (Fragrant Hills Park). *Haidian District*. Open 8am–sunset daily. Admission 10 yuan.

original, most of it 300 to 500 years old, although extensive re-modeling and fresh materials have been added.

The look and the feel are authentic enough, once one is on the wall itself, out of sight of the shops, vendors, tour buses, parking lots, and cable cars below. The hordes of tourists are another modern addition, of course, but it is possible at all these sites to walk beyond the crowds. The steep mountain scenery is spectacular and the air is usually quite clear. The sheer steepness of the wall's stone stairs and the precarious footing provided by the irregular treads are what most surprise first-time visitors. As it snakes up and down the peaks and ridges, the wall conforms to a challenging topography, one that leaves many tourists gasping for breath. But the views from China's ancient Dragon of Stone make the journey unforgettable.

Carefully restored in 1957, the Great Wall at **Badaling**, 67 km (42 miles) northwest of Beijing, is the most-visited portion of the wall. The mountain setting is spectacular and the wall rises and falls steeply as it winds up and down the ridges. About 7 m (24 ft) high and 5 m (18 ft) wide, this Ming Dynasty fortification is built of tamped earth, stone, and brick. Beacon towers of stone and brick are mounted at regular intervals. It is possible to walk the stairs of the restored section for about 2 km (1½ miles) before reaching the crumbling remains of the original wall on either end.

At the northern terminus, there is a cable car connecting the wall to a parking lot below. The parking lots at the base of the wall are filled with vendors, stores, restaurants, and other modern attractions, including a cinema and a KFC fast-food outlet.

Badaling is crowded, especially from June through September, but it is quite beautiful. Equally attractive is the second-most visited section of the Great Wall at **Mutianyu**, 88 km (55 miles) northeast of Beijing. Mutianyu was opened to tourists in 1986 to relieve the crowding at Badaling. There is also a cable car at Mutianyu, eliminating the 20-minute hike up to the wall, and at the foot of the wall there is again a village of vendors, shops, and cafés. Mutianyu is one of the oldest restored sections of the Great Wall in the Beijing area, thought to have been built under the Ming rulers nearly 500 years ago.

Visitors can walk well over a kilometer (nearly a mile) atop these ramparts from watchtower to watchtower. At either end you can view the crumbling wall running to the horizon, broken but still visible. Surrounded by its renowned green forests, the Great Wall at Mutianya is a pleasant alternative to Badaling.

The Great Wall at **Juyongguan**, 58 km (36 miles) northwest of Beijing on the way to the Badaling section, is the newest portion of the wall open to tourism (1998) and the nearest to the capital. Juyongguan contains a massive guard tower marking one of the Great Wall's most celebrated mountain passes. This guard tower, built in 1345, is decorated in Buddhist carvings, with inscriptions in Chinese, Tibetan, Sanskrit, and languages of the northern tribes. Some of the temples and parks clustered at the pass in the days of the Ming dynasty have also been restored here. The wall can be walked for 4 km (2½ miles) as it winds over the peaks of the Taihang Mountains.

The Great Wall

The least restored, least crowded major segment of the Great Wall near Beijing is at **Simatai**, 124 km (77 miles) northeast of the capital. Not only is Simatai rather far from the capital, it is also quite uncrowded and unreconstructed. Its stairways and watchtowers resemble those crumbling edifices one can only glimpse from Badaling, Mutianyu, and Juyongguan. The natural scenery is dramatic, and the ruined state of the wall gives Simatai a romantic feel (although there is a cable car to the top). It is also dangerous, with broken stairways leading up some of the 70-degree inclines. Other portions are in such ruins that one must walk along the outside of the wall on steep, narrow paths, where the footing is sometimes difficult.

With its ruinous nature and dramatic scenery, the Wall at Simatai casts its own spell.

From the village at the base of Simatai there is a half-mile gravel path to the first stairway, which skirts the small Simatai Reservoir. The reservoir divides the Simatai wall from another section, known as Jinshanling, which adventurous hikers can also tackle. Simatai consists of 14 beacon towers, each about 400 m (a quarter mile) apart, which were once used to transmit fire and smoke signals — tower by tower — to the Chinese armies encamped below should an enemy be sighted. The highest of the beacon towers (known as Wangjinglou) stands at an elevation of 986 m (3,235 ft), affording a grand view southwest toward Beijing. Locals say the lights of the capital are visible on clear evenings from here.

Ming Tombs

The valley of the **Ming Tombs**, 50 km (31 miles) northwest of Beijing, is the final resting place of 13 of the 16 Ming emperors. Courtyards and elaborate pavilions, similar to those in the Forbidden City, cap underground burial chambers where the emperor, with his empress and concubines, is entombed.

Buried treasure: the Ming Tombs reveal the royal desire to be buried in style.

Here, a Spirit Way (Shen Dao) 6½ km (4 miles) long — the most renowned graveyard entrance in China — forms a grand introduction to the valley. It is lined with arching entrance gates and an avenue of stone animals (12 pairs of creatures, including lions and elephants) and court officials (6 pairs), the statuary dating from 1435. Inside the Dragon Phoenix Gate are the tombs, of which three have been restored and opened to visitors.

The tomb of Emperor Yongle (Chang Ling) is the largest, although its underground palace, where the emperor and his empress are buried, has not been opened. Nor have the 16 satellite vaults, where Yongle's concubines are entombed. The massive courtyards and pavilions above Yongle's burial chambers have been restored, and they house some of the Ming Tombs' excavated treasures, including imperial armor.

The burial palace of Emperor Wanli (Ding Ling) honors the 13th Ming emperor, who ruled from 1573 to 1620. His burial vaults, 27 m (88 ft) below ground, are made of marble and cover 1,200 sq m (13,000 sq ft). His white marble throne, golden crown, and red coffin (along with the coffins of his wife and first concubine) remain in the tomb. The Zhao Ling tomb is also open but is less impressive.

The Ming Tombs were once a staple of tours to the Great Wall at Badaling, but foreign tourists have seldom been impressed by the site, finding it dank and poorly restored. A more interesting imperial cemetery is the Eastern Qing Tomb site, although it is located at a much greater distance from Beijing.

Eastern Qing Tombs

Nearly as vast and monumental as the Forbidden City, the **Eastern Qing Tombs** (Dong Qing Ling), 125 km (78 miles) northeast of Beijing, require a considerable daytrip to view. The journey over country roads, while scenic, is slow. Emperor Sun Zhi (1644–1911), the founder of the Qing Dynasty, selected this remote spot in a large mountain valley while on a hunting expedition. It is China's largest royal cemetery, with the tombs of 5 emperors, 15 empresses, and over 100 members of the Qing court. Three of China's most famous rulers are buried here, including Emperor Qianlong (1711–1799), Emperor Kangxi (1654–1722), and the notorious Empress Dowager Cixi (1835–1908).

> Since 1997 smoking has been prohibited on all public transportation and at public attractions where posted. Violators are subject to fines on the spot.

Like the Ming Tombs, the Eastern Qing Tombs are entered via a long Sacred Way, lined with 18 pairs of stone animals and court officials. The oldest tomb (Xiao Ling) is that of the founder of the Qing Dynasty, Sun Zhi. His tomb is unopened, but the 28 pavilions and halls on the site can be visited. The tomb of Emperor Kangxi (Jing Ling) is also unopened, but its magnificent above-ground halls contain many original imperial treasures, including Kangxi's Dragon Throne. The tomb of Emperor Qianlong (Yu Ling) is open. Located 54 m (177 ft) underground, it consists of nine immense vaults and the marble coffins of the Manchu emperor and his five favorite consorts.

The most lavish tomb is that of Empress Dowager Cixi. Above her underground palace, inside a sacrificial hall, is a wax museum showing Cixi in full regalia as Goddess of Mercy (her favorite Buddhist deity). The underground palace contains her gold-and-lacquer coffin. Unfortunately, the coffin was desecrated in 1928 by a warlord who also plundered the tomb's treasures, including 25,000 pearls and a burial quilt studded with rare pearls. Many of the treasures survived, however, and are now on display in the galleries above her tomb.

Peking Man Museum

The **Peking Man Museum** is located 50 km (31 miles) southwest of Beijing in the village of Zhoukoudian, whose name has become synonymous with Chinese paleontology. In the hills and caves of Zhoukoudian archaeologists found the skull of a new ancestral link to mankind, *Homo erectus pekinensis* — Peking Man. This 1929 discovery suggested that man's closest ancestor might have lived in Asia as well as Africa. Excavations of the site continued until 1937, when most of the fossils were carried out of war-torn China by foreigners, never to return.

The cave on Dragon Bone Hill, where Peking Man lived 690,000 years ago, showed evidence of a community numbering up to 40 individuals. Nearby caves contained fossils and artifacts from more-recent Stone Age settlements (20,000 to 50,000 years ago). These caves may now be visited, their treasures housed in the nearby Peking Man Museum. Here there are molds of the missing skulls, an array of stone tools, the bones of prehistoric beasts, some human fossils, and a modern statue of Peking Man himself.

The royal summer palace at Chengde has everything an emperor might need, including eight Buddhist temples.

Chengde

The small city of **Chengde** (formerly known in the west as Jehol), 250 km (155 miles) northeast of Beijing, requires an overnight stay for visitors based in the capital. But it's worthwhile for anyone interested in seeing the monumental remains of the Qing Dynasty, as well as its most spectacular Buddhist temples. Chengde became the imperial resort of the Qing rulers, who built a royal city and park here rivaling that of the Forbidden City and Summer Palace in Beijing.

The Qing rulers never forgot their nomadic Manchu roots, and Emperor Kangxi developed this remote valley in the countryside as a summer court and hunting ground in 1703. It was here that Kangxi's grandson, Emperor Qinalong, received the first official delegation from the West ever to visit China, a British team headed by Lord Macartney in 1793. And it was here that Lord Macartney refused to kow-tow (bow) before the emperor, ending any hopes for a peaceful opening of the door to trade in the 18th century.

The Chengde Summer Palace today is demarcated by a wall 9½ km (6 miles) around, and its grounds comprise the largest surviving imperial garden in China. Among the palaces and halls still in place are the Front Palace, where the emperors conducted official court business, and nine courtyard halls in plain, rustic style. Beyond this cluster of imperial halls and residences is a large park with lakes, bridges, pavilions, rockeries, and the grasslands and hills where the court enjoyed sports on horseback. There are copies of famous Chinese gardens here, as well as small temples and multilevel viewing pavilions.

Chengde's other main attractions are the temples in the hills outside the park Many of these "Eight Outer Temples" have a strong Tibetan flavor. All were built under Emperor Qinalong between 1713 and 1779. The Mount Sumera Longevity and Happiness Temple (Xumifushou Miao) commemorates the Panchen Lama's visit to Chengde in 1779. A copy of the lama's residence in Shigatse, Tibet, it is crowned by a pagoda decorated in green and yellow tiles. The Small Potala Temple (Putuozongsheng Miao), built in 1769, is even larger and more lavish, covering 22 hectares (54 acres). Its great red hall evokes the Potala Palace in Lhasa, and the arcades within are filled with Buddhist treasures, including sensual figures related to the esoteric Buddhism of the Red Hat sect.

Beyond these and the other temples is Hammer Rock (Bangchui Shan), a massive stone pinnacle that can be reached by ski lift or hiking trails. The view from this 18-m (60-ft) natural tower of the valley below, the imperial park, and the surrounding Buddhist temples reveals the wealth and scale of the Qing Dynasty at its height. In 1820 this imperial summer villa was all but abandoned after Emperor Jiaqing was killed here by a bolt of lightning. Less than a century later, the Qing Dynasty itself was destroyed by Republican forces, ending China's last period of imperial rule.

Museums

Ancient Observatory. *2 Dongbiaobei Hutong, Chaoyang District*. Open 9am–5:30pm daily. Admission 10 yuan.

Beijing Art Museum. *In Wanshou Temple, Xisanhuan Lu, Haidian District*. Open 9am–5:30pm daily except Monday. Admission 10 yuan.

China Art Gallery. *1 Wusi Dajie, Dongcheng District*. Open 9am–5pm daily. Admission 15 yuan.

Eastern Qing Tombs. *Malanyu, Zunhua County, Hebei Province*. Open 8:30am–4:30pm daily. Admission 81 yuan.

Forbidden City. *Chang'an Jie, Dongcheng District*. Open 8:30am–5pm daily. Admission 40–60 yuan.

Mao Zedong Mausoleum. *Tiananmen Square, Chongwen District*. Open 8:30am–11:30am (also 2pm–4pm Tuesday and Thursday); closed Sunday. Free admission.

Ming Tombs. *Changping County*. Open 8am–5:30pm daily. Admission 50 yuan.

Museum of Chinese History. *East side of Tiananmen Square, Chongwen District*. Open 8:30am–3:30pm daily except Monday. Admission 30 yuan.

Museum of the Chinese Revolution. *East side of Tiananmen Square, Chongwen District*. Open 8:30am–5pm daily except Monday. Admission 2 yuan.

Natural History Museum. *126 Tianqiaonan Dajie, Chongwen District*. Open 8:30am–5pm daily except Monday. Admission 20 yuan.

Peking Man Museum. *Zhoukoudian Village, Fangshan District*. Open 8:30am–6pm daily. Admission 20 yuan.

Prince Gong's Mansion. *17 Qianhai Xi Lu, Xicheng District*. Open 9am–5pm daily. Admission 5 yuan.

Soong Ching-ling Residence. *46 Houhai Beiyan, Xicheng District*. Open 9am–4:30pm daily. Admission 8 yuan.

Summer Palace. *Haidian District*. Open 7am–sunset daily. Admission 30 yuan; an additional 10–25 yuan for the Old Summer Palace.

WHAT TO DO

O nce a sleepy capital with little to do but sightsee by day, Beijing has opened considerably to the outside world since the days of Chairman Mao. Entrepreneurs have enlivened the shopping scene and given the capital its first dose of nightlife in recent years. Beijing is becoming a modern international capital, but one with strong Chinese characteristics that keep it an interesting and distinctive place to visit.

SHOPPING

Beijing has some of the world's best places to shop for Chinese-made goods and traditional arts and crafts, often with prices far below those paid in the West. The capital is renowned for its selection of silk fabrics and clothing, embroidery, pearls, jade, porcelains, cloisonné, lacquerware, carpets, furniture, antiques, and artwork (both contemporary and traditional).

The most popular shopping streets are Wangfujing Dajie downtown, Liulichang Culture Street and the Dazhalan Mall south of Tiananmen Square, and Xidan Street west of city center (the favorite of locals). All three of these avenues are superb for strolling and window-shopping. Most shops and stores stay open seven days a week from about 9am to 8pm or later. Some English is spoken in most shops. Few stores accept credit cards, so carry plenty of Chinese cash. ATMs are appearing in the capital, but don't count on finding one when you need it (see MONEY, page 115). Sunday is the most crowded day of the week to shop.

You can survey the variety of goods available in Beijing (from crafts and souvenirs to jewelry and carpets) and determine their fair market prices by visiting the city's most comprehensive department store for tourists, the Friendship

Store, located well east of the Forbidden City (at 17 Jianguomenwai Dajie).

Although small shops, department stores, and large modern shopping plazas carry a wide range of goods these days, the best places to find bargains are the street markets and bazaars scattered throughout the city. Although their numbers are dwindling as Beijing modernises at a breakneck pace, these open-air markets are still the most interesting places to shop in Beijing.

Hidden treasures — Markets are full of intriguing items, and at bargain prices, too.

Best Buys

Antiques. Beijing has antiques galore — and plenty of fakes, too. Any item created between 1795 and 1949 must have a red wax seal to allow export from China. Hotel shops and the Friendship Store are the most reliable antiques dealers, and they often provide international shipping services for purchases. The antiques shops along Liulichang Culture Street are worth browsing, as is the Panjiayuan Market on Sunday mornings (see page 81). Among the most popular antiques for sale in Beijing are Qing- and Ming-era furniture, porcelains, jewelry, wood carvings, screens, and scrolls.

Art. Beijing has a number of contemporary art galleries in the Wangfujing area and in some of the leading hotels (notably the China World and Holiday Inn Crowne Plaza).

A number of Beijing's artists are developing international followings. Reproductions of classic and traditional landscapes and Chinese masterpieces are sold at most galleries as well, as are low-priced painted scrolls that can be framed at home.

Arts and crafts. The traditional handmade items of China, including paper kites and fans, ceramic teapots, bamboo knickknacks, lacquerware, chopsticks, and cloisonné bracelets, are widely available in department stores and from vendors at tourist sites. They should be quite inexpensive, particularly when purchased from streetside vendors. Craftworkers in China are turning out an increasing number of fine ornaments aimed at foreign shoppers; these make perfect Christmas presents to carry back home.

Carpets. Chinese carpets of silk or wool should be inspected carefully. The colors should not be fading and the threads should be fine and tightly woven. Handmade carpets from the far western provinces and from Tibet are popular in Beijing. Begin shopping at the Friendship Store or the Beijing Carpet Import and Export Corporation on the first floor of the Hong Kong Macao Center (Third Ring Road East).

Cashmere. Cashmere sweaters and other wool creations have been popular with recent shoppers. Department stores and clothing stores in shopping plazas carry a full range of wool and cashmere garments in Western sizes, well made and priced far below overseas retail markets.

Chops (seals). Everyone who was anyone in China had their own carved stamp, called a *chop,* usually a palm-sized stone block that was dipped in a special red ink. This ink stamp served as an official signature and seal. *Chops* are still used widely in modern China. At the Friendship Store, in the markets, and in some hotels, master carvers can quickly create a personalized *chop* with the purchaser's name engraved in any language, including Chinese characters, for an inexpensive and unique souvenir or gift.

Collectibles. Nearly every open market, sidewalk stall, and alley bazaar has plenty of old collectibles for sale. The Mao buttons and Mao posters have become highly collectible. Old Chinese coins, Buddhist statues, wood carvings, and handpainted plates can all be had cheaply on the street if you bargain long and hard.

Jade. China's most prized precious stone is also quite difficult to judge. Unless you are with an expert, buy only what you like at a price you can easily afford. Some jade is fake. Color, transparency, smoothness, and the skill of cutting determine the price. Check the Friendship Store first to see what you get for your money.

Pearls. The Chinese gem traditionally associated with love can be an extremely good buy in Beijing. The third floor of the Hongqiao Market (see page 81) has become the capital's leading outlet for freshwater and saltwater pearls, usually sold in tassels. Prices range from as little as 20 yuan to over 20,000 yuan. Look for uniformity in the size, shape, and color of a string of pearls. The best pearls are large and highly lustrous.

Silk and embroidery. This "Land of Silk" has excellent selection and prices in silk fabrics and finished garments. Department stores, the Friendship Store, some hotel shops, and specialty silk shops carry good selections in Western sizes. Many of these outlets also carry inexpensive embroidered goods, such as tablecloths and sheets. Try the Yuanlong Embroidery and Silk Store at the south entrance to the Temple of Heaven or the Ruifuxiang Silk and Cotton Store on the Dazhalan Mall off Qianmen Dajie.

Tea. Packaged teas are quite affordable in the land that invented this drink. Small tea shops along Wangfujing and Liulichang streets are good places to shop for loose-leaf green teas and teaware. Trustworthy outlets include the Jiguge Teahouse at 132 Liulichang Dong Jie and the Bichu Tea Shop at 233 Wangfujing Dajie.

Shopping Malls and Plazas

The Friendship Store on east Chang'an Avenue and the aging Wangfujing Department Store (255 Wangfujing Dajie), once purveyors of Beijing's most up-to-date fashions and top merchandise, have been superseded by the sudden eruption of huge shopping malls and plazas. Boutiques with an international flair, designer-label outlets, specialty stores, fast-food restaurants, coffee shops, supermarkets, department stores, and cinemas — linked together by mezzanines, escalators, and glass elevators — have all gathered under single roofs across the capital. Although the prices are high by local standards and much of the merchandise is imported, careful visiting shoppers can still find bargains at the Beijing malls.

Beijing's premier mega-malls are located along Wangfujing Street. The vast malls at the Oriental Plaza and the six-story Sun Dong An Plaza together feature hundreds of shops ranging from a Chinese supermarket and silk and clothing outlets to McDonald's and London Fog. The Xidan shopping district, about 2 km (1½ miles) west of the Forbidden City, and the Beijing New World Center by Chonguenmen also host massive shopping centers to rival those of Wangfujing.

The Lufthansa You Yi Shopping Center serves those staying at the international hotels in northeast Beijing on the Third Ring Road. China World Trade Center's shopping plaza (at 1 Jianguomenwai Dajie) has been enlarged by the opening of more shops and an ice-skating rink. This mall is also home to an Internet café and China's first Starbucks coffee shop. Finally, for those who tire of shopping for Chinese

At Friendship Stores, the vibe is international. Lots of imported items for sale here, and a multilingual staff.

goods, there's the Palace Hotel Shopping Arcade, the most upscale collection of shops in China, with such international names as Gucci and Armani.

Markets and Bazaars

Beijing's open-air markets are disappearing as the city modernizes, a number of them having been (permanently) closed or otherwise relegated to indoor spaces. Nevertheless Beijing's markets and bazaars still offer the most interesting shopping ventures in the capital. Bargaining is the rule. The vendors are experts, language presents no barrier to negotiations, and buyers should exercise patience and caution. It helps to have a notion of the market value of the merchandise by first checking out prices in stores. Street markets

Homespun — China has been producing coveted silk goods for hundreds of years.

should have the lowest prices of all, but the initial price set by the vendor is always on the high side.

The Silk Alley Market (Xiushui Shichang), on Jian-guomenwai Dajie within a few blocks of the Friendship Store, is Beijing's most popular clothing market. The passageways are jammed with stalls. Although silk goods are becoming scarce, design-er-label sportswear, ties, and luggage are abundant and cheap if the buyer is willing to haggle.

> If you pay more than half of a market ven-dor's initial asking price, you've proba-bly paid too much.

The Lido Market, across from the Holiday Inn Lido Hotel on the way to the airport, has 100 stalls — all indoors — carrying many of the same goods as the Silk Alley Market often at better prices. The Panjiayuan Antique and Curio Market (variously known as the "Dirt Market," "Ghost Mar-ket," and "Sunday Market") is the most interesting to browse in Beijing. Located well south of city center inside the Third Ring Road, it goes into full swing at sunrise every Sunday morning, when over 100,000 visitors sift through wares ranging from antiques and collectibles to ceramics and family heirlooms.

Other markets specialize in certain merchandise. The Chaowai Flea Market, north of Ritan Park, is known for its antiques, carvings, and furniture. Adjacent to the Chaowai Flea market is the Yabaolu Market (known as the "Russian Market"), which has a good collection of wool and leather goods. The shoe market is also located here, right by the north gate of Ritan Park. The Lotus Flower Market (He Hua Market), at the southern edge of the Back Lanes (Hou Hai), sells hand painted scrolls and old books. The Hongqiao Market (also known as the Chongwenmen Market and the Farmers' Market), on the northeast edge of the Temple of Heaven (Tiantan) Park, is the best place to shop for jewelry bargains, especially pearls.

More adventurous shopping experiences can be had at one of Beijing's numerous so-called Flower and Bird Markets, which primarily cater to Beijingers. The Guanyuan Market, south of Chegongzhuang subway stop along the Second Ring Road West, and the Farmer's Market by Nongkeyuan South Gate in the Haidian District, are fascinating to browse and often have the cheapest prices for scrolls and antiques.

ENTERTAINMENT

From traditional Chinese entertainment to modern Western music, Beijing offers a fairly full calendar of events for visitors, headlined by performances of the Peking Opera and China's best acrobatic troupes. Your hotel concierge or tour desk has current schedules and can book tickets for you. Check also the English-language newspaper *China Daily* or the free weekly and monthly guides published for foreigners, such as *City Weekend, That's Beijing,* and others that are distributed to hotels and cafés. They list a wide range of entertainment possibilities as well as special events and concerts. Beijing also has several teahouse theaters presenting samplers of traditional entertainment forms along with snacks or dinners. Finally, the capital has a growing number of late-night spots (some with live pop music) and discos that welcome foreign visitors.

Peking Opera and Acrobatics

Peking Opera (Jing Ju) today varies little from the form it assumed during the Qing Dynasty about 250 years ago. The costumes, choreography, instruments, and singing — all quite unique to China — might seem strange to Westerners, but these highly stylized elements are part of a familiar tradition that many Beijingers love. Other areas of China have their own regional styles of opera, but Peking Opera is definitely the most famous.

Chinese opera becomes more comprehensible and enjoyable when the plot is known (it's usually a historic drama or tragic love story) and when subtitles (in English) are projected on a side-screen. It is also helpful to know that the masks, painted faces, and costumes identify each character's social role and personality, and that the live music, with its gongs and cymbals, often functions like a film score to emphasize the action on stage.

With the closing of the centuries-old Zhengyici Theater (an opera venue since 1713), the best place to take in an evening of exotic opera Beijing-style is the Liyuan Theater in the Qianmen Hotel (175 Yong'an Lu). Here spirited excerpts from three or four operas are performed most nights, with simultaneous English subtitles provided (as well as a choice of snacks).

Other opera theaters of high repute include the Chang'an Grand Theater (7 Jianguomenwai Dajie), and the new Dawancha Opera Tower, located just around the corner from the famous Laoshe Teahouse, on Qianmen Street West. Admission prices vary widely depending on the seat location and snack or meal options, ranging from as little as 20 yuan to over 200 yuan for the best seat and treats in the house.

Acrobatics are part of most opera performances, but this 2,000-year-old tradition in China has produced its own highly entertaining performers. Some of the best acrobatic groups are based in Beijing. When not on an international tour, the Beijing Acrobatic Troupe performs at the Wansheng Theater (95 Tianqiao Market). The Sichuan Acrobatic Troupe often uses the Chaoyang Theater, and the Chinese National Troupe performs at Tiandi Theatre (10 Dongzhimen Nan Dajie).

The traditional opera, an age-old Chinese art form, proves that heroes and villains are the same in any language.

Teahouses

To see snatches of China's traditional performing arts in a setting appropriate for an imperial banquet, try one of Beijing's special teahouses. At these intimate dinner theaters, decorated in Qing Dynasty fashion (carved wood trim, paper lanterns, and red columns), customers can enjoy local snacks or full Chinese meals at their tables while viewing a variety of acts on stage, including opera highlights, acrobatics, magic shows, ethnic dancing, puppetry, storytelling, and comedy.

The two top teahouse theaters in the capital are the Lao She Teahouse (3 Qianmenxi Dajie), with nightly variety shows and snacks, and the Tian Qiao Happy Teahouse (113 Tianqiao Market), with balcony seating and a staff outfitted in Qing costumes. The Tian Hai Teahouse (Sanlitun Lu) offers an even more intimate theater on Friday and Saturday nights only.

Nightlife

Much of Beijing's contemporary music scene is centered in the Sanlitun area, a favorite of expatriates and foreign visitors looking for comfortable bars and late-night international cafés. Local Chinese also frequent these spots, where the live music ranges from rock to jazz. Prices for drinks (especially for imported wines, spirits, and beers) are high for Beijing but are about on par with those in the West. Sanlitun Lu features several dozen café bars in the space of a few blocks, some of which never close.

Among the most popular Western-style café bars in Beijing are Frank's Place (east of Worker's Stadium), an American-style bar founded by an American in 1990; John Bull Pub (44 Guanghua Lu), a very English-style pub with darts and a British menu; and Henry J. Bean's (1 Jianguomenwai

Dajie), a bar and grill with rock bands and dancing. Local Chinese pop and rock groups can be heard in the Sanlitun area at Hidden Tree (12 Dongdaqiao Xie Jie). Beijing even has several Western-style sports bars, including the Grandstand in the Holiday Inn Lido Hotel, the Pit Stop in the Harbour Plaza Hotel, and the immense Sports City Café in the Gloria Plaza Hotel.

For live jazz, the best bets are the CD Jazz Club (Nongzhanguan, Third Ring Road East) on weekends and the Sanwei Bookstore (60 Fuxingmenwai Dajie) on Friday nights. Beijing's plushest jazz club — often attracting international performers to its piano bar — is Aria, an upscale bar and grill located in the China World Hotel (1 Jianguomenwai Dajie). Open nightly and featuring a Cajun-style menu and atmosphere, the new and very popular Big Easy (Chaoyang Park South Gate) hosts jazz and blues bands that you can enjoy from the lounge or the second floor balcony. For fans of disco Vogue (Gongrentiyuchang Street East, northeast of Worker's Stadium), serves foreign drinks in its Art-Deco lounge, while the wild Hot Spot (south of the Jiangguang New World Hotel), has stage shows every night. Other popular venues include NASA (2 Xitucheng Lu, Haidian District), and Poachers Inn the Park (Tuanjiehu Park), with its English pub

Beijing's nightlife is vibrant.

and stone dance floor. The most international late-night dance floor is at Beijing's own Hard Rock Cafe (8 Dongsanhuan Bei Lu), the first such franchise in China.

RECREATION AND SPORTS

Although most visitors to the capital do not come for out-door pursuits or sports, Beijing does have a variety of recreational activities. Most international hotels maintain full-service fitness centers with exercise machines, saunas, indoor swimming pools, and other facilities such as tennis courts, with day rates for non-guests. The city parks are fine places for jogging, exercises, *tai chi,* walking, and other early morning workouts. Golf, bowling, and billiards are the three most popular recreational sports.

Beijing also offers bungee jumping (at the Shidu Bungee Jumping Facility in the Fangshan District), paintball (at Color Me Purple in Wanfangting Park), rock climbing (at the Qidagudu Climbing Club in the Xuanwu District), horse-back riding (check with the Movenpick Hotel), and shooting (at the China North Shooting Range near the Great Wall Badaling — where even machine guns are for rent).

Golf. Beijing's top course is the Beijing International Golf Club, located near the Ming Tombs. The Beijing Grand Canal Golf Club, east of Beijing, has night golf. Near the air-port, the Beijing Country Golf Club provides 36 holes. The newest championship golf course, designed by Graham Marsh, is the Huatang International Golf. The closest course to the city is the Chaoyang Golf Club, a 9-hole course with a driving range. All these courses are open to the public (make reservations through your hotel), and they rent clubs and provide caddies. Greens fees start at about 1,000 yuan.

Bowling. Modern bowling lanes enjoyed a boom in Bei-jing during the 1990s, with alleys located in the Holiday Inn

Lido, Beijing International, and other hotels. The bowling alley in the lower basement of the China World Hotel has special off-hour rates during the day.

Ice-skating. Beihai Park and the Summer Palace both offer superb outdoor ice-skating in the winter, with skate rental at stalls on the shoreline. Indoor skating is available at the Ditan Ice Arena in Ditan Park and at the underground shopping center connecting the Traders and China World hotels (1 Jianguomenwai Dajie).

Spectator sports. Beijing's two professional teams, the Beijing Ducks (basketball) and the National Guardians (soccer), play at Workers' Stadium in northeast Beijing. Both have strong followings in a country where fans know European football stars by name and Michael Jordan is a household name (known in China as Fei Ren, the "Flying Man").

ACTIVITIES FOR CHILDREN

Beijing has dozens of attractions for its children, and many of these can be enjoyed by visiting families. The Beijing Zoo (see page 62) has long been a prime attraction with its pandas and tigers, and next door there's the new and elaborate attraction, the Beijing Aquarium. At the south gate of the Workers' Stadium there's also the Blue Aquarium, with its 100-m (328-ft) underwater tunnel. Water parks with sluices, slides, and swimming pools include the Yuyuantan Water World (in Yuyuantan Park, on the Fourth Ring Road East), Beijing's largest, and the Tuanjiehu Manmade Seashore (in Tuanjiehu Park, on the Third Ring Road East), with its artificial white-sand beach and outdoor swimming pool. Inside Daguan Park, Tongle Yuan houses an animal game farm and holds performances daily, twice before noontime and twice in the afternoon at 2pm and 4pm.

The Beijing Amusement Park (west side of Longtan Lake

Calendar of Events

January–February. *Lunar New Year* — also called "Spring Festival" — is China's biggest celebration, held every year on the first day of the lunar calendar (1 February 2003, 22 January 2004, 9 February 2005, 29 January 2006, 18 February 2007). On the first three days all offices and banks and many shops close down in the capital. Gifts are given, the year's debts are paid off, relatives and hometowns are visited, and everyone celebrates with large meals and get-togethers. Parks, temples, and markets hold special celebrations all over the capital. An ice-sculpture display is held at Longqingxia Park. For many people, this celebration stretches out for fifteen days.

February. The *Lantern Festival* falls exactly fifteen days after the Lunar New Year, on the first full moon. Parks and temples display decorative paper lanterns and hold celebrations punctuated by fireworks and ethnic dances.

April–May. During International Labor Day, held on 1 May and observed for five days, most places are closed except hotels, restaurants, and major sights. The Buddhist Goddess of Mercy (Guanyin), is honored each year with lively temple festivals. Celebrations take place on the 19th day of the second lunar month, about 50 days after the Lunar New Year. April is also the time of the *Qing Ming Festival,* known also as "Grave-Sweeping Day," when families visit the graves of ancestors and make offerings of food, wine, and special "spirit money," which is burned for use in the afterlife.

June–July. The *Dragon Boat Festival* occurs on the fifth day of the fifth lunar month, in early summer. Dragon boat races are held in Beijing at the Chinese Cultural Park (1 Minzu Lu), and the festival is marked by the eating of one particularly special treat, *zongzi*, a sticky rice ball wrapped in bamboo leaves. This water-spirited holiday marks the suicide of an ancient poet, Qu Yuan, who protested the politics of his time by drowning himself.

September. *Mid-Autumn Festival*, also known as the "Moon Festival," celebrates the harvest moon and a revolt against the Yuan Dynasty by ethnic Han Chinese. Held on the 15th day of the eighth lunar month, it is a favorite of Beijing's children, who march with colorful lanterns through the parks and feast on a special treat, moon cakes (sweet biscuits with red bean, bean curd, sesame, or date paste, sometimes spiced with a duck egg).

October. *National Day*, held on the first day of October, commemorates the founding of the People Republic of China on 1 October 1949. The largest National Day celebration is in Beijing at Tiananmen Square, where a patriotic rally fills the square and nearby streets. The *Beijing International Marathon* is staged annually in the third week of October, attracting thousands of international entrants who race through the streets of the capital.

October–November. The *Red Leaf Festival* is held at the Fragrant Hills Park in the Western Hills as the autumn leaves change color. The scenery is fine and the park's markets and temples hold celebrations. In mid-November there is the *China International Jazz Festival*, staged throughout Beijing annually since 1994.

Park) is the old-fashioned standard, with a Ferris wheel, go-carts, and a looping roller coaster. China's largest theme park, World Park, is located near the Fourth Ring Road in the Fangtai District. It is stocked with scale models of 100 of the world's greatest monuments, landmarks, and skylines. At the Chinese Ethnic Culture Park (Beichan Lu, on the Fourth Ring Road) costumed representatives of China's 55 minorities live in model villages and put on cultural performances.

Children are also entertained by the special effects and Hollywood sets assembled at Universal Studios in the basement of the Henderson Center (18 Jianguomenwai Dajie). Fans of miniature golf gather for a round at Kaite Mini-Golf (north entrance, Ritan Park). An indoor playground with games and slides for younger kids, Fundazzle, is located near the Workers' Stadium on Gongren Tiyuchang Lu, and a chance for children to learn such crafts as paper-making, embroidery, and pottery is provided by the Five Colours Earth Craft Center (10 Dongzhimen Nanlu, near Poly Plaza).

The Sony Explora Science Center in Oriental Plaza (Wangfujing Street) features fun and interactive science and technology exhibits that both entertain and educate. Kids will also enjoy Beijing's outdoor attractions: the Great Wall, the Summer Palace or Behai Park, the Temple of Heaven, and strolling the alleys and streets of Beijing's new and old neighborhoods.

Beijing is rich in amusements for children.

EATING OUT

Beijing offers a sumptuous banquet of eating choices unrivaled in variety by any other city in China. Every regional cuisine — from Sichuan to Cantonese — is well represented among the capital's restaurants, headlined by such Beijing specialties as Peking duck, Northern China pastries, Mongolian hot pots, and imperial dishes prepared according to recipes once used in the Forbidden City. Beijing also offers a full range of international and Western-style restaurants, both inside and outside its major hotels. The favorite dishes of many Beijingers (for low price as much as for taste) consist of local favorites prepared by vendors who line streets, alleys, and night markets with their small coal-burning stoves ablaze.

When and How to Eat

Meals are a primary concern of Beijingers, perhaps the most important events of daily life. Chinese restaurants and cafés keep fairly limited hours, serving breakfast 7am–9am, lunch 11:30am–2pm, and dinner 5pm–8pm, although hotels have longer hours (often maintaining 24-hour restaurants). International buffet brunches are popular in hotels on Sundays (11am–3pm). Night markets serve local snacks and favorites from dusk to midnight, although there is no assurance of proper hygiene. Café bars in the Sanlitun district and elsewhere serve Western foods and snacks well into the wee hours.

Chinese cuisine is usually served "family style," meaning that diners help themselves to each item or course from a single large platter at each table. Chopsticks are the norm (practice at home if possible), but Western-style utensils are becoming quite common in most restaurants that regularly serve foreign visitors, as are English-language menus.

At banquets, service is also "family style." The evening's dishes are served one at a time, fresh from the kitchen. Each new dish is placed on a small platform tray that can be rotated by the diners. The host often serves guests with the first sampling from each item; thereafter, guests can serve themselves. It is not impolite to leave unfinished portions on one's plate. In general, follow your host's lead.

> **Don't leave your chopsticks standing upright, embedded in rice or food. This is a traditional symbol of death.**

Rice is normally served at the end of a meal, but guests may request a bowl of steamed rice at any time. Appetizers on small plates come first, followed by a soup and the main entrées. Fruit slices constitute dessert at a typical Chinese banquet or large meal. Rice is typically eaten with the bowl held near the mouth; soup may be slurped, and noodles may be "inhaled."

The key element is to enjoy the meal and not to stand on ceremony. Meals are a time of enjoyment and relaxation, although in a traditional banquet there is seldom time at the end to converse. The host simply stands up, signaling an abrupt end to the feast.

The Chinese food in Beijing is prepared to local tastes, and it is quite different in flavor and presentation from that served overseas, being more bold than delicate, more basic than subtle, but usually quite delicious.

Beijing Cuisine

No Beijing visit is complete without a sampling of the local specialties, especially the famous Peking duck. Since Beijing is located in the north of China and experiences cold

For a quick breakfast try jian bing (egg pancakes) or youtiao, deep fried bread sticks.

weather, it has developed a hearty fare that relies more on bread, noodles, potatoes, cabbage, and vinegar than on rice, seafood, and chili sauces. The local food is not known for its fiery seasonings, but garlic, salt, ginger, and other pungent spices are common.

Peking duck is Beijing's most famous specialty, and there are some venerable restaurants that feature this as their mainstay. The duck is roasted whole over an open flame, presented at the table, then carved into small strips. Noted for its crispy skin and fat, the duck is placed on a thin pancake, seasoned with plum sauce and spring onion, rolled up, and eaten with the fingers or chopsticks. The Quan Jude chain of duck restaurants has been in business in Beijing for over a century.

Equally famous in Beijing are its *jiaozi* (bite-sized steamed dumplings) filled with vegetables, meats, or seafood. These resemble what's known in southern China and around the world as *dim sum.* Diners often season these treats with vinegar. The capital's wonderful dumplings are available from streetside vendors or at special *jiaozi* restaurants, or as part of a complete dinner with spring rolls and noodles at the Sihexuan Restaurant in the Jinglun Hotel.

Imperial cuisine comes from the recipes developed for the royal court in Beijing's Forbidden City. Elaborate and complex, using exotic ingredients (swan's liver, lake turtles), it survived China's last dynasty, the Qing (1644–1911), and in the hands of former court chefs appeared in some of Beijing's finest restaurants. The Fangshan Restaurant at Beihai Park serves its version of imperial dishes and banquets (using noodles, pork, duck, and winter vegetables) in an old mansion. A newcomer, the Li Family Restaurant, housed in a traditional courtyard house in a *hutong,* uses the same dynastic recipes and has become the capital's most popular (and difficult to book) eating experience among visitors.

Cultural Revolution cafés are also trendy newcomers in Beijing, specializing in the simple countryside fare of steamed breads, oily noodles, and steamed cabbage that many Beijingers experienced during the bleak years of social upheaval (1966–1976). Cafés such as Heitudi (Black Earth) and Sunflower Village have spare, unadorned interiors, clay dishes, and Mao posters to evoke the era.

Mongolian hot pot restaurants are popular all over Beijing, in summer as well as winter. Lamb is the favored meat, sliced so the diner can dip it into the cauldron of boiling oil in the center of the table and cook to taste. A variety of other cook-it-yourself items are on hand, including fish, noodles, bean vermicelli, cabbage, and potatoes. The nomadic Mongolian tribes to the north (who eventually conquered China and ruled it under Kublai Khan) introduced this cuisine to the capital, along with the barbecue. Diners at the Mongolian Gher (Movenpick Hotel) can try either the hot pot or the barbecue, prepared by Mongolian chefs and served in a traditional *yurt* (a round felt tent).

The night markets of Beijing serve up samples of *jiaozi,* noodles, and lamb kebabs from their streetside stalls. The largest such market is Donghuamen, a downtown street running west from Wangfujing and east of the Forbidden City. Any time of day, street vendors all over Beijing dish up the favorite local snacks, including *baozi* (stuffed steamed buns), *huntun* (won-ton soup), *jian bing guozi* (crepes with hot sauce), *miantiao* (noodles), and *youtiao* (deep-fried dough strands), as well as more exotic fare such as scorpions and other delicacies for the daring.

Regional Chinese Cuisine

The most popular regional fare in Beijing — and in fact around the world — is Cantonese. Known for its seafood, sauces, exotic ingredients (snake, monkey), and such delicacies as shark's fin and bird's nest soup, southern cooking (including Chaozhou as well as Cantonese) graces some of Beijing's most upscale Chinese restaurants. Notable among these are Summer Palace in the China World Hotel, Shang Palace in the Shangri-La Hotel, Fortune Garden in the Palace Hotel, and Tingliguan, located in an old pavilion at the Summer Palace. There are several good restaurants specializing in the spicier foods of Hunan province and the fruits and vegetables of southwest Yunnan. A popular Cantonese breakfast, Dim Sum is best enjoyed at the award-winning Sampan Restaurant in the Gloria Plaza hotel. Growing in popularity are Beijing's Shanghai restaurants, famed for

(near the Second Ring Road East) and the Metro Café (near Workers' Stadium).

Fajitas, enchiladas, and other Mexican dishes are best sampled at the Texan Bar and Grill in the Holiday Inn Lido. Fanciers of British fish and chips have the John Bull Pub (near the Second Ring Road East). American fare is superb at Louisiana (Beijing Hilton), an elegant restaurant with the best wine list in Beijing, and quite good at Frank's Place (near Workers' Stadium), the Hard Rock Cafe (Third Ring Road East), and Henry J. Bean's (China World Trade Center).

Finally, should one succumb to fast-food cravings, Beijing has an abundant supply of quick burgers, fries, pizzas, and chicken seemingly on every corner, with over 50 McDonald's, over 20 KFCs, a smattering of Pizza Huts, A&Ws,

The Pop Food Invasion

American fast foods and drinks are so popular in Beijing that many Chinese parents complain about the impact on their children's health. But despite a campaign in the 1990s to launch a counter-offensive by encouraging local fast-food venues, the foreign brands have triumphed. The world's 10,000th Kentucky Fried Chicken outlet opened in Beijing in 1998. KFC was the first US fast-food chain to enter China, establishing its 700-seat flagship site near Tiananmen Square in 1987. McDonald's came to Beijing later, in 1992, but it has become the fast-food king in the capital. According to a recent survey, many Beijing students eat at McDonald's as often as ten times a month, despite the fact that a hamburger, soda, and fries cost five to ten times more than a meal of traditional snacks in the streets.

and Kenny Rogers Roasters, and even outlets for Haagen-Dazs, Dunkin' Donuts, and Starbucks.

What to Drink

China invented tea *(cha)* and has thousands of years' experience in its brewing. The light green tea is favored, although the darker "red" teas (known is the West as "black") are sometimes available. Coffee *(kafei)* is available at most restaurants, and Western-style coffeehouses are starting to catch on. Better restaurants, especially in hotels, are now brewing up lattés and some stronger coffees that are more to Westerners' taste than the watery instant coffees that are common throughout China. Bottled water, imported and local, can be purchased at stores and on nearly every street corner.

Foreign-brand sodas and soft drinks *(qishui)* are a staple at Beijing cafés, groceries, and street stalls. Coca-Cola *(kekou kele),* made under license in Beijing, has long been available in the capital. Beer *(pijiu)* is perhaps the most favored drink — next to tea — among diners in the city. Imported beers are widely available and microbreweries are springing up, but the most popular beers are China's own Tsingtao (distributed worldwide) and Beijing's local product, Yanjing.

China's own wine industry is still in its infancy, but several joint ventures with overseas vintners may yet produce some world-class white wines. China's classic *huangjiu* (yellow wine made from corn millet or glutinous rice) has a high alcohol content and a 4,000-year history; it is sweet and rough. Banquets are routinely interrupted by toasts from small glasses filled with *baijiu,* a Chinese "fire water" made from sorghum. This clear spirit tests the mettle of experienced whiskey drinkers and is best drunk in modest amounts — even on the most festive occasion.

HANDY TRAVEL TIPS

An A–Z Summary of Practical Information

Note: China's international phone code is 86; Beijing's city code is 10. To dial the local Beijing phone numbers listed in this chapter from outside China, dial your international access code and then **86+10** before the eight-digit number. To dial from elsewhere in China, first dial **010**.

A

ACCOMMODATION

Until a decade ago, most Beijing hotels were little more than crash courses in culture shock, in part because China had learned the "modern" hotel business from the Soviet Union in the 1950s. Today, however, China is learning from the West, and its hotel services and facilities are often of international caliber.

Beijing hotels are graded with one to five stars by the government, with the ratings largely determined by the hotel facilities (that is, by swimming pools rather than by quality of service). One- and two-star hotels are quite basic affairs, often shabby, with indifferent service. The few budget hotels that are officially approved for foreign guests are favored by adventurous backpackers and those willing to rough it.

Beijing's three-star hotels represent a major step up in comfort and price. They possess a range of modern conveniences, including reasonably clean and usually functional private bathrooms, money-exchange and tour counters, business centers, restaurants, satellite TV, and a few staff members conversant in English. Service and housekeeping levels are well below those of four- and five-star hotels, however.

In fact, Beijing's stable of deluxe accommodations is impressive: almost all four- and five-star hotels are of international level. Some have foreign management teams, particularly those affiliated with international hotel chains (Shangri-La, Gloria, Holiday Inn, Swissôtel, Radisson, Kempinski, Mövenpick, Hilton, Sheraton). The dozen or more five-star hotels in the capital are quite grand, but so are their room rates (on par with fine hotels in Europe and North America). Prices are steep, too, in hotels of lower rank, and decent choices in the moderate and budget classes (three stars and below) are nearly nonexistent. There are no B&B, hostel, or camping options in or near Beijing.

From late November through early April, however, many hotels do lower their rates, and competition year round often leads to special rates, particularly when a visitor books ahead (which one must do in May and October, the busiest months). Most business and independent travelers make reservations long before arriving in Beijing. While excellent deals are sometimes offered at the hotel counters in the Beijing Capital Airport, counting on last-minute reservations is not for the faint-hearted or the wise traveler.

AIRPORT

The Beijing Capital Airport was renovated in 2000, and is China's largest, as well as one of its oldest (1980) and most crowded. The domestic and international terminals adjoin but have separate outside entrances. Located just 27 km (17 miles) northeast of city center and connected to Beijing by a modern tollroad, the airport is still about an hour's drive from most hotels (due to traffic congestion within the city). There is no rail connection.

Arrival. Passports (with a China visa) and health and customs forms are required to pass through the immigration and customs checkpoints. The process is usually quick. The arrival hall is always chaotic. Ignore touts hawking taxi rides. Near the exit is a branch of the Bank of China offering currency exchange (6am to midnight daily), as well as automated currency exchange machines. There are no airport porters, but there are self-service luggage carts.

To reach downtown Beijing, there are three options. The hotel counters near the main exit provide their own shuttle bus and limousine service (requiring reservations in advance). The Air Bus, an inexpensive public bus, departs from the front of the terminal every 30 minutes. Buy a ticket (16 yuan) at the Air Bus counter in the arrival hall. Air Bus "A" stops near the Kunlun Hotel and the Beijing Railway Station. Air Bus "B" stops near the Friendship Hotel and the

Shangri-La Hotel. A local taxi can then be hailed. The third option is an airport taxi. Ignore taxi hustlers, line up in the taxi queue at the curb, and be sure your taxi has a working meter. The taxi charge should come to about 120 yuan, including the expressway toll.

Departure. Allow at least 90 minutes to return to the airport, whether by hotel shuttle or taxi, and arrive at least two hours before scheduled departure (as ticket and security lines are long). Begin by paying the departure tax at the clearly marked tax counter (50 yuan for domestic flights, 90 yuan for international flights). This tax can be paid for only in Chinese currency. Then proceed to your airline's check-in counter on the first floor.

B

BICYCLE RENTAL

Bicycling is an excellent way to see the city, which is filled with over 8 million bikes. Major streets have special bicycle lanes. Rental by the hour, half day, or full day is offered at many hotels and by bicycle shops on the streets. The charges are inexpensive (about US$5–$10 per day) but a deposit (typically 100 yuan) is often required; avoid giving your passport or other forms of ID as a deposit. Bicycle repair is provided by curbside mechanics who set up on sidewalks all over the city. New "mountain bikes" can be hired. Always be sure the brakes work. Traffic is thick, but it is easy to get into the flow with so many bicycles on the streets.

BUDGETING for YOUR TRIP

Beijing costs are rising quickly due to constant inflation. But aside from major fixed expenses such as accommodations, prices are lower than in most Western capitals, except for imported goods and services. The US$ equivalents below are approximate.

Taxi. 15–40 yuan (US$2–$5), depending on distance.

Subway. 3 yuan (US$0.36).

Beijing

Meals. Lunch seldom costs more than US$5 and dinner buffets even in expensive hotels can be enjoyed for under US$15. Food from street vendors is much cheaper. Drinks are rather expensive, with coffee 20 yuan (US$2.50), soft drinks 10 yuan (US$1.25), and beer in a bar or restaurant 25–50 yuan (US$3–$6), but tea is often free. Western-style supermarkets stock imported goods at roughly the same prices charged overseas.

Tickets. admission to most popular attractions is 10–80 yuan (US$1.25–$10).

Guided day tours. 250–400 yuan (US$30–$50), often including lunch.

Summary. After budgeting for accommodations and overseas air tickets, travelers can expect to spend an additional US$10–$100 per day, depending on what they buy at shops and what restaurants they select.

C

CAR RENTAL

Renting a self-drive car, motorcycle, or scooter in Beijing is not an option for tourists because a Chinese driver's license and residency permit are required. Major hotels can rent chauffeured sedans to guests, although the rates are exorbitant (at least US$100 per day).

CLIMATE

Beijing is extremely hot and humid in the summer (mid-June through late August), making spring (late April through mid-June) and fall (September–October) the high tourist seasons. Winters (November through March) are cold, although usually not rainy or snowy, but few tourists visit and many attractions are closed or only partially open.

The rains are heaviest in July and August; dust storms are most frequent in March and April. Air pollution is not as large a problem as in previous years. Overall, the best weather conditions are from mid-

September through mid-November, when the capital is most crowded with tourists.

Approximate monthly average temperatures are as follows:

	J	F	M	A	M	J	J	A	S	O	N	D
°C	-4	-2	4	13	20	25	26	25	20	13	4	-3
°F	25	28	39	55	68	77	79	77	68	55	39	27

CLOTHING

Above all pack a pair of comfortable, durable walking shoes. The sidewalks take a toll on shoes and the dusty air is hard on clothing. Cotton shirts and pants are best for coping with the heat. Shorts are acceptable in summer, although few Beijingers wear them. Warmer coats and gloves are necessary from November through early April. A waterproof jacket and umbrella should be packed for changes in the weather, whatever the season. A sweater and light jacket are handy.

Temples and historic sites do not have clothing rules. Informal attire is acceptable nearly everywhere, including most fine restaurants. Sportswear is common; formal wear (skirts, dresses, suits, ties) is seldom required, except for business travelers. Most hotels provide slippers but not robes.

COMPLAINTS

Complaints may be made using the Beijing tourist hotline (Tel. 6513-0828). A quiet word to a guide, concierge, or hotel desk about poor service can be productive; losing one's temper usually solves nothing.

Complaints commonly arise over excessive taxi charges. Many hotels now provide tourists with a card identifying each taxi as it is boarded. Use this card or copy down the taxi's number to file a complaint with your hotel bell desk. Complaints can also be directed to the Beijing Taxi Administration Bureau (Tel. 6835-1150).

COMPUTERS and the INTERNET

Hotel business centers provide e-mail access for guests, and if you've brought your own computer, you can easily access the Internet from your room via Beijing's free service provider. The fee is smaller than the numerous local Internet cafes (equivalent to placing a local call). Ask the front desk how to do this.

Many hotel business centers also have personal computers and printers for rent, usually by the hour, with a full array of standard software available. Computer rental, word processing, scanning, and printing — as well as faxing and copying — are also available 24 hours a day at Kinko's (on the Third Ring Road East, north of the Jing Guang Hotel, at A11 Xiang Jun Bei Li, Dong San Huan Lu; Tel. 6595-8020; fax 6595-8218).

CRIME and SAFETY

Although Beijing remains a very safe city compared to most world capitals, petty street crime (particularly pickpocketing) is on the rise. Assaults and muggings of foreign visitors remain rare. The main office of the Public Security Bureau is at 9 Qianmen Dong Dajie, south of the Forbidden City. The emergency telephone number for the police is 110.

CUSTOMS and ENTRY REQUIREMENTS

Foreign visitors are required to have a valid passport (good for at least six months after arrival date) and a visa issued by a Chinese embassy or consulate. The stamped visa is valid only for the dates specified.

Visas. Obtain a visa application from the Chinese embassy or a Chinese consulate in your country. Send the completed application form, valid passport, and payment to the embassy according to instructions, allowing at least one month for return. A 30-day single-entry tourist visa is the most common document issued, although visas covering longer stays are available. Business travelers require special visas. If you are entering China through Hong Kong, you can obtain a Chinese visa in as little as 24 hours from authorized Hong Kong travel agents. Note that no vaccinations or inoculations are currently required.

Customs. You may bring into China up to four bottles of alcohol and three cartons of cigarettes. Guns and dangerous drugs are forbidden.

Upon departure from China, Chinese antiques must contain a red wax seal for export.

Customs allowances when returning home are as follows. *Australia:* A$400 of merchandise, 250 cigarettes or 250 grams of tobacco, 1.125 liters of alcohol. *Canada:* $500 of merchandise, 200 cigarettes, 2.2 pounds of tobacco, 50 cigars, 40 imperial ounces of alcohol. *UK:* £145 of merchandise and 200 cigarettes, 250 g of smoking tobacco, 50 cigars, 1 liter of spirits, 2 liters of wine. *New Zealand:* NZ$700 of merchandise, 200 cigarettes, 250 g of tobacco, 50 cigars, 1.125 liters of liquor or 4.5 liters of wine and beer. *US:* US$400 of merchandise, 200 cigarettes, 100 cigars, 1 liter of alcohol.

Currency restrictions. Amounts of foreign currency equaling more than US$10,000 must be declared on customs forms before entry, although there is no restriction on the amount brought in. Chinese currency (yuan) must be exchanged before departure at the Bank of China, since it is not convertible and may not be exchanged in your home country.

D

DRIVING

The Chinese drive on the right side of the road. Rules, highways, traffic signals, and road signs are similar to those in Western nations. So are Beijing's rush hours and traffic jams.

E

ELECTRICITY

The standard is 220-volt, 50-cycle AC. Hotels supply adapters, as the outlets come in a variety of configurations, the most common being the slanted 2-prong, the narrow round 2-pin, and the 3-prong types. Bring your own set of modem adapters and transformers.

Beijing

EMBASSIES

Australia	21 Dongzhimenwai Dajie; Tel. 6532-2331
Canada	19 Dongzhimenwai Dajie; Tel. 6532-3536
Ireland	3 Ritan Donglu; Tel. 6532-2914
New Zealand	1 Dong'erjie, Ritan Lu; Tel. 6532-2731
UK	11 Guanghua Lu; Tel. 6532-1961
US	3 Xiushui Beijie, Jianguomenwai Dajie; Tel. 6532-3831

EMERGENCIES

Dial the following numbers in Beijing:

Police 110. *Fire* 119. *Ambulance* 120.

If you don't speak Chinese, contact your hotel front desk or the Beijing Tourism Administration's 24-hour hotline: Tel. 6513-0828.

G

GAY and LESBIAN TRAVELERS

Beijing's homosexual community is not well organized or particularly visible, so there are no groups or organizations to contact in the capital. A few nightspots have been identified with lesbian, gay, and transsexual customers, but these places change constantly. China is strict about displays of sexual behavior, gay or straight, and even in the capital tolerance of homosexuals seems extremely limited. Nevertheless, gay and lesbian travelers will feel no discrimination. Being foreign is far more "peculiar" and overwhelming in the eyes of most Chinese than one's sexual orientation.

GETTING THERE

By air. Beijing is served by over 30 international airlines, including its own Air China. The trip is about 10 hours from the UK, 11 hours from the West Coast of North America, 12 hours from Copenhagen, 13 hours from Australia, and 15 hours from the East Coast of North

America. The flight times depend on wind conditions and the number of stops made along the way.

Most airlines offer a choice of economy, business, or first-class cabins, with some of the finest in-flight services in the world. APEX fares are considerably lower than regular full fares, but they require advance purchase (14 days) and have other restrictions. Travel agents who use ticket consolidator services might be able to find even cheaper tickets (but often of the nonrefundable variety). Bargain fares sometimes show up on Internet travel sites. Many airlines code-share internationally, meaning you will start out on one nation's airline and transfer to another nation's to reach Beijing, all on the same single ticket. Flights to China are often heavily booked, so reserve as far ahead as possible.

By train. Beijing is connected to virtually all Chinese cities, including Hong Kong, via an extensive passenger rail system. There are also connections to Moscow via the Trans-Siberian Railway. Customs and immigration procedures are handled on board. China's most deluxe train connects Hong Kong to Beijing, a 29-hour trip. The new Beijing West Station (Tel. 5182-6253), Asia's largest, and the old Beijing Railway Station (Tel.6512-8977) both have special ticket counters and waiting rooms for foreigners. Train tickets can be purchased through hotel travel services, which add a nominal service charge.

GUIDES and TOURS

Because of language barriers, sharp cultural differences, and the relative infancy of the Chinese travel industry, most visitors come to Beijing the first time as part of a group tour. Travel agents can also set up customized trips for independent travelers who wish to book a hotel in advance and be met by a local English-speaking guide in Beijing. Group tours are the more expensive option, but they are efficient and convenient.

Fully independent travelers can get their bearings in Beijing by signing up for a few of the day tours with English-speaking guides that are offered in all hotels. These tours provide a quick survey of Beijing's major sites. Taxis, the subway, and bike rental are also inexpensive means to tour the capital on one's own.

For sites outside Beijing, such as the Great Wall, independent travelers can sign up for a day tour or hire a chauffeured car with an English-speaking guide at the hotel travel desk. Adventurous travelers might want to take the slow, crowded, but interesting local and intercity buses to sites (as Beijingers do) or hire a taxi in the streets for a day's touring. The taxi fare must be negotiated with the driver.

China International Travel Service (CITS), with offices at 103 Fuxingmen Nei Dajie (Tel. 6601-1122), offers a wide range of group tours, creates customized itineraries, and provides multilingual guides.

H

HEALTH and MEDICAL CARE

Medications. There are no vaccinations required for entry into Beijing. It is easiest to bring your own prescription medicines with you, although there are hospitals that can fill Western prescriptions. Colds, upset stomachs, and diarrhea are the most common ailments among travelers. Bring your own remedies, since pain relievers and other nonprescription medicines can be difficult to locate in Beijing.

Water. Refrain completely from drinking water from the tap. The only water in Beijing that is safe to drink is bottled water (for sale everywhere) and the boiled water in hotel room flasks and thermoses. Tap water is suitable for washing, but it is not safe for drinking.

Hospitals. Several hospitals and clinics provide international-caliber care for foreign residents and tourists. The Beijing United Family Hospital, the Beijing AEA International Clinic, and SOS International (Tel. 6462-9100) all maintain 24-hour emergency facilities and pharmacies. Prices are similar to those in the West. Check if your health insurance covers you in China. If it does not, consider purchasing a short-term policy for overseas travel.

HOLIDAYS

National and local holidays observed in Beijing are listed below. Spring Festival (Chinese New Year) is the biggest holiday, lasting as many as 15 days for some people and concluding with the Lantern Festival. On the first three days, all banks, offices, and many shops are closed. Banks, offices, and many businesses close again for two days starting on 1 October, National Day, commemorating the founding of the People's Republic of China in 1949; large celebrations are staged at Tiananmen Square.

1 January	*New Year's Day*
January or February	*Spring Festival (Lunar New Year)*
January or February	*Lantern Festival*
	(15th day of first lunar month)
March or April	*Guanyin's Birthday*
	(50th day on lunar calendar)
April	*Ching Ming Festival*
1 May	*International Labor Day*
June	*Dragon Boat Festival*
September or October	*Mid-Autumn Festival (Moon Festival)*
1 October	*National Day*

LANGUAGE

While every city and region of China has its own distinct dialect, Beijingers speak a version of Chinese that is the basis for the official spoken language of the nation (called *putonghua,* or Mandarin Chinese). Nearly all Beijingers have taken classes in English (required by all schools), but outside of hotels and tourist spots, English is not well understood or commonly spoken. Nevertheless, for ordinary shopping, dining, and touring in the capital, no Chinese language skills are required, as there are enough signs in English or *pinyin* (the official system for romanizing Chinese words) to navigate by and enough clever vendors with whom to bargain.

The Berlitz *Mandarin Chinese Phrase Book and Dictionary* covers most of the situations you are likely to encounter in China. (See page 121 for a selection of useful Chinese expressions.)

LAUNDRY and DRY CLEANING

Most hotels offer excellent same-day or next-day laundry and dry cleaning services at reasonable prices. Self-service Laundromats are rare, and laundries outside of hotels are inconvenient for tourists to use.

M

MAPS

City maps are for sale in hotel gift shops and from street corner vendors. The most useful maps label streets and sites in Chinese script, *pinyin* (romanized Chinese), and English or other Western languages. Beijing maps can be purchased in advance from bookstores abroad.

MEDIA

Newspapers and magazines. China's official English-language newspaper, *China Daily,* is available free at hotel desks Monday through Saturday. It includes world news, China news, and entertainment listings for Beijing. Free monthly Beijing newspapers in English, focusing on tourist sites and entertainment, are also distributed to many hotels and cafés. Foreign magazines and newspapers — including *International Herald Tribune, USA Today,* Hong Kong's *South China Morning Post,* and Asian editions of the *Wall Street Journal, Time,* and *Newsweek* — can be purchased at kiosks and gift shops in major luxury hotels.

Television. Most major hotels carry via satellite two channels of Chinese Central Television (CCTV) and three channels of Beijing Television (BTV), all in the Chinese language. Other common selections include Star TV (Hong Kong-based, with one English-language station), CNN, CNBC, BBC, ESPN, MTV, and NHK (Japanese language). The five-star hotels offer a wider selection, including stations from Europe and Australia. In-room movie services usually include closed-circuit videos or HBO.

MONEY

Currency. China's currency, called *renminbi* ("the people's money") and often abbreviated as "RMB," is based on the *yuan,* commonly referred to in the streets as *kwai.* The yuan is divided into 100 *fen.* Ten fen equal one *jiao* (also called *mao).* For most transactions, you will use yuan notes in denominations of 1, 2, 5, 10, 20, 50, and 100. Chinese money is currently not convertible to foreign currencies outside China.

Currency exchange. Foreign currency and traveler's checks can be exchanged for yuan at the Bank of China, hotel exchange counters, and a few tourist shops. The Beijing Capital Airport maintains a branch of the Bank of China specializing in currency exchange. The exchange rates at each outlet vary only slightly; you will receive a better exchange rate for traveler's checks than for cash. A passport is required for all currency transactions. The airport also has new fast and convenient automated currency exchange machines.

Credit cards. Major credit cards are increasingly accepted at shops and restaurants in tourist areas. Look for the familiar emblems (Visa, MasterCard, American Express, Diner's Club, JCB). The Eurocard is accepted at very few locations. Major hotels accept credit cards for payment of all bills, including hotel restaurants. Some branches of the Bank of China and some hotels can also make cash advances on credit cards, but with daily limits on the amount advanced (usually no more than US$1,000).

ATMs. There are ATMs all over Beijing, but many only honor Chinese credit cards. Look for ATMs that feature Visa, American Express and other international credit card logos. Larger branches at the Bank of China (at Wangfujing, Jianguomen and elsewhere) are the most reliable. Before visiting, ask your credit card company or bank for a list of ATMs in Beijing. ATM cash withdrawals require the cardholder's pin number.

Cash. China is still a cash society, and Beijing is no exception. Most transactions outside large hotels, restaurants, and shops catering largely to Westerners require payment in yuan.

OPEN HOURS

Most government offices and banks are open Monday through Friday 9am–5pm, although some close for the lunch hour (noon–2pm). Tour desks and bank branches in major hotels keep longer hours and are usually open on Saturdays. Stores are typically open seven days a week 9am–7pm and might keep longer hours in the summer. Temples, parks, and other tourist sites are usually open from sunrise to sunset daily, although museums sometimes close on one or two weekdays each week. Hotel restaurants usually keep long hours, but independent restaurants keep shorter hours, typically 6am–9am, 11:30am–2pm, and 5pm–9:30pm. Late dinners are the exception, not the rule, but bars and cafés catering to foreigners stay open well past midnight.

POLICE

Beijing police are usually quite courteous and helpful. Their main office (the Public Security Bureau) is at 85 Beichizi Lu, on the east side of the Forbidden City. The police emergency phone number is 110.

POST OFFICES

The International Post Office, located on the Second Ring Road East (Jianguomen Bei Dajie), is open every day 8am–6pm (Tel. 6512-8120), and there is a branch near the Friendship Store on Jianguomenwai Dajie. Hotels often sell postage stamps and will mail cards, letters, and packages.

Overseas postcard stamps cost 3.20 yuan; overseas letter stamps for up to 20 g (0.5 ounces) cost 5.40 yuan. The aerogramme rate is 5.20 yuan. Overseas delivery can be rather slow (from 7 to 14 days).

PUBLIC TRANSPORTATION

Beijing is a vast, flat, sprawling city. The subway is the fastest form of public transport. City buses are the cheapest but also the most crowded, slow, and difficult way to get around. Taxis are plentiful and relatively cheap. Bicycles are sometimes the fastest way to get through the busy streets.

Subway. This is the quickest way through the city, and all rides cost just 3 yuan (US$0.25). There are two lines (operating 5am–10:30pm): the circle line traces the route of the Second Ring Road around downtown Beijing, while the crosstown line runs along Chang'an Avenue. Fuxingmen and Jiangnomen stations are the free transfer points between the two lines.

Tickets are sold at booths one level above the train platforms. No magnetic cards, passes, or tokens are used — just a paper ticket. Maps of the system (in Chinese and in romanized *pinyin* letters) are posted above each door inside the train car. A recording announces in Chinese and in English each upcoming stop. Exit signs along the platform point to main streets and sights in Chinese and *pinyin*. There are escalators only at exits, and there is no air-conditioning in the cars. But the cars themselves are surprisingly clean and the subway is fast, reliable, and seldom crowded.

Beijing

Buses. Beijing's public buses cost just 1–5 yuan for a short trip in the city, but they are bewildering to use. Come armed with a city map labeled in Chinese. A roving conductor collects fares and asks for destinations after you board. The red-and-white buses service every downtown bus stop, with buses #103 and #104 running up and down the length of Chang'an Avenue. Be sure to watch backpacks and purses while on the bus, as these can be targets for thieves.

Taxis. The most popular means of transport for those visiting Beijing, taxis are cheap and convenient. Small older taxis, usually painted red, are cramped but widely available, and they charge 10 yuan (US$1.25) for the first 4 km (2½ miles) and 1.6 yuan (US$0.20) for each additional kilometer. Newer and larger taxis, often painted black, charge a few cents more. Short trips usually cost about 20 yuan (US$2.50) in good taxis; to cross town, the fare can rise to 50 yuan or more (US$6.25). Tipping is not necessary, although most drivers are happy to receive a few yuan extra. Always make sure the taxi meter works and pay the price it shows. Don't bargain for the ride.

Bicycles. Bikes can be rented at many hotels and in some bicycle rental stores on the streets. The hourly rate varies from 10 to 20 yuan (US$1.25–$2.50) at hotels, with half-day and full-day rentals proportionately cheaper. Check for good brakes, full tires, a working bell, and a functioning bike lock; bikes must be parked in official bike parks located on sidewalks near subway stations, big stores, and tourist sites. Once you get into the Beijing bike flow, you're free to enjoy the city at your own pace.

R

RELIGION

Fewer than ten percent of Beijingers are affiliated with any religious organization, although Daoism, Buddhism, and Christianity are gaining many new adherents. The Daoist and Buddhist temples in

Beijing, best known as tourist sites, are also quite active institutions, especially on traditional festival days. Beijing also has over 200,000 Muslims and 40 mosques, with the Ox Street (Niu Jie) area south-west of Tiananmen Square the largest Muslim quarter.

Beijing's main Catholic congregation worships at the South Cathedral (Nan Tang), where masses are conducted in Chinese, English, and Latin. There are Protestant congregations and churches as well. Check with your hotel about service times and locations.

T

TELEPHONE

The international country code for China is 86. The city code for Beijing is 10.

Calling from abroad. To place a long-distance call to Beijing from overseas, dial the international access code used in your country, then 86, then 10, then the 8-digit Beijing phone number.

Calling from inside China. *Domestic calls:* To call Beijing from other destinations in China, you must add a zero to the city code: 0+10. To call from Beijing to another city in China, dial 0, then that city's code and the local number. *International calls:* to reach an overseas destination from Beijing, dial China's international access code, 00, then the country code, then the area/city code and the local phone number. The country code for the US and Canada is 1, for the United Kingdom 44, for Australia 61, for New Zealand 64, for Ireland 353, and for South Africa 27. You can reach an international operator by dialing 115 in Beijing.

All major hotels in Beijing have IDD (International Direct Dial) in-room telephones (but some hotels charge a connection fee). Hotel business centers also provide IDD telephone services (with a 15 percent surcharge). Calling-card calls can be made from IDD phones, but check with your card company or hotel, as a local access number might be required.

Beijing

Public phone booths (requiring local phone cards, which can be purchased in hotels and shops) can be found on many major downtown Beijing streets. Some are equipped to handle long-distance and international calls.

TICKETS

It is easiest to book tickets for entertainment and events — such as the opera or acrobatics — through hotel travel desks or the hotel concierge, rather than directly at the venue's crowded and often distant ticket office.

TIME ZONES

Although China stretches across four time zones, all of China set their clocks to Beijing time. Beijing is eight hours ahead of Greenwich Mean Time (GMT+8). It is 8 hours ahead of London, 9 hours ahead of Western Europe, 13 hours ahead of New York, 16 hours ahead of Los Angeles, and 2 hours earlier than Australia.

The following chart lists the times in selected cities in winter months when it is 8pm in Beijing. China does not employ Daylight Savings Time in the summer, when times in most of the rest of the world are one hour later.

Los Angeles	New York	London	Paris	**Beijing**	Sydney	Auckland
4am	7am	noon	1pm	**8pm**	10pm	midnight

TIPPING

By law, tipping is not allowed in the People's Republic of China. However, in current practice bellmen, room-service waiters, and hired guides are usually tipped 10–20 yuan and taxi drivers appreciate finding their fares overpaid by a few yuan.

TOILETS

For many tourists, public toilets are a tale of woe and terror in much of Beijing (and throughout China): they tend to be thoroughly unclean, with the "squat" toilet still common. Carry your own toilet paper (and even your own disinfectant spray, if queasy). Don't expect hand-washing facilities or privacy. Some public toilets (those that charge a small admission) have Western-style facilities and attempt cleanliness.

Public toilets are often down sidestreets, with a "WC" sign posted on the corner. It is usually best to search out a good hotel or fine restaurant when in need.

TOURIST INFORMATION

In Beijing your best sources of tourist information are your hotel tour desk or concierge and the free local monthly papers in English that cater to foreigners with news of sites, restaurants, and entertainment.

Tourist information is also available at the main office of China International Tourist Service (CITS) at 103 Faxingmen Nei Dajie (Tel. 6601-1122). The Beijing Travel Agency is located at 28 Jiangnomen Nai Dajie (Tel.6515-7111). In addition, there is a tourist hotline: Tel. 6513-0828.

Before your trip. Overseas, CITS has opened several China National Tourist Offices (CNTO) to provide tourist information.

New York City	350 5th Ave., Suite 6413, New York, NY 10118; Tel. (212) 760-9700
Los Angeles area	333 W. Broadway, Suite 201, Glendale, CA 91204; Tel. (818) 545-7504
London	4 Glentworth St., London NW1; Tel. (0171) 935-9427
Sydney	44 Market St., Sydney NSW 2000; Tel. (02) 9299-4057

China travel on the Web. CITS posts a helpful planning and reservations site for Beijing visitors on the Internet at <www.citsusa.com>. Another useful website for planning a trip to Beijing is <www.chinesebusinessworld.com>, which includes ac-

Beijing

cess to a biweekly newsletter put out by the International Community in China (ICIC).

Two more Beijing tourist sites are at <www.tour-beijing.com > and <www.beijinghighlights.com>. The Beijing Tourism Administration's tourist magazine, *Beijing This Month,* along with its monthly calendar, feature stories, city map, and useful advertisements, is also available online at <www.cbw.com/btm>. Using these sites, it is possible to map out a trip to Beijing well ahead of time. There are also links for making online hotel reservations. (Americans can even download visa application forms and instructions from <www.China-embassy.org>.)

The travel sections of such websites as Microsoft Expedia (<www.expedia.com>), Travelocity (<www.travelocity.com>), and Yahoo! (<www.yahoo.com>) can make planning your trip to Beijing — from reserving air flights to making hotel reservations — an armchair affair.

WEIGHTS and MEASURES

Length

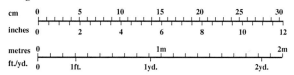

Weight

Temperature

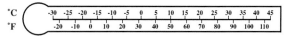

USEFUL EXPRESSIONS

Accommodation

I'd like a single/ double room.	**wo shiarng yao yee- ge dan-ren/shwarng- ren farng-jian**	我想要一个单人/ 双人房间。
I'd like a room with a … bath/shower.	**wo shiarng yao yee- ge yo yü-garng/lin- yü de farng-jian**	我想要一个有浴缸/ 淋浴的房间。

Communications

Where's the post office?	**yo-jü dsai na-r**	邮局在哪儿？
A … yuan stamp, please.	**ching gay wo yee- jarng … yüan de yo-piao**	请给我一张… 元的邮票。
Where's the mailbox?	**na-r yo yo-tong**	哪儿有邮筒？
Where's the nearest telephone?	**foo-jin na-r yo dian-hwaa**	附近哪儿有电话？
I'd like to send a fax.	**wo shiarng song yee-fen chwan-jen**	我想送一份传真。

Customs and Entry Requirements

I have only the nor- mal allowances.	**wo j dai le jung- charng shian-e**	我只带了正常限额。

Emergencies

Call the police!	**kwai jiao jing-cha**	快叫警察！
Danger!	**way-shian**	危险！
Fire!	**sh-huo la**	失火啦！
Get a doctor!	**kwai jao yee-shung**	快找医生！
Help!	**lai-ren na**	来人哪！
I'm ill.	**wo shung-bing le**	我生病了。
I'm lost.	**wo mee-loo le**	我迷路了。
Stop thief!	**jwaa-dsay**	抓贼！

Health and Medical Care

It hurts here.	**jer-lee tung**	这里疼。
headache	**tou-tong**	头痛
sore throat	**sarng-ds tung**	嗓子疼
stomachache	**way-tung**	胃疼

Beijing

Language Tips (General)

I don't understand.	**wo boo dong**	我不懂.
Please.	**ching**	请.
Thank you.	**shie-shie**	谢谢.
Yes. (correct)/No. (incorrect)	**dwee/ boo dwee**	对 / 不对.
Excuse me. (I'm sorry.)	**dwee-boo-chee**	对不起!
I need to contact the ... consulate.	**wo shü-yao gen ... ling-sh-gwan lian-shee**	我需要跟 ...领事馆联系.
Hello./Hi!	**nee-hao**	你好.
Good morning/ afternoon.	**dsao-sharng hao/ nee-hao**	早上好. / 你好.
Good evening.	**wan-sharng hao**	晚上好.
Good night.	**wan-an**	晚安.
Good-bye.	**dsai-jian**	再见.
good/bad	**hao/hwai**	好 / 坏
big/small	**da/shiao**	大 / 小
cheap/expensive	**pian-yee/gway**	便宜 / 贵
quiet/noisy	**an-jing/chao-nao**	安静 / 吵闹
old/new	**jio/shin**	旧 / 新
old/young	**nian-lao/nian-ching**	年老 / 年轻
beautiful/ugly	**piao-liarng/cho-lo**	漂亮 / 丑陋

Lost Property

I've lost my ...	**wo de ... dio le**	我的...丢了.
wallet	**chian-bao**	钱包
handbag	**sho-tee-bao**	手提包
passport	**hoo-jao**	护照

Money

Can I exchange foreign currency here?	**jer-r nung dwee-hwan wai-bee ma**	这儿能兑换 外币吗?
I want to cash some traveler's checks.	**wo shiarng yong lü-shing-j-piao dwee shie shian-jin**	我想用旅行 支票兑些现金.
Where's the nearest bank?	**foo-jin na-r yo yin-harng**	附近哪儿有银行?

Useful Expressions

Numbers

0	ling	零	20	er-sh	二十
1	yee	一	21	er-sh-yee	二十一
2	er (liarng)	二	22	er-sh-er	二十二
3	san	三	30	san-sh	三十
4	s	四	40	s-sh	四十
5	woo	五	50	woo-sh	五十
6	lio	六	60	lio-sh	六十
7	chee	七	70	chee-sh	七十
8	ba	八	80	ba-sh	八十
9	jio	九	90	jio-sh	九十
10	sh	十	100	yee-bai	一百
11	sh-yee	十一	101	yee-bai-ling-yee	一百零一
12	sh-er	十二	200	er-bai	二百
13	sh-san	十三	1,000	yee-chian	一千
14	sh-s	十四	10,000	yee-wan	一万

Photography

I'd like a ...	wo yao yee-ge ...	我要一个...
black and white film	hay-bai jiao-jüan	黑白胶卷
color film	tsai-ser jiao-jüan	彩色胶卷
battery	dian-ch	电池
I'd like this film developed, please.	ching gay wo chong-shee jer-ge jiao-jüan	请给我冲洗这个胶卷。

Restaurants

Asking the waiter:

A table for ..., please?	yao yee jarng ... dsuo-way de juo-ds	要一张...座位的桌子。
The bill (check), please.	ching gay wo jarng-dan	请给我帐单。
I'd like (some) ...	wo yao ...	我要...

rice wine	mee-jio	米酒
beer	pee-jio	啤酒
green tea	lü-cha	绿茶
jasmine tea	muo-lee hwaa-cha	茉莉花茶
mineral water	kwarng-chüan-shwee	矿泉水
noodles	mian-tiao	面条

Beijing

chicken	**jee-ro**	鸡肉
pork	**joo-ro**	猪肉
rice	**mee-fan**	米饭
fruit	**shwee-guo**	水果
vegetables	**shoo-tsai**	蔬菜

Reading the menu:

bamboo shoots	**joo-swun**	竹笋
dim sum	**dian-shin/shiao-ch**	点心 / 小吃
wonton soup	**hwun-twun-tarng**	馄饨汤
egg-fried rice	**dan-chao-fan**	蛋炒饭
glazed (Beijing) duck	**bei-jing-kao-ya**	北京烤鸭
hot and sour soup	**swan-la-tarng**	酸辣汤
Szechuan-style pork	**hway-guo-ro**	回锅肉
spring roll	**chwun-jüan**	春卷

Signs and Notices

Entrance	入口	No photography	禁止拍照
Exit	出口		
Elevator (lift)	电梯	Danger	危险
		Information	问询处
Emergency exit	紧急出口	Warning	警告
Closed	关门	Pull	拉
Stop	停	Push	推
Occupied	有人	No smoking	禁止吸烟
No entry	禁止入内		
		Do not touch	请勿触摸

Taxi

Please take me to the …	**ching song wo chü …**	请送我去…
How much will it cost?	**yao duo-shao chian**	要多少钱？

Toilets

Where are the bath-rooms (toilets)?	**tser-suo dsai na-r**	厕所在哪儿？
Men	**nan**	男
Women	**nü**	女

Tourist Information

Where is the tourist information office?	**lü-yo foo-woo-choo dsai na-r**	旅游服务处在哪儿?

Transportation

I'd like a ... ticket to Shanghai.	**wo shiarng mai yee-jarng chü sharng-hai de ... cher-piao**	我想买一张去上海的...车票。
one-way (single)/ round-trip (return)	**dan-chung/ warng-fan**	单程/往返
How much is that?	**duo-shao chian**	多少钱?
Is this the right bus/tram to ...?	**chü ... sh jer cher ma**	去...是这车吗?

PLACE NAMES

City and sight names that are well-traveled by tourists are listed with *Putonghua* (Mandarin) pronunciations.

Ancient Observatory	**goo gwan-shiarng tai**	古观象台
Beihai Park	**bay-hai gong-yüan**	北海公园
Beijing Art Museum	**bay-jing ee-shoo-buo-woo-guan**	北京美术馆
Beijing Zoo	**bay-jing dong-woo-yüan**	北京动物园
Bell Tower	**jong-lou**	钟楼
Big Bell Temple	**da-jong-s**	大钟寺
China Art Gallery	**jong-guo may-shoo-gwan**	中国美术馆
Confucius Temple	**kong-miao**	孔庙
Drum Tower	**goo-lou**	鼓楼
Eastern Qing Tombs	**dong ching-ling**	东清陵
Five Pagoda Temple	**woo-ta-s**	五塔寺
Forbidden City	**ds-jin-churng**	紫禁城
Fragrant Hills Park	**shiarng-shan gong-yüan**	香山公园

Beijing

Guanghua Temple	gwarng-hwaa-s	广化寺
Great Hall of the People	ren-min da-hwee-tarng	人民大会堂
Great Wall	charng-churng	长城
Jingshan Park	jing-shan gong-yüan	景山公园
Lama Temple	yong-her-gong	永和宫
Liulichang Culture Street	lio-lee-charng jie	琉璃厂街
Mao Zedong Mausoleum	mao-joo-shee jee-nian-tarng	毛主席纪念堂
Ming Tombs	sh-san-ling	十三陵
Monument to the People's Heroes	ren-min ying-shiong jee-nian-bay	人民英雄纪念碑
Museum of Chinese History	jong-guo lee-sh buo-woo-gwan	中国历史博物馆
Museum of the Chinese Revolution	jong-guo ger-ming lee-sh buo-woo-gwan	中国革命历史博物馆
Natural History Museum	ds-ran lee-sh buo-woo-gwan	自然历史博物馆
Prince Gong's Mansion	gong-warng-foo	恭王府
Ritan Park	r-tan gong-yüan	日坛公园
Silk Alley Market	shio-shwee-jie sh-charng	秀水街丝绸市场
Soong Ching-ling Residence	song-ching-ling goo-jü	宋仲龄故居
Summer Palace	yee-her-yüan	颐和园
Temple of the Azure Clouds	bee-yün-s	碧云寺
Temple of Heaven Park	tian-tan gong-yüan	天坛公园
Temple of the Sleeping Buddha	wo-fuo-s	卧佛寺
Tiananmen Square	tian-an-men gwarng-charng	天安门广场
Wanshou Temple	wan-shou-s	万寿寺
Western Hills	shee-shan	西山
White Pagoda Temple	bai-taa-s	白塔寺

Recommended Hotels

Most travelers prefer four- and five-star hotels (as rated by the government), as these have clean, modern facilities and English-speaking staffs. Some of the top five-star hotels are affiliated with major hotel chains and have international management teams. Full Western breakfast buffets are not routinely included in room rates, nor is airport transportation, so inquire ahead about both.

Reservations well in advance are strongly recommended from May through October. Many Beijing hotels are completely booked in May and October. To phone a hotel from abroad, be sure to dial China's country code (86) and Beijing's city code (10) before the eight-digit local number.

Major hotels (three-star and above) add a 15 percent service charge and levy a small city development tax (neither reflected in the prices listed below). Nearly all of these hotels accept international credit cards (although few Beijing hotels currently accept the Eurocard).

As a basic guide, we have used the symbols below to indicate average prices, per night, for a double room with bath. (Note that the symbols are not necessarily equivalent to the star ratings provided by the Chinese government.)

✪✪✪✪✪	above 1,600 yuan
✪✪✪✪	1,000–1,600 yuan
✪✪✪	750–1,000 yuan
✪✪	400–750 yuan
✪	below 400 yuan

Central District (Dongcheng)

Beijing Hotel (Beijing Fandian) ✪✪✪✪ *35 Dong Chang'an Jie; Tel. 6513-7766; fax 6513-7703.* Original section of Beijing's historic hotel opened in 1917. The west wing was added in 1954 and the east wing, on Wangfujing Dajie, was added in

1974. Extensive remodeling and modernization have left only a few reminders of Old Peking, but the ballroom and long lobby have touches of pre-revolutionary days. 850 rooms. Major credit cards.

Beijing International Hotel (Beijing Guoji Fandian) ✪✪✪ *9 Jianguomenwai Dajie; Tel. 6512-6688; fax 6512-9961.* A 15-minute walk east of the Forbidden City, this massive 29-story Chinese-managed hotel has more than 12 restaurants and its own bowling alley. Rooms are large and well-appointed, but housekeeping is a problem. 1,008 rooms. Major credit cards.

Beijing Song He Hotel (Songhe Da Jiudian) ✪✪ *88 Deng-shikou Jie; Tel. 6513-8822; fax 6513-9088.* This former Novo-tel, just off Wangfujing Dajie, is now locally managed. It remains one of Beijing's best three-star values. Rooms are fairly large and modern, with a few basic amenities. 310 rooms. Major credit cards.

Grand Hotel (Guibinluo Fandian) ✪✪✪✪✪ *35 Dong Chang'an Jie; Tel. 6513-7788; fax 6513-0048; www.grand-hotelbeijing.com.cn.* The west wing of the historic Beijing Hotel, this deluxe modern addition with seven-story marble atrium is the closest hotel to the Forbidden City. Its elegant rooms, with separate baths and showers, are large and feature a full range of amenities. 218 rooms. Major credit cards.

Grand Hyatt (Dongfang Junyne Da Jindian) ✪✪✪✪✪ *1 Dong Chang An Jie; Tel. 8518 1234; fax. 8518-0000; www.hyatt.com.* Situated in the Oriental Plaza this hotel is ide-ally situated for Wangfujing Street, Tiananmen Square, and the Forbidden City. Opened in 2001, this is Bejing's newest and most modern accommodations. 531 rooms. Major credit cards.

Holiday Inn Crowne Plaza (Guoji Yiyuan Huangguan Jiari Fandian) ✪✪✪✪✪ *48 Wangfujing Dajie; Tel. 6513-3388; fax 6513-2513.* Art is the theme of this five-star boutique hotel (with its own contemporary Chinese art gallery), located on Beijing's top shopping street. Rooms face either the street or the nine-story atrium, where classical music is performed in the evenings. Service, particularly at the bell desk, is exceptional. 385 rooms. Major credit cards.

Palace Hotel (Wangfu Fandian) ✿✿✿✿✿ *8 Jingyu Hutong, Wangfujing Dajie; Tel. 6512-8899; fax 6512-9050.* Downtown's grand hotel, with its fleet of Rolls-Royces at the door and a waterfall in the lobby, the Palace contains two floors of high-priced international shops and superb restaurants. Rooms are spacious, with every amenity imaginable, from robes to safe drinking-water dispensers. 530 rooms. Major credit cards.

Eastern District (Chaoyang)

Beijing International Club Hotel (Guoji Julebu Fandian) ✿✿✿✿✿ *21 Jianguomenwai Dajie; Tel. 6460-6688; fax 6460-3299.* A member of the ITT Sheraton Luxury Collection, this stylish new grand hotel boasts the most spectacular lobby in Beijing. Health and athletic facilities are shared with the adjacent Beijing International Club (built 1911). Spacious rooms come with all the amenities, including 24-hour butler service. 287 rooms. Major credit cards.

China World Hotel (Zhongguo Da Fandian) ✿✿✿✿✿ *1 Jianguomenwai Dajie; Tel. 6505-2266; fax 6505-3167; www.cwtc.com.cn.* Widely regarded as Beijing's best hotel (a favorite of diplomatic and corporate officials), this Shangri-La hotel is located on the eastern extension of Chang'an Boulevard next to a subway station on the Third Ring Road. The business center is Beijing's best. The hotel is inside the China World Trade Center, a shopping and office plaza. Rooms are large, elegant, and well-maintained. 738 rooms. Major credit cards.

Jianguo Hotel (Jianguo Fandian) ✿✿✿✿ *5 Jianguomenwai Dajie; Tel. 6500-2233; fax 6500-2871.* China's first joint-venture hotel (1982), renovated in 1996, the Jianguo is a longtime favorite of the expatriate community. Rooms are average in size and some are a bit worn, but all have good amenities. 399 rooms. Major credit cards.

Jing Guang New World Hotel (Jingguang Xinshijie Fandian) ✪✪✪✪✪ *Jingguang Centre, Hu Jia Lou (Third Ring Road East at Chaoyangmenwai Dajie); Tel. 6597-8888; fax 6597-3333.* This 52-story blue tower, the highest building in Beijing, contains large, well-maintained, and brightly furnished rooms on floors 8–23, with numerous shops, restaurants, and offices (including the Bank of China) in the same complex. 446 rooms. Major credit cards.

Jinglun Hotel (Jinglun Fandian) ✪✪✪✪ *3 Jianguomenwai Dajie; Tel. 6500-2266; fax 6500-2022.* Managed by Nikko Hotels International, the Jinglun has excellent service and upkeep. Silk Alley and the Friendship Store are a few blocks away. Rooms are clean, bathrooms are compact. There's one of the city's best local restaurants here (Sihexuan) and a French bistro in the lobby. 558 rooms. Major credit cards.

Kerry Centre Hotel (Beijing Jiali Zhongxin Fandian) ✪✪✪✪ *1 Guanghua Lu; Tel. 6561-8833; fax 6561-2626.* One of Beijing's newest hotels, managed by Shangri-La, this hotel has highly efficient service and deluxe facilities, headlined by a roof garden with jogging track, in-line skating, and a children's play area. The rooms are in high-tech style, with data jacks and duvets. 487 rooms. Major credit cards.

Swissôtel (Beijing Gang Ao Zhongxin) ✪✪✪✪✪ *Dongsishi Tiao Li Jiao Qiao, Hong Kong Macau-Centre; Tel. 6501-2288; fax 6501-2501; www.swissotel.com.* Presided over by the Swissair Swissôtel Management Group, this sterling five-star hotel has a European feel, well-maintained rooms, and excellent facilities, including a medical clinic. The fourth floor is barrier-free for travelers with disabilities. 421 rooms. Major credit cards.

Traders Hotel Beijing (Gumao Fandian) ✪✪✪✪ *1 Jian-guomenwai Dajie; Tel. 6505-2277; fax 6505-0818.* Perhaps Beijing's best four-star hotel, Traders (managed by Shangri-La) has close links to the five-star China World Hotel next door. Its new underground shopping center includes an indoor ice-skating rink. Rooms are spacious, the marble bathrooms are luxurious, and the large hotel business center has an excellent bookstore. 564 rooms. Major credit cards.

Northeast District (Chaoyang)

Beijing Hilton Hotel (Xierdun Fandian) ✪✪✪✪✪ *1 Dong-fang Lu, Dongsanhuan Beilu; Tel. 6466-2288; fax 6465-3052.* The Hilton is a fine international hotel, popular with Western business travelers. Services and maintenance are first-rate, and the rooms come with robes and slippers, dataports for PCs, and even umbrellas. 363 rooms. Major credit cards.

Great Wall Sheraton (Changcheng Fandian) ✪✪✪✪✪ *10 Dongsanhuan Beilu; Tel. 6590-5566; fax 6590-1938.* The first internationally managed five-star hotel to open (1984) on the Third Ring Road North, the Great Wall sets a high standard with its services and many facilities. The spacious rooms feature in-room PC dataports for Internet use and compact marble bathrooms. 1,007 rooms. Major credit cards.

Holiday Inn Lido (Lidu Jiari Fandian) ✪✪✪✪ *Jichang Lu, Jiangtai Lu; Tel. 6437-6688; fax 6437-6237.* Located halfway between city center and the airport (16 km/10 miles), this hotel is a place unto itself and the largest Holiday Inn in the world. The facilities, including a bank, a bowling alley, and a Western supermarket, are unequaled in China. The rooms are more basic but come with king-sized beds, 44-channel satellite TV, and clean modern bathrooms. 720 rooms. Major credit cards.

Kempinski Hotel (Kaibinsiji Fandian) ✪✪✪✪✪ *50 Liang-maqiao Lu, Lufthansa Centre; Tel. 6465-3388; fax 6465-3366;*

www.kempinski-beijing.com. With impeccable service and up-keep and German management, the Kempinski is popular with Europeans. The hotel has a deli and a German brewpub, and it is attached to the You Yi shopping center. Rooms are large, the fitness center is comprehensive, and a shuttle bus serves both the airport and downtown. 529 rooms. Major credit cards.

Mövenpick Hotel Beijing (Guodu Da Fandian) ✪✪✪✪ *Xiao Tianzhu Village, Capital Airport, Shunyi County; Tel. 6456-5588; fax 6456-5678.* Situated beyond the urban smog belt, this is Beijing's only deluxe airport hotel (15 minutes on the free Mövenpick shuttle) — and its only resort hotel. Rooms are large, and the atmosphere is European. Resort facilities include the capital's only natural thermal hot springs pool, interconnected indoor and outdoor swimming pools, and beach-sand volleyball court. 408 rooms. Major credit cards.

Radisson SAS Hotel (Huangjia Da Fandian) ✪✪✪✪ *6-A Beisanhuan Donglu; Tel. 6466-3388; fax 6465-3186.* The most stylish rooms in the capital come in three décors: Oriental, High-Tech, and Art Deco. All rooms are large and well maintained. The service is excellent, facilities extensive, and the atmosphere European. This is the best four-star hotel in northeast Beijing (as well as the priciest in its class). 362 rooms. Major credit cards.

Northwest Districts (Xicheng, Haidian)

Beijing New Century Hotel (Xin Shiji Fandian) ✪✪✪✪✪ *6 Shoudu Tiyuguan Nanlu; Tel. 6849-2001; fax 6849-1103.* Well managed by ANA, a Japanese hotel group, this five-star, 32-story tower near the Beijing Zoo is long on facilities, including a Bank of China branch and golf driving range. Each spotless room has a window nook with extensive views of the Western Hills or downtown Beijing. 738 units. Major credit cards.

Exhibition Centre Hotel (Zhanian Guan Binguan) ✪✪ *135 Xizhimenwai Dajie; Tel. 6831-6633; fax 6834-7450.* Located between the zoo and a subway stop (six blocks away), this three-star complex is one of the few good budget choices in Beijing. Everything is showing wear and tear, but the staff is friendly (if not always knowledgeable). Rooms are compact, with brown carpet and small TVs. 250 rooms. Major credit cards.

Holiday Inn Downtown (Jindu Jiari Fandian) ✿✿✿ *98 Beilishi Lu; Tel. 6833-8822; fax 6834-0696.* Not exactly downtown, but just a block from the Fuchengmen subway station and Vantone shopping plaza, this internationally managed Holiday Inn is highly efficient and comfortable: a good deal for the price. 346 rooms. Major credit cards.

Shangri-La Beijing Hotel (Xiangge Lila Fandian) ✿✿✿✿✿ *29 Zizhuyuan Lu; Tel. 6841-2211; fax 6841-8002; www.shangri-la.com.* One of the top hotels in China, the Shangri-La has set high standards for service and elegance since it opened in 1986. The classic Chinese garden is a focal point and symbol of its serene atmosphere, far from the jarring energy downtown. The rooms are among Beijing's largest and best appointed. 640 rooms. Major credit cards.

Southern Districts (Xuanwu, Chongwen)

Jinghua Hotel (Jinghua Fandian) ✿ *Yongwai Xiluoyuan Nanli, Fengtai District; Tel. (6722-2211); fax 6721-1455.* Ten kilometers (6 miles) south of city center, this popular backpacker's hotel has some very economical, no-frills double rooms, small but fairly clean, with private baths. There's a tour desk, bicycle rental, and a helpful staff that speaks a little English. 168 rooms. No credit cards.

Qiaoyuan Hotel (Qiaoyuan Fandian) ✿ *135 Dongbinhe Lu (Xuanwu District); Tel. 6303-8861; fax 6318-4709.* About 10 km (6 miles) south of downtown, this budget travelers' hotel has remodeled to achieve a two-star rating. The rooms are small but clean, with few amenities. Some of the staff speaks limited English. 440 rooms. Major credit cards.

Recommended Restaurants

Dining for foreign visitors was once confined to the expensive fare offered in the big hotels and a handful of small, independent outlets. That has changed. While many of the finer restaurants are still in the hotels, there are scores of independent cafés today competing for visitors with good cuisine, hygienic conditions, English-language menus, and generally lower prices.

Nor is Northern Chinese food your only choice on the menu. Beijing has the largest collection of regional Chinese and international restaurants in China (outside of Hong Kong), not to mention hundreds of familiar fast-food chains and coffee outlets (the world's largest KFC, over 50 McDonald's, and China's first Starbucks).

Most restaurants, including many in hotels, keep traditional Chinese hours, which are typically 7am–9am for breakfast, 11:30am–2pm for lunch, and 5:30pm–9pm for dinner, although some stay open later. Many hotels have 24-hour lobby restaurants serving Western and Asian dishes. Chopsticks are the rule at Chinese restaurants, although knife and fork can often be requested.

Beijingers spend more on food than on housing, but restaurant prices in Beijing are lower than in most Western capitals. Reservations are recommended in the more expensive establishments, particularly on weekends. Tipping is not necessary in private restaurants, but a small gratuity is acceptable; most hotel outlets include a 15 percent service charge on the bill. The following symbols indicate the cost of an average dinner, per person, excluding drinks:

✿✿✿✿	above 240 yuan
✿✿✿	120–240 yuan
✿✿	80–120 yuan
✿	below 80 yuan

Central District (Dongcheng)

Courtyard ✦✦✦✦ *95 Donghuamen Lu; Tel. 6526-8881; www.courtyard-gallery.com.* This upscale contemporary bistro, located on the moat of the Forbidden City, is among the city's most popular spots. The East-West fusion dishes blend Chinese and fresh Western ingredients in everything from salads to blackened salmon. A gallery features contemporary Chinese artists, and there's a cigar divan for a relaxing drink. Open daily 6am–10:30pm. Major credit cards.

Green Tian Shi ✦✦✦ *57 Dengshi Xikou Lu; Tel. 6524-2349.* Beijing's finest "New Age" vegetarian restaurant, Green Tian Shi has an English-language menu laced with Chinese dishes that have the texture, appearance, and sometimes the taste of meats, including a Gong Bao "chicken" and a braised "eel." Open daily 10am–10pm. Major credit cards.

Plaza Grill ✦✦✦✦ *Holiday Inn Crowne Plaza, 48 Wangfujing Dajie; Tel. 6513-3388, ext. 1132.* The French cooking here, often with Asian ingredients, ranks among the best in the capital. The setting is romantic: on the mezzanine overlooking the hotel's nine-story atrium, which is filled each evening with live performances of Chinese or Western classical music. The salads are fresh and the entrées are typified by the breast of duckling in a morel mango sauce. Open daily 6:30pm–10pm; Sundays for dinner only 6pm–10pm. Major credit cards.

Uncle Afanti ✦✦ *2 Houguaibang Hutong, Chaoyangmennei Dajie; Tel. 6525-1071 and 6527-2288.* Beijing's Muslim minority has had a strong influence on local cuisine, and Uncle Afanti is an entertaining place to sample the food of the Uighur people who populate the far-western province of Xinjiang. The skewers of barbecued lamb *(yang rou chuanr)* and the noodles with tomato sauce *(lamian)* are zesty, but the belly dancing stage show is more rousing yet. Open daily 11am–11:30pm. Major credit cards.

Eastern District (Chaoyang)

Aria ✿✿✿ *China World Hotel, Levels 2-3, 1 Jianguomenwai Dajie; Tel. 6505-2266.* Jazz is the focus at this stylish "uptown" grill with a piano, open kitchen, well-stocked wine bar, and excellent American and Continental dishes. The entrées range from rotisserie-grilled fish to imported steaks and pastas. Open daily 12–2pm and 6–10pm. Major credit cards.

Bleu Marine ✿✿✿ *5 Dongdaqiao Lu; Tel. 6500-6704.* Run by two Frenchmen and a Chinese investor, this Mediterranean-style bistro was an immediate hit. Seafood is the centerpiece, but fresh ingredients dictate many of the courses. Sidewalk seating in the summer. Open daily 11:30am–10:30pm. Major credit cards.

Henry J. Bean's ✿✿ *China World Trade Center, West Wing, 1 Jianguomenwai Dajie; Tel. 6505-2266, ext. 6334.* Beijing's top American-style grill and bar, Henry's offers a well-trimmed hamburger, a good chicken Caesar salad, potato skins, and fajitas and nachos, as well as many imported beers. The décor is splashy American kitsch. Live rock music on weekends. Open Sunday–Thursday 11:30am–1am, Friday–Saturday 11:30am–2:30am. Major credit cards.

Justine's ✿✿✿✿ *Jianguo Hotel, 5 Jianguomenwai Dajie; Tel. 6500-2233, ext. 8039.* French cooking and a touch of European elegance, complete with chandeliers and crystal, have made Justine's a favorite with romantics. Normandie shellfish dishes, fresh oysters, goose liver, and the rack of lamb headline the menu. Open daily 6:30am–10am, noon–3pm, and 6pm–11pm. Major credit cards.

Ritan Park Restaurant ✿✿✿ *Southwest gate, Ritan Park, Guanghua Lu; Tel. 6500-5939 and 6500-5883.* This imperial garden court restaurant has plenty of Old Peking atmosphere and a view of Ritan Park's goldfish pool. The menu has Sichuan and Beijing specialties, including chili-pepper chicken, noodles,

Beijing steamed pastries, and crispy duck. Open daily 11am–1:30pm and 5pm–9pm. Major credit cards.

Sihexuan ✪✪ *Jinglun Hotel, 4th floor, 3 Jianguomenwai Dajie; Tel. 6500-2266, ext. 8116.* Beijing specialties as good as any from the local night markets are prepared in an open kitchen and served in a fitting atmosphere of red lanterns and long-spout teapots. Traditional choices from the bilingual menu include spring roll and *wu si tong* ("five shredded buckets"), which consists of a thin egg pancake filled with duck, pork, celery, ginger, scallions, and plum sauce. An excellent introduction to Beijing cuisine at its best. Open daily 11:30am–2pm and 5:30pm–11pm. Major credit cards.

Summer Palace ✪✪✪ *China World Hotel, Level 2, 1 Jianguomenwai Dajie; Tel. 6505-2266, ext. 34.* With cuisine, service, and décor consistently impeccable, this might be the best Cantonese restaurant in Beijing, and not a bad place to try the capital's own specialty, Peking duck. The atmosphere is upscale but informal, the waiters skilled but not pushy. Open daily 11:30am–2:15pm and 6pm–9:45pm. Major credit cards.

Xihe Yaju ✪ *Northeast gate, Ritan Park, Ritan Dong Lu; Tel. 6501-0385 and 6594-1915.* Located in an old Qing Dynasty courtyard mansion, this is a fine place to try reasonably priced Sichuan and Cantonese dishes, with patio seating in the summer. The chicken with peanuts (*gong bao jiding*) is cheap and not very spicy. The same can be said of the steamed grass carp. Open daily 11am–2pm and 5pm–10pm. No credit cards.

Northeast District (Chaoyang)

Berena's Bistro ✪✪ *6 Gongrentiyuchang Dong Lu; Tel. 6592-2628.* Beijing's favorite Sichuan restaurant among foreign residents, this casual candlelit café has attentive service and well-prepared dishes that aren't too spicy. The sweet-and-sour soup, chicken with almonds, sizzling *gong bao* chicken, and sweet-and-sour pork are popular and reliable. The Chengdu roast duck is less greasy than the renowned Peking duck. Open daily 11:30am–11:30pm. Major credit cards.

Borom Piman ✿✿-✿✿✿ *Holiday Inn Lido, Jichang Lu, Jiangtai Lu; Tel. 6437-6688, ext. 2899.* Beijing's best Thai restaurant, Borom Thai has an elegant traditional décor, skilled wait staff, nice set lunches, and an array of fine dishes starting with spring prawn soup and including a scrumptious curry chicken. Open daily 11am–2pm and 5pm–10pm. Major credit cards.

Gold Cat Jiaozi City ✿ *East gate, Tuanjiehu Park, Third Ring Road East; Tel. 6598-5011.* Economical examples of Beijing's famous *jiaozi* (steamed dumplings with meat or vegetable fillings) are the focus of this no-frills courtyard emporium, with dozens of fillings available, including seafood and vegetables. A noisy nightspot. English menus. Open 24 hours daily. Major credit cards.

Kebab Kafé ✿✿ *Sanlitun Bei Lu; Tel. 6415-5812.* Among scores of Sanlitun café bars offering Western-style food, the Kebab stands out with its excellent German and Continental cuisine ranging from sandwich-style kebabs and fresh salads to a chicken breast Cordon Bleu, vegetarian pizza, ratatouille, and Swiss fondues in the winter. Inside, it's a compact informal bistro, while outside it's a busy sidewalk café for those looking for good German beers. Open daily 8:30am–midnight. Major credit cards.

Lao Shanghai ✿✿✿ *Holiday Inn Lido, Jichang Road, Jiangtai Road; Tel. 6437-6688.* With crystal settings and photographs of old Shanghai, Lao Shanghai is a relaxed but upscale new restaurant staffed by Shanghai chefs. Pleasingly presented — encircled with bamboo shoots and cucumbers — the white eel and river shrimp are delicious, as is the superb liquefied hairy crab. A three-piece jazz combo entertains nightly. Open daily 11:30am–2pm and 6pm–10pm. Major credit cards.

LaxenOxen ❖❖❖❖ *Radisson SAS Hotel, 6-A Beisanhuan Dong Lu; Tel. 6466-3388, ext. 3430.* The best Scandinavian restaurant in town, worth dressing up for, the LaxenOxen has a fine wine list and excellent Atlantic salmon, herring, grilled steaks, blue mussel soup, and — for lunch — robust open-faced sandwiches. Open daily 11:30am–2:30pm and 6pm–10:30pm. Major credit cards.

Louisiana ❖❖❖❖ *Beijing Hilton Hotel, 2nd floor, 1 Dongfang Lu; Tel. 6466-2288, ext. 7420.* A superb American-Cajun restaurant with Beijing's best wine list, elegantly decorated with a Dixieland jazz theme, Louisiana has Creole salad and gumbo for starters, smoked rack of lamb and wood-roasted baby pork ribs on coconut mashed potatoes for entrées, and pecan pie for dessert. Open Monday–Saturday 11:30am–2:30pm and 6pm–10pm, Sunday 6pm–10pm. Major credit cards.

Mongolian Gher ❖❖❖ *Mövenpick Hotel, Beijing Capital Airport, Xiao Tianzhu Village, Shunyi; Tel. 6456-5588.* With food served in a traditional round tent *(yurt),* this Mongolian restaurant is the nicest place in Beijing to try summer lamb barbecues and winter hot pots from two multicourse set menus. After dinner, costumed Mongolian dancers and musicians provide spirited performances. Open daily 6pm–11pm. Major credit cards.

San Si Lang ❖❖ *52 Liangmaqiao Lu; Tel. 6506-9625.* Beijing's least expensive Japanese restaurant, very popular with the foreign community, San Si Lang has great sushi and tempura. First-floor seating is divided into comfortable booths; upstairs are *tatami*-mat rooms. The multilingual menu has a picture of each dish. Usually crowded for lunch. Open daily 11:30am–11pm. Major credit cards.

Western Districts (Xicheng, Haidian)

Carousel Revolving Restaurant ❖❖-❖❖❖ *Xiyuan Hotel, 26th floor, 1 Sanlihe Lu, Xicheng District; Tel. 6831-3388.* Excellent views, formal table settings, and a wide-ranging Asian buffet (Thai, Malaysian, Japanese, Vietnamese, Chinese), as well as a salad bar and Western desserts, make this a place to linger and relax. Open daily 11:30am–2:30pm and 6pm–10pm. Major credit cards.

Fangshan Restaurant ❀❀❀ *Beihai Park, Jade Isle, Xicheng District, Tel. 6401-1879.* Beijing's first and oldest imperial restaurant is a courtyard mansion on the north shore of a former royal pleasure park. Imperial Beijing cuisine consists of hearty, simple fare: steamed pastries, stir-fried peas, roast duck and chicken, and beancurd cakes. But you'll also find expensive delicacies such as poached lake trout *(tian xiang bao yu)*. The décor is straight out of Old China. Open daily 11am–1:30pm and 5pm–7pm. Major credit cards.

Li Family Restaurant (Li Jia Cai) ❀❀❀❀ *11 Yangfang Hutong, Deshengmennei Dajie, Xicheng District; Tel. 6618-0107.* Set in the humble rooms of a typical courtyard house located deep in a *hutong* (alley) neighborhood, this is Beijing's most popular restaurant among visitors, requiring advance bookings. The recipes — created for the Qing Dynasty Empress Dowager — employ fresh, simple countryside ingredients prepared in the home kitchen. Flavors are odd and rustic; the Li version of Peking duck is neither crispy nor oily. Open daily 6pm–10pm. No credit cards.

Nishimura ❀❀❀❀ *Shangri-La Beijing Hotel, Level 2, 29 Zizhuyuan Lu, Haidian District; Tel. 6841-2211.* Beijing's first Japanese *robatayaki* (grill) restaurant also includes a take-out counter and two *teppanyaki* counters, but the long grill is the place to sit. Order any item from the counter and the chef will grill it to perfection. The bacon roll with asparagus, a potato with butter, and the giant prawn are divine. Come at lunchtime for cheaper fare. Open daily 12:30–2:30pm and 6–10pm. Major credit cards.

Shamiana ✿✿ *Holiday Inn Downtown, 98 Beilishi Lu, Xicheng District; Tel. 6833-8822, ext. 7107.* Upscale but fun, this is Beijing's best Indian restaurant, with chef and fresh ingredients from India. Set menus feature vegetable *samosa* (crunchy fried pastries), curries, flat breads, mango chutney, and *phirni* (rice pudding), with à la carte choices range from vegetarian plates to grilled chicken. Indian dancers and musicians in the evening. Open daily 11:30am–2:30pm and 6pm–midnight. Major credit cards.

Southern Districts (Xuanwu, Chongwen)

Gongdelin ✿✿ *158 Qianmen Nan Dajie, Chongwen District; Tel. 6511-2542.* With Beijing's most comprehensive vegetarian menu, the government-run Gongdelin turns out delicious dishes despite its ugly institutional interior. Entrées taste and look like popular Chinese dishes usually made with pork duck, chicken, or fish. There's even a vegetarian Peking duck *(su yazi).* Open daily 10am–8:30pm. Major credit cards.

Quanjude Hepingmen ✿✿ *14 Qianmen Xi Dajie, Xuanwu District; Tel. 6301-8833.* The Quanjude chain of Peking duck restaurants began in the capital 115 years ago. Hepingmen is its most modern and inexpensive branch. Side dishes can be inspected and selected from a freezer section, but the real action is the crispy, fatty duck, carved at your table and rolled into a thin pancake with plum sauce and onions. Open daily 10:30am–1:30pm and 4:30pm–8:30pm. Major credit cards.

Quanjude Kaoyadian ✿✿✿ *32 Qianmen Dajie, Chongwen District; Tel. 6511-2418.* The Quanjude chain's most elegant Peking duck restaurant enjoys its reputation for serving the best roast duck in the world. Dining rooms come in a variety of sizes; all are ornately imperial. Best appreciated as a banquet with four or more diners. Open daily 10:30am–1:30pm and 4:30pm–8:30pm. Major credit cards.

INDEX

Berlitz Puts The World In Your Pocket

Berlitz Spain pocket guide

Berlitz puts *Spain* in your pocket!

Berlitz Spanish phrase book & dictionary

Travel with ease... communicate with confidence!

Berlitz speaks the language of travel.
Its Pocket Guides take you to more
than 110 destinations and its phrase
books, pocket dictionaries, and
cassette and CD language packs help
you communicate when you get there.

Berlitz